A Contract of Words

To Freya

Thanks so much for your continued support!

Laura x

Published by Scout Media

ISBN: 978-0-9979485-2-3

Cover & chapter headers designed by **Amy Hunter**

Visit: **www.ScoutMediaBooksMusic.com**
for more information on each author and all volumes
in the *Of Words* series.

Table of Contents

NO WAY

Signature F. A. Fisher

F.A. Fisher sat in his office, hands on the keyboard, eyes fixed intently on the screen of his laptop. The only problem was that the screen was blank.

And his fingers weren't moving.

And his brain cells weren't firing.

With a sigh, he leaned back in his chair. He'd made a promise to himself that he would submit a story to the anthology, *A Contract of Words.* But now the deadline for submission was practically on him, and he still hadn't started.

Maybe he should just give up. He'd broken promises to himself before. But this particular promise held him with an almost supernatural power. He'd stopped attending to his usual tasks, let his business fall by the wayside, and given up on his other writing. It was even hurting his family relationships. He *had* to get this story written.

And yet the only story ideas he could think of containing a contract all involved that beaten-to-death idea of a deal with the Devil. Probably two-thirds of the submissions would fall into that category, and he did *not* want his to be one of them.

Still, all that came to mind was: the Devil, the Devil, the Devil . . . He'd even started imagining the odor of burning sulfur on occasion. He'd developed a fixation. Maybe it was time to see a psychiatrist.

He groaned and buried his face in his hands—and there it was again. Burning sulfur. Brimstone. He jerked his head up, determined to sniff out the source, but his attention was caught by the computer screen. The blank page was now full of words. What . . . ?

Before he had a chance to start reading, the page faded and was replaced by the leering, behorned face of the Devil.

That's it. I've totally lost it. He reached out and slammed the lid on his laptop.

It popped back open.

"Now, now," Satan said. "That's no way to treat a fellow who's trying to do you a favor."

Right. Even if it was only a hallucination, he was *not* going to make any deals with that . . . that . . . Well, with *that.*

"Don't decide so quickly," Satan went on, apparently reading his mind. "You haven't even heard what I have to say."

"Don't have to. Don't want to."

"Tut-tut. No need for petulance." With a *poof!* accompanied by the smell of fried electronics, Satan stood next to him.

"*Aah!*" Fisher jumped away so hard he and his chair fell over backwards. He rolled off carefully—he wasn't as young as he used to be—stood, and backed against the wall. His laptop, still on the desk, smoked. *Huh. Yeah, some favor.* "Just beat it, will you?"

Satan grasped the overturned chair with one red hand. "Allow me." He set the chair on its feet, leaving a charred handprint in the wood. "Have a seat." He snapped his fingers and another chair appeared, already on fire. Satan took that seat for himself.

Fisher hesitated but finally sat. He wasn't going to get out of this by closing his eyes and clapping his hands over his ears. Satan clearly wouldn't leave until he'd had his say. Best listen and get it over with. "Go on, then."

Satan grinned. "That's better. Now, we both know the problem you're having. I can solve it for you."

"At what price?"

Satan shrugged. "The usual. But payback's a long way off—"

"Like hell—uh, I mean . . . I'm over sixty already."

"But think of how miserable you are!"

"Yeah, yeah." Fisher closed his eyes. "Go on." No point arguing. Let Satan make his pitch and then refuse.

"I can give you a thousand great story ideas you could use for this anthology. Pick one, write the story, and submit it. And then, even if it turns out your anxiety over the issue really has nothing to do with this story but is just because . . . well, you know . . . because you're a little crazy—"

"Ha!" Of course he was crazy! Talking to the Devil. He didn't even *believe* in the Devil. Which didn't make him any more inclined to bargain. No point taking chances.

"Don't interrupt. Even if that's the problem, I can fix it. Well . . ." Satan waggled his hand. "I can fix it like you were before you found out about this anthology. No crazier than that. I'm not all powerful, you know." He cast a nervous glance in the direction of the ceiling.

Fisher shook his head. "Not interested. I can't write stories based on other people's ideas. They've got to come from inside me—"

"Then that's exactly what we'll do!" Satan beamed. "The ideas will well up from your subconscious, bringing all the excitement your own ideas generate. You won't be able to tell your ideas from the ones I supply."

"But . . . if I can't tell, how will I even know I've picked one of yours? I might have my own idea and write that—" He caught himself. Why was he arguing? Just say, *No!*

"Not to worry!" Satan waved his hand carelessly, nearly setting fire to some papers on the desk. "If you get your own idea, why should I care? If you write a story and submit it and feel better about the whole thing, then I've done my part, right?"

The barest glimmering of a way out tickled the back of Fisher's mind. "You mean it doesn't matter what story I write? If I submit it, you'll still guarantee that I'll feel better? *And* you guarantee that I *will* be able to write something?"

"You got it, bud."

"How do I know you'll keep your word?"

"Hey, don't I always? And, uh,"—Satan glanced at the ceiling again—"if I ever, even once, go back on my word, all the souls I've harvested get set free. That would be a disaster. I'd lose the respect of all my subordinates, you know?"

Fisher shook his head. "Listen, Satan—"

"That's *Mr.* Satan, to you."

"Whatever. I just don't know—"

"What's not to know?"

"Well, there's my computer—"

"A trifle." Satan snapped his fingers. The laptop stopped smoking, the screen flickered, and the blank page reappeared.

"*O-o-o-o*-kay." That was easier than he'd expected. Might as well try for the kicker. "One more thing. The story I submit has to be *accepted.*"

Satan narrowed his eyes. "You trying to trick me?"

"Who, me?"

"Yeah, you. You're smarter than you look. Of course, you look rather stupid." Satan thought a moment. "Okay, we'll do it this way—yeah, if the story isn't accepted, the contract is void. But *you* have to submit a story that meets the requirements. So no submitting a story that doesn't have a contract in it or that's over seventy-five hundred words. And you have to write it as well as you can—no deliberate grammar or stylistic errors. If you fail in any of those regards, I win."

Rats! Those were exactly the things he'd been planning.

"So, then. Here's the contract."

Fisher read it. Not that he was going to sign, not with Satan having figured out his dodge. But how often does one get a chance to read an actual contract with the Devil? To his surprise, it wasn't full of legalese. It was, in fact, very clear and easy to understand and had exactly the conditions they'd arrived at.

And then Fisher had another thought, one that Satan couldn't possibly have read in his mind and guarded against in the contract, because he hadn't *had* the thought till after the contract was prepared. "Yes," he said. "I'll sign this. Uh, what with?" He hated getting his finger pricked and didn't think doing so would supply enough blood anyway.

"Try your pen," Satan said. "Maybe you aren't so smart after all."

Fisher signed the contract.

Satan ran his finger underneath Fisher's signature, burning the name *Lucifer Satan* into the paper. Then he snatched the contract and said, "See you in a few years, sucker," and disappeared.

Fisher smiled. His spirits weren't dampened, not even by Satan having left his burning chair behind. The ideas were popping up in his head already, and *wow!* they were good.

But he didn't plan to use any of them. Not for *this* anthology. He was going to write what actually happened.

It met all the requirements, after all. But it was one of those make-a-deal-with-the-Devil stories. It would never get into the anthology. No way would a story like that be accepted.

No way in Hell.

The course of F.A. Fisher's life was determined in utero, when he was introduced to science fiction and fantasy by way of his mother reading *The Chronicle of Narnia* to his older sister. Though he grew up among the first generation where television was commonplace, he was of a contrary nature and spent most of his time reading. That contrariness continued in college, where he ignored his adviser and chose an area major, which allowed him to take whatever he wanted, with the result that his degree didn't prepare him for any job whatsoever—except perhaps writing.

He was raised in an era without computers or even hand calculators, so naturally he got a master's degree in computer science. And though he loved learning, he always hated school, so of course he got his second master's in education. He'd wanted to become a writer from an early age, so it followed that he went through a number of other jobs, including two self-start companies, before putting out his first book.

Somewhere along the way he developed a deep and abiding hatred for typos. Fortunately, by now his contrariness has abated, so if you find a typo in any of his books, let him know, and he'll fix it.

Pandir Decloaked, the sequel to *Cloaks,* is his second novel. His third *Cloaks* novel is due out in May 2018.

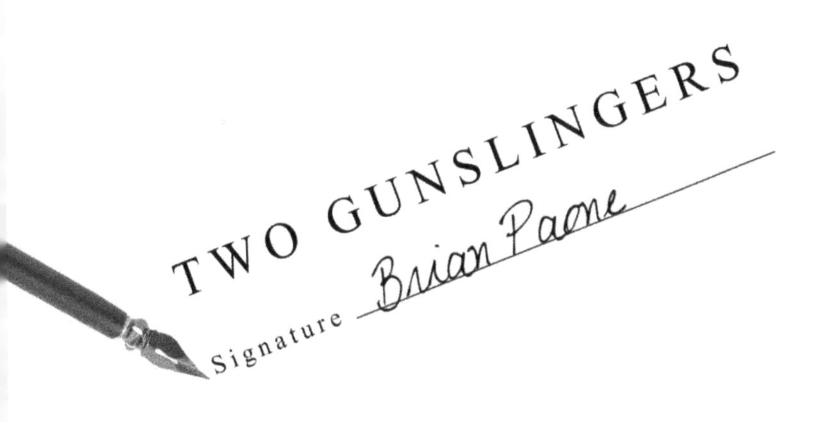

Jack panicked and flailed his arms, trying to grab hold of any part of Billy, the man pressing Jack's face into the puddle in the middle of the street. The water's surface engulfed Jack's forehead and eyes; his nose and mouth scrunched into the mud at the bottom. He knew he had only a few more moments before his lights went out.

Jack sprawled out his arms, like a bird in flight, in a final effort to grip anything as a potential weapon to smash his assailant's head before he lost all consciousness. The clock wound down. The end was nigh.

And why weren't any of the onlooking pedestrians helping a man obviously being drowned in a shallow puddle? What kind of blind-eye town had his home become?

Jack felt the leather of the man's chaps and danced his fingertips toward the man's knee—the epicenter of the force keeping Jack trapped underwater in a four-inch puddle.

Maybe he should open his mouth and take a breath of water, like a reverse fish out of water. Just stop fighting and let the fluid fill his lungs, and he could drift into a peaceful slumber. That would teach them all—a selfish martyr inflicting psychological retribution, even if he wasn't alive to reap the satisfaction.

A fist closed around his mangled and knotted long blond hair to lift Jack's submersed face from the puddle of rainwater.

Jack gasped, inhaling as much clean air as possible, blinking to suppress the black dots that had invaded the back of his eyelids while underwater.

Billy's lips and scratchy facial hair grazed Jack's earlobe. "It's over now."

Jack nodded, swallowing forcefully to purge the stench of Billy's alcohol-laden breath from his nostrils.

"Get on your feet," Billy whispered.

Jack and Billy rose, and Billy released his grasp on Jack's cowhide vest.

Jack adjusted his gun belt and quickly touched the handle of his revolver to confirm it had not been swiped during the fray.

Billy stepped onto the sidewalk to get out of the pathway of an oncoming horse-drawn carriage.

Jack scanned the onlooking crowd that had congregated to watch the tiff.

"And none of you had the decency to intervene?" Jack yelled at the slowly dispersing and disappointed crowd. "I could've died!"

The swinging doors of the Golden Rose Saloon opened, and Jericho stepped outside, clapping slowly, mocking both Billy's benevolent mercy and Jack's near-death experience. Jericho stopped and laid a hand atop one of the doors and removed a matchstick from his mouth.

"That's what they wanted. A show. The whole bloodthirsty lot of 'em." He stepped closer. "You should've run him through, Billy. This town'd be a little . . . cleaner without that dirty rodent hanging 'round."

Jack brushed the dust and sand off his pants and glared at Jericho. Jack's horse, tethered to the hitching post next to the Golden Rose's entrance, snorted and shook his mane.

Jericho tossed his matchstick into the road and gestured for both men to cross the street. "Come. Two drinks. On the house. Let's settle your squabble like gents, . . . like civilized businessmen."

Jericho turned and disappeared into his saloon—the swinging doors came to rest, one door slightly misaligned with its mate.

Jack shoved Billy in retaliation before they headed into the Golden Rose.

The doors swung shut behind them, and Jericho stood behind the bar, pouring three gills of whiskey.

"Sit. Both of you."

Jericho turned his back to his only two patrons and replaced the whiskey bottle in the trough behind him.

Jack glanced at his drink and then eyed the barkeep suspiciously.

"Drink!" Jericho instructed when he turned around and noticed both glasses remained untouched.

Billy lifted his glass off the counter. He tilted his head ever so slightly to bring Jack into his peripheral vision.

"Truce?" Billy asked, not committing to full-blown eye contact yet with the man he had just tried to drown in a muddy puddle on Main Street.

Jack raised his glass to agree, swallowing his pride and his manhood.

Jericho slammed both hands onto the bar. "No!"

The move startled Billy and Jack, a small wave of brown liquid capsizing over the rim of Billy's glass.

"Did you guys see how many gawking lookie-loos couldn't help but stop and watch?"

Jack brought his glass to his lips; Jericho's perspective of the situation intrigued him. He tilted the glass so the alcohol rushed toward his open mouth.

Jericho slapped the drink from Jack's grasp with the back of his hand, sending the cup and the liquor across the empty saloon.

"Not . . . for . . . you," Jericho said, leaning on his elbows to level his gaze with Jack's. "You already owe me too much."

Billy slowly removed his glass from his lips and cautiously set his drink on the bar without taking a sip. He cleared his throat and rubbed his sweaty palms on his chaps.

"Not you, partner," Jericho said, shifting his gaze to Billy. "You drink up. It's this one here who has an unpaid tab."

Jack swallowed hard and leaned backward on the stool.

Jericho stood upright and downed his gill of whiskey in one gulp. He slammed the empty glass on the counter and clapped once loudly.

"How much *do* you owe me now, Mr. Jack?"

Jack shook his head. The tab had been increasing, running for years now—first with just the occasional drink, then the occasional lady, then the frequent gambling, then the even more frequent—

"Answer me!"

Jack met his gaze. "I've lost count."

Jericho wiped the bar with a dingy yellowed dish towel. "It's more than the worth of your life at this point, I can tell you that much."

Jack picked at a cuticle on his index finger and nervously adjusted the weight of his holster.

"And you, Mr. William," Jericho said, facing Billy. "I don't suppose you have that post letter about your wife."

Billy's eyebrows furrowed, and his lips pursed. "What the hell do you know about that?"

The barkeep leaned across the counter. "I'm the one who mailed it. I know where Mary Jane is."

Billy grabbed Jericho's lapel. "And what's it to you?"

Jericho looked at Billy's hand and grabbed his wrist. He pulled the fistful of fabric from Billy's grip and calmly stepped backward.

"The facts are simple. Your wife is missing, and I know where she is. And this whoremongering yack"—he tilted his chin in Jack's direction—"owes me a pretty penny."

"What's the play?" Billy asked, wringing his hands, afraid to take a sip of his whiskey.

Jericho topped his own glass again and scratched his scruffy chin. "A situation where we all come out winners."

The Golden Rose's double doors swung open, and a couple men

entered, their spurs clack-clack-clacking on the uneven wooden floor.

"Closed right now, gents," Jericho called out. "Be open in a jiffy, depending on what these two decide and how quickly they decide it."

The newcomers nodded, respectfully dipping their broad-brimmed hats between their thumb and index fingers, and exited the saloon.

"Go on," Jack said.

Jericho circled the rim of his glass with his fingertip and cocked his head. "A duel."

"'Scuse me?"

"A good ol'-fashion gunfight. Right out front them doors. A showdown at high noon. This weekend."

Billy cleared his throat and shifted on his bar stool. "Usually people don't *tell* me what I'm to do or where. That's for me to decide."

Jericho slapped his dish towel over his shoulder. "Not this time, partner. I'll get your wife back to you, if you prevail. And, Jack,"—Jericho turned to face the man sitting next to Billy—"if you prevail, your debt with me is settled."

Jack scratched his nose and unholstered his revolver. "I smell something mighty fishy." He placed the weapon on the bar.

"If you're trying to intimidate me, it's not working. Let me take care of the details. You two just make sure you're out front, high noon, on Saturday."

Billy tossed back his drink. "Sounds all right with me." He turned to Jack. "Come wearing your big-boy britches. You're gonna need them. Don't want to be staining your pants before I run you through."

Jack holstered his revolver as Billy slid off the bar stool and headed for the door.

"Not so fast, partner," Jericho advised. "I need this in writing. Can't have you two welching on me."

The barkeep slid a piece of parchment across the counter for the pair of gunslingers to sign.

Jericho finished painting the advertisement on a piece of wood from a broken crate. Without waiting for the paint to dry, he hung it on the outside of the Golden Rose. The townsfolk stopped to read the announcement in droves.

Within minutes, Jericho's saloon was cramped with men and women throwing money at him, placing bets on who would win the duel. Within hours, he had recouped enough money to satisfy Jack's debt and then some, no matter which gunslinger won.

"You don't have to do this," Mary Jane said to Jack as she rubbed his shoulders. "We could just ride on outta here and never look back. I'd put a smile on your face every night. I promise."

Jack turned toward her. "I signed a deal, honeybee. Jericho has been selling tickets all week. It's become more of a spectacle than anything at this point. But that's what he wanted. He's a surefire ringleader. He might be crazier than a run-over coon, but I'm not a coward."

"I know you aren't," she said and stroked his arm.

Jack lifted his gun belt and fastened his holster to his side. "Plus, if I win, years of debt and regret die outside that bloody fool's saloon."

"But if you lose . . ."

"Then I wasn't the best man today. And Billy gets his wife back. Don't you see? No matter who wins, there is a happy ending."

Mary Jane removed her hand from his arm and looked at the floor. "I know we've only known each other a short time, but please don't leave me alone."

Jack pressed his lips to hers so forcefully she stumbled backward. "No matter what happens today, at least my debt will be paid."

"To that bugger who dreamed up this mess!" Mary Jane said and stormed from the room.

Jack took a deep breath and inspected himself in the bedroom mirror. He tugged on his gun belt and drew his revolver with lightning speed, pointing it at his reflection.

"You still got it, old hoss."

Pigeons congregated in the empty market square as the townsfolk lined Main Street, most converging outside the Golden Rose Saloon. Jericho appeared through the swinging doors.

"Ladies and gents. Today's the day we've all been waiting for, the day you've all paid for. Today I give you two of the county's more . . . interesting vermin."

Jack peered through the saloon's window at the growing crowd. He glanced at Billy, who looked through the slits next to the other side of the swinging doors. The saloon was empty. A low-hanging haze of stale tobacco enveloped the two gunslingers. Jack clicked his tongue to get Billy's attention.

Billy shook his head and looked at his boots.

Jericho worked the crowd. "Some of you have placed your hard-earned money on the womanizing and gambling Jack Campbell."

A cheer rose up from some of the crowd.

Jack noticed a few children clap and jump up and down at the mention of his name.

"Who brings their young'ns to a gunfight?" Jack whispered.

Billy glanced at him. "The whole town is out there. And everyone has picked a winner. They've placed bets on us. Some of those young'ns will go hungry for the next week because of this fight."

Jericho continued to address the townsfolk. "And some of you have placed your worth on the deceitful and betraying Billy Tench."

Another cheer rose from the remainder of the crowd.

"If the Golden Rose Saloon can promise you one thing, it's

a show worthy of the money you spent betting on your favorite gunslinger."

Jack watched Billy tighten his gun belt.

"You want a drink before we do this?" Jack asked.

Billy finished adjusting his belt and confirmed a single round was in his revolver's chamber.

"I think that's fitting," he answered.

They approached the empty bar and heard Jericho spewing clichés like some circus barker to the assembled crowd outside, spurring them on and sustaining their enthusiasm for the upcoming duel.

Billy reached behind the bar and placed a bottle of scotch on the counter.

"Now you're talking," Jack said.

Billy poured two glasses and raised his. "To keeping our promises."

Jack nodded and clinked his glass to his adversary's.

Billy swallowed his scotch in one gulp, growled, and slammed down the glass. "Let's do this."

"And here they are, ladies and gents! Just as promised, today's main attraction."

Jack shielded his eyes from the sunlight with his forearm as the crowd erupted in a ruckus.

"No matter who you have placed your bets on, today's show, ladies and gents, is sure to be one for the ages!"

Jack and Billy approached Jericho, who stood in the middle of the intersection, acting like a deranged conductor of the townsfolk's emotions and monetary stability.

"Don't you dare come out here acting like friends," Jericho hissed. "These people have bet on a gruesome bloodbath, and I shall deliver. You're both fighting for your lives. Remember that. Your signatures say so."

Billy nodded and turned his back to Jack.

"There you have it, ladies and gents!" Jericho announced. "The showdown is about to begin."

The crowd applauded, and a few conscientious mothers tucked their wee ones behind their legs. Jericho bowed and trotted toward the curb in front of his saloon. He shook the sheriff's hand, slipping a hefty note into it, and turned to see the two gunslingers place their backs against each other.

The crowd's roar consumed any conspiring words the men spoke among themselves just before the duelists took their predetermined number of steps. The crowd's frenzied excitement also masked the gunslingers' understanding nods after they turned to face each other . . . their weapons still holstered.

Everyone hissed and booed after too many minutes of this stalemate.

Then the two gunslingers shook hands, mounted their horses, and rode off together down Main Street.

A man in the crowd angrily waved a handwritten blue ticket containing one of the duelists' names. He turned to his wife in disgust at the gunslingers' anticlimactic exit. "That's the last one of these gunfights you're ever gonna drag me to."

He dropped the ticket in the empty roadway. The man pushed through the crowd toward the saloon. "Jericho! You owe my family and many of these fine people a refund!"

The barkeep made his way to the back of the Golden Rose and manhandled his shotgun.

"C'mon in and get it!"

The sheriff pushed through the swinging doors and raised a hand. "Whoa, now. Put that away. Just refund these people what they bet, and business here can continue as usual."

Jericho quickly eyed the angry mob entering the Golden Rose—people demanding refunds on the botched duel, money he didn't have anymore. He scurried through a side door behind the bar, and the scorned and angry townsfolk followed suit.

The two gunslingers refused to look back at the godforsaken town as their horses trotted deeper into the uncharted West.

"Want some?" Billy asked.

Jack nodded and took the flask. "I didn't want to fight either."

"I think you've settled your debt with Jericho," Billy said. "And I don't think it has anything to do with profit."

Jack spit out his mouthful of alcohol in laughter. "Yeah, I guess he really got his this time, huh? I hope they looted his joint when he couldn't pay up."

"Yessiree, you got him good there. Jericho used your debt to manipulate you and then tried to make money off your death. Despicable."

Jack handed the flask back to Billy. The sun cast elongated horse shadows on the desert sand.

"That idiot," Billy said as he wiped a dribble of whiskey from the corner of his mouth, "never realized I knew he was shacking up with that wench I call a wife. That's why my end of the contract was such a farce. He had my whoring wife all along."

Jack rode in silence for a moment. The galloping muscles of the steed under his legs gave him the courage he didn't usually have.

"I guess I should thank you," Jack said.

"We both won today," Billy replied. "If we had dueled, one of us would have lost, and, no matter who lost, Jericho would have won *his* money. It was the only way to beat that rodent. Plus, he can have and do whatever he wants with Mary Jane . . . that floozy. Here he was, trying to fool me into believing he knows where my wife is when he was the one plugging her the whole time."

Jack's eyes widened as he swallowed hard and subconsciously patted the butt of his revolver. "I'll take another swig, if you don't mind, friend."

Billy handed Jack the last of the drink in the flask as the two gunslingers rode into the sprawling, barren landscape ahead.

Brian Paone was born and raised in the Salem, Massachusetts area. Brian has, thus far, published four novels: a memoir about being friends with a drug-addicted rock star, *Dreams Are Unfinished Thoughts*; a macabre cerebral-horror novel, *Welcome to Parkview*; a time-travel romance novel, *Yours Truly, 2095,* (which was nominated for a Hugo Award, though it did not make the finalists); and a supernatural, crime-noir detective novel, *Moonlight City Drive*.

Along with his four novels, Brian has published three short stories: "Outside of Heaven," which is featured in the anthology, *A Matter of Words*; "The Whaler's Dues," which is featured in the anthology, *A Journey of Words*; and "Anesthetize (or A Dream Played in Reverse on Piano Keys)," which is featured in the anthology, *A Haunting of Words*.

Brian is also a vocalist and has released seven albums with his four bands: Yellow #1, Drop Kick Jesus, The Grave Machine, and Transpose.

Brian is married to a US Naval Officer, and they have four children. He is a retired police officer and worked in law enforcement for sixteen years from 2002 - 2018. He is a self-proclaimed roller coaster junkie, a New England Patriots fanatic, and his favorite color is burnt orange. For more information on all his books and music, visit www.BrianPaone.com.

"What's the difference between a drunk and an alcoholic?" the guy asked, sprawled on a dirty tarp, a bottle in a twisted paper bag and a crumpled, empty cigarette pack beside him.

On the brick wall behind him, someone had crudely spray-painted: *Graffiti is a crime.*

"I don't know," Mike said. "What?"

"A drunk doesn't have to go to all those damn meetings."

Mike studied the man. He was about the right age—seventy or so. Although, these hard drinkers were often lots younger than they looked. His shoulders were wide and his facial bones sharp. Thinning gray hair, complexion of a redhead. Yellowish teeth, but all there. He looked a lot like Buster. He could be Buster's brother.

"So, which are you?" Mike asked.

"Take a wild guess."

A drunk was Mike's guess, but he didn't say this aloud. He moved a step closer to the man and took a discreet sniff. The body odor wasn't as bad as he expected.

"How do you bathe?"

"How do I *bathe*?" the guy said, his mouth twisted in disgust. "How do *you* bathe? With water and a goddamn bar of soap! What a question. How do I *bathe*."

"I mean, how do you bathe, living on the streets?"

The man dropped his jaw in incredulity. "On the streets? Why in the name of Christ would you assume I live on the *streets*?"

Mike glanced at the tarp, the trash strewn about, and said, "I don't know. Sorry. Where do you live, then?"

The man stood, stumbling a little. He turned around (a flask poked out of his back pocket) and pointed up at the shabby brick building he now faced. "Up there on the third floor. I have a room. On the *streets*. Christ Almighty."

"Sorry," Mike said again. "My mistake."

So, the guy had a home. Good. And broad shoulders and a bony face and an easily offended personality. All good.

"What's your name?" Wouldn't it be freaky if the guy's name was Buster?

"My name's Mackie. Who wants to know?" His chin jutted forward. He reached behind him and pulled the flask from his pocket, unscrewed the cap and took a swallow.

Mike extended his hand. "Good to meet you. I'm Mike."

After a moment of hesitation, the man tucked his flask back into his pocket and grasped Mike's hand. His handshake was firm. Mike's father had drilled the importance of a firm handshake into him from the time he was a toddler. To hear his dad tell it, the firmness of a handshake was the truest measure of a man.

"Do you have a criminal record, Mackie?" Mike cringed at the reaction he knew was coming.

"A criminal *record*? Do I have a criminal *record*? Jesus, what a question for a complete stranger to ask!" He looked around as though wanting backup for his outrage.

"The reason I ask," Mike said, taking a step back, "is, I have a proposition for you, kind of a job offer, and I need to make sure you're not a criminal before I hire you. If you're interested. And if you're free from four 'til seven every day."

Mackie replaced his flask, and in a caricature of Man Thinking, rested an elbow in one hand and stroked his stubble with the other. "A job? You for real?"

Mike nodded.

"I'm not a criminal. Unless you call drunkenness a crime, and if you do, you're an asshole. I've had a few DUIs—why do you think I live in a *room* instead of a *house,* for God's sake? But that's not criminal, it's just stupidity. Drunks are stupid, idiotic, friggin' morons—but not criminals." He raised his eyes to the heavens. "Does that answer your question?"

"Yes," Mike said. "It does. So, you've lost your license?"

"My license, my car, my wife, my goddamn kids, my humanity . . . but I'm no criminal."

He really should be doing background checks on all these guys, but this project was costing enough as it was. His wife, Sara, would freak if she knew the extent of it. He told her he'd gotten the bar (an intricately carved oak beauty, complete with beer tap and back mirror and shelves and brass foot rest) for $100 from the friend of a friend who was closing down a pub due to lack of business, but the true story was he bought it from a salvage shop in the trendy part of the city for $2,700, and he'd dipped into the money market account to do so. But it was so perfect, so authentic.

"For this job, you won't have to have a car. It's only a few blocks from here, so you can walk. It's kind of an acting gig."

Mackie stood a little straighter when he heard those words. He probably always figured that someday he'd be discovered.

A man in khakis walked past Mackie's tarp, and without so much as a glance at him, tossed a dollar to the ground.

"What the goddamn hell!" Mackie shouted after the man. "I'm not homeless! Christ Almighty!"

But he picked up the bill and stuffed it in his pocket.

"The thing is," Mike said, "I can't pay you in cash. I can only pay you in beer. Four beers a day. Maybe five if another actor doesn't show up that day. And one or two shots of hard liquor. The hours are four o'clock until seven. You'll be drinking your pay in a bar." He looked at Mackie. "You still interested?"

He looked interested. Mackie again stroked his stubble. "Is this a movie?"

"No. It's . . . kind of hard to explain. Easy gig, though. You'd be going by the name of Buster. Really important. Your name would be Buster, and you'd be in Chicago. You ever been to Chicago?"

Mackie snorted. "Have I ever been to *Chicago*? How far away do you think Milwaukee *is* from Chicago?" He threw his arms out dramatically and muttered, "Have I ever been to Chicago. Damn. Who hasn't been to Chicago?"

Mackie could not be more perfect for the part of Buster if Mike had used a casting service.

"Okay, okay, you've been to Chicago." Mike paused as a garbage truck rumbled by. "So, you're Buster, you're in Chicago, and you're a regular at Sully's. Got that? Sully's is the name of the bar. Sully is actually dead now, and the bar is run by new people, but that isn't important."

"I might be a drunk, but I'm not stupid."

"I see that. Okay, now, here's the most important part. In Sully's, there's a regular, like you'd be. His name's Charlie. He's a really important regular in this gig, so part of your job would be to engage with Charlie, to interact with and talk to Charlie, to act like you've known him for years and years and you're old drinking buddies. Kind of like that show *Cheers*—you know that show?"

"Christ," Mackie answered with a snort. "Everybody knows *Cheers*. I have a TV in my goddamn room. Do I know *Cheers*. Do *you* know *Cheers*?"

Mackie was the king of dripping sarcasm—but then, so was Buster.

"So, you in?"

"Name's Buster, four 'til seven at Sully's, four beers, maybe five, two shots, from goddamn Chicago, friends with my old buddy,

Charlie." Mackie thrust his hand towards Mike for another firm shake.

His dad would have liked this guy whose grip crushed Mike's bones.

"I'm in."

"Okay, then." Mike pulled a folded sheet of paper from his front pants pocket. "I've got a contract here." At Mackie's raised eyebrows, he said, "I'm not asking your social security number or anything. This is just an agreement that you'll follow the terms I've laid out. No stealing, no fighting with any of the other bar patrons, stuff like that."

"Do you employ a bouncer?" Mackie asked.

"No. But I'm the bartender—one with the authority to kick patrons out on their asses. Violating the contract means you're booted out the door."

Mike had always been a runner, but in preparation had been hitting the gym daily in case any bouncing duties actually presented themselves. He hoped that just the sight of his impressive biceps would be enough. He flexed them now, thinking about it. He felt them strain at the sleeves of his button-down shirt.

"One more thing," Mike added. "Maybe tone down the whole taking-the-Lord's-name-in-vain thing. It doesn't bother me, but our important bar patron Charlie's not a fan."

Mackie's reddish eyebrows shot up. "You think I'm an idiot? I can do that. Christ."

Mackie took the paper from his hand and, to Mike's surprise, pulled a pair of reading glasses from his shirt pocket. He rested them on his nose and studied the contract.

"It says here I get all the popcorn and peanuts I want."

"Yes! Popcorn, peanuts, and if you like pickled eggs, there'll be a jar of them on the bar top, too."

Mike had never seen anyone eat a pickled egg at Sully's; those eggs might have been fifty years old for all he knew, but they were part of the Sully's scene, so they'd be there.

"Where do I sign?" Mackie asked, already playing a part since the Sign Here line at the bottom was plain to see.

Mike handed him a pen and Mackie signed his name.

Mike looked at the spiky signature: *Andrew M. McCallister.* "I guess Mackie comes from McCallister."

"We've got us an Einstein here." Mackie rolled his eyes.

Mike told him exact directions to the bar, and they parted ways with the agreement that the job started tomorrow at four o'clock.

Mike headed toward the house he'd lived in for the past three years. He'd left Sara home to fix dinner and handle things. Guilt quickened his step. As he got closer to home, the gentrification of the neighborhood became more evident; stoops grew less crumbly, shutters hung straighter, flowers and grassy lawns appeared.

He felt pretty good about the find of Mackie. Perfect, perfect Buster. And at a seedy bar named Drink, he'd found skinny, bald Jimmy (real name Greg), who actually used to live in Chicago. Jimmy was giddy at the prospect of free beer and peanuts so was more than willing to play a passionate Sox fan.

Buster and Jimmy were the only regulars he could really remember with certainty. He hadn't paid close enough attention back then. So after several days of searching, he'd picked up a couple of generic regulars. He vaguely remembered a short guy and a fat guy; so, behind the breakfast counter of Mornin' Biscuits, he'd found Norman with his substantial belly and endless supply of bar jokes (a three-legged dog walks into a saloon demanding to see the man who shot his paw; a guy walks into a bar with a chunk of asphalt, orders a beer for himself and one for the road—nice, simple jokes, easy to follow). Norman's nose was big and red with an abundant roadmap of capillaries, his eyes bloodshot and bleary as he ladled gravy over Mike's biscuit, so Mike knew he'd found a drinker. And at a halfway house he found Shorty, who was probably five feet tall. He looked like he belonged on a horse at the races. Shorty's name was actually Fredrick, but Mike changed it to Shorty because it sounded more authentically Drunk-Guy-at-Sully's. Authenticity was key. (He'd have to tell Norman a good Shorty joke: "Sully's likes to keep Shorty around because it makes the drinks look bigger.")

When this was all over someday, he might need to look into getting these guys into AA. For now, though, he needed them to drink.

His brick house sat on a corner. It looked a lot like the single-story brick house he'd left behind in Chicago. Sara's potted red geraniums flanked the front door.

Mike rounded the corner and walked down the steep street. His lower-basement level became evident, with its heavy mahogany door and the substantial leaded glass window beside it. Mike stood in front of the door, which he installed just last week, to admire his handiwork.

Not bad, not bad at all.

The next day was the first day.

Mike took the day off (he worked for himself, so that was easy to do) to deal with the finishing touches: installing a blue BAR sign in the window, getting the pickled eggs, picking up a keg, sorting through glass liquor bottles at the recycling center, rinsing them and filling them with colored water, lining them up on the shelves in front of the mirror. And a few bottles with real liquor, of course, since he'd promised the occasional shot to the drunks. He'd have to see how his money held out.

He had five barstools at the beautiful, gleaming bar and two pub-type tables with captain's chairs. The real Sully's had probably eight or ten barstools and five or six tables, but Mike had space limitations to deal with. The floor was authentic linoleum—the real stuff, not the sheet vinyl crap—and the walls had wood on the lower half and chipped plaster on the upper, kind of a blotchy brownish yellow to simulate years of cigarette smoke. He'd had to experiment with various stains and rags to get the effect just right.

Sara leaned in the doorway one recent night past midnight,

arms folded and shaking her head while watching Mike smash a crumpled rag repeatedly into the wall's corners. She didn't understand—and yet, she did. She knew this project was important to him, and that was one reason he loved her so.

Now it was four o'clock, and right on the money, here came his drunks. Turns out they'd been at the curb watching Norman's wristwatch, waiting for exactly four. They didn't want to screw up the first day on the new job.

He welcomed them in, reviewed the terms of their contracts, and poured them each a beer from the tap. They each took a seat at a barstool, but Mike told Norman and Shorty to go sit at a table. Authenticity was key. They objected, but Mike pointed out that it was a contractual obligation, and the legal speak caused them to shuffle meekly to a table, where the two strangers awkwardly began conversing.

"I'll take that shot now," Mackie (Buster! Mike needed to remember that) said.

Buster looked around the bar, nodding his head a little as though pleased by what he saw. He rubbed his hand along the polished wood.

Mike didn't want to start pouring shots so soon but did anyway.

Jimmy, the sports guy, leaned toward Buster, lifted his beer, and asked, "You a Sox fan?"

Buster looked down at his argyle-clad ankles. "What do you mean by that? Am I a *socks* fan? What does it look like, Einstein? What a question. Am I a *socks* fan."

He tossed his shot of whiskey down his throat and slammed his shot glass to the counter.

Mike gnawed at a hangnail.

Luckily, his Jimmy was an affable guy. "*Naw*, not socks, man. Sox! The White Sox! You a fan of them?"

"Am I a *White Sox* fan?" Buster began, and Mike looked forward to hearing the rude answer, but at that moment, his cell phone rang.

He turned his back to answer. In the mirror, he could see Jimmy nodding and grinning at Buster, and, beyond them, Norman and Shorty starting a game of chess.

It was Sara.

"The cops are here," she said. "Mike, I'm sorry."

"Where?"

"At the front door of our house."

"Oh, God." Mike glanced behind him. He needed to deal with this, but how could he leave a bunch of drunks in an untended bar?

He was probably nuts, but something about Mackie—Buster!—made Mike trust him. Maybe it was that handshake.

"Buster," he said.

Buster turned his head at hearing the name. He'd already learned his part.

"Buster, I've got to run out for just a minute. I'll be back in a jiff. You okay bartending for a few minutes?"

Buster stood. "Am I okay *bartending* for a few minutes? Jesus Christ, how hard is it to pull a lever? Am I okay bartending. Are *you* okay bartending?"

Buster came around to the other side of the bar, grabbed a rag, and began swiping at the clean bar top as though he'd been doing it all his life.

"How you doing over there, boys?" he called out to Shorty and Norman.

Mike dashed out the door, got into his car, and took a short drive to the front of his house. He could have walked but didn't want any questions about where he'd come from. He didn't need the police asking questions about his unlicensed bar. No money was changing hands, and he could claim he was just having drinks with friends—but it was much easier just to avoid questions altogether.

Two uniformed officers stood on the porch. A gray-haired man, his cardigan sweater misbuttoned, sat on the porch swing, staring at his lap.

Mike climbed out of his car and ran up the porch steps.

The man in the sweater looked up at Mike's face. Light came into his eyes. "Mikey!" he said happily. "Mikey!"

"Hi, Dad," Mike said. "Hello, officers."

"Hey, there," the taller of the two said. "This time he got as far as 11th and Main. That's a long walk for an old guy. And traffic was really flying. I worry about him crossing the street."

"Dad," Mike said, joining his father on the swing. "Dad, that was a long walk."

His father looked at him with his pale-blue, watery eyes. "Mike, I just want to have a beer at Sully's. That's all. I just want to have a beer at Sully's."

"That's what he told us, too," the cop said. "I told him, just like I did last time, there isn't a bar called Sully's *in* Milwaukee. And then he insisted, just like last time, that he's not in Milwaukee, that he's in Chicago. We just can't get through to him." The cop looked at Mike's dad and shook his head. "My mom had dementia pretty bad, and she'd take off, too. Once she got all the way to the zoo, wearing a nightgown with her bra on the outside. Said she wanted to see the monkeys. It was tough."

The other cop, the shorter one, asked, "How long's your dad been living with you?"

"Almost three months now. And every day, four o'clock, he wants to head for Sully's."

His father had gone to Sully's from four 'til seven every day for probably the bulk of his adult life. At 6:45 each day, it had been Mike's job to set the kitchen table because Dad would be home soon.

"Routine's huge with these dementia folk," the tall cop said. "You might want to consider a nursing home. They're used to dealing—"

"Thanks for bringing him back," Mike interrupted. "Again. I really appreciate it. I don't think you'll have to do it again, I really don't. We're going to be so careful to watch him closely from now on."

The short cop gave his dad's shoulder a squeeze before he left.

Mike's throat clenched.

His dad stood. His knees were perpetually bent. He reached out and touched Mike's sleeve. "Are we going to Sully's now? I need to catch up with the boys."

Mike poked his head inside the door. Sara was right there. She'd probably been listening.

"Sorry, Mike. I know you wanted today to get things ready. He slipped out the door so fast. I thought he was snoozing in front of the game. Are the 'regulars' there alone?"

"Yep."

"Leave your dad with me. Go back. I'll watch him really hard this time."

"No," Mike said. "He wants to go to Sully's *now*. So, I'm taking him to Sully's." He gave Sara a quick kiss and turned to his father. "Come on, Dad. Let's go to Sully's."

In the car, his father sat staring ahead with his hands folded in his lap.

"Buckle up for takeoff, Dad."

It's what his father always said to Mike and his brother when they were kids: *"Buckle up for takeoff."* Then he'd rev the engine, and Mike would tingle with excitement as though the station wagon were about to make liftoff.

He pulled away from the curb and headed away from his house. Down two blocks, a right turn, another right, another . . .

"Is this the way to Sully's?" his dad asked.

"Yep, sure is. You haven't been there in a while, that's why it seems different."

"What?" His father looked at him, eyebrows raised. "I go there every day!"

Mike swallowed. He turned his last right and pulled the car into the gravel parking spot he'd created. "Here we are, Dad."

His father climbed out and stood staring at the basement level of Mike's house. The mahogany door, which was almost an exact replica of the entrance to Sully's—Mike had driven to Chicago to photograph and sketch and measure—and the leaded glass window with its blue BAR sign. He'd even put one of those sand things for cigarette butts outside the door.

"Is this Sully's?" his dad said.

The real Sully's stood in the center of a whole row of brick buildings, and Mike's house stood alone, the way houses do. He'd hoped his dad wouldn't notice.

"Yeah, Dad. Did you hear the buildings on each side of Sully's had to get torn down? Dry rot. That's why Sully's has space on each side now."

His father kept standing, his pale eyes fixed on the door. A slight tremor shook his head—a tremor that Mike knew appeared when his dad was stressed.

"C'mon, Dad, I'm dying for a beer. Your old pals, Buster and Jimmy, might be in there."

He pulled the heavy door open—it really was a fantastic door; it would likely add value to their home—and stepped inside with trepidation. Who knew what these alcoholic strangers might have done in the ten or fifteen minutes he'd been away? But when they walked in, there was Buster, still behind the bar, tossing peanuts expertly into Jimmy's open mouth. Norman and Shorty were still at their chess game, their beer glasses empty.

"Hey, everybody!" Mike shouted, his voice hearty. "Here's Charlie!"

Buster, Jimmy, Norman, Shorty—all four men shouted, nearly in unison, "Charlie!" Bless them.

Buster, overplaying his part, rushed out from behind the bar, grabbed Charlie's hand, and pumped it vigorously. "Long time no see, buddy!"

Charlie looked bewildered. "I come to Sully's every day."

"Of course you do," Buster said. "And so do I! I'm a drunk! You know the difference between a drunk and an alcoholic? A drunk doesn't have to go to all those damn meetings."

"Here, Dad, sit at the bar."

Once his dad was seated, Mike got behind the bar, tied on an apron, and poured his father a beer. He turned on the little TV he'd mounted in the upper corner. It had always been on at Sully's, even though bar noise drowned out the sound. He searched through channels until he found a bowling tournament, which seemed authentic enough.

"Where's Sully?" his dad said.

Sully had died, oh, sometime back in the mid '90s, but his dad's mind was apparently stuck somewhere in the '90s, too.

"Didn't I tell you, Dad? Sully hired me to bartend now and then!"

Why did this charade make him speak with such forced heartiness? He might have to go on the hunt for a Sully. Sully hadn't been a drinker, though, so would he have to pay him in cash? And half of Sully's face had been covered by a strawberry birthmark. That wouldn't be an easy find. Of course, there was always makeup . . .

Charlie turned to the man beside him. "What's your name again?"

"Name's Buster," Mackie answered. "Ol' drinking buddy, ol' pal."

Mike gave him a warning look: *Don't go overboard.*

His dad gestured toward Mike there behind the bar. "That's my boy. Sully hired him to tend bar. He's a college boy, a smart one, too. Reads books, college books, big thick college . . ." His voice trailed away.

"Textbooks?" Buster said.

"That's it! Textbooks!" Charlie clinked Buster's beer glass with his own.

Mike was forty-four and had graduated over twenty years ago, but he just smiled and shouted, "Another round, fellas?"

Jimmy leaned past Buster and said, "Remind me, you a Sox fan like me?"

Charlie was silent for a long moment as though trying to

remember just who he was a fan of but finally answered, "No! I'm a Cubs man!"

"Oh, Cubbies, little baby bears, *waah, waah, waah!* Bunch of crybabies, blaming everything on a goat. A goat! So they won the World Series. It was a fluke. Just you watch, when they start losing again—and they will, mark my words—it'll be the goat's fault."

Mike's dad put his beer down, looked hard at the man. Then, "Jimmy? That you?"

"Hell yes, I'm Jimmy. Jimmy, the world's biggest Sox fan!" Jimmy reached past Buster and clinked Charlie's glass.

Beer sloshed onto the polished bar top, and Mike was swift to wipe it up. This basement bar would add value to his home, someday, especially if he kept it in tip-top condition.

Charlie turned his head back to face the mirror.

Mike poured himself a beer, watching his father watching himself.

He hooked a finger, calling Mike close.

"Yeah, Dad?"

His father pointed towards the mirror. "Who's that old guy? The one with the white mustache? Is he new here?"

Mike looked at the mirror. His father was pointing at himself.

"That's you, Dad."

If his father was stuck in the '90s, he likely pictured his own face as that of a younger man. Dark-haired and strong-jawed, a smile with straight, white teeth, a bend to his nose from a fight he'd had in Vietnam.

Buster, listening, said, "Charlie, that white mustache is the foam on your upper lip!" He roared with laughter.

Damn it. Mike might have to use his muscle right now, right now.

His dad reached up and swiped his lip, looked at the foam on his finger in bewilderment. Then he threw back his head, and he laughed. *Laughed.* Mike hadn't heard his father laugh since he'd brought him to Milwaukee.

"Bartender," his dad said, glancing at Mike without recognition, "pour me another beer, would you?" He turned to Buster. "How about you? You like the Cubs?"

Buster rolled his eyes. "What a question. Of course I like the goddamn Cubs. Who doesn't like the Cubs?"

Jimmy raised his hand. "*Aw*, the Cubs stink worse than my undershorts," he said. "And my undershorts haven't been washed in a month."

His father slid his glass toward Mike for a refill, but his eyes were on Buster and Jimmy. His pale blue eyes had come alive. His dad was home. He'd found his home again. His four 'til seven home that occupied his heart for the rest of the hours.

Mike filled the glass and slid it towards his father, who took it and nodded the way you'd nod at a stranger. Mike blinked, swallowed, wiped the bar top fiercely with the rag.

His dad made eye contact with the old guy in the mirror, the one whose white mustache had reappeared. He tipped his glass toward the man; the man tipped his back simultaneously.

"I have a college boy," he told the man. "Real smart, reads big books, big college books—"

"Textbooks," Buster interjected.

"Textbooks, that's right."

Norman and Shorty ambled up to the bar.

Mike's father said, "Next round's on me."

Mike was pretty sure this was beer number four already, but what the hell. He filled their glasses from the tap, angling them to get the head of foam just right.

"To Charlie!" Buster shouted, and the other drunks chimed in.

Even the one in the mirror.

S. Lyle Lunt grew up in a small Midwestern river town. She attended college in Wyoming, where she fell in love with the wild west, the cowboy she ended up marrying, and the bar and its inhabitants which inspired her story, "A Guy Walks Into a Bar."

She now lives in Georgia with her husband and dachshund, Charlie.

She plans to release her debut novel, *A River, A Canoe, Glug Glug, Lindy Lou*, in 2018.

www.facebook.com/SLyleLunt

DON'T FORGET ME

Signature *Laurie Gardiner*

"If I forget who you are, I want you to kill me."

Anthony choked on his wine.

Kate handed him a napkin. "Don't spew, darling. It's unbecoming."

He watched her through narrowed eyes as he dabbed his mouth. Kate Templeton was renowned for her sarcasm, but she rarely joked.

She leaned back in her chair and took a long drag from a cigarette. The jewels on her manicured fingers flashed in the glow of the setting sun.

"Care to explain?" Anthony asked.

Kate looked up, one perfectly waxed dark brow arched.

That look always unnerved him, but his unwavering gaze held hers.

She inhaled deeply, exhaled in a sigh, and stubbed out the cigarette in a nine-hundred-dollar Baccarat crystal ashtray.

"Because that's what happens with Alzheimer's. First you forget where you put your keys, then you forget who people are, and eventually you forget how to eat and use the toilet." She shuddered. "I know. I watched it happen to my mother. Add stage-four cancer to the mix, and I don't stand a chance. I don't want to live my last days bedridden and helpless while some stranger changes my diapers and feeds me purees."

Anthony shifted in his seat. She talked about her illnesses as though discussing the weather.

"Why me? Why not Holly?"

"Don't be an idiot. I would never ask Holly to kill me. It's a very unmotherly thing to do. And besides, she wouldn't have the stomach for it."

And I do? I feel bad when I have to kill a spider.

Kate was right about Holly though; she was much softer hearted than her mother.

"Go to Switzerland then. You can afford it."

"Why would I want to die in a foreign country surrounded by people I don't know?"

"True. At least you tolerate me and Holly. Your threshold for strangers is uncomfortably low at times."

"Are you saying I make you uncomfortable?"

"You know that's exactly what I'm saying. And we both know you enjoy making people uncomfortable. Let's not pretend it's an insult."

Anthony grabbed the wine carafe and topped off both glasses as he mused. "An overdose of painkillers and booze then. After all, isn't that how the rich and famous do it?"

The corners of Kate's mouth lifted slightly. "That was my thought as well."

Anthony blinked in surprise. "But you could do that yourself."

"No, I can't."

"Why not? What's the difference? Either you take them yourself or I give them to you and you take them. Either way, you'll know what's happening."

Her voice dropped to a low growl. "How will I know? By then, my brain will be Swiss cheese, and I won't have a clue what's going on. Hell, by then, I may not even remember this conversation." She averted her eyes. "You'll have to put it in my drink without me knowing. It can't be suicide."

Anthony's eyes widened as realization hit him. "Oh my God. You're afraid if you commit suicide, you'll go to Hell."

Kate's hand trembled slightly as she reached for another cigarette.

"But no concern whatsoever for my soul?" Anthony continued. "We're talking murder here."

Her eyes flashed. "Oh, please. You don't believe in God or Hell or sin. Don't pretend it matters to you."

He relented, shrinking a little beneath her accusing glare. "You've been divorced twice, and you're sleeping with a bisexual man nearly half your age. I think it's a little late to worry about sin."

"I've confessed those sins. I can't confess and be forgiven after I'm dead." She lit the cigarette and took a long drag before waving it in his direction. "No one will ever find out, if that's what you're worried about. My doctor and Holly both know my propensity for mixing pills and booze. They'll think the Alzheimer's made me careless."

"I suppose . . ."

"You'll do it then?"

Anthony sighed. "Of course I will. You know I'd do anything for you."

The self-satisfied smile on her face made it clear she felt she'd won. He shrugged off a twinge of resentment. Everything to Kate was a competition, and anything less than a win was a failure. He'd learned long ago not to take it personally.

She touched his hand and leaned in closer. "Now, we need to discuss the terms and conditions of the agreement."

An hour later Anthony returned to the solitude of the guesthouse. He went straight to the bar, poured two straight-up fingers of scotch, and sipped it as he surveyed the room. She owned it all: the apartment, the leather furniture, the Porsche in the garage, the silk Armani shirt on his back.

Hell, she owns me. Terms and conditions? Seriously? Is everything business to her? Even our relationship? With a short, sardonic laugh, he tossed back the rest of the scotch. Of course it was.

He poured a more conservative drink and paced, rehashing the conversation. Nothing could be in writing, and no one else could know about the deal—not even Holly. No evidence, no witnesses, no way to connect him to Kate's death. She had given him a small window of time within which to do it—before she became bedridden and incoherent but not until her quality of life was compromised.

"What if I can't bring myself to do it?" he'd asked.

Kate had raised a brow and stared down her nose at him as though, by asking, he had already failed her.

"You're asking me to kill you," he reminded her.

"I'm asking you to help me die peacefully, without suffering. It's not murder if it's what I want."

He waved his hand. "Semantics. I doubt anyone else would see it that way."

"Regardless, I've already thought of that."

Anthony rolled his eyes. The woman would argue that the sky wasn't blue simply for the sake of arguing. "Please, go on."

"If you can't do it, you're to stay with me until I die. I've already told Holly and my doctor that I'm to die at home, not be put into a facility. You'll hire nurses to do my physical care, and Holly will pay them. She and I have spoken to the lawyer, and I've already appointed her my power of attorney for the estate as well as my medical care. If, at any point, the doctor declares me incapable of making decisions, Holly will step in. She's aware of my wishes concerning you. Questions?"

"I'm not sure what I can do for you that nurses can't."

"Keep me company. Read to me. Eat with me. Make me a drink, and bring me a cigarette when I ask for one, even when Holly and the doctor forbid it. Do what you know I would want, not what others think is best. You'll know when it's time. I believe you can do it, Anthony." She swallowed hard and looked away. "But if you can't, just be a friend. I have a feeling the few I have won't stick around long once I start acting like a lunatic."

Anthony snorted into his glass. She'd always been a lunatic. But the sight of tears in her eyes softened his heart. He had never seen Kate cry. He doubted anyone had.

After draining the last of his wine, Anthony stood and leaned over to kiss her cheek. "That I can promise, Kate. I will always be your friend."

She touched his hand as he turned to leave. "I know you will. That's why I chose you. Now, don't you want to know what's in it for you, what *you* will get out of this agreement?"

He shook his head. "No. I get to be with you until you're gone. That's enough."

Those words haunted him already. Anthony slugged back his drink and slammed the glass on the bar. God, he was an idiot. He had gone and done what he vowed not to do when he first met Kate—he had fallen in love with her.

Anthony ordered a chai latte and a black coffee and sat on a leather loveseat near the fireplace. Holly *would* choose the trendiest, most expensive place in the city to meet.

A moment later, she strode through the door. As always, he was struck by how much she resembled her mother. Their height, always exaggerated by heels, intimidated some men. Anthony found it refreshing to effortlessly look a woman in the eye.

He stood to greet her.

"Anthony!" She placed a hand on his arm and leaned in close, her lips barely brushing his cheek. "How long has it been?" She took a seat in the armchair across from him.

He handed her the coffee. "Too long. Kate and I don't get out much these days."

She curled her bottom lip in a small, sad smile. "And I've been working too much and haven't taken the time to visit."

"Yes. Kate complains daily what a bad daughter you are."

Holly threw her head backward and laughed. "You say that sarcastically, but it wouldn't surprise me at all if it were true."

"Actually, she may not say it, but I know she's quite proud of you."

"She's proud that I turned out to be a strong, independent woman with a good head for business, like her. And I turned out that way because I respect and look up to her for those things. It doesn't change the fact that we don't really like each other very much."

"She's not an easy person to like."

"No need to tell me that. Why do you think I grew up living with my father? For the same reason Mother's been divorced twice. She's impossible to live with."

"Which is why, even after three years, I live in the guest house."

"Oh dear. Please tell me you're not bitter about that. You must know it's for the best."

"Not bitter. Resigned, I suppose. I know it wouldn't work any other way, but there are times I wish for more." Anthony heard the longing in his voice and cringed. He had revealed more than he meant to.

A look of surprise flashed across Holly's face before turning to sympathy. "Oh, you poor thing. You're in deep, aren't you?"

Heat crept up his neck. "I suppose I am. What other reason could I have for staying with her?"

"Well, there is the money."

His eyes darted to her face. "You don't believe that's why I'm with her, do you? Because I have no doubt she plans on leaving it all to you."

Holly said nothing as they stared at each other. Finally, she smiled and shook her head. "No. I do believe you're with her for the right reasons. Which is why I asked to meet with you today."

"To find out my intentions?"

Her eyes danced with humor. "Don't be offended, darling. I'm only looking out for my mother's best interests, and you've put my mind at ease. She says she wants you to be in charge of her care. Is that what you want as well?"

"We discussed it, and I agreed."

She leaned forward. "You agreed, or she coerced you? I know how intimidating she can be, Anthony. This won't be easy. If you think she's hard to please now, wait until all reason has left her."

"I know. Believe me, I've thought of that. I've pictured Kate at her very worst, and I still can't imagine leaving her." He straightened in his seat and stared intently into Holly's eyes. "There's no choice. I have to do it. I promised her I would."

What Anthony had pictured as Kate's worst did not come close to reality. In the three months following their agreement, she became even more difficult. Depression and paranoia set in, and her memory declined rapidly.

Anthony struggled to deal with the changes. He dreaded doing what he had agreed to. He also dreaded *not* being able to do it. And yet, there were days when the thought of killing her did not seem so daunting. Today was one of those days.

That morning, Anthony joined Kate in the dining room.

Colette came out of the kitchen with two plates. She served Kate her breakfast with a smile and a pleasant "*Bonjour, Madame*," before turning to drop a plate on the table in front of Anthony. Two slimy, sunny-side-up eggs stared back at him, causing his stomach to somersault. Colette knew very well he liked them over hard.

"I'm not hungry anyway," he called as she marched into the kitchen.

There was no response. She had not spoken to him since he complained about the overcooked asparagus three nights ago.

With a shrug, he pushed away the plate and reached for his coffee cup. It was empty. He sighed and went to get the coffee pot from the buffet.

When he returned a moment later, Kate leaned in close and spoke in a loud whisper. "I don't trust that woman."

Anthony glanced toward the kitchen door. "Colette? I thought you liked her."

"I think she's been stealing from me."

Anthony did not care much for Colette. He found her bossy and condescending, but even he could not call her untrustworthy.

"Why do you think that?"

"My favorite diamond earrings are missing, and this morning I couldn't find my rings."

Anthony looked pointedly at her hands. "Obviously you found the rings. Where were they?"

"She *conveniently* found them on my sink when I asked if she had seen them. I always leave them on my nightstand when I take them off before bed, so how could they have been in the bathroom?"

"You *have* been a little forgetful lately . . ."

Kate's back stiffened. She put down her fork and stared at him. "Are you taking her side?"

"No, I'm not. I'm just saying—"

"You're saying you don't believe me. You think I'm making this up."

"No, that's not what I said. Of course I believe you, but remember what the doctor said—"

"I don't care what the doctor said!" Kate screamed as she rose from her chair. The coffee cup flew from her hand and smashed against the wall. She spun toward Anthony and loomed over him. "You're in on this with her, aren't you?"

He stood to face her. "Of course I'm not! Stop acting crazy."

Her hand lashed out and struck his face. They both stood in shocked silence for a moment before Kate erupted into tears and ran from the room, leaving Anthony speechless.

"What did you do to *Madame*?"

He looked up to see Colette glaring at him from the kitchen doorway.

"Fuck off, Colette."

Not even the sight of the housekeeper's agape mouth placated him as he strode from the room. He stormed down the hallway to Kate's bedroom and stopped outside the door. His fist hovered, ready to knock. He hesitated, unsure of how to best deal with the situation. The old Kate was always in control of her emotions—cool and calculating and sure of every word. This was a side of her he had never seen. Perhaps it was best to give her time to cool down.

His hand dropped to his side and he walked away.

An hour later, he charged into the laundry room.

Colette dropped the towel she was folding and clutched a hand to her heart. "*Mon Dieu*! What do you want now?"

"Where's Kate?"

"I do not know, *Monsieur*. I have not seen her since you made her upset. She must be in her room."

"She's not. I checked. I've looked everywhere."

"Perhaps she is in the pool."

He shook his head. "I checked."

"*Le jardin—*"

"No. I'm telling you. I've looked everywhere."

Colette's thick brows knitted together, deepening the crease between them. "*Madame's* car. It is in the garage, *oui*?"

"I didn't check. The doctor took her license away . . ."

They exchanged a knowing look. Kate did not take orders; she gave them. Anthony ran out the room and down the hallway with Colette following close behind. He burst through the interior garage door and stopped at the sight of one empty bay.

Colette plowed into him, grabbing his arm to steady herself. "*Merde*! She is gone."

Anthony's phone rang, and he activated his Bluetooth. "Any luck?"

Holly's voice filled the Porsche. "No. She's not at the office. I'm sure you'll find her at the beach house. Are you close?"

"About five minutes out."

"Five? For God's sake, Anthony. Slow down. You can't help her if you get yourself killed."

"Don't worry about me. If she's not there, I'm calling the police. I still think we should've called them right away."

"She's only been missing three hours. The police aren't going to do anything yet."

Anthony gripped the steering wheel tighter and clenched his teeth to keep from snapping. How could Holly be so calm when he was a ball of anxiety?

"Anthony? Are you still there?"

"Yes."

"She'll be there. It's where she always goes when she's upset."

Anthony turned onto the beach road, barely registering the vast expanse of the brilliant blue ocean before him. As he rounded the bend, the beach house and Kate's black Mercedes came into view. He let out a deep, audible sigh.

"I take it she's there."

He jumped at the sound of Holly's voice and let out a short bark of relieved laughter. "Yes. My God, you scared me. I forgot you were still on the line."

"Because I was quiet, and you're not used to that?"

"You said it, not me. I'm going in. Stay on the line, and I'll switch you over to my phone."

The door was unlocked.

Anthony pushed it open and called out from the foyer. "Kate? Hello?"

His voice bounced off the twenty-foot ceiling and echoed through the house. He crossed the main floor to the living room, opened the sliding door, and stepped onto the deck.

A lone figure sat huddled on the beach.

Anthony brought his phone to his mouth. "She's here. She's fine."

Holly's voice radiated relief. "Oh, good. Call me later."

He slid the phone into his pocket and traipsed across the sand toward Kate.

She sat, knees hugged tight to her chest, so close to the water's edge that the waves licked her toes. The cool wind flattened her thin dress against her body, revealing the gaunt angles of disease-ridden bones.

Not wanting to startle her, Anthony stopped a few feet away and said her name.

She turned to stare at him with eyes that bled misery. Lines of pain creased her pallid face. "I came here to be alone."

"I know. Holly and I needed to know you were okay."

Her voice sounded hoarse and bitter when she laughed. "Why? I'm dying anyway."

Anthony settled in the sand beside her, removing his shoes and socks as he spoke. "We don't want you dying alone in a ditch somewhere."

She gazed across the water and spoke in a voice so low the wind nearly swept it away. "I made a fool of myself this morning."

"Yes, you did."

Her head swiveled, and she glowered at him through narrowed eyes.

He brought her hand to his mouth and kissed it. "But it doesn't matter. I still love you."

She scooted closer until their bodies touched. "I know. That's why I chose you to be with me at the end."

Anthony ignored the pangs of disappointment. It wasn't what he had hoped to hear, but he doubted she had ever said *I love you* to anyone.

When he had discovered her missing that morning, so many scenarios had played out in his mind. The reality of losing her struck hard, and the pain nearly brought him to his knees. Even now, with her safe at his side, the thought was unbearable.

He wrapped an arm around her shoulders, pulled her tight, and buried his face in her hair. *I'm not ready to lose you. Please, don't forget me.*

Kate's health deteriorated quickly over the next few weeks. She barely ate, and her body went from gaunt to emaciated in days. Sickness shrouded the house with despair. The nurses came and went silently, barely speaking a word to avoid being the target of one of Kate's verbal assaults. Two had quit, despite being offered substantially more money to stay.

Anthony couldn't blame them. Even he could barely stand to be near her some days. This was one of those days.

Kate's mood was exceptionally vile that morning, so Anthony made himself scarce. He sat at the table, sipping coffee and scrolling through his emails. Collette worked wordlessly around him, setting the table for breakfast. A *bang*, followed by the sound of raised voices, floated down the hallway.

Colette paused. "Perhaps you should see what is happening."

Anthony dismissed her with a shrug. "The nurse knows where I am. If she needs me, she'll call."

Minutes later, the nurse called his name. Ignoring the smug look on Colette's face, Anthony left the room. The nurse met him in the hallway, frustration etched into her features.

He offered her a sympathetic smile. "What is it?"

"I'm sorry. I've tried hard to remain professional and compassionate. I can deal with the insults, but I draw the line at physical violence."

"Oh no. What did she do?"

"When I asked her to take her meds, she accused me of trying to poison her and tried to slap me. Then she threw a brush at me."

"What will it take to get you to stay?"

"I never said I was quitting."

Anthony blinked in surprise. "You're not?"

"No, I'm not. I've had clients worse than Ms. Templeton, and I haven't quit a job yet. But, it's too much for one person to handle. From now on, a second person needs to be present to help keep her calm during her morning and evening care. You, her daughter, Colette, another nurse—whatever you decide."

Anthony resisted the urge to hug her. "I'll talk to Holly, and we'll figure it out."

"Another thing. I'm afraid Ms. Templeton has become so weak that she's at risk for falls. I believe it's time to order a wheelchair." She lowered her voice and leaned closer. "She also needs to start wearing incontinence products at night. Would you like me to order those as well?"

Anthony cleared his throat. "Uh, yes, please."

After the nurse left, Anthony stood in the hallway feeling stunned. Kate—his Kate—in diapers and a wheelchair. Her words floated in his head: *I don't want to live my last days bedridden and helpless while some stranger changes my diapers . . .*

Anthony swiped the dampness from his eyes and shambled to Kate's bedroom. He tapped on the door and listened. The only sound was the murmur of the television. He opened the door partway and peeked into the room. Kate lay on the chaise lounge, wrapped in a thick blanket.

Anthony crossed the room and took a seat beside her. He brushed a strand of hair from her face.

Kate stared at him. "What are you doing here?"

"The nurse said you're having a rough morning. Is there anything I can do to make it better?"

Her gaze darted around the room as she fought to sit up. "No. You shouldn't be here. Get out. Get out!"

Coldness seeped into Anthony's body. He placed a hand on her arm. "You just woke up. You're tired and confused and—"

"No! Get your hands off me."

Her arm flew up and hit him in the face, knocking him off the lounge. His forehead glanced off the coffee table with a *crack*, and he landed on the floor. He lay there, unmoving, until a line of wet warmth trickled down his face. He wiped it, and his hand came away covered in blood.

"Shit."

Kate looked at him. "Get out! Get out of here now." She clawed at the blanket, struggling to escape its weight. "Philip, help me!"

Anthony closed his eyes. Kate's yelling and the pounding in his head made it nearly impossible to think. Philip was her second ex. They had divorced a few months before Kate hired Anthony as her personal assistant.

The realization hit him hard; her memories had retreated to a time before they met. She didn't know who he was. Hot tears stung the backs of his eyelids, and he squeezed them shut harder.

"*Mon Dieu, que s'est-il passé ici?*"

The sound of Colette's voice brought the strange combination of relief and dread to Anthony. With a groan, he rolled onto his side and wiped his eyes dry with a shirtsleeve.

Colette leaned over him and clucked her tongue. "You have bled all over *Madame's* white carpet. Must I call *une ambulance*?"

"No! No ambulance. I'll take care of it."

He grabbed the side of the coffee table and pulled himself to a sitting position. The room tilted, then straightened. He turned to Colette, but she had already forgotten him.

She spoke to her employer in soft, soothing tones, and in no time, Kate became calm.

Anthony left the room and retreated to his apartment to lick his wounds. He cleaned his face and placed a suture strip on the gash above his brow. With both hands on the sink, he leaned toward the mirror and gazed at his reflection. His face was creased with worry. Dark shadows haunted his eyes.

Their bargain kept him up at night. He couldn't stand to watch Kate waste away, but how could he kill the woman he loved?

Nothing is in writing. She probably doesn't even remember making the deal. No one will ever know if I don't carry out my end of the bargain. A hoarse half sob, half laugh erupted from him. *Who am I kidding? I'll know. And Kate will haunt me forever. What the hell have I done?*

Resisting the urge to slam his fist into the mirror, he turned and left the room. He couldn't stand to look at himself any longer.

The next morning, Anthony stayed out of sight until Kate was seated in the dining room. After Colette served breakfast and retreated to the kitchen, he went to the buffet and poured a cup of coffee. He turned and studied Kate over the rim of his cup.

"Come sit, darling," Kate said without looking up from her plate.

Anthony's shoulders slumped as a wave of relief washed over him. He had spent a sleepless night in dread of the morning light, worrying she might have forgotten him forever. He crossed the room and took a seat beside her.

She pushed away her plate and studied Anthony's face. Her eyes lingered on the dressing above his brow. "What happened?"

He touched a finger to the wound and winced. "I fell and hit it on the coffee table."

"One of the things I've always liked most about you is that you're not afraid to tell me the truth. Don't stop now, just because I'm dying. Tell me what really happened."

"It was an accident. I startled you awake, and when you pushed me away, I fell and hit my head on the table."

"Why did I push you away?"

Anthony hung his head in his hands.

"I didn't know who you were, did I?"

Her words rang through his head: *If I forget who you are, I want you to kill me.*

"Anthony?"

"No."

Silence hung heavy in the room.

Anthony lifted his cup, saw it was empty, and placed it back on the table.

"Let's not talk about it anymore," Kate said. "I'm having a good day, and I don't want to ruin it. Call Holly, and tell her to come for lunch."

Holly arrived at noon and joined Kate and Anthony on the patio. She leaned over to drop a quick peck on her mother's cheek before sitting beside her.

"Thank you for coming on such short notice, my dear." Kate lifted her champagne flute. "Anthony, be a darling, and pour Holly a glass."

Holly shot a perplexed glance in Anthony's direction. "Are we . . . celebrating something?"

He filled a glass and handed it to Holly without a word.

"A toast," Kate said, raising her glass in the air between them. "To good days."

After lunch, the nurse took Kate to her room for a nap.

Holly tapped a finger on the table while Colette cleared the lunch dishes. As soon as the Frenchwoman went inside, Holly asked, "What was that really about?"

Anthony opened his mouth and closed it. His first instinct was to protect Holly's feelings with a lie, but that wouldn't help anyone now. "Kate doesn't have much time left, and she knows it. I think she woke up this morning feeling like she needed something to look forward to."

Holly reached for her napkin and dabbed at the corners of her eyes. "I suppose when you're dying, waking up in the morning is a reason to celebrate."

"Stop, or you'll have us both in tears."

Holly's lower lip trembled as she attempted a smile. She reached across the table to cover his hand with hers. "Thank you for loving my mother."

Kate slept most of the afternoon and woke in good spirits. Anthony helped her outside to the patio. She removed a cigarette and inhaled as he lit it for her.

"I'd like to have dinner by the pool tonight. Late, so I can enjoy the stars."

"Of course. I'll let Colette know. Casual, or shall we dress for it?"

Kate's face glowed at the suggestion. "Let's dress for it."

"Perfect. I'll tell Colette to prepare something special."

Later, when the light faded and the sky blushed pink, Anthony placed a vase of white roses on the table and lit the candles. Colette had dressed the table in linen and laid it with Kate's finest dishes. All around the patio, strings of tiny white lights sparkled, their reflections shimmering on the surface of the pool.

Anthony paced, resisting the urge to down a shot of scotch. He stopped in front of the sliding door and adjusted his tie. As he ran a hand through his dark hair, a movement caught his eye. Through the glass, he watched Kate walk toward him, arm in arm with the nurse. Despite her slow, awkward gait, she still managed to look regal.

The full-length gown hung from her body, where a few short months ago it would have hugged her curves. Her hair, pulled into a bun, revealed a long, slender neck draped in diamonds. Red lipstick-stained lips turned up at the sight of him. The nurse left Kate at the door.

Anthony slid it open and offered his arm. "You look beautiful."

Her smile widened. She took his arm, and they crossed the patio to the table. Kate bent over the roses and inhaled deeply before she sat.

"White are my favorite."

"I know. Can I get you anything?"

"A gin and tonic would be lovely."

After dinner, Anthony refreshed their drinks, and they moved to the sectional beside the fireplace. He tucked a blanket around her lap.

"Are you warm enough?"

"I'm fine. There's no need to fuss over me. I get enough of that from the nurses."

He sat beside her and pulled her close.

"Look," he said, pointing toward the sky.

The green glow of fireflies winked against the darkness.

Kate rested her head on his shoulder and gazed upward. "My father used to catch fireflies for me. He'd put them in a jar and let me keep them in my room as a nightlight. But only if I promised to let them go the next day so they didn't die. I feel like . . . someone put me in a jar and forgot to let me out, and now I'm running out of air, and my light is fading."

Anthony's arm tightened around her. His heart hurt, and he had no words.

Kate looked up at him. "It's almost time."

"I know."

They watched the fireflies dance and the stars emerge from the darkness until Kate's eyes drooped with exhaustion. When she drifted off to sleep, he gathered her in his arms and carried her to the bedroom.

Anthony had sent the nurse home early, so he helped Kate prepare for bed and slipped beneath the blankets with her. He snuggled close, cradling her against the warmth of his body, and whispered, "I will always love you, Kate."

Hours later, Anthony left the room and shuffled through the

moonlight to his apartment. Without even stopping to turn on a light, he went to the bar and filled a glass with scotch.

He could still feel her in his arms. The light snoring that assured him she was still breathing had become fainter and fainter until, with a soft rattle, it ceased, and his Kate left him forever.

The glass slipped from his hand and shattered at his feet. Anthony sank to his knees amid the shards of glass. Screams of pain caught in his throat and echoed in his head. He welcomed the pain.

He deserved it for what he had done.

Anthony closed the last box and placed it by the front door with the others. There hadn't been much to pack: clothes, books, photos, and toiletries. What little he owned fit into a suitcase and a few boxes. He scanned the apartment and blinked back tears.

Holly had let him stay these past couple weeks since Kate's death, but it was time to move on. Sad memories haunted him here. He couldn't go into the house or sit by the pool or look at Holly without guilt consuming him.

"I hope you were planning to come say goodbye."

He swung around at the sound of Holly's voice. "I certainly was. And it's not goodbye. We'll stay in touch, won't we?"

"We will. In fact, I'm sure you'll get sick of me visiting you so often at the beach house."

"What do you mean?"

"I just came from a meeting with Mother's lawyer. She left you the beach house and the Porsche and five million dollars. Oh,"—she handed him an envelope—"and this."

He slowly took it from her and stared blankly at his name, written in Kate's meticulous handwriting on the front of the sealed envelope.

"I . . . don't understand."

"You don't have to. No one ever understood my mother. But she always took care of the people she loved."

"I don't . . ." Anthony shook his head in disbelief. "But what about you?"

Holly shouted with laughter. "Oh Anthony, darling, don't worry about me. The business, the house, the cars . . . I have more than I'll ever need." She closed the space between them and wrapped him in a hug. "Thank you for everything you did for her. You deserve this."

After Holly left, Anthony sank into the nearest chair and gazed at the envelope in his hand. He had wanted so badly to tell Holly how wrong she was. He did not deserve this.

He ripped open the envelope and unfolded the letter.

Anthony,

If you are reading this, it is because you chose to stay with me until the end. I left concise instructions in my will regarding you. I did not mention our arrangement, but I made it clear that you would receive nothing if you left me before I died.

I have every confidence that you will someday read this letter. You always do the right thing.

I do love you.

Kate

The letter slipped from Anthony's hand. His head dropped to his hands as sobs of relief tore from him. The sobs turned to laughter. Leave it to Kate to get what she wanted, even in death. He retrieved the letter and read it again, eyes lingering on the last line.

I do love you.

A smile spread across his face. He folded the letter, slipped it into his pocket, and picked up his suitcase.

If he left now, he could watch the sunset from the beach.

Laurie has loved writing as long as she can remember. Her most recent works include short stories, "Retribution" and "Thief," appearing respectively in Scout Media's 2016 and 2017 anthologies, *A Journey of Words* and *A Haunting of Words*.

Over the years, her poetry has also been published in various anthologies.

Her debut novel, *Tranquility*, published in 2015 by Escargot Books and Music, was inspired by her work as a personal support worker specializing in dementia care.

In 2015, she graduated with honors from Conestoga College's Creative Writing program. She's a Canadian, an avid reader, a yogi, and a Gemini. She grew up on a farm in remote northern Ontario and now lives in Cambridge, Ontario with her husband and cat.

You can find Laurie's work on Amazon: amazon.com/author/lauriegardiner and follow her on Facebook: www.facebook.com/www.lauriegardiner.me.

It was one of those muggy summer days when the feeling of malice hung in the air like the lingering odour of an old, wet dog. Or the smell could have actually been coming from Max, my old, wet dog. Thing is, when you're a private eye like I am, your senses become honed to a keen edge, so when the small hairs on the back of your neck stand up straight and you get that nagging feeling something is out of place, you make sure the barber cuts them shorter next time so it stops happening.

Sam Stale is my name, and danger is my game. Unless of course there is any chance of physical injury to my person, then pinochle is my game.

She sauntered into my office and looked around like a piranha that had been dropped into the guppy tank. She was tall enough to hang a powerline on, and she had more curves than a roadmap of the Ural Mountains. I looked her up and down, and a cold wind sent a chill through my body. I made a silent note to pay the heating bill.

Gorgeous dames don't just stroll into my office off the street every day, and I had no idea what kind of trouble she was selling. Whatever it was, I hoped I could afford lots of it.

"I'm looking for a private investigator," she said.

"That'd be me," I told her. "Sam Stale P.I., like the sign on the door says."

"Actually, the sign on the door says you clean rain gutters."

"That's me also," I said. "It's seasonal."

"Mr. Stale, you came highly recommended by a mutual friend."

Now I was really suspicious. "When did I clean his gutters?" I asked.

"He said you could find anything, anytime, anywhere, Mr. Stale."

That was news to me. I usually had a hard time locating my sock drawer in the morning.

She said her name was Kitty Cookie. Or it might have been the other way around—I wasn't sure. Like most of my customers and every woman I date, she was desperate. The huge rock on her finger said, "Money," which startled me, 'cause I had never heard jewelry speak before.

"What can I do for you, Mrs. Cookie?"

I crossed my arms on my chest, put my feet up on the desk, and toppled the chair over backwards, my head colliding with the wall on the way down. When I came to, she was kneeling over me, fanning my face with her ample bosom.

"My husband, James, is missing," she said, her full cleavage hovering over me. "I want you to find him for me."

"If he's lost in there," I said, looking up, "we may never see him again."

I brushed myself off and sat back down in my chair. Unfortunately, it had broken in the fall, and a splinter from the seat the size of a Ginsu paring knife speared me in the butt. I wanted to scream, but when you're a seasoned P.I. like I am, you learn to control things like pain, thirst, and flatulence. Well, pain and thirst anyway. I stayed completely composed, determined not to show even the slightest sign of discomfort.

"Why are you crying?" she asked.

"How long has your husband been missing, Mrs. Cookie?"

"Since breakfast. I'm worried sick."

It didn't add up. There were too many questions unanswered.

Why hadn't Mrs. Kitty Cookie gone straight to the cops? Why would any sane man leave this beautiful woman in the first place? Why can't they make cling wrap easier to use?

"Lady, you must think I'm some kind of rube." I had no idea what a rube was, but it sounded right. "You expect me to believe a wild story like that and drop everything—"

She reached into her purse and extracted a roll of bills big enough around to choke a Baleen whale. She laid the wad on the table, and then she leaned back, lit a cigarette, and waited to see what I'd do.

I looked at the money, at her, and at the NO SMOKING sign on the wall. Then I cupped my hand and put it in front of her in case she needed an ashtray.

"You put up a strong argument," I told her. "Show me a picture of your husband."

An hour after Kitty Cookie departed, I was lost in deep reflection, staring at the money she had left on my desk. I thought long and hard about things, mostly how much a new bass boat was going for these days.

Suddenly, a man burst into my office in a panic and said, "Are you Sam Stale?"

"Sorry," I said. "Gutter cleaning season is over."

"I need you to find my wife, Mr. Stale."

Two customers in one year; business was picking up. I examined him a little closer, and I realized he bore an incredible resemblance to Mrs. Cookie's lost husband. Could it possibly be?

"Is your name James Cookie?" I asked.

"Jim Cookie," he said.

Darn, wrong guy.

I said, "Sorry pal, I'm already working on a big case."

He reached into his pocket and pulled out a roll of bills identical to the one Kitty Cookie had put on my desk and laid it down beside its sister. I wondered if they were having a sale on large rolls of money somewhere that I didn't know about.

"I'm not making any promises," I told him, "but I'll see what I can do."

He went into his pocket again and took out another roll of bills, which he placed on the table next to the other two.

"I swear I'll find her," I said. "Or your next gutter cleaning is ten percent . . . okay, fifteen percent off."

He showed me a picture of his wife, and by some incredible twist of fate, she looked just like Kitty but with darker hair. I slapped my forehead—that was two meaningless coincidences in a row. The odds against that must be astronomical.

Y'see, Kitty Cookie was blonde, and the lady in the picture was a redhead. Sure, they had the same last name and the same facial features, but when you're an experienced P.I., you learn not to be led astray by murky clues. Having faith in your gut instincts is what it's all about, not dubious, superficial resemblances.

I spent the rest of the afternoon in feverish investigation mode. Most of the time I was on the phone doing interviews, but I also scoured the internet, searching for any tiny scrap of information I could find. By supper, I had gathered all the data I needed to make a decision on a bass boat.

Then, as an afterthought, I called a psychic I knew from previous cases. She went by the handle Vancouver Vicky, but her real name was New York Nancy.

I told her about the two cases I was working on, and I asked if she would gaze into her crystal ball, or rub it, or do whatever the hell it is she does with it and see if it could give me even a small clue about the missing Cookies.

All she came up with was some cryptic talk about looking under my nose and being closer than I thought to cracking the case wide open. I listened to her riddle-speak for a while, and I realized it was getting me nowhere. The situation was hopeless. It had been nearly three hours since Kitty hired me, and I was still no closer to solving the case. It was time to admit defeat.

I called Kitty and asked her to meet me in my office. When she arrived, I sat her down and was getting ready to give her the bad news. That's when Jim burst in and saw the woman sitting in the chair. I was stunned to see him run to her and sweep her up in his arms. They embraced deeply and stared into each other's eyes like long lost lovers. The truth hit me as suddenly as the time I walked into the open manhole.

Adultery.

Jim and Kitty were going to have an affair. The pressure from the loss of their respective mates had driven these two lonely souls into each other's arms. It just goes to show how emotionally fragile people are. The two illicit lovebirds left together arm in arm without a word, and I sat down at my desk and pondered the situation.

It was another unsolved case for my files, just like all the others. One burning question remained though, and I couldn't shake it. Did I have enough time to make it to the boat dealership before they closed?

The pen hovered inches from the paper—a huge expanse of unblemished white, screaming out for a signature. Nina wasn't even sure why she was hesitating. Her eyes flickered once more over the lengthy terms, the legal jargon fogging her brain.

"I just sign here?" she clarified, even though the answer was obvious.

The man from Mayhem Productions nodded, a cold smile on his thin lips. He was handsome, Nina noticed, in that way men often are once they put on a suit. He looked suave, like he'd know how to treat a girl. She put the pen to her lips in what she hoped was subtle flirtation.

"Just sign right there, Mrs. Roberts, and we can get the ball rolling."

"And it's definitely five million?"

"That's the prize. It's right there in the contract. You understand participation doesn't guarantee a win, though?"

"Of course. I have to earn it."

"Absolutely. But I've read your application; you've a strong chance of impressing the judges. We're very excited to have you on board, Mrs. Roberts." A smile touched his lips again, this time extending its reach to his bright blue eyes.

Nina batted her eyelashes a little before lowering the pen once more towards the paper. "Call me Nina."

She took a deep breath and swept the nib across the pristine page, leaving a glistening trail of black.

The man plucked the paper out from beneath her hand as soon as the last letter was formed. He held it gingerly, like some sort of ancient relic. "Thank you . . . Nina. And welcome aboard."

Miles shifted his weight from one foot to the other and fluttered his fingers—a habit from childhood. "Please, Alex. I know it's a lot, but I really need it."

Alex rubbed her face in an attempt to mask her frustration. "You promise it's not for drugs?"

"I swear."

Miles had spent a great deal of his teens and early twenties on a drug known as Tiger. It was a legal high and worked with e-cigarettes, but it was nasty. Several MPs were campaigning to get it criminalised, but so far, their crusade seemed to be nothing more than hot air.

"It's a lot of money, Miles."

"I know, I know. But this thing, oh Alex, it's so cool. We get to watch the contestant twenty-four/seven."

"That's basically *Big Brother*."

"No, it's really not. It's so much more than that. The contestant knows they're competing but none of their friends or family do. And it's not just watching them go about their day-to-day life—the production company arranges pranks and sets challenges, and we get to rate the contestant's participation. Jez watched the last one, and he said it was just, like, so deep, like it took TV to a whole new level. This company, seriously, they are reinventing everything. Nothing much has changed in TV since streaming became the main viewing method, but this—it's so interactive. It's going to change the world. Good entertainment's worth paying for, isn't it? I mean, how much did you pay to see Beyoncé last year? And that was—what—three or four hours of entertainment?"

Alex blushed. Those Beyoncé tickets had been ridiculously expensive but worth every penny.

"Shit, I know it's a lot of money, and I know you've bailed me out so many times, but this isn't you bailing me out, this is just you helping me. This show is going to give me something to focus on. It'll keep me off the T, you know it will. I've been working, you know, coding for this little start-up—I mean, only a bit here and there, but they're really interested in my ideas. I need to stay off the T, I know I do, and this will help me. I'll be more focused on my work and—"

"Okay, okay," Alex cut her brother off. "I hear you." She paused, and a frown creased her brow. "This is the last time though, okay? No more bailouts. No more *loans*."

"Definitely. Definitely." His fingers fluttered again but slower, calming.

Alex got out her phone and, with a few swift taps on the screen, sent him the five hundred pounds.

A message popped up on the screen: *Do you want to share this transaction to your timeline?*

She clicked *No* without hesitation. She was embarrassed enough at the frequency she had lent her brother money, much to her friends' disgust. She did not need to publicise it.

The anesthetist was busying herself behind where Nina lay in a surgical gown and stockings. Nina gasped at the sharp pain of the nurse inserting the cannula into the back of her hand.

"You okay?" the nurse asked, fixing the equipment in place with tape.

Nina nodded. "Just a bit nervous, I guess."

"It's to be expected. You're one of only a handful of people to have this done. I feel privileged to be on your team today."

Nina gave a weak smile. "I knew this was part of the deal when I signed up, but . . . It feels a little scary now I'm here."

"It'll be over in minutes; it's such a simple procedure. The only reason they put you under is because, well, it's practically impossible to do anything to an eye when the patient is awake—the movement's so involuntary."

"Do you think it will hurt?"

"They explained this, right? They must have done. You won't feel a thing. You'll wake up and not feel any different. But the implant will stream everything you can see. It's so clever." He was practically gushing now, and Nina wished he would shut up.

They had explained the retinal implant before she had signed. Mayhem Productions had been very clear about what was going to happen. At least, that was how Nina had felt when she left that first meeting, when they had brought her a cup of quality coffee and then shown her into the other room where the suited man with the blue eyes had watched her sign.

But an hour or so later, she realised she didn't have much more of an idea what was going to happen than she had when she first saw the innocuous advert online, sandwiched between a hilarious meme about parenthood and a friend's rant about the Tesco car park.

Do you dare? the advert asked. *Think you've got what it takes to become the newest kind of television star? Play to win and walk away with a life-changing amount of money.*

Nina had toyed with the idea of trying to get on television before but never seriously. The promise of a life-changing amount of money was what piqued her interest.

Sean was taking her for everything in the divorce. He was taking the kids, he was taking the house, he was trying to make Nina out to be a bad mother and a general scourge on society. With enough money, she could buy a bigger, better house, as well as a vicious lawyer to make him suffer the way he was making her.

She clicked the link and tapped her details into the application form, embellishing slightly as she assumed everyone always did.

She had been told very little before the meeting in Hackney, but from the small amount she had gleaned, only one thing stuck in her mind as she got off the train at London Fields, searching for the unassuming building housing the plush offices: the prize was five million pounds.

It was win or lose—she knew that much; no runners-up, no booby prize. You either won the money or you didn't.

The first meeting had been touted as an informal interview, but they didn't ask her many questions at all. There were two of them, a man in skinny jeans and a porkpie hat and a barefoot woman in a kaftan. They greeted her like a long-lost friend and proceeded to tell her more about the game show—if you could call it that.

The game would last eight weeks, and during that time, she was forbidden to tell anyone about it. Doing so would breach her contract and forfeit the prize money. She would continue her day-to-day life but would be monitored twenty-four hours a day by hidden cameras in her house and the local area. A retinal implant would also stream everything she saw.

Occasionally, things would happen that were out of the ordinary. Sometimes she would be set a particular task. Her participation would be rated continuously by the judges. If at the end of the eight weeks her rating had stayed above an average of 7.8, then she would walk away with five million pounds. If it averaged less, she would leave with nothing.

The pair spoke with such enthusiasm it was hard for Nina to spot any flaws in the concept.

"It's kind of like *Big Brother* meets *Punk'd*," the man, Fenn, effused. "But even better. It's a new generation of TV show. There's nothing like it out there. It's going to be huge. Our first season was small to start off with—we only offered the contestant five hundred thousand—but the ratings picked up so quickly, and we felt like we could just take this so much further, you know. Extend. Enrich. Captivate."

He's just saying random words now, Nina thought and suppressed a laugh, but she couldn't deny the pull of his charisma or that of the woman at his side who mostly stayed silent but offered Nina the warmest smiles at every opportunity and repeated several times what a perfect contestant she thought Nina would make.

Their smiles were contagious, and Nina was swept up in the flurry of excitement that seemed to emanate from their pores.

As she walked back to London Fields, the image of her signature, dark and solid on the white sheet, still imprinted on her vision, the elation sloughed away, and she wondered what the contest actually entailed—the extent of the pranks, the difficulty of the tasks, and whether she would be able to tackle them with the necessary motivation and showmanship to earn the coveted prize.

Miles sat at his desk, his hands fluttering by his side. Alex made tea, adding three sugars to Miles' cup with a grimace.

"You going to watch from there?" she asked.

"This chair's ergonomic. Much better for my posture than being slumped on a sofa. And they say it's better to have your keyboard on a desk than your lap too."

Alex smiled. Trust Miles to care about things like posture when he could barely do his own laundry.

"Can I put it on the big screen too though?" she asked, taking her own position on the sofa.

"Course." He threw her the remote. "You just won't be able to interact the way I can, but I think they wouldn't accept multiple players on one account anyway."

She powered up the wall-mounted screen and connected the input to the source on Miles' computer. Immediately, an image appeared of a skinny woman with an equine face and long, dark hair. The camera viewed her from the side and above but showed her in crystalline high definition. She was making a sandwich.

Not exactly scintillating viewing, Alex thought, sipping her tea.

"It's a lull," Miles explained. Of course, he knew exactly what she was thinking. "They happen. They have to. She'd be worn out if they didn't."

A couple of voiceovers narrated, recapping for those just tuning in. "Nina's making a sandwich right now, as you can see. I'm not surprised she's hungry," said the first voice. A banner across the bottom of the screen revealed this to be quasi-celebrity Bantz, a radio DJ who had made it big for no other reason than his ability to keep up an incessant level of inane chatter.

"Neither am I," came the reply. "Nina has had a stressful morning, for those of you who missed it. We asked her to head to her local supermarket, and there we gave her a rather bizarre shopping list. Many of the items would not be available in your average supermarket, but we wanted Nina to request them from a member of staff and to get irate when they were unavailable. We also asked her to fill her trolley with random items and to act suspiciously around security staff. As you know, on *Who Dares Wins*, we cannot ask our contestants to break the law, but we can certainly let them give the impression they might." The strapline named the second speaker as "Doctor" Sammi Stone, an agony aunt who had a PhD in something or other and liked to pretend this made her an accredited clinical psychologist.

Alex pulled a face, wondering if she could tolerate the commentary.

"Nina dumped the trolley just inside the entrance," Bantz continued, "and legged it all the way home. I'd be starving too."

Miles tapped away furiously at his keyboard.

"What you doing?" Alex enquired.

"Just updating my scores," came the reply. "We can adjust our rating every twenty-four hours. Look, I'll flick it across."

He swiped the air in front of him, and an additional window appeared on the screen Alex was watching. Within it, a data cloud surrounded three categories: enthusiasm, obedience, and entertainment value. Miles moved the cursor around, and as he did so, various data appeared relating to each word.

Alex could see the contestant's raw score for each category and that was broken down by area, time of day, specific tasks and pranks, and a range of other fields. It could be viewed in a variety of different visualisations selected by the player.

Miles added his scores for the last twenty-four hours, and the data was recalibrated.

"She's doing well," he observed. "Her raw scores are staying pretty high, which is good for her overall rating at the end of the show. She's scoring much higher for enthusiasm than the last guy did. She's motivated, and it shows."

"So, you just vote once a day?" Alex sipped her tea.

"Yeah, but that's only part of it. We also get to share ideas for pranks and tasks. At any one time there's an average of one hundred thousand players online, so you post your idea, and if it gets a thousand likes within five minutes, they incorporate it into the show. It's great because it levels the playing field. It's not like those stupid votes on other social media platforms where it all comes down to who has the most friends. This is completely open within the game platform, so all one hundred thousand people can see your idea. And if you hashtag it, then people can search through the hashtags to find the sort of tasks they're interested in. And then, after five minutes, it disappears from the timeline so you know you're not voting on something too late for it to count."

"So, you can suggest anything? And if it gets a thousand votes, then they have to do it?"

"Well, yes and no. Obviously, the successful suggestions are vetted. And all the players know the limitations and rules. They can't suggest anything illegal."

Alex frowned. "Nothing illegal but . . . what about immoral?"

"I guess there's a fine line."

A heavy, sick sensation settled itself in Alex's stomach. She watched the woman on the screen take a bite of the sandwich she had just made. She looked up towards the concealed camera that watched her. Her eyes were dark and hollow, her expression unreadable.

"Don't worry about it, Alex." Miles shifted in his chair and took a swig of his sugary tea. "This company is absolutely dedicated to providing top-notch entertainment. They don't want cheap thrills, they want quality TV. The rules are there to keep everyone safe. Last season, the contestant nearly broke one, and they came down on him hard. They want the experience to be authentic for everyone."

Alex chewed on her lip, unconvinced. The narration rabbited on, and a message flashed up across Nina's face. *PRANK,* it said. *Suggested by user aimless429.*

"I saw this one!" Miles yelped with excitement. "I voted for it."

Alex read the caption below with mounting horror.

Nina took another bite of her sandwich. It tasted bland and empty, like bad air. Her body ached, and her legs were leaden. Her breathing was still slightly laboured after her sprint home from the supermarket.

A knock at the door made her jump and bite her tongue. Blood filled her mouth. *At least that has some flavour*, she thought. She shook her head, as though the odd thoughts that had begun to populate her psyche could be shaken away.

The knock came again, harder. Then a voice. "Nina! Open up!"

Sean.

She forced her weary legs to carry her towards the front door and stretched her face into an expression of enthusiasm. This must have been instigated by the production company. Sean never bothered coming round any more. His mum conducted the handovers of the children ever since Sean had told Nina he couldn't bear to look at her. She wondered how they were. It had been over a week. They were due again tomorrow. Was that why Sean was here? To try to stop her from seeing them again?

She gripped the latch so hard her knuckles turned white. She could see Sean's silhouette through the front door's frosted glass.

"Nina." The voice was angry, bitter.

Nina twisted the latch and pulled the door open. Sean stood on the step, his face shrouded in disappointment.

"Hi, Sean." Nina stood to the side to allow him to enter.

Sean strode into the shabby hallway of Nina's rental property—all she could afford in the wake of the legal action he had taken against her.

"What the fuck is this?" He brandished a folded piece of paper.

Nina raised an eyebrow. "Am I supposed to know?"

"I'm not pissing about, Nina. You need to stop behaving like a spoilt child."

"Thanks for the suggestion, but I've no idea what you're talking about."

Nina kept her expression blank, but her mind was scurrying through every possibility. What had she done? Or was this just another set up for the cameras? She wondered momentarily what Sean's response would be if he knew he was being filmed right now. Her stomach lurched, and she felt the burning sensation of acid at the back of her throat.

"This." Sean thrust the piece of paper at her, and Nina unfolded it slowly.

It was a credit card statement in Nina's name and registered to the family home where Sean now lived with their kids. The account was maxed out to its ten-thousand-pound credit limit. Nina knew for certain it was nothing to do with her, which meant the people from *Who Dares Wins* were responsible for it. Nina tried to keep a lid on her bubbling thoughts.

How did they want her to respond? She knew her reaction to each task and prank was carefully measured by scientific algorithms and fed back to the judges. She had to think about how her demeanour would translate onto television. What was this prank hoping to achieve?

She decided to go with an honest reaction to start with until she could get a better idea how the land lay.

"I have no idea what this is, Sean," she insisted. "It must be credit card fraud."

Sean gave a humourless laugh. "Right."

"Come on, Sean, you know I wouldn't do this."

"See, you say that Nina, but I know nothing of the sort. Besides, this is something of a giveaway."

He reached over and pointed at an item halfway down the statement. "Jardine Topiary," Nina read. "So what?"

Sean spat out a laugh and shook his head. "So what? So, why are they in your front garden, if you didn't buy them?"

Nina didn't answer. She crossed the hall and went out the front door. Sure enough, two manicured trees stood in ornamental pots either side of her front door. They must have appeared since she arrived back from the supermarket. The pristine pots made the house look shabbier still.

"Good taste at least," Nina muttered for the audience, hoping Sean couldn't hear.

She threw a wink towards the house, assuming there was a camera mounted somewhere in the vicinity.

Sean stood in the doorway, arms folded. "This is all a joke to you, isn't it?"

"It's really not, but Sean, I swear I didn't order these."

"So who did? The tooth fairy?"

Nina watched Sean disappear inside the house. How to handle this? She decided to stick with her original plan. The production company must have some kind of end-game planned out for this prank, after all. Maybe she could say the topiaries were a gift, but from whom?

Her name floated out from inside the house, and she followed the sound into the living room, where Sean stood beside the under-stair cupboard. "I'm sick of this, Nina. I'm giving you ample maintenance. I'm paying for the kids. I'm not asking you for anything, even though they're with me far more than they are with you. Pulling shit like this is just taking the piss."

"I didn't buy those pots, Sean, I swear—"

She stopped when she realised why Sean was standing next to the cupboard. Inside, it was an array of expensive items, mostly electrical. She imagined they probably tallied perfectly with the credit card statement Sean had found.

"I'm not paying this, Nina, no matter what you think. If they start calling or coming round demanding payment, I'm sending them here. I suggest you return this stuff and cut the card up."

"Sean, I really didn't—"

It was pointless. Nina sighed. Wasn't this almost exactly out of a film? She was sure it rang a few bells. Couldn't they come up with something original, for fuck's sake?

A voice came through the temporary aural implant she wore. "New instruction: try to have sex with Sean."

Nina blanched. Did they really want her to do that? Her stomach roiled, and she could once again feel the burning taste of acid at the back of her throat.

Five million, she thought. *Five. Million. Pounds.*

It was worth it.

She smiled at Sean—a shy, lopsided grin that had worked wonders when they first met. "Look, you got me. I was going to return all this stuff anyway. I just wanted . . . Oh, it's stupid."

"What, Nina? What's your ridiculous excuse this time?" Sean's frosty exterior had yet to be melted.

"I just wanted to see you. I figured this was the only way to get you to come round." She paused and took a step closer to him. She dropped her voice to a husky whisper. "I missed you."

Sean's lip curled in disgust. "Nina, what the fuck? This kind of behaviour is exactly what's landed you in the mess you're in."

"Come on, Sean. For old time's sake." She moved another step closer and placed a hand on his arm.

"What do you think you're doing?"

Nina wished she could tell him, wished she could explain; he just needed to go along with it, but then that would spoil the satisfying sensation of informing him she was a multimillionaire in a few weeks' time. She inched closer and pressed herself against his body. She felt stirrings of excitement from him, however reluctant.

"I need you, Sean. I want you so bad."

He grabbed her shoulders and pushed her away, holding her at arm's length. "This is fucked up, Nina."

Enthusiasm, Nina thought. *Obedience. Entertainment value.*

She reached out and grabbed Sean's crotch, giving a gentle suggestive squeeze. His body responded, and she heard a sharp intake of breath close to her ear.

In for a penny, in for a pound, Nina thought. *In for five million.*

She hooked a finger behind Sean's belt, pulling it loose from the buckle as she sank to her knees.

"Come on, it's a gorgeous day, and Mum would love to see you."

Alex hovered inside the front door she had opened herself in order to not drag Miles away from the screen. She stood at an angle that kept the action on the screen and out of her direct eye line.

"I'm not saying I won't come, I'm just saying not now," Miles protested, tapping away at the keyboard as he spoke.

"She hasn't seen you in ages. I've been telling her how well you're doing, but she'd really like to see it for herself."

"Like I said, maybe in half an hour or so."

Alex clenched her fists and took a deep breath. "You need to take a break from this, Miles. It's not healthy."

Miles jabbed a finger at the screen in front of him, forcing Alex to track her eyes across to where a second window was open full of indecipherable code. "I'm working, look."

"But how much are you getting done with that other window open? I don't know how you can focus."

Miles waved a dismissive hand at her as his attention was drawn back to the other window and a flurry of new comments on a thread he was following.

"Miles, I'm serious. This is almost as bad as when you were on T. Your work must be suffering, you're hardly sleeping, and I . . . I mean, the subject matter is really . . . It's unsavoury."

Alex tried to block out the mental image of the contestant attempting to perform fellatio on her unsuspecting ex-husband. The conflict that flared across his face as he momentarily relaxed into the familiar act of intimacy with someone he used to love and then the venom with which he pushed her away and stepped across her cowed body had made Alex's blood run cold. For a second, she had been impressed at how real it looked, and then she had reminded herself that of course it looked real—it was. These were real people, unsuspecting people, with real feelings.

Miles turned his body towards his sister but somehow kept his face towards the softly glowing screen. "This is nothing like when I was on T. Nothing. I can't believe you would even say that."

"No, of course not. It's not like you're addicted to this show and can't even stop to sleep or eat. It's totally different."

"There's no need to be sarcastic. I'm not addicted. I've eaten, look." He waved an empty delivery pizza box at her.

"Oh, well, that's all right then," Alex snapped. "Look, I'm going to see Mum. I'd really like you to come. But if you can't be bothered—"

"I said I'll come in a bit. Stop trying to guilt trip me."

Alex shook her head in disappointment as her brother's gaze stayed resolutely fixed on the screen before him. "It's sick, this programme. It's immoral and unethical. It's glorified voyeurism. That poor woman is being tortured and so are her innocent friends and family."

"It's revolutionary. It's changing the face of television."

"Yeah, into something distasteful and cruel."

"You just don't understand. The contestant knew what she was signing up for."

"Did she? You know that for sure?"

"Of course."

"And even if she did, the people in her life don't."

"Look, it's just a game. Chill the fuck out. She stands to win millions. She only has to last a couple more weeks, and she will walk away into a completely different life from anything she's ever known. A life a million times better than anything she's ever known. Look at the way she lives now. That money will change everything."

"No, this show will change everything. Her ex-husband's already trying to stop her seeing her kids at all because of the way she's been behaving. But she's only been behaving that way because someone is telling her to."

"She has a choice, Alex."

"Hardly. If she doesn't do as she's told, her obedience ratings will drop right down. If she wants that money, she has to do as they say."

"And then she wins the money, gets a shit-hot lawyer, and gets her kids back."

"You are so naïve. I'm off to see Mum."

"Laters," Miles called after her, his fingers flickering over the keys as he debated the merits of Nina's response to the last task with the strangers who were now his closest companions.

Nina's heart pounded and her legs throbbed as she hurtled up the stairs. The stale urine stink made it hard to breathe, but she pushed onwards and upwards. She rounded the corner—another flight, then another. Her lungs burned, and she gasped for breath as she threw open the door at the top and stepped out into the cold air of the multi-story car park.

The area was sparsely populated with cars, most patrons preferring the new car park attached to the shopping centre on the other side of town. The voice in her ear was silent for now, her instructions complete.

Nina approached the far wall of the car park and stepped over the low metal barrier. The wind whipped through her hair, and it billowed like smoke behind her. She placed her hands decisively on the concrete precipice in front of her and leaned over the edge, looking down. She was six stories up, and the world looked like a child's play mat.

Joey had one like that, she remembered, thinking back to when her youngest was three or four.

The silence in her ear felt thunderous and vast. In the early days, there had been encouragement, pep talks, even goading. But now, with less than twelve hours until she walked away with the prize money (she hoped; oh God, she hoped), they delivered their instructions and stayed silent, waiting for their obedient little puppet to comply.

Nina braced her hands on the top of the wall and pushed, lifting her feet off the floor. She managed to get a knee over the top and scrambled the rest of her body up, clinging on to the rough concrete with trembling fingers. She lay across the length of the wall, her stomach pressed to the slightly convex surface, the cold leaching through the thin T-shirt she wore. The wind buffeted her as she tried, slowly, to sit up, and her fingers clawed at the flat surface, searching for purchase.

She steadied herself and swung her legs out over the edge.

Miles mindlessly stuffed a handful of popcorn into his mouth, barely registering the flavour. The contestant was up on the top floor of a multi-story car park and threatening to jump.

Of course, she wouldn't really jump. This was all part of her latest task. Miles had been part of the conversation that had conceived the idea, even though he hadn't been the one to post the suggestion and receive the accolades. He didn't mind though. The wonderful thing about this game was how collaborative it was.

The screen in front of Miles showed the view from the contestant's retinal implant. The elevation was incredible. The people below looked like die-cast models. It reminded him of a trip he and Alex had once taken to Legoland when their dad had still been alive.

The view cut back to the cameras at ground level. Now there was an assembly of police, friends, relatives, and curious onlookers; the production company had been able to get a hand-held camera on the scene without it seeming out of place.

The crowd was large—Miles seriously doubted the contestant had that many people in her life, so he suspected the majority were rubberneckers. A smug smile crept across his face as he considered the fact he was happily rubbernecking from the comfort of his own home. He shifted his weight. Despite the ergonomic chair, his neck ached, and his buttocks were getting particularly painful.

Near the front of the crowd, Mile recognised the contestant's ex-husband. His face was haggard and grey, coated with several days' worth of stubble. Beside him stood two children—a girl of about eleven and a boy of about eight—they had their arms around each other, and the boy was crying. Their presence was what had caused Alex to flee Miles' flat earlier. Miles tutted again at the thought. Alex just didn't appreciate genius; she couldn't see this show for the revolutionary concept it was.

The police were deep in conversation. One of them held a loudhailer. The camera cut away again to show the view of the contestant from below. Her legs dangled, ragdoll limp, over the edge of the concrete wall she sat upon. Her face was indecipherable from such a distance, which would make it hard to select a rating for enthusiasm.

Sound came from somewhere out of view—a commotion. The screen displayed the crowd once more, and it became apparent someone was pushing their way through the throng.

A woman came into view. She was shouting at the rubberneckers, telling them to get lost, pleading with the man holding the camera to turn it off. She ran to the contestant's husband and grabbed him by the shoulders, screaming unintelligible words in his ashen face. An onlooker—probably someone from the production company—pulled her away, and she struggled free and fell to her knees.

Miles took in the blonde bob, the rounded face, and the slim build and pushed back from the computer screen in horror.

"Fuck!"

Nina hugged one arm around herself, trying to keep warm. The other hand clung tightly to the edge of the precipice. She could see Sean below with Savannah and Joey. She wondered if they would ever forgive her for this stunt, whether the money would be enough of a balm to soothe the chaos she had wrought.

It made no difference. She had come too far now to admit defeat. She had to see this through to the bitter end, whatever the cost.

There was a hubbub below. The crowd parted and swirled like a school of fish. A woman pushed forward and spoke to Sean, then someone pulled her away, and she fell to her knees. Nina watched as the woman clambered to her feet and sprinted away from the crowd into the stairwell of the multi-story. A police officer followed.

The wait whilst the woman and her pursuer climbed the stairs seemed to last hours. Nina sat in endless silence, watching the tumult below with a strangely detached sensation. Finally, the door opened with a bang, striking the wall beside it, and the woman—short, blonde, breathless—placed her hands on her knees for a moment, fixing Nina with an enigmatic stare.

Nina looked back at the crowd below, and a wave of vertigo hit her. She dug her fingers into the concrete surface, barely noticing when a nail snapped off close to the nail bed. She looked back towards the door to see the woman had advanced several paces. A police officer—just a local beat bobby, clearly unsure of protocol—hung back in the doorway.

Nina's tired mind waded through the possibilities like treacle. Was this woman part of a final twist from the production company?

Was the cop? How was she supposed to handle this? *Enthusiasm, obedience, entertainment value.* The mantra repeated itself in her mind.

"Stay back!" she shouted, the panic in her voice surprising even her. "Stay back, or I'll jump."

The suicide bid was supposed to look convincing. Those were her instructions. She wasn't sure what direction the task was taking now, but she had to stick to the brief, show obedience.

The advancing woman faltered, but only for a moment. "I know this isn't real, Nina," she called across the half-empty car park. "This isn't real, and you don't need to do it. These people are manipulating you for their own entertainment. And that's wrong. It's so wrong."

Nina raised her eyebrows at the strange blonde in front of her. What was she playing at?

"I'll jump," she repeated. "I mean it."

"No, you won't," came the reply, and the woman took yet another slow step towards her. "You won't jump because then you won't win, and that's the whole point isn't it?"

Nina shifted uncomfortably. She didn't understand where this was going.

"Those are your kids down there, Nina. Your kids!"

The police officer still hadn't moved from the doorway but was talking fast and low into his radio.

The woman was now only a few feet from where Nina sat. The wind whipped Nina's hair across her face for what felt like the millionth time, but she was relieved to lose sight of those wild green eyes, even if just for a moment.

"My name is Alex," the woman continued. "I've been watching. But I can't bear what I've seen. It's not right. It's not right."

She looked like she might break down and cry, but then she took a breath, crossed the remaining distance between them, and looked straight into Nina's eyes. Nina flinched, but the woman grabbed her face and held it in her hands.

"This woman's name is Nina. She is a person. She has children.

They are down there crying for their mother right now. She is a person. She has feelings. Her name is Nina."

Miles sprinted out of the Uber and through the growing crowd. His muscles were nearly seizing up after so little use over the last few weeks, but he persisted through the pain, despite feeling like he was running into the wind.

The police stopped him at the entrance to the stairs.

"You don't understand. That's my sister. I need to get her. I need to stop her."

They weren't going to let him through. He felt a lump rise up in his throat and a sob build in his chest. This was so unfair.

One of the officers answered a call on his radio, and the other was momentarily distracted by a shout from the crowd. Miles snatched the opportunity and pushed between them, taking the stairs two at a time, even though his thighs felt like they were made of marshmallow and throbbed as though acid ran through his veins.

He had to pause halfway up, the breaths ripping in and out of his battered lungs. His throat was hot and raw. He felt nausea swell in his stomach, and a thin stream of vomit poured out of his open mouth. He wiped his lips dry with the back of his hand before resolutely plunging onwards, desperate to find Alex and stop her.

At the top of the stairs, he encountered another police officer, this one less sure of himself than the ones at the base of the stairwell. Miles pushed past without a second glance, and the officer did little to prevent him.

Alex was standing beside the contestant, talking to her in earnest. The wind carried her words faintly across the open space. "How much more will they make you do, Nina? What crazy, damaging sacrifices will they ask you to make? And for what? Money." She spat the final word like a mouthful of rotten fruit.

"Five million quid. That's not just money, you stupid bitch, that's another world, a new life. Why are you trying to fuck this up for me?"

"I'm not," Alex insisted. "I just want you to see—to truly see—what you're doing. Each task gets more risky, more twisted, more likely to alienate everyone you've ever known."

"I've got less than twelve hours left. I mean, I'm down to my last hour or two now." Nina looked at her empty wrists, wishing she hadn't forgotten her watch. "I'm almost there. What more can they do to me?"

Alex looked deflated for a brief moment, but she ploughed on. "But look what they have done. Look where you are. Look at your children down there, distressed because they genuinely believe you're threatening to kill yourself. Can't you see that's the kind of thing that will scar them for life?"

Miles couldn't listen to another word. "What the fuck are you doing, Alex?"

Alex jumped. Miles was the last person she expected to see.

"How did you—?"

"I was watching, you idiot. How do you think?"

"This isn't right, Miles. You know that. I know that. They all know that." She directed this last sentence to the people watching through Nina's eyes. "If I can just convince her too, then this sick experiment can all be over."

"This isn't a sick experiment, Alex, this is TV. It's entertainment. This is the future, and you're just too stuck in the past to see it."

"You're sick, Miles. Everyone involved in this is sick. It needs taking down. You're all sick and horribly, horribly twisted," she told the viewers.

She looked back towards Miles, and her mouth fell open. He followed her eyes and saw several large men, suited in black and armed with semi-automatics, flowing out of the door to the stairwell. They were accompanied by a smaller man in an expensive-looking suit with startling blue eyes. The contestant looked panicked at their arrival.

"I'm doing it. I'm doing what you said," she protested, her tone reminiscent of a sullen teenage girl.

"What have you done, Alex?" Miles chided.

"What I had to. And I don't regret it."

Miles shook his head. "You've ruined it. You've ruined it all."

"I don't care, Miles. I'm glad." Alex's smile looked nervous.

Miles felt a hand close around his wrist followed by the cold touch of metal. He looked up and saw a stern face set on a solid neck glaring back at him. Miles' mouth felt suddenly dry, as though the water had been wrung out of it. He tried to ask the man what was happening, but all his tongue could manage was a hapless, "*Whaa?*"

The shorter man with the bright blue eyes approached him. "Breach of contract, I'm afraid," he explained with no hint of regret.

"What do you mean?" Alex asked, her voice taut and high pitched.

"Participation does not entitle the player to share the programme with any non-users. Not only did he do so, but his actions have caused this . . ." He waved his hand in Alex's direction. ". . . fiasco. Miles Jarvis, you are in breach of your contract with Mayhem Productions and will be dealt with accordingly. Take him downstairs please, Grantham."

The heavyset man who had handcuffed Miles prodded him in the back, directing him towards the stairwell. Miles' arms ached in the unnatural position the handcuffs created. Alex ran over and grabbed the man's arm.

"No," she cried. "Please stop. He didn't do anything."

"I'm afraid he did. This is very serious."

Alex's pleas did nothing to stop the party moving en masse towards the stairwell. Nina watched as the group filed back through the doorway whilst Alex's protestations echoed from the stairwell, leaving her once again alone on the roof. She looked around the empty space and then down at the crowd who were mostly distracted by the appearance of the officials from Mayhem Productions rather than her ersatz plight.

The silence, once again, felt boundless.

She spoke into the void. "Did I . . . Did I win?"

Laura Ings Self lives and writes in the suburbs of London. When she isn't writing, she is home educating her five-year-old twins or taking the stage at her local community theatre. "Who Dares Wins" is her second published work, after her short story "Home" was published in Scout Media's previous anthology, *A Haunting of Words*.

She is currently working on a stage play about our darkest fears and also seeking representation for her two middle-grade novels, one of which was long-listed for The Times/Chicken House Children's Fiction Competition 2016.

CATCH UP

Signature *Kari Holloway*

What if *all your dreams could be made with a single whack of the bat?*

"Joe, wait up!" Beni leaned over on his knees, huffing and puffing for air. He'd been chasing Joe for two blocks, but Joe always seemed to be another block ahead.

"Come on, Beni," Joe yelled back. "The game's about to start!" He waved his friend along, but the anticipation of watching the local team's baseball game pulled him along. He patted his pocket and smiled. He'd been saving every penny from his paper route to go, and the coins jingled in his pocket with each step.

The stands were packed for the end of summer fling. Kids shouted their wares, offering peanuts and bottled drinks, while some people brought their own snacks.

The town mayor stood on the pitcher's mound, thanking the people for coming to the last game, and even with the microphone, his voice was drowned out by the shuffling of people.

Joe and Beni climbed up the back of the bleachers, taking the tiny spot near third base line.

"Joe, why can't we stand at the fence? At least then we can see the game," Beni began to whine.

Joe shoved his hand into his glove and flexed it. "We can't, Beni. Almost all the fly balls and pop ups land this way." Tonight would be his night to catch a ball, he was certain. "But you go on ahead."

Beni crossed his arms and sat down on the hard bleachers.

The crowd clapped and cheered, giving it their all. High-pitched whistles pierced the air, and the patrons began to stomp their feet, causing the seats to vibrate from one end to the other.

Joe smiled wide. "One day, Beni, I'm going to play, just like Babe Ruth." Even with the glove on, Joe pretended to swing a bat and watched the imaginary ball spiral out past the wall. "One day." He licked his lips and joined in with the crowd cheering.

The umpire supervised as the first batter took a stand in the box. The catcher flexed his knees and squatted. The pitcher tossed the ball into his glove before checking his basemen. He nodded to the catcher, and the first ball flew across the plate.

Joe leaned over, captivated by the fluidity of baseball. His tongue stuck out between thin lips, and the entire crowd disappeared for him. For the next nine innings, his entire world existed within the baseball diamond.

The score stayed close. The occasional ball followed down the third base.

"I wanna go, Joe." Beni fanned his face, tired of sitting there, bored out of his mind.

"Then go. I'll see you tomorrow." Joe's eyes tracked the latest ball, and his grin got a little wider as an outfielder caught it with ease.

"Come with me. We can listen to the radio at my house." Beni looked over the side of the bleachers. His head spun, and his stomach knotted. He didn't remember the climb being so high. He clutched Joe's sleeve. "Come on, Joe."

Joe turned, shaking Beni loose. "You didn't have to come." The whack of the bat connecting with the ball punctuated Joe's sentence. Joe turned back to the game. His eyes tried to scan for the ball, and the movement from the corner of his eye came too late.

"Joe!" Beni's voice sounded far away as Joe succumbed to the darkness.

The stadium brimmed with fans, despite the July heat. Women waved their programs, trying to find relief while complaining behind their husbands to the other wives. Kids ran amuck, oblivious to patrons trying to ease down the steep steps with arms full of popcorn and soda.

Yet all of that stopped when the Yankees came on the field, dressed in their iconic pin-stripes with NEW YORK emblazoned across the front.

The crowd clapped and cheered. One thought was on everyone's mind. *Would Joe DiMaggio make number fifty-seven?*

For two months, the true Yankees fans had watched in wonder as the center fielder put every pitcher through their paces, gaining a hit in every game. As May turned to June, and July hovered on the horizon, even non-fans became fans, leaving the Cleveland stands packed with a variety of patrons for a change.

Their voices flowed over the field, singing "Take Me Out to the Ball Game," and sales of Cracker Jacks peaked after each time.

DiMaggio stood in the dugout, rotating his shoulder and trying to shake the pressure building. If he made a hit this evening, he'd be one step closer to matching his minor league record: sixty-one consecutive hits.

A newspaper fluttered down from the stands, and the muggy breeze swept it in front of DiMaggio. He snatched at the paper before it twirled farther onto the field. Out of habit, he glanced at the front page. Instead of pictures of war happening thousands of miles away, he was above the fold, swinging his lucky bat.

His dark eyes stared at the replacement he was just beginning to get used to. He sighed, missing *his* bat.

He paused, his gaze captured by the bold font at the top of the column: IS THE DEAL WITH HEINZ TRUE?

His brow furrowed as he crumpled the paper and tossed it

in the trash. Even the papers had wind of the deal that could be unmade today. He tried to push the contract from his mind. Ten thousand dollars was a lot of money—more money than he'd ever seen. Maybe enough to even buy stock in a team after he retired.

DiMaggio picked up the bat and went on deck. He swung a few times, loosening up. He watched as Al Smith threw another strike. Swallowing the lump in his throat, he moved to the batter's box. He ground his toe into the dirt and tightened his grip on the bat. He blinked, and his gaze focused on the white ball in Smith's hand.

The ball came charging across the plate, and he swung. He dropped his bat and began to run toward first plate. The ball careened down the third base line, going . . . going . . . caught by Ken Keltner, who threw him out at first.

This was not what DiMaggio had hoped for.

The first inning came and went, followed by three more. Each time the Cleveland Indians shook the center fielder, the ball grounded, and Al Smith walked him, causing Jim Bagby to come from the bullpen. The eighth inning gleamed vacant from the scoreboard.

DiMaggio tightened his hands on the handle, choking up on it. He swung the bat a few times before stepping into the box. Everything was eerily silent.

The crowds vanished.

The outfield blurred.

His gaze narrowed on Bagby, whose face hid beneath the brim of the cap.

He licked his lips, and his breath left him as he swung. The ball *thunked* into the catcher's glove.

Strike one.

Two and one. DiMaggio knocked the dirt from his cleats. He swung the bat up to his shoulder as he stepped into the box.

Bagby tossed the baseball into his glove. His eyes never left home plate. He nodded to the umpire.

DiMaggio shifted his weight to his right leg, arms extended as the bat connected with the fastball.

The whack echoed through the stadium, and silence filled the stands.

Lou Boudreau, the shortstop, had caught it on a hop, ending DiMaggio's streak with a double play.

DiMaggio walked back to the dugout. His head throbbed, and despite his teammates telling him it was okay, he felt like the biggest loser.

Joe's ears throbbed. His eyelids felt heavy, and each time he tried to open them, he felt like he was being shaken by an earthquake.

"Joe." Beni's voice was high and squeaky, just like the time he fell off his bike and scraped his knee.

Something wet and cold pressed against his head. A drop of liquid rolled down his face, settling in his ear. He turned his head away and carefully opened his eyes.

"DiMaggio. You okay? Want me to get Vince?" Mr. Costa, the middle school's baseball coach, asked.

Joe groaned when he sat up. Through squinted eyes, he looked around the ground. Clutched in his hand was his glove, and inside the worn-out leather was the ball. "Did I catch it?"

"Against the side of your head." Mr. Costa chuckled. "I'll give you a ride home."

"No. I wanna stay." He rubbed the knot on the side of his head. "Was I saying anything?" he asked Beni.

Beni rubbed the back of his head, smoothing his hair. He had a puzzled look on his face. He wrinkled his nose. "Does ketchup ring any bells?"

Kari Holloway is an American writer who grew up in Leesburg, Georgia. She dabbles in southern romances filled with iconic components of sexy cowboys and firefighters (*Laughing P*), explored the unexplained in her paranormal series (*Devil's Playground*), found her way to the battlefields of the Civil War, and to love's first kiss under the weeping willow through various anthologies.

Unsure of what her future holds, Kari enjoys writing what captures her attention in the evenings. During the day, she chases her kids around, laughing at their sassy ways and the depths of their curiosity.

Her motto in life: Show the world the best version of you, for our actions of today make tomorrow.

For more information, check out her website www.kariholloway.com, or follow her on social media: facebook.com/authorkariholloway, kariholloway.tumblr.com, and lunanara87.tumblr.com.

"When I'm grown, if I have two babies, I'll give you one, and then we'll be mummies together."

"What if I have two babies first?"

"Then I'll have one of yours, silly. If you don't give me one, I won't be your friend anymore."

"Pinkie promise?"

"Pinkie promise."

Arms linked, the expectant couple made their way across the retail car park towards the baby superstore, the flutters and gentle kicks causing a smile to cross the expectant mother's face as she looked up at her husband.

"Blimey, they're really moving around today. Walking normally sends them to sleep."

"Clearly they know we're buying their bedroom stuff."

"Nursery furniture, Robert! How many times?" She gave him a jab in the ribs for the eye roll she received.

"Bedroom, nursery, it's all the same thing, Allie."

The automatic doors made way for them with a hiss, and Robert's eyes were bombarded with all manner of baby-related items. He had done his best to avoid this place for the last eighteen weeks. As excited as he was about having twins, the thought of throwing away his savings wasn't as exciting. He had seen the circled baby items in the numerous catalogues that were scattered around the house in the same fashion Alice did when Christmas or her birthday was approaching.

"Really, it isn't." Alice slid her fingers between his and guided him towards the mock nurseries. "Robert, look!" His arm was almost pulled from its socket as Alice speedily made for a set that had caught her eye. "It's perfect for us!"

"I don't think I'd fit; it's even smaller than my rack."

"Oh, *haha*. When did you get a sense of humour?"

While his wife looked over the nautical-themed design, Robert took a peek at the price tags, which had conveniently been absent from the catalogues. He was just beginning to think that the price wasn't that bad when he spotted the tags hanging from the other items. He gave a low whistle as he looked over at his wife.

"Maybe we should take your weirdo friend up on her offer after all."

"What?" Alice looked up from the cot bedding, her furrowed brow easing. "Oh, you mean Lucy. Well, I wasn't the one who replied, *lol*. I mean how was her comment remotely funny? Idiot."

"Well, *Piss off, you weirdo* would probably have come off a bit harsh, don't you think?"

"You could've ignored it, you know, like I did. I told you; she sounds as crazy as her oddball mother. I mean, who writes on a pregnancy announcement: *Which one's mine?* It's not normal. Nor is making jokes about it, Robert," she stated with a pointed look as she approached him and glanced at the price tag that Robert was still holding. "You have to let the moths out of your wallet sooner or later."

She ran her hand across the curved, white-painted wood of the cot, looking at him through those long lashes of hers.

"I take it this is the one we're getting then?" he questioned, knowing there was no point in trying to negotiate with her on how much they were going to spend.

"Can we?"

"Might have to tighten our budget on the pushchair, but if you love it, we might as well start their fascination with the sea early."

"Forget it. Just because I love you doesn't mean I want my boys joining the Navy. Oh my! Look over there, matching clothes," she gasped as she headed off towards the clothing section.

"Pretty sure their clothes don't have to match their bedroom," he muttered at her retreating back.

For someone growing two humans, she sure could move fast when she wanted to.

Alice was adjusting the blue and white anchor bunting that hung above each cot when the rattling of keys and the metallic click of a lock alerted her to Robert's return from sea. Stepping back with hands on hips, Alice surveyed the room. It had taken three weeks to finally pull it together, and she knew that he wouldn't be impressed with her doing it all while he was away, but she just couldn't help herself. Looking at the empty room with boxes stacked in the corner had been driving her insane. She had ensured she took regular breaks and skipped a few days here and there so that no one could really complain.

"Alice?"

This time the flutter in the pit of her stomach had nothing to do with the two infants growing inside her but everything to do with their father, the loneliness she felt when he was away being almost unbearable. It had always been the difficult part of their relationship, but now with the impending birth, Alice worried even more about how she would cope with him not being around.

The door opened, and she was pulled from her thoughts as Robert stood in the doorway, looking at the room with wide eyes.

"You've done their room."

"Do you like it?"

Alice inhaled deeply as she watched Robert scan the room, taking in the pale blue walls, the furniture, the small nautical-themed objects scattered around. His eyes rested on the wooden lettering on the opposite wall, and she watched as a grin spread across his face, and the creases under and around his eyes became more evident.

"Finally agreed then?" Robert stepped into the room and wrapped his arm around her extended waistline. "Rufus and James. It's perfect." Kissing her temple, he placed a hand on her firm bump. "And how have these two been?"

"They protested a little, but, as usual, they are perfect. Quick. Take a photo."

Obliging, Robert pulled out his phone, and lining his wife up so that she stood directly between both names, he laughed as she posed. Snapping the scene, he showed it to her before sending it on to her before she started nagging him for it.

"Now, you,"—he glanced at her as he stowed his phone away in his pocket—"downstairs. You need to rest; I told you I would sort all this out."

"And what if you were late home? Look how many of your leaves have been cancelled or emergencies that have come up. With the Navy, the boys could be six weeks old before they got their nursery."

"It's not *that* bad."

Alice gave him a look which he chose to ignore as he made his way out of the room, Alice following behind.

Settling on the sofa, Alice picked up her phone and scrolled through her messages so that she could upload the photo of the twins' nursery to Facebook. Choosing to be close to Robert meant that her family and friends were all back in London and using social media, and technology was their way of keeping everyone up to date.

"Here you go." Robert placed a cup of tea down beside her before sprawling out at the other end of the sofa.

"Comfortable?" she asked as he placed his sock-clad feet up against her leg.

"Better if you came over here." He smirked with a wriggle of his eyebrows.

"In case you haven't noticed, I am the size of a beached whale, so I'm not going anywhere."

"I've seen plenty of whales, and none look as good as you."

"Oh, shut up."

Her phone chimed, and Alice hastily picked it up, eager to see what people thought of her hard work. Checking her notifications, Alice saw that her photo had been well received.

"Your mum loves it. So does mine."

Scrolling through the comments, Alice stopped at one in particular.

"Damn, Crazy is back," Robert said as he looked at her over his own phone.

"Yeah I saw. Why would she write that? *I don't like James, I think I'll choose something else.* What does that even mean?"

"Maybe she's suggesting we change it? Not that it has anything to do with her. Or she's still trying to be funny."

"Well, she's not!" Alice didn't know where it came from, but suddenly, her eyes filled with tears. "It's a horrible thing to put!"

She sobbed as Robert scooted over to console her.

"Those hormones are playing havoc already, I see."

"So, I'm not allowed to be annoyed?" she snapped, trying to pull away.

"I didn't say that. It's just normally you'd have just been abusive to her over Facebook. Crying isn't normally your thing."

"Robert, look at this. It comes in red and blue." Alice held up two all-in-ones. "Aren't they adorable?"

"Yes, along with the other thousand-or-so outfits you've already bought. Leave something for others to buy. What about these?"

Raising an eyebrow, Alice looked at the wellies that Robert was holding.

"What?"

"Will wellies not exist next year? I don't think there is much call for babies to wear wellies."

"I meant if we wait till the sale, we could grab them for—"

"You're unbelievable."

Walking to the next rack, Alice flicked through the items a little more zealously than browsing normally required.

"Hardly, just remembering that you're not going back to work after they're here. We may have money to spend now, but it won't last more than a few weeks."

"So you're going to throw that back at me? Let's remember I didn't choose to have twins. That wasn't the plan."

"I'm not saying that, Al! I'm just trying to stop us from drowning in debt. We're buying two of everything, Al. This wasn't our life plan. Remember? Have one, both work, then once it was at school, have the second and repeat."

Alice looked at him before giving a heavy sigh. Adjusting her handbag strap, she made her way around the clothing racks and linked her arm through his, leaning her head against his shoulder.

"I'm sorry. I know you're just trying your best. And I know exactly how much you're taking on with me being at home. You know if my job covered childcare for both of them and my share of the bills, I wouldn't leave it all to you. Right?"

"Of course, I know."

"And I will try and find a way to help with the bills. I might not be able to go out and work, but I'll do something. I love you."

Robert gave her a small smile before placing his lips against her forehead.

She closed her eyes and enjoyed the moment. She was aware that she had been snapping at him a lot lately. Especially when it was money related. Neither of them was used to watching the pennies.

"Alice!"

Her eyes snapped open and took in the tall woman standing before her. She was instantly recognisable from her photos on her profile. Lucy Hanningfield stood there, her bright flowery dress and flowery perfume overpowering to Alice's senses.

"Look at the size of you!"

Lucy placed her hands on the large protruding belly before Alice could manoeuvre it out of reach. She threw a look at Robert who seemed amused.

"How far now? Thirty-four weeks and . . . four days?"

Alice swallowed; her stomach tightened at the fact that this distant so-called friend knew exactly how far along she was. Even her mother lost track of the weeks. Unable to speak, Alice nodded and tightened her grip on Robert's arm.

"I noticed you never said on Facebook, but I'm guessing it was . . ." Lucy waved a hand over the bump, and her chunky plastic jewellery clanked against each other. ". . . you know, IVF?"

Alice felt Robert stiffen besides her. This was a common question it seemed; people automatically assumed that because they'd been married for three years and were expecting twins that it must be the result of fertility treatment.

"No. Twins run in the family, and I'm in the Navy, so things took a little longer."

Alice gave a swift kick to Robert's ankle. "Lucy doesn't need to know all *that*. It's lovely seeing you, but we need to go. We've got an appointment." Alice gave a false smile and went to sidestep the other woman.

"Of course, of course. I just love the photo of the nursery, by the way. It'll be lovely for their sleepovers."

"What—"

Robert's question was cut off as Alice dragged him towards the exit. Lucy's comment had shaken her up, and while part of her wanted to fend off her crazy former schoolmate, the mother instincts wanted her to get the hell away from her. For someone so heavily pregnant, she made short work of reaching their car, Robert on her heels the whole time, not that that was any effort for him.

Once in the safety of the car, Alice leant her head against the headrest and let out a heavy sigh. "She is just like her mother."

"What was that comment about?"

"I don't know, but she scares me, Robert. I know it sounds silly, but I feel like she's stalking me. She knows how far along I am, and she has never mentioned being in the area."

"People are allowed to travel."

"She lives in London; she's never moved out of the town she was born in. I have her on Facebook. She still lives with her crazy-arsed mother, and I think she is too."

"Look, I agree that it's weird, but let's not jump the gun and get yourself in a panic. She comments on all your stuff. She just remembered stuff, that's all." Robert looked at her before raising both hands. "Yeah, okay. Even that sounded stupid to me. What do you think she meant by sleepovers?"

"I don't know, and honestly, I don't care or want to find out."

Placing her bag on top of her bump, Alice began rummaging through her handbag. Pulling out her phone, she hit the screen multiple times before throwing it back into the depths of the bag.

"There. I unfriended her and blocked her. She can't see any more of my stuff."

Robert's hand rested on her leg, and she placed her hand on top, giving it a light squeeze.

"Come on, let's get you home. I think a take-away is in order."

"Yes, because I'm not fat enough already."

"You're not fat." Leaning over, Robert kissed her and smiled. "I love the three of you, and if that crazy woman tries to contact you again, I will personally see her off. With a stick, up her arse, after I have beaten her with it."

Leaning against the pillows, Alice rolled her head to the side, taking in the sight of her boys. The labour had been long, and without Robert there by her side, it had been far scarier than she had imagined. The perfect, peaceful labour she had read and planned for had gone out the window as she had screamed and cried her way through it. Now she was finally alone, she was able to relax slightly, waiting for the next whimper to come from one of her boys. She had been moved to a side room so had the peace and quiet, even if she was feeling particularly lonely with nobody to talk to. The boys had arrived a few days earlier than planned, meaning that Robert was away on a patrol but due back by the end of the week. Until his return, the other wives and girlfriends were taking it in turns to keep an eye on her.

The sound of footsteps made her look towards the door, and she smiled as Veronica, one of the midwives, entered.

"Here they are. Now, they do need their rest, so not too long."

Veronica stepped aside, and Alice was horrified to see Lucy standing there. She watched the midwife leave, wanting to beg her not to but was too worried about looking silly.

Once the door closed, Alice sat up slowly, keeping her eyes on her boys.

"What are you doing here?"

"I would have called beforehand, but I seem to be having some trouble getting through to you. You seem to have disappeared off of Facebook."

"I, er, deleted it. I didn't want anyone else to know when I went into labour. You know, you read horror stories about people announcing it before the parents do, and with Robert's job, it was important that we had some privacy."

"Where is Robert?"

"He's popped home for some stuff. He'll be back soon."

Alice watched as Lucy approached the cots. Protectively, she reached out, grasping onto Rufus's cot. Suddenly wishing she had a cot on either side of her, she watched as Lucy turned the tags on James's ankle.

"He's lovely. I can't wait to hold him." Lucy reached into the cot and gently stroked the sleeping infant's face. "Such a chubby cheek for someone so small."

"How did you get in? It's family only."

"Oh, I saw your sister couldn't make it until Friday. She posted on Monday that she hoped her nephews stayed put so she could be here. Lucky for me, they didn't." Lucy turned to look at Alice, and it felt like she was bearing deep into her soul, questioning every inner thought Alice was having. "Do you remember when we were at school? How we used to walk around and around the playground holding hands?"

Alice nodded, her eyes on James the entire time.

"We always said we'd be mummies together. We were going to marry them brothers. What were they called again?"

When Alice didn't answer, Lucy flapped a hand in her direction.

"That's right, baby brain, silly me. I think it was David; his brother was . . . Derrick? Yes, that was it. Derrick was in year six, and David was year four. We'd have been sisters. Proper aunties to our children."

Lucy placed her hand on Alice's leg, and though it was covered with the hospital sheets, Alice could feel the tightness of the grip.

"Do you remember the promise we made?"

Alice had a sickening feeling in the pit of her stomach; memories began coming back to her of her time as Lucy's best friend. They had been great times, filled with skipping games and laughter. Lucy had been a sweet, little thing and so shy around others.

"Let me remind you. We always said if one of us had two children when the other had none, we'd share. We made a pinkie promise. Do you remember that?"

Alice did. Suddenly, she remembered it as if she had never forgotten. It had been a beautiful day in the playground. They'd been walking around with their pretend pushchairs, playing mummies, their usual game. Alice had offered up the scenario first, and it had been Lucy who enquired about if she was to have the children first.

"I never met the right man; you did though. He's just right for us—"

"Sorry to interrupt, but is it okay if we take the babies to see the paediatrician?" Veronica peered around the door, her bright smile a relief to Alice.

"Yes!" Alice was already pulling off the bed sheets and climbing out of the bed. "I'm sorry, Lucy, but I best go with them."

"That's okay. I'll wait."

Alice looked at her surprised before helping the midwife wheel the second cot out of the room and across the hall into the examination room.

"Alice? Is everything okay?" The midwife looked between her and the paediatrician.

"Yes, fine."

Unable to relax, Alice stood by the door, staring across at the closed door to her room.

"We can ask your sister to join us, if you're worried. I understand your husband is at sea? This is just procedure to make sure they are ready to go home."

"No. I'm fine."

Sighing, Alice closed her eyes before resting her forehead against the cool glass. She needed help with this. She couldn't take her babies back in there.

"She's not my sister. She lied."

"Excuse me?"

The doctor looked at her seemingly to see if she was somehow responsible for the deception. The doctor's expression relaxed, and she walked over, placing a hand on Alice's arm.

"Come sit down. Would you like her removed from the premises?"

Alice nodded, her eyes filling with tears as she broke down.

"I just want Robert." She sobbed quietly into her hand.

A tissue was passed to her, and she heard the click of a handset lifted from its cradle. The midwife was speaking in a low tone.

"You can wait in here until security arrives to remove her. Do we need to call the police?"

"I don't know. I think she wants one of my babies. I think she wants James."

The doctor took her hands in her own and squeezed them reassuringly. "The only person leaving this hospital with James and Rufus is you and your husband, if he arrives home in time. It is our job to ensure our babies go home with none other than their parents. Neither of your boys will leave this hospital with anyone other than you. No matter who she tries to impersonate."

Shortly after, a scream pierced the peacefulness of the maternity ward, and Alice jumped to her feet and turned to face the door. Through the slim panel of glass, two men in security uniforms were dragging Lucy from the side room.

Lucy stared straight through the glass at her. Her eyes were wild, and her usually well-styled hair was beginning to fall out of place as she struggled and kicked.

"You promised! He's mine, Alice. You won't get away with this! He's mine."

Alice watched as she was dragged out of view, and only once she could no longer hear her did she feel that she could relax.

"How are they doing back there?"

Alice made eye contact with her sister through the mirror. "They're sleeping. Thanks again for rushing down here, B. I mean it, the way you dropped everything."

"You're my sister. Of course, I dropped everything. One of us had to get here. Mum and Dad are just making arrangements so they can extend their stay."

"Robert will be back in two days. I told them they didn't need to."

"Someone is threatening you. Of course, they will."

"You told them? I told you not to!"

Their eyes met once again, and Alice did her best to convey her annoyance silently, not wanting to wake either of the babies.

"I had to. They knew something was wrong with me rushing down here. They thought something was happening to you."

Alice rolled her eyes and fidgeted with James' clothing. "I just hate the thought of them worrying."

"Me too, but with Robert away, it's our job to protect you. What have the police said?"

"They're investigating. They have my statement, and last I heard, they were going to speak to the hospital. Left here."

Alice looked at the familiar houses as they passed. Five days ago, as her friend Jenna had driven her to the hospital, she had felt excited that she was close to meeting her babies, lonely at the absence of Robert, and anticipation of what labour would be like and how she'd cope being a mum. Now she was full of dread. Her family were rallying around, but Robert wasn't here, and Lucy had reared her ugly head and upped her scare tactics.

Bethany pulled expertly onto their drive as if she had been here many times before instead of twice.

"You remember which one was mine?"

"Not all of us have a hunky sailor to ogle, and I have been here twice. That's more than enough to be able to remember where my sister lives."

The engine off, Bethany climbed out and proceeded to remove James from the car while Alice slid out and made her way towards the door.

A small blue bear sat upon the stoop, a ribbon around its neck and a small card between its paws. Reaching out, Alice read the card before knocking the bear over with a feeble kick of her foot.

"Alice?" Bethany placed James' seat beside her on the drive and looked from her sister to the overturned stuffed toy.

"It's from her. She's been here."

Pulling her hair into a high ponytail, Alice poked her head around the nursery door to check on the twins.

"Robert!"

Her heart pounded as she took in their empty cots.

Robert's voice came over the monitor, informing her that they had stirred while she was sleeping and were downstairs with him.

With a huff and a mutter of annoyance, Alice hurried down to the living room.

"You scared me," she stated as she leaned on the bottom post, watching as her husband sat with his back against the sofa, playing on his PlayStation, a foot on each bouncer, gently rocking the babies as they slept.

"Sorry. I forgot ten-day-old babies are known for escaping and running away. Relax, please, or none of us will ever sleep again." He glanced up from his controller and smiled. "Who says men can't multitask, eh?"

"You better be joking, or you can forget just waiting six weeks."

"Just?"

"Don't push your luck. What d'you fancy for dinner?"

Robert turned his attention back to his game, giving a shrug for a reply.

"Helpful," she muttered as she hopped off the last step and made her way to the kitchen. The sudden coldness caused her to glance at the back door, which stood wide open, as well as the pantry. "Rob, seriously? I don't have the heating set to the right temperature for you to leave the back door open! You know they have to be kept warm. Not to mention I don't want next door's cat helping itself to our pantry again."

When there was no reply, Alice stood in the kitchen doorway, watching Robert as he stared at the television, his brow furrowed and mouth hanging open in a rather unattractive way.

"Robert!"

"Uh?"

"You left the pantry and back door open."

"Haven't touched it," he mumbled as his eyes never left the screen.

"So, it just opened its self?"

"You must of." Throwing the controller down, he growled, "Great. I lost my concentration."

"At least you were concentrating on something, I suppose."

Returning to the kitchen, Alice opened the door to the pantry, and grabbing one of her pre-made meals from the freezer, threw it into the oven before returning to the stairs.

"I'm going for a shower."

While dinner had failed to get Robert's attention, the idea of supervising the babies again did.

"But you've just had a nap," he argued, putting the controller down.

"Yeah, in bed, not the bloody shower."

"I haven't had a break."

Alice stared at him before moving to stand over him. "Are you freaking kidding me? When was my break when I was pregnant? When I was in labour? Did you push two humans out of *your* vagina? Which one of us gets to go away for weeks on end?"

"Working! You seem to forget that what I do could get me killed. I'm not sitting around watching TV."

"And I am? You've looked after them on your own for, what? A few hours? They're ten days old! I've been in the same room or building as them since they were born! You've been to sea, to the pub, and to a stag-do. I really don't think watching them while I have a rare nap and shower is too much to ask!"

They glared at each other before Alice bent down and removed Rufus from his bouncer.

"Seeing as it's too much to ask, I'll manage like I always do."

Snatching the monitor from the seat of the sofa, Alice stomped upstairs to place her eldest infant in his cot. Covering him over, she turned the dial on the mobile and watched as he stirred before settling. Turning, she found Robert in the doorway, not to apologise but holding James ready for her to place him down. Jaw clenched, she took him as she glared at her husband before setting James down just like his brother.

"Right. I'll try and have a shower then, shall I?" she asked no one in particular.

The hot water rained down on her upturned face. With eyes closed, she enjoyed the feeling of the high-pressured water hitting her skin, especially her tired eyelids. Rinsing the shampoo from her hair, she wrung out her waterlogged hair. Pushing it back off her face, she froze as the sound of the monitor fought to be heard over the running water. Shutting off the tap, she paused before the monitor came to life again with the sound of a door clicking shut. Throwing back the curtain, Alice grabbed the nearest towel and hastily wrapped it about her as she stumbled into her postnatal underwear.

"What's wrong?" she called out.

When Robert didn't answer, she opened the door and looked out onto the landing. The blaring sounds of gunfire and profanities told her Robert was playing his game still.

"Are they okay?" she called down the stairs. "Robert?"

"What!" he hollered over his game.

"What's wrong with the boys?"

The television went quiet.

"Well, you're the one up there with them!"

"Just stop being an arse! I heard you up here!"

"I haven't been up there!"

Robert appeared at the foot of the stairs, his cheeks flushed and the top of his ears red.

"I heard their door," Alice called over the bannister as she headed along the landing and into the nursery.

The boys were in their cots, Rufus still asleep while James

lay staring at a small blue bear. Alice felt her heart leap into her mouth as she recognised it from the one that had been sat upon her doorstep on her return from hospital.

"Isn't that the—"

Robert stood behind her, staring at the soft toy that his wife now held in her shaking hands. Taking it from her, he opened the nappy bin and threw the toy in before slamming the lid down.

"If you didn't put it there, then how did it get in his cot? How did it get in the house?" Alice looked at Robert with wide eyes, shaking her head as she began to process the information.

Leaning into the cot, Alice lifted James out and took him into her arms, checking him over in the process. A movement on the landing caught her eye; her reaction caused Robert to turn and break into a run. Clutching James to her chest, Alice buried her face into his thin covering of hair, his familiar baby smell doing nothing to ease her apprehension.

As Robert ran along the landing, she heard footsteps on the stairs, followed swiftly by Robert storming down them as he shouted at their intruder. Deep down, Alice knew exactly who it was, and her stomach twisted in knots knowing Lucy had been in her home.

Alice heard Robert screaming abuse after Lucy, and then the back door slammed. He returned shortly, this time his face hardened and pale. There was an anger in his eyes that she had never seen before. She realised that this was the part of him she never saw—the hardened sailor who risked his life every time he left, the sailor who never knew what he would encounter when boarding other vessels.

He placed an arm around her, one hand brushing her wet hair back. "They went out the back door, but by the time I got to it, there was no sign of them. I checked the garden and found the side gate was open." He attempted a reassuring smile. "It's locked now and the back door as well, but I'll sleep downstairs tonight in case they try getting back in."

"It's not they, it's her. It can only be her."

"I didn't see her face. Whoever it was had a hood up. I'll call the police. Why don't you bring the boys down, and we'll have dinner?"

"I'm not hungry."

"You've got to eat something. I'm not letting you make yourself ill."

Reluctantly, Alice let Robert take James from her so that she could get dressed and bring Rufus downstairs. Even after checking that both doors and windows were secured and locked, Alice couldn't help but shake the feeling that they were still being watched. Alice found herself peering out between the curtains each time she heard a car or saw a shadow flit across the wall.

It took Robert a number of hours to convince her to go to bed. The police weren't coming out until the following morning as Lucy was no longer on the premises, and in the end, he had to turn everything off and virtually sit in darkness before she admitted defeat and made her way upstairs with the twins in her arms.

He followed her up and helped her with the bedtime routine, along with settling them both. Not wanting to be far from them, Alice decided to sleep in the nursing chair. With a pillow and duvet fetched by Robert, she settled down for what she assumed would be a long and sleepless night, until she felt her eyelids begin to drop, and slowly sleep took over.

The creak of a stair brought Robert out of his slumber. The room was dark. The streetlamps outside were off, telling him it was the early hours of the morning. Rubbing his eyes, he rolled his head to the side and watched as the figure of his wife moved slowly up the first few stairs.

"Alice?"

When she didn't acknowledge him and continued up, Robert stood up from the sofa and moved across the room to the foot of the stairs.

"Alice? What's wrong?"

The figure reached the top of the stairs, and with no reply, Robert reached across to the light switch. The sudden light blinded him for a second but not enough for him to still think it was Alice on the stairs.

"What the hell are you doing? . . . *Alice!*"

Lucy looked down at him before turning onto the landing silently.

Alice opened her eyes at the sound of Robert's voice. It took a moment to register where she was. The landing light was on. Instantly, she knew something was wrong. They never turned the light on at night if the other was asleep, as neither of them found it easy to drift off to sleep once woken up. It felt like she had only just fallen to sleep after the twins' midnight feed.

The feeling of dread washed over her, her stomach once again turned in knots, and her mouth went dry. Begrudgingly, she opened the door to the landing, coming face to face with Lucy.

Before she could do anything, Lucy lunged for her, pushing her back into the room.

Robert shouted something, but his words were lost in Lucy's endless barrage of shouts, accusations, and Robert's feet on the last few stairs as he raced towards the two struggling women.

Suddenly, the fear left Alice, and determination set in. She knew why Lucy was here, and it wasn't happening. Nothing was going to stop Alice from keeping James. If Lucy wanted her child, she would have to kill her.

Alice pulled an arm back and struck the other woman across the face. Her hand burned from the impact, but it disorientated Lucy enough for Robert to be able to yank her backwards along the landing towards the stairs. That's when Alice saw it—the small knife from their kitchen that Lucy was pulling from her pocket. She backed away in fright briefly and realised too late that the knife wasn't aimed at her. It was a decision that Alice could never have imagined needing to make, but as soon as it came to her, she knew she was going to do it. She was going to do everything she could to protect her family, even if it meant doing the worst.

Alice lurched forward, shoving Lucy square in the chest, forcing her back towards the top of the stairs. Robert had yet to see the knife and grabbed Lucy before Alice could stop him. She watched as Lucy stumbled over the top step with Robert still holding onto her. There was a tangle of feet and both fell backwards.

The crashing of their bodies against the stairs and wall awoke the twins, or was it her as she screamed out for her husband? She wasn't sure. Nor was she sure about who to run to. Her sons were wailing, that desperate cry that newborns had to remind their caregivers that they had been yanked from their world of safety into an endless world full of bright lights and loud noises. She could hear the panic in their young cries as if they assumed they had been abandoned because of the lack of her familiar comfort, no doubt startled and unsure of what was happening in the strange new world they were still getting used to.

Should she run to the two bodies that now lay at the bottom of the stairs? The two bodies that were there because she had pushed Lucy? To her relief, Robert moved slightly, a groan barely audible over the two infants. Lucy lay across him, her head at a strange angle, blood oozing from a temple wound, her eyes unblinking, staring at the ceiling.

Alice wasn't even aware that she had decided until she found herself by the cot of Rufus. She placed a hand gently on his chest and rocked him slightly, her other hand expertly turning the dial to his mobile so that soft lullaby music would play. She moved to do the same to James, but he was more worked up than his brother. Lifting him from his cot, Alice rocked him back and forth, making shushing noises into his ear until he calmed enough for her to hear Robert's calls for help. With Rufus settling nicely, she hurried back to the stairs, James in her arms.

Robert had pushed Lucy off of himself slightly, and now the

scarlet patch seeping through his T-shirt was visible. He had a hand over it in an attempt to slow the bleeding.

"Alice . . . Alice, get help. I can't move her anymore."

Alice stared back at him, rooted to the spot, her mind going blank. He was hurt, she had left him. She had pushed Lucy. She had killed Lucy. Lucy was dead. It was over. The relief was short-lived as she remembered Robert. She knew he needed help, but at the very moment, with her son in her arms, she had no idea on how to help him. Finally, she had the motivation to move.

Running back to the nursery, Alice placed James down and shakily opened the window. She needed other people here; her mind raced as she tried to think how, if she used her phone, she would be alone until an ambulance or the police arrived. No, she couldn't be stuck on the phone. She needed to get to Robert to help him, and she needed witnesses.

"Help! Please! Somebody help us! We need an ambulance!"

A light across the street came on, followed by others. A few moments passed before doors began to open, and light spilled out into the dark street.

"What's happened?"

"Did anyone else hear that?"

Alice waved desperately, drawing attention to her house and begged those starting to come out into the street to call the police and an ambulance. Once the collective knew where they were heading, there was a rush towards her house. Closing the window, Alice raced along the landing and down the stairs, doing her best to avoid looking at the motionless figure where Robert lay.

"I've got to let them in."

Stepping over him, Alice fumbled with the keys as she tried to find the right one. After a few attempts, the right key slid into its lock, and the cool morning air rushed in along with their neighbours.

"Jesus! What happened here? You okay, fella?" The man from Number 15 knelt down at Robert's head.

"I have a hole that shouldn't be here, but I'm better than that nutcase."

Arms reached under him and he dragged him away from under the dead weight of Lucy.

"Has someone called the police? She's been stalking us. I found her going up the stairs. I thought I chased her out earlier, but she must have slipped into the pantry. She must have walked past me. I think she was going to hurt Alice. Alice? You okay?"

Robert tried to stand, but a number of hands pushed him back down.

Normally, his admission of not checking that the house was free from intruders earlier would have annoyed her, but seeing him hurt and knowing it was because of her quelled her temper.

"Stay there, fella. Best you wait for the ambulance and police."

"It was an accident. I was trying to get her away from Alice. I must've pulled her down the stairs with me."

Robert looked at his blood-covered hand that was pressed against his wound as he rested his back against the wall, his eyes avoiding looking at Lucy.

Alice watched him for a moment before deciding that what he said was what he believed had happened. The nag of guilt began at the back of her mind, but she silenced it. It had been self-defence—that was what she had needed to do. It wasn't murder if you were protecting your family. Normally, she was one for the truth. Already the thought of lying to the police was a daunting one, but she had read the news where people protecting their home and family from home invaders were prosecuted. She had the twins to think about. She couldn't leave them if she was punished for her actions. It would be easier to go along with Robert's version of events. Their neighbours had found him underneath Lucy's body. Everything corroborated his version of events. She knew Robert; he wouldn't feel guilty about this. In his eyes, this was justice. He had always said, if anyone broke in, he would kill them and suffer the consequences.

Moving to his side, Alice placed a hand over his and helped him apply pressure. Her other ran through his hair as she rested her lips against his temple.

"You'll be fine," she whispered as she rested her head against his, and he would be.

She was going to make sure they both were.

Gemma Lambart, born and raised in the London borough of Dagenham, now lives in Maldon, Essex with her husband, two sons, and their cat.

Gemma has been writing for twenty-two years, encouraged by both grandmothers. While one listened to her stories, the other shared her collection of books, broadening her imagination.

Gemma's writing spans many genres, but she often finds enjoyment creating thrillers, horror, and supernatural works.

DANCING IN THE DARK

Signature Jan Maher

"Hold the door!"

Oh God, she recognizes that voice. The imperious tone, the assumption that his command is any reasonable person's wish. She sees him now, huffing across the lobby. As soon as he knows he's been heard, he stops running, too self-centered to realize that the polite thing to do is wait for the next car, when this one is already packed full.

No, Claire will not hold the door for him. Will not lunge on his command for the button. But another woman in the elevator does.

Victor has the grace, at least, to hurry the last few steps. He thanks the little gray-haired lady with her thumb on the door-open icon, shoves his way in, and says to her, as if she's the operator, "Twelve . . . Oh, it's already lit. Going to twelve?" he asks jovially.

"Oh, no," she says, speaking to his chest because there's no room to lift her gaze without stressing her neck. That's how crowded it is. "I get off at five. The American Lady Gym."

Taller than average, he's able to turn his gaze to take in the rest of the people in the car. And sees the one pressed in the far corner, watching through narrowed eyes.

"Claire!"

"Hello, Victor."

"I didn't even see you."

"I know."

"Going to twelve?"

"Yes, of course."

Victor. What a perfect name. Victor. A self-centered jerk who always has to have his way.

Claire. What an irony, he thinks. A name that means *clear*, for such a muddle-brained broad.

Four people get off on two. For a moment, the unspoken thoughts in Claire's and Victor's minds merge. They couldn't have taken the stairs?

The little lady gets off at five.

"Enjoy your workout," Victor tells her.

They ride in silence, except for the cheery chirping of "Raindrops Keep Falling on My Head" that surrounds them as the elevator discharges three more of its passengers on six and two on seven.

"By the way—" Victor clears his throat as the elevator doors close, leaving them alone together in this tiny box. "I'd like to switch this weekend for next so I can take Sean and Jenny to the ballgame. Margie's mom got us free tickets."

"You know we agreed to stick to the parenting plan for the sake of stability. Besides, I've already got plans for this weekend," Claire lies, planning an impromptu trip to the zoo.

They listen to the Muzak. Victor clears his throat. Claire shifts her weight. The raindrops keep falling, but the elevator itself has stopped humming.

Claire looks up at the floor indicator.

"We're not going anywhere," she says.

"I thought you just said you had plans."

"No, I mean we're not going anywhere. You and I."

"We've already signed off on the big stuff. But you know what they say about the Devil being in the details."

"No. We are not moving in this elevator. There's no movement in the elevator."

He stares at her blankly.

"The elevator is stuck." She says it slowly, her voice serrated.

He hates that way she has of talking to him like he's an idiot. Harvard doesn't give doctorates to idiots, not the last time he checked; maybe at that diploma mill where she got her so-called masters.

"Stuck," he says.

"Maybe we should press the emergency call button."

"No need to panic."

"I'm not panicked. But I have no desire to be late to this meeting. You know both of these guys are going to charge us, whether we're on time or not."

"You could have picked a cheaper attorney."

"Victor, don't start. You could have, too."

"So, should I hit this button?"

"I say hit it."

There is no response to the alarm button.

"What does that panel say?"

"Where?"

"By the buzzer."

"It says, *in case of emergency, open door and lift phone*." He opens the little door and lifts the receiver that is tucked inside. "What should I tell them?"

"That we're stuck!"

Jesus, she thinks.

"Hello? Yes. Yes. Looks like ten. Yes, I see. Oh, my! . . . Yes, uh-hum, yes."

"What?" she demands.

He puts his fingers to his lips in a shushing gesture.

Fuck you, she silently mouths to him.

"Thank you," he says aloud to the person on the other end of the receiver. He hangs up. "We're stuck," he says.

"No duh," she says.

"The whole building is out. A computer glitch of some kind."

"How soon will they fix it?"

"They don't know. First they have to figure out what's causing it."

"Don't they have a back-up system or something?"

"I didn't ask."

"Call back and ask."

"I don't think I should bother them."

"Bother them?"

"They're trying to figure it out. I don't think we should interrupt them."

"I'm sure the person who answers the phone isn't part of whoever's trying to figure it out."

"He said *we*."

"Huh?"

"He said, 'We're trying to figure it out.' He didn't say, 'They're trying to figure it out.'"

This is when the lights go out. Claire screams.

Victor hates darkness too. He's never told her how much, because he was always the one who comforted her or the kids when they were afraid. He's remembering Jenny's third birthday when they lived in Savannah, and Hurricane Dave took out the lights. Jenny was scared out of her wits, and Claire was no help at all. She yelled, *Somebody get the candles!* and started to cry. Jenny picked up on it and began to wail too. He kidded her about that for years.

He can hear Claire breathing. Short, terrified breaths. He knows she is shaking. He doesn't need a light on to know that. He's held that shaking person tightly in his arms more than once.

"Claire?"

"What?" Her breathing makes her voice raspy.

"Got any birthday candles?"

Claire's labored breath splutters just a bit. He hopes it's a little giggle in spite of her fear.

"Not with me."

"A lighter?"

"I stopped smoking."

"You did? Good for you! Actually, I may have some matches. Here we go, I've got three."

"Strike anywhere?"

"No, just book matches."

"What do you have matches for?"

"For the joint I also have. Want to share it?"

"Victor!"

"What?"

"You can't smoke marijuana in a public elevator."

"Who's going to know?"

"They're going to rescue us any minute. Everybody knows what pot smells like. Besides, you know I haven't smoked since Jenny was conceived."

"Pot."

"What?"

"You haven't smoked pot since Jenny was conceived."

"Implying?" Claire stopped smoking cigarettes two months ago, on the lawyer's advice. You never know who you're going to get on the bench, the attorney had pointed out.

"Nothing, Claire. It was just a point of *clar*-ification, no pun intended."

"What pun?"

"Never mind."

There is a moment of silence. Finally, Victor says, "We could go over the terms so we'll have something to show for the time we'll probably be billed for anyway."

"Okay."

"Why are you insisting on every other Christmas when you're not even Christian?"

"Because that's when they get time off from school." Claire is distracted by a wave of panic. "Victor, would you sit where I can feel you? Just, you know, so I know you're there?"

"I'm here, Claire." Victor is distracted himself.

The scent of her fear is mingling with the touch of lime that she wears because someone told her it's calming. He gropes his way around the perimeter of the elevator until he's near her. He rejects the vivid images of having wild lime-scented sex with Claire right there on the elevator floor that are flooding his mind.

God! I used to love this woman, he thinks. *What happened?*

"Victor?"

"I'm right here."

"Victor?"

"What?"

"Can we call that guy again? See if the phone works?"

"Of course, we can. Why don't you call this time?"

"No, you. I'm too . . . I-I don't want them to hear how scared I am. Victor, what if this is it?"

"What?"

"You know. *It.* Maybe today is the day the terrorists pulled it off again. Or the Earth's crust shifted or the North Koreans lobbed a bomb. What if civilization as we know it has just ended."

"Claire, get a grip. The elevator's stuck. It's not the end of the world."

His condescending tone suddenly reminds her of a decade of marriage. "Give me the phone," she snaps, tight-lipped.

Her demand suddenly reminds him of a decade of marriage. "It's over there," he says, refusing to obey, "by the buttons."

"Light one of your matches so I can see," she says.

"Can't you just feel your way?"

"Oh, Jesus, Victor, just do it, will you? Why do you have to be so controlling?"

"Me controlling? Who's giving orders here?"

"Just do it."

There's the sound of rooting in the darkness of this box they occupy together.

Victor listens for a moment, then has to ask, "What the hell are you doing?"

"I'm looking for something I just remembered I have in my purse."

"In the dark?"

"Well, obviously. Since you won't light your precious match. Here it is. Now. Will you please light just one match?"

"What you got?"

"An ear candle."

"A what?"

"An ear candle. It's something I bought to try cleaning my ears out. It should burn a lot longer than a match."

"An ear candle."

"Victor, will you stop repeating me. It drives me crazy."

"An ear candle," he repeats. "Don't hit me, or I'll eat the matches."

She laughs despite herself. "Victor, intuit my lips. Light a match."

He does. She's holding a waxy tube.

"Now, light this. Let's see how it works."

He holds the match to the end of the tube, and they both watch the ear candle take fire and begin to burn.

"So how is this thing supposed to clean your ears?"

"You put the little end in your ear, and as the other end burns, it pulls your ear wax up the tube."

"Yeah, right."

"Well, you asked."

"And I was answered. Call the guy."

She looks at him through the flickering light. *Ten years I spent living with this sonofabitch. Still, he was a steady presence.*

He looks at her through the flickering light. *Ten years I spent living with this dingbat. Still, the sex was good.*

"Call him."

She makes her way across the elevator and lifts the small receiver from its cradle. "Do I have to dial anything?"

"No, they pick it up auto—"

He is interrupted by her speaking to the man at the other end of the phone.

"Yes, yes, we had just passed the ninth floor when it stopped, and then a couple of minutes later, after my—" She stops herself from saying *my husband.* "—after my about-to-be-ex-husband called, the lights went out, too. Oh, you know? Oh. Oh, I see."

Victor's fantasies are subsiding now of their own accord. He's trying to figure out how he likes being referred to as an about-to-be-ex-husband.

"What'd he say?"

Her answer is drowned by the sound of the smoke alarm, triggered by the spirals of gray that curl off the end of the ear candle. She drops the flaming tube, slams her foot onto it, plunging them once again in darkness.

"What?" She is shouting into the phone. "An ear candle . . . A *candle*, okay? Something we lit so we could see. It's out now. How do we get this thing to stop? I said, *how do we get this thing to stop?*"

Victor is yelling, too. "Tell them to turn the damn alarm off!"

"Shut up, Victor! I'm trying to hear how to do that! Okay, okay, I think I got it," she says now, into the phone. She gropes the floor-number panel in front of her and feels her way up two buttons from the bottom. "Okay, I got it. Okay."

The alarm stops wailing. Claire laughs.

"What's so funny?"

She ignores him. "Really! Like two weeks in Philadelphia!" She laughs again, falls silent for a moment.

This annoys Victor. He has always hated being the outsider in the presence of an in-joke.

"What in blazes was that all about?" Victor is suddenly aware that he sounds like he cares too much.

"They've got a crew working on it."

"No shit."

"Victor, that phrase. It makes you sound so middle school, you know what I mean?"

She's sassy. That's what he had fallen for when he first met her. He knows he tends to be pompous, and she was one of the few women he'd met who could take him down a peg. She was witty. And she wasn't afraid of him. Then. And she apparently isn't afraid of him now. Of the dark, but not of him.

He isn't really middle school, she thinks. *He's sort of . . . classy.* He knows which wines go with which main courses. He'd even have the nerve and knowledge to send a bottle back at a restaurant if he didn't think it was up to standards. And when she used to tease him about his pretensions, he delighted in it.

She closes her eyes in the pitch-dark cubicle and smiles at her memories. And he is a good father. When things went to hell between them, he didn't bail on the visits and child support the way some do.

"What are you thinking?" His voice intrudes, reminds her that she dislikes telling him what she is thinking. She used to love confiding in him. He doesn't seem to have realized that was then, this is now.

She is silent.

Victor is not a man who can stand much silence. He fills it quickly. "I'm thinking, let's get back to our lists, see if we can come to some agreements while we wait."

She sighs. "We can try."

"All right then. I want the kids at Christmas on alternate years."

"What am I supposed to do?"

"What do you mean?"

"I don't want to be alone on Christmas."

"Hey, guess what? Neither do I."

"But your family—"

"Isn't Christian. Good lord, Claire, what is this, the Spanish Inquisition?"

"I just mean it's not an emotional family time for you."

"Oh? Number one: it's very emotional to have the entire world around you act like Christmas is everyone's holiday whether it is or not. Number two: what's so special about your family's tradition of overcooked turkey and stewed uncles? You never go to church. You're not a Christian either. You're a damn Buddhist. Isn't that what you told me?"

"It's not a religious thing. It's cultural."

"Claire, we're talking about basic fairness here. Cut the crap."

Silence. Claire admits to herself that she's been talking crap. Out loud: "Okay. I get them this year."

"Fine."

"What's next?"

"I went first. How about you bring up something from your list."

"A college fund."

"What?"

"I want you to make regular contributions to a college fund."

"Look, they'll do better keeping their grades up and getting good scholarships. It was how we both did it."

"And if they don't keep a four-point-zero?"

"They have to. You have to have impeccable records."

"Reality check, Victor. Jenny is not like you and me. She works hard for a B-plus."

"I don't have a lot of extra cash lying around, Claire. This divorce has cost me plenty already."

"And it's almost over, isn't it? So your cash flow is going to improve. Four hundred dollars a month. Two hundred dollars each until they're out of college—"

Victor should admit to himself that she's got a point. But come to think of it, Jenny might not even go to college.

"And what if—"

"—or twenty-three, whichever comes first."

"You've got it all thought out, don't you?"

"I've had time." She is appalled to hear her voice catch.

"You're the one who wanted out."

"Yes. I was."

"And you still want out?"

"Victor, I *am* out. It doesn't matter whether I want it or not."

"I wish I could see you."

"Huh?"

"It's weird talking to you in the dark. I don't like not being able to see you."

Something in his voice makes her want to rush to him and cradle him, stroke his hair, tell him everything is going to be all right. He sounds just like Sean when he saw a monster in his closet one night. She turned on the light for him to prove it was his Nerf-ball hoop with the ball balanced atop. Then said, *See? It's all right, honey. You can go back to sleep.*

As she turned to leave, she heard that voice. *Mom? Can I have a hug good night?*

And then she got the Nerf ball and said, *Tell you what. I'll take this monster's head with me and put it in my closet. That way, if he sees me, he won't have any legs to walk on. If his body wants to walk, he won't be able to see which way to go. We'll divide and conquer.* She hugged him fiercely.

Mom?

Yes, honey?

What does conquer mean?

A moment of silence. He sits with his back against the wall of the elevator. He hears tiny noises, brushing, whishing sounds of movement across the carpeted floor and then feels the electric touch of her hand. It hits his upper arm first as she waves through the air to locate his body. From there, it travels down to his elbow, forearm, wrist, and comes to rest by lacing its fingers into his own.

"Victor," she says.

He has never heard such heaviness in her voice. Such weariness. Has it never been there before or has he never listened to it before?

"I'm sorry," she continues, "that it didn't work out. I did love you once."

He embraces her, accepting comforting from this woman who

left him, this mother of his children, this enigma. He almost asks if she wants to try again. He murmurs her name and leaves it at that.

The Muzak comes on first. It has moved, apparently played on during their wait. The raindrops have finished falling, and "Dancing in the Dark" now oozes from the sound system.

She pulls into herself. He lets her go. They never did dance together, really. She grabs the rail and hauls herself up.

The lights return, a flicker, another, and then they creak on the way fluorescents do. The elevator lurches ever so slightly, and there are whirring sounds somewhere in the distance.

Claire crosses the cubicle to get her purse. Victor stands and kicks his left leg out to banish the kink in his knee.

"What time is it?" Claire asks.

"Two thirty."

"We should make sure they aren't billing us for this time."

"For sure. And we're agreed on the Christmas schedule?"

"Yes."

"Cross your heart?"

"Cross my heart. And the college fund?"

"Yes. Cross my heart."

She pushes the button for twelve. The elevator hums of facing the music together. They continue their slow ascent.

Jan Maher's novel, *Earth As It Is*, has won the 2017 Best Fiction and Grand Prize awards in the Great Midwest Book Festival competition and is listed by Kirkus as a 2017 Best Indie Book. Other writing credits include a novel, *Heaven, Indiana*; plays *Ismene, Intruders, Widow's Walk,* and *Most Dangerous Women;* and books for educators, *Most Dangerous Women: Bringing History to Life through Readers' Theater* and *History in the Present Tense: Engaging Students through Inquiry and Action.* Her short stories and poetry have been published in online and print journals and anthologies, including

Ride 2: More Short Fiction about Bicycles, Meat for Tea: The Valley Review and *Straw Dog Poetry Anthology: Compass Roads: A Dispatch from Paradise/Poems about the Pioneer Valley.*

She lives with her husband, best friend, most helpful critic, and occasional co-writer, Doug Selwyn, in Greenfield, MA. Her website address is www.janmaher.com.

"Sign here, please," a grubby and snotty clark with eyes like beryl said, handing me an obscenely large clipboard over the counter. "Then initial and date, bottom right corner. Good, good. One more, just here, and we'll get on with it."

So I signed. Why wouldn't I? It's what I came here to do, after all.

I pretended to read the pages over, peering over the frames of my glasses, before asking, "Is this it? Just these sheets?"

Though not quite, the final flourish of my signature felt like the last rung of a pair of handcuffs clicking shut far tighter than they ought to be and digging into my flesh. I had signed my life away before for student loans, a mortgage, marriage, even for a handful of parking tickets, but never like this. Never with a peacock-feathered fountain pen.

"Well done. This way, please, for the first part of your orient*aaa*tion," the clark said, drawing out the *a* in *orientation* for several beats.

He snatched the clipboard from me, and it disappeared under his desk. What other eccentric treasures was he hiding under there? I probably shouldn't even wonder.

He was slow to get up, both because of a mandatory shuffling of paper to prove his fastidious attention to detail and because of the arthritic popping in his knees and hips. Ever fall over in slow motion? First collapsing to your knees, then onto the palms of your hands, not yet out of the woods, and finally ending the whole drama flat on your face? Well, this is how the clark stood.

He sidled past me and down the hall, pausing to urge me to follow. "Please, we haven't time to d*aaa*wdle. Dawdling leads to idleness. Idleness to—"

"Too much snacking? Obesity? Perhaps a new outlook on life," I offered. He wasn't amused.

I followed, sure to keep well behind him. When I lost him around one of the labyrinth of an office's dozens of corners, he wasn't hard to find. I just had to listen to my nose. The song of him was as dissonant as Thai food left in the garbage disposal during a weekend trip to the dump.

Abruptly, he stopped.

I'd been busy admiring the starkness of our journey. Each corridor was the same, complete with evenly spaced fluorescent bulbs, plain white-tiled floors, and silver name plaques to the left-hand side of nondescript doors with monograms like C.A. JOHNSON and B.S. SMITH.

In one room, a break room of sorts, its door wide open, a blonde-haired woman paced back and forth. She held a cup of coffee, occasionally bringing it up for a good chug, and talked through a wireless headset to someone named Horrible Jackass. She said something about the keeping of appearances and clouds and little men in diapers, but I didn't quite catch her meaning. For a second, she had ivory, feathered wings. Or maybe she didn't. When she made eye contact with me, they disappeared with my memory of them just before she slammed shut the door.

I nearly ran into the mole of a man but managed to avoid him with a well-executed swim move. He didn't seem the least fazed.

"Here we are, sir. Orientation is just through that door. Step through. Have a seat, please. You will be orient*aaa*ted shortly. It won't hurt . . . for long. Good luck."

"My last job," I said, hand hovering over the doorknob, "they sent me first-class to California for a week of training. I cruised the bay, sipped champagne, ate room service steaks every night, and kissed all the right—"

"Orientation is nothing like that, sir. You won't be kissing any posteriors here, I assure you. It will be nothing like anything you've ever experienced. Now, please, go in and have a seat. Your file did say you weren't a man to w*aaa*ste time."

We didn't shake hands. We didn't so much as nod to each another. The clark turned and waddled back towards his desk and I, given no other choice, opened the door and took my seat.

It was a bright, wide-open room, inhabited only by a single folding chair.

"Hello, Sam," a deep, god-like voice boomed down at me from tiny speakers on the walls and ceiling.

"Uh, hi there," I said.

"Relax and avert your attention to the screen, if you will. I want to show you a short motion film."

"What motion?"

Suddenly, a projection screen dropped down on the wall in front of me, and an old-timey movie reel appeared behind me without as much as a *puff.* It whirred to life, and the tape clicked as it wound through the feed. Indecipherable words flashed by, and the grainy *beep, beep* of an equally antiquated countdown sequence began.

At zero, a man appeared in black and white. It was the same voice that had greeted me.

"*Ahem.* Is this thing on? Check, one two. Check, check. Good. Ready to begin, young man?"

"Do I get popcorn or anything?" I said under my breath. "Or some nachos?"

"Absolutely not," the man on the screen said. "Pay attention."

"Do I get anything?"

"Yes," he sighed audibly. "You get orientated. You get freedom. You get an eternity. Most of all, you get a job. Nay, a career."

"Fair enough. Please, the show must go on."

Without warning, the show indeed went on. An indeterminate amount of time passed. Image after image, scene after scene flashed across the screen. Even if I wanted to, I wouldn't have been able to look away. I was hypnotized. The whole of the universe revealed itself to me, written and directed and narrated by the man behind the curtain.

I witnessed the murder of Abel, the burning of witches young and old, the slaying of kings. I tried to blink away the piles of bodies in the streets of London, only to blink to existence people leaping from burning buildings in Chicago, New York, and Berlin. All the death, all the horror, all the atrocities of the past, present, and future unfurled on that screen.

But there was more to it than that. The full screen side of the movie, the side most viewers liked to play, showed beauty and hope and all the other empty words people use to try to explain life. A rose opened its bud to reveal pale pink petals. A doe walked on wobbly legs seconds after birth. A doctor handed a mother her newborn, when forty others had already told her she'd never be able to bring a child into the world.

For the first time, I understood the duality of it all. For the first time, I believed in something greater than myself.

When it was over, my first thoughts were about how big the film reel must have been. Did they even make them that size? My second thought was that I knew it all, everything, and that I had arisen from the dust of my old life to do this job.

Second chances don't come often. Thirds are a blessing.

The deep voice again: "Now, if you'll please exit the way you came, and follow Walter to the next part of your orientation. Your time here is drawing to an end. Thank you for watching."

"There's more? What else could I possibly need to know?"

"There is always more to know, sir. And things we must . . . unknow. Now, please exit in an orderly fashion, and follow Walter to the staging area. Don't make me ask again."

I saluted. I can't say why, but it felt like the right thing to do.

That godly disembodied voice deserved as much. Then I left the room, which was once again empty aside from the folding chair, because it was the only thing left to do.

"This w*aaa*y, please."

"Can I ask you something, Walt?" I said as we made our way farther into the belly of the beast.

I knew the way to our final destination and no longer needed the clark but was nonetheless thankful for his company. Company would be a rare commodity where I was going. All the people in the world would be around, but no one to talk to.

"Certainly, sir, though I suspect you already know the answer."

I did, of course. I'd asked a lot of questions over the years, as most people do. They seemed impossible puzzles and riddles, only solvable through God or the clever application of science or the taking of various mind-enhancing drugs. The video made all the answers seem so simple. Simple enough for a monkey throwing poo to answer. Even Walter could answer them, if he put his mind to it.

"Will I ever have to visit my family?"

"In time, you'll have to visit everyone, sir. What has a beginning must have an end. It is your duty to bring that end."

"But, when I do, will they be able see me for who I really am? Will I have to see them as I once did?"

We arrived at the end of the long passageway, which stopped at a brick wall painted stark white like the rest of the office complex. The clark snorted noisily and cleared his throat before running his hand clockwise, then counterclockwise, on the surface of the wall. One by one, the bricks folded in on themselves, revealing a . . . locker room?

Several angels clad in matching white tracksuits swung tennis rackets back and forth as they exchanged bits of high-spirited camaraderie. They noticed me, bowed solemnly, and avoided eye contact. Two demons across the way, dressed similarly in red and black, stood erect and triumphant. They grinned toothily at me.

I winked at both parties and went on, following Walter past a stretch of beings—some winged, others horned, both recognizable and familiar. One wore a clock around her neck. Another sharpened a heart-shaped arrow. None of them showed any sign of bashfulness, despite their apparent sex.

At a bend in the locker room, steam rose from underneath a shower curtain. Its occupant hummed a tune, oblivious to anyone's presence.

"Proceed, sir. The staging aw*aaa*its."

"Thank you, Walter. I hope to see you again someday soon."

"Not too soon, I pray," he sniggered.

I nodded and made my way towards the shower and the singing bather. As I came closer to the curtain, the humming stopped, as did the gentle, silvery tinkle of cascading water. The song continued to play in the background of my consciousness, as it would for the rest of eternity.

"Hand me a towel, would ya?"

I hadn't seen a towel anywhere, but I looked around just in case. Then, draped neatly over my extended left arm, hung a blue towel, soft as a lamb, with the initials J.C. embroidered in gold lettering across the bottom. I handed it over the retention bar, and the man snatched it away with a grunt.

"Thanks, mate. Just finishing up. Don't worry, I left you some hot water," he said, stepping out completely naked.

I won't lie, I was impressed. His bald head shone like an eight ball as he leaned forward to squeeze water out of his beard and onto the floor.

He winked at me. "See ya on the other side, yeah?"

"Uh, sure. Where, exactly?"

"Everywhere, mate."

He was gone just as quickly as I had arrived, leaving me alone with my thoughts and the dirty shower stall. I loosened my suit and left it in a messy pile on the floor before willing myself in. All I had to clean myself with was the remnant of an orange soap bar covered in curly black hair. A pile of the same stuff clung to the edges of the stall.

The naked man hadn't lied, though. Hot, cleansing water washed over me. No matter how many times I turned the handle, it refused to cool down. So, I let it scald my skin as I ran my fingers through my hair.

Filth I hadn't even known I was covered in swirled down the drain between my legs. I found myself humming the same tune—a song I knew but still couldn't place—as my sins and my desires and every memory I'd ever had washed away. I hummed louder and louder until nothing was left besides me, the tune, and my new job.

Eventually, the water stopped. I don't remember turning it off. At the time, I was sure I must have drained the world dry. Every stream, every lake, even the oceans. It all belonged to me, in a way; both sides of the beautiful, hopeful coin.

I stood there dripping wet and as red as a newborn, taking it all in. I should have felt overwhelmed. I should have trembled with terror or at least shaken with nerves, but I didn't. I saw what lay before me, was blind to where I had been in the past, and knew here was exactly where I was supposed to be.

On the other side of the curtain, right where they promised to be, hung my black cloak and bone-white scythe, the tip of which glinted and seemed to say *shing*. Instead of the ambient hum of office lighting, I heard only the ticking of a billion clocks and the hissing of a thousand-billion hourglasses. Sunlight seeped in through a cracked window. On the other side came the whining of horses and clacking of hooves.

A familiar voice said, "Whoa, there. T*aaa*ke it easy, girl."

Finally, I caught the whiff of leather bound books, volumes of them, each labeled by name. They reminded me of all the work that still needed to be done. There was a lot of it, no matter how many centuries I'd been at it or how many more were to come.

All I could do was attend to it as best I could, one soul at a time.

Harlow sat surrounded by a teetering pile of discarded wrapping paper and boxes, trying not to look disappointed. She wasn't an ungrateful girl by any means, but it was just that—on this, her eighteenth birthday—she'd hoped for the gift she'd wished for since she was twelve years old.

She mentally added the money she'd received in cards from her grandma and Aunt Lucy to the cash she'd stashed away from her part-time job at the throwback record store in the mall, Sympathy for the Vinyl. Still about $500 short.

"Thank you, everyone," she said. "I love you guys."

Her mom clapped her hands together and said, "On to the cake!"

Harlow stood and brushed a kiss on top of her mother's blonde head. She towered above that side of the family. They all looked like pixies, with their pale skin and hair, while she'd inherited her father's height, curly dark hair, and brown skin. Her green eyes were the only feature that she could call her own, a surprising result of the combination of her mother's bright blue eye color with her father's deep brown.

"Soulful eyes," her dad always said. "No wonder you're a musician."

A musician without her own instrument. Oh, well. Maybe she could save up enough by Christmas.

Her dad headed into the dining room first. He drew up short and turned to look at her with sparkling eyes. "Oh, wow. I think we forgot a present. What do we have here?"

From inside the doorway, he withdrew a long, bulky box.

Harlow's heart skipped, and her vision danced. She must've swayed because she felt hands press against her back, and her Aunt Lucy laughed.

"I think she knows what it is, Daniel."

Harlow ran and threw her arms around her father, nearly causing him to drop the box. She knew, indeed.

With trembling hands, she ripped into the paper, then ran her hands over the classic, brown Gibson hard-shell case.

The guitar inside stunned her, though she'd looked at pictures of it a thousand times. A Les Paul Standard in Blueberry Burst. It was the most beautiful thing she'd ever seen, its gleaming surface the color of cornflowers and denim.

Her cousin Tara begged her to play something, but her father seemed to understand her hesitation.

"Let's cut that cake. We'll have the concert on a different day, after Harlow and her new friend have a chance to get acquainted."

Somehow, she made it through the cake and ice cream, though she honestly couldn't remember tasting a thing.

Finally, people began to leave. Her parents looked at each other, then at her.

"You may be excused," her dad said.

Harlow gave them both another fierce hug, grabbed her guitar, and ran upstairs to her room. She lay the guitar across her lap, her fingers reverently trailing on the slick, shining surface. She looked up at the posters on her wall: Jimi Hendrix, Lita Ford, Eric Clapton, Orianthi, Nancy Wilson—guitar gods, every one of them.

She made some adjustments, then strummed a riff of "Satisfaction" by the Rolling Stones. A cloud of blue smoke filled the room. Harlow froze, unsure what was happening. When it dissipated, she yelped.

A skinny white dude with frizzy bleached hair and heavy black eyeliner stood at the foot of her bed.

Harlow swallowed a lump of bitter disappointment and clutched her guitar. This had seemed so real, but obviously it wasn't. In a minute, she would wake up from this crazy dream with no Blueberry Burst Les Paul, no aging glam guitarist staring at her.

She squeezed her eyes shut.

"Are you okay?" he asked. "Is it a bad trip?"

Harlow opened one eye and stared at him.

He pursed his Pepto pink lips. "Well?" he demanded. "Can you speak? Don't you know who I am?"

"You're C.C. DeVille. Former guitarist for Poison." She sighed. "Figment of my dream world."

He laughed. "As if! I'm as real as it gets, sweetheart, and I've come for what's mine."

Harlow clutched the guitar. "You can't have it."

He rolled his eyes. "Not it. You."

"*Ew,*" she said. "No offense, but . . . *ew*. You're older than my dad."

C.C. scowled. "Not that, either. I still have groupies. Hundreds of them. I'm here for your soul."

Harlow laughed. For a dream, this was lit as fuck. She decided to play along.

"So, you're like the Grim Reaper? Am I dead?"

If possible, he only looked more impatient. "No, to both."

"Are *you* dead? I can't remember."

He gritted his too-perfect white teeth. "No."

From his pocket, he withdrew a crumpled piece of paper and thrust it at her. Harlow recognized her handwriting.

"I, Harlow James, hereby sell my soul to the DeVille, for fortune, fame, and guitar god superstar status."

It was witnessed by her sixth-grade boyfriend, Keith, and sealed with a glossy pink kiss that smelled faintly of strawberries. In the corner, beside the word *DeVille*, she had sketched a cartoon version of C.C. shredding on his guitar. She'd been such a weird kid.

Harlow laughed. She couldn't stop laughing.

"Excuse me," C.C. said. "Are you finished?"

She wasn't, but she tried. She wiped her eyes and said, "This can't be legally binding."

"It is," he insisted.

"I was, like, twelve when I wrote that."

"Age doesn't apply in these transactions," he said. "But, even if it did, wouldn't you still want it?"

Harlow gave him an amused glance. "Let's say I did agree to sell my soul to the . . ." She snickered. ". . . DeVille for all those things. How are *you* going to help *me*?"

He looked mortally offended. "I was great. Hell, I *am* great. I just got sidetracked by the trappings of fame. Girls, drugs, Aquanet. I can make sure you don't."

"We're off to a good start," Harlow said. "I don't do any of those things."

"Smartass," he said, but she caught the ghost of a smile. "You don't even know who you are, do you?"

She opened her mouth, and he held up a palm.

"What do you know about your father's side of the family?"

"Not much." She shrugged. "He was adopted."

"What if I told you that you are a descendent of the great Sister Rosetta Tharpe?"

"I'd say you're too short to be that full of shit."

"Do you even know who that is?"

"The Godmother of Rock 'n' Roll? Of course I do."

C.C. smiled. "Good girl. You have talent. With my help, you can have all that you desire. You can be better than any of them." He gestured at the posters on her wall. "And you're attractive. That always helps. Together, we can bring back glam metal and hair ballads."

Harlow snickered. "Really?"

"Why not?" he asked, a bit defensively. "That's when music was *fun*. Life was a party, bright and festive and light. Those were the best days of my life. Then all those mopey, grunge people came around. They hated themselves, hated each other. It was nothing but depression and heroin. And flannel." He shuddered. "So much flannel."

"As opposed to what? Cocaine and spandex?"

"Smartass," he said again. "Life *was* better then. The world was a happier place when it was singing 'Paradise City,' 'Unskinny Bop,' and 'Girls, Girls, Girls.' Look, let me show you what I can do for you." He motioned for her to pick up the guitar. "Play something."

Harlow strummed the guitar riff from "Talk Dirty to Me."

C.C. nodded his approval, then he stepped forward and touched the guitar.

Harlow felt something hum through the wood, vibrate the strings. She had a vision of herself on stage, hair flying like Slash, thousands of people screaming her name.

It felt good.

"Now play it again," C.C. said.

She did. It sounded amazing, better than she'd ever played. The guitar screamed and wailed the sweetest riff she'd ever heard.

"Glam is transcendent. Transportive. It takes people back to the good times when they were young and carefree. We can change the world, Harlow. I can give it all to you. I promise you the best years of your life, and when it's over, you give me your soul."

He sent her another vision. She stood on stage, shredding the clearest, most amazing solo she'd ever heard. When she finished, the stage trembled from the vibrations of the audience's applause, from their screams.

It was all she'd ever wanted.

Still thinking it must be a dream, she said, "Okay."

When she woke in her bed, clutching the guitar, she was even more convinced it was a dream. A strange, vivid one, but a dream nonetheless.

Within months, Harlow James was on track to becoming the greatest guitar player of all time. New bands, old bands—they all clamored to hire the beautiful virtuoso.

Nearly ten years later, she was playing a sold-out show in Madison Square Garden when she looked out into the audience and saw C.C. smiling at her from the front row.

It's time, he mouthed.

Harlow shook her head. She was too young. This wasn't part of the deal, surely. But then she felt it—a sudden, sharp pain in the center of her chest. The heart attack dropped the young musician in her tracks. She died still clutching the Blueberry Burst Les Paul.

C.C. shook his head with more than a little regret. She'd been the best of them. Brought back the best music of all time, in his opinion. At least that part of her would live forever, along with the mystery of her sudden, drug-free death.

At 8:23 p.m. that cool September night, Harlow James became the latest and most-mourned member of the 27 Club—a group of talented, young musicians who'd all died before their twenty-eighth birthday. It was a club that C.C. himself had avoided only by offering up souls in his place.

He pushed his way through the crowd, which was clamoring to see what was happening onstage. Harlow's new husband, the lead singer of the most popular band on the planet, was on his knees beside her, trying to resuscitate her.

Although it was impossible to hear over the noise of the crowd, C.C. was humming "I Won't Forget You" as he made his way through the throng of people.

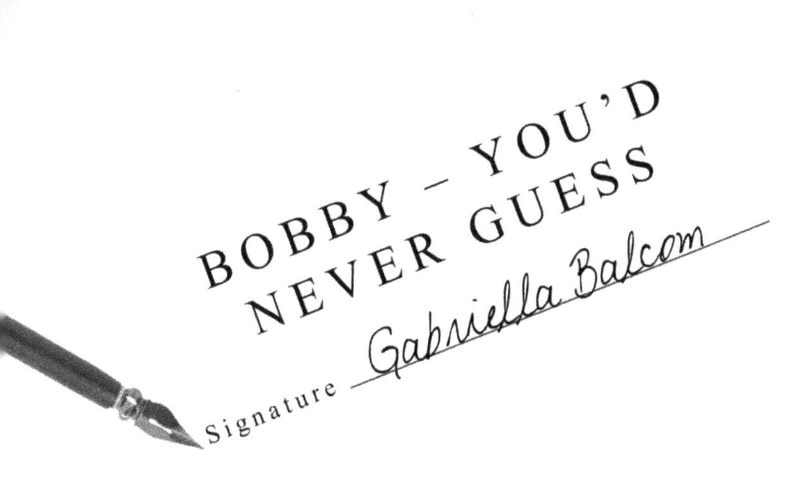

Friday, February 2

Ted Bundy and Jeffrey Dahmer are interesting. That's why I chose both instead of one when Mrs. Smith told us to write three pages about a serial killer. Everyone else griped about the assignment, but it didn't bother me. I didn't know so many people admired killers until I saw all the websites and information online. When Mrs. Smith handed our graded papers back, she said she didn't expect anyone to have anything positive to say and gave me extra points for "thinking outside the box" and "being creative."

Writing this is strange. I've never kept a journal before but Pain-in-the-Ass Wilson's been hounding me to. She's the counselor at my school. Nothing describes her better than "pain," and she's a total ass. Somehow she got this screwy idea I'm lonely and hurting. She said I need an outlet so things don't build up inside. Makes me want to gag! Stupid old bat! Where the heck was her concern the first time I told her Josh wouldn't leave me alone? Or the second time, or the next thirty? Nowhere—that's where!

I'm Bobby, by the way, and this is enough for now.

Tuesday, February 6

Mom narrowed her eyes and her brows went up when we were watching a movie earlier. It was one of those let's-do-stuff-together-as-a-family and let's-bond things she pushes. We go along with her so she'll shut up! If we don't, she says stuff like, "Someday we might not be able to do things as a family," and starts sniffling. No, thanks! The crying gets irritating. Makes me want to smack her. I wonder if Josh or Tim the Bastard ever feel the same way. Josh is my older brother—he's 16—and we live with Mom, Lacie, and the Bastard. That's what I call Mom's husband, Tim—my stepfather. Lacie's my little sister. She's four. The show we watched was good guy/bad guy, and the bad man killed people before the police got him. Thing is, I laughed at the wrong place when he hurt some smugster instead of when he was taken down. I'll have to be careful not to do that again.

Thursday, February 8

I went fishing but did something different this time. It was okay but not as much fun as I thought it'd be. I got the idea from a horror movie Mom didn't know I watched one night after she went to bed (I'm not allowed to see them yet). A man in the movie threw gas on people, tossed matches, and burned them alive. Another put bags over men's heads and suffocated them. The way the dying people looked—eyes bulging, clawing at their heads and necks, and unable to breathe—looked interesting.

It would've been strange putting a bag on a fish's head, but they need water, right? So I dropped the one I caught on the ground instead and watched. It flopped all over the place, its mouth open the whole time, trying to get air. That was sort of disappointing. I'll try a squirrel next time.

Monday, February 12

School called Mom to come talk with them this morning and bring me along. Today's Teacher Preparation Day, so classes were cancelled. I didn't know what to think when Mom asked what I'd done wrong, but I told her, "Nothing." They don't know about me.

Mr. Moore, the principal, sent us to see Wilson the Pain. I didn't pay attention to everything, but she told Mom I was intelligent but "failing to meet his full academic potential." She pulled out papers, showed Mom, and said testing showed I had an IQ of 139. The Pain started on me next. "You can be anything you want in life, Bobby. Don't let things get you down. You're real intelligent—a handsome boy with those blue eyes and blonde hair. Girls are going to chase you someday . . ." Blah, blah, blah. She wouldn't stop running her mouth.

Mom was so excited about the IQ thing when we got home, she talked fast and didn't make a lot of sense. The Bastard was his usual self and said he didn't think I'd amount to much no matter what. He spews crap like that to all of us now and then, and I've heard Lacie crying sometimes at night. There's no telling what he's said to her. Listening to him put me down today, I imagined him with no air—like a dying fish—and smiled. That just made him call me a weirdo.

I never thought of myself as good looking. My hair's the color of butterscotch pudding (with a little vanilla mixed in maybe, making it a bit lighter). My eyes are between bluebell and cornflower blue and go cooler depending on what I'm thinking about. My nose tilts up at the end. I've got a few freckles, a small gap between my two front teeth, and Mom says the padding in my cheeks is leftover baby fat. I'm thin and average as far as my height, or so I'm told. Personally, I think I look ordinary, but maybe that's because I'm used to myself. "Real intelligent" is what the Pain said. Yeah, that part I already knew.

Wednesday, February 14

I got an idea when we visited Grandpa after school. He's big on hunting, fishing, and trapping. He stuffs the animals he catches or makes things out of their skins. I've gone out with him before and seen him shoot animals and skin them. You know, their eyes change when they're dying, going kind of empty or glassy.

Grandpa offered me a snare of my own for rabbits and squirrels.

I didn't want to show too much interest, though, so I just shrugged and said, "I don't know if I'd use it or not. Well, maybe—"

Friday, February 16

I haven't had this much fun in a long time. The snare I put out Wednesday night worked and trapped a rabbit. I had to smack it on the head with a rock a couple times because it tried to get away. Man, oh man, it got upset, kicking and hissing at me. That thing did *not* like being squashed! I gotta agree; getting squashed isn't fun. I've been through that myself. First, I used my foot to press down on the rabbit, then large rocks, and it whined and made a weird noise like it was grinding its teeth. Then it shrieked like a girl with a worm thrown in her face or a bug dropped down her shirt. I tried to memorize the sound and what the rabbit looked like. Watching it trying to breathe was more satisfying than with the fish.

But that wasn't even the best part! I started skinning it and wow! Rabbits bleed like we do! They feel pain! I didn't know that. Fish hardly make a sound, but my rabbit screamed like a little girl being murdered! I got goosebumps and felt a little lightheaded. I got real close to it on my hands and knees so I could watch its eyes.

I wanted so badly to play with it longer, but I had to kill it eventually. The blood didn't bother me, or the sound—I liked those parts—but the screaming made me a little nervous. What if someone heard and came to check? What if they found me?

I've replayed everything over and over in my mind since then, and I think this might have been the best day ever.

Saturday, February 24

Last night, I slept over with Mark Snow. Mom was so pleased, I thought she'd hug me to death (what would that be like?) or start singing or crying. Her eyes were gooey bright as she told me, "Friends are great. They're there for you no matter what, and you deserve a good friend!" She's always blabbing about me needing to be more social and make friends, telling me, "Bring your buddies home, Bobby." I figured if I told her I had no buddies and didn't want any, she'd get worried and take me to a shrink or something.

She saw one after my baby sister died. Not my sister Lacie, but my other sister, Tami. Tami was eight months old when she died. Mom cried like crazy for a long time. It didn't affect me or my brother or Lacie as much, because we didn't spend a lot of time with Tami, her being a baby and all. She did nothing but sleep, eat, cry, and crap. The Bastard and Mom were the ones who spent the most time with her.

When the Bastard heard I was going to Mark's house, he was rude. That's normal for him, and I know he won't change. He had Lacie crying again two nights ago; I heard as I was falling asleep. Yesterday after school, I went to ask her what she was so upset about, but Mom yelled for me to hurry up so she could get me to Mark's place before she went grocery shopping. I guess I'll ask Lacie another time.

Mark and I have been sitting together in school for about a week because we were assigned a science project. I was bored at first, but his sweat band broke three days ago. He wears it under his watch on his left wrist, and I saw what he was hiding. He has scars, maybe 15 or 20 of them. He has no idea I saw, but I did. I wondered if they're from cutting himself. I heard people do that to deal with problems or because they like the pain.

At Mark's house, I made a big deal over his video games. It wasn't hard because I like them. He has a Playstation 4 and a Nintendo Switch like me, some of the same games I've got, and several new ones I don't have.

He showed me his wrist and where he cuts his thighs up high. He even let me in on where he hides his blades. He takes them out of cheapie razors his mother uses. I tried one on myself when he asked if I wanted to. I'd been wondering about cutting anyway, how it felt, and if I'd like it. When I pushed the blade into my skin, it stung a little, and I liked watching the blood oozing up. The blood smelled metallic and tasted salty. Mark said he never thought of tasting it, but he tried some. Later he told me, "You can use the blades if you come over more. This is fun, and I'd get to hang out with you more." I liked the idea. I wouldn't have to sneak any razors myself if I used his. I wonder if Mark would let me taste his blood.

We promised each other we won't tell about cutting for the rest of our lives. If one of us does, he has to give his savings to the other guy. I have $22.53 from helping Grandpa, and Mark has $37.10 he told me he saved from allowances. The tattletale would have to be the other's slave for two months also. I was good with our agreement, but Mark wanted something stronger, like a blood pact. I like blood so why not? He made a new cut on his wrist, and I made one. We held them together so our blood would mix, and he said, "There! We sealed it, and we're blood brothers now."

I think I'll invite him over next Friday.

Monday, March 19

I'm bored. All Mark wants to do is play video games, cut, or watch fish out of water flop around with their mouths open. I haven't shown him my snare or animal skins.

We tried cutting deeper, but Mark got scared and said, "I'm afraid I'll kill myself by accident." He told me his mother revealed she used to cut when she was younger too, and she worried he might die.

Sometimes he says how he felt before he had a friend, how he used to think about dying because he was lonely and had no one to talk to. When he tells me that stuff, he ducks his head, his brown hair falls into his eyes, and he starts crying. He wanted us to hug last time he cried. Sheesh!

Listening to him gets boring fast, especially when he's boo-hooing. I wonder how he'd feel if I stopped being his friend.

Saturday, April 14

Mark's funeral was today. Everyone says he killed himself,

either on purpose because he failed a math test and his dog died the next day, or by accident when he cut his wrists too deeply. I didn't think I'd miss him, but I do. I guess I got used to doing things with another person. Maybe I'll get a new friend. I've noticed a kid sitting by himself all the time at lunch. I don't know his name, but I think he's a grade below me. I wonder if he likes video games. I wonder if he's ever cut.

Sitting through Mark's memorial service was hard because it lasted forever, was boring as heck, and I had other stuff I wanted to do. A lot of the kids in our class were there, although they never liked Mark and a few were mean to him. I heard two girls whispering behind me. One said, "I heard the nurse caught him cutting last year." Number 2 said, "Like cutting his skin or something?" I snorted and thought, *Stupid cow.* The first girl said, "Yeah. He must've been real, real sad to be cutting himself, but I guess he's not sad anymore now." The second girl said, "I don't know. I tried cutting before and it was okay—"

Mom told me twice to get in line with her to see Mark's body, but I didn't want to. Why would I? I knew what he looked like, but I did what she said so she'd shut up. I guess she was right, though. If I didn't go see him and say "Bye," it would've seemed strange since we were best friends. Lacie started crying when Mom and I walked off. She didn't want to be left with the Bastard. I didn't blame her, so I picked her up and we took her with us.

Looking at Mark lying in the casket, pale and quiet, I expected him to say, "Hey, Bobby. I snuck us a new razor." Remembering things, I smiled and couldn't help but laugh a little. I didn't realize his mother had come up by me until she asked, "Are you smiling?" She looked horrified. Anyone could tell she'd been crying. Her nose was red, and her eyes looked puffy. I told her, "He must have been real, real sad to be cutting himself, but I guess he's not sad anymore now."

Bursting into blubbery tears, she started wailing! She looked ugly, with the blotches on her cheeks and crud dripping from her nose, and she started blowing it and wiping it on her sleeve. I thought she'd go medieval on my butt for a second, but she grabbed me and hugged me super tight. It felt weird, and I worried about her getting snot on me, but everyone was looking our direction, so what could I do? I guess she figured I cared about Mark and was glad he wasn't sad anymore. She kept going on and on and on. "You were the best thing that happened to him, Bobby. You were such a good friend to my baby." I said, "I tried my best." I wanted to show modesty.

Thursday, April 19

Josh smacked Tim around today during recess. Josh picks on everyone, but Tim's one of his favorites to mess with. Tim starts whimpering and snuffling like a baby so fast. Me, I stopped crying years ago. It's not as much fun for Josh when there are no tears. When Tim was punched in the nose, he started bleeding and boo-hooing. I guess he couldn't breathe, because he had his mouth open. It reminded me of the animals I play with. Seeing the blood, I stopped to watch like everyone else.

I wanted to get a better look at the blood and Tim's eyes, so I leaned in. I must have gotten too close because Josh noticed. He sneered and taunted me. "Wanna join him, huh? You missing your boyfriend?" I didn't expect him to hit me, but he did. He didn't notice Pain-y Wilson coming down the hall. It was good timing! Between her and the principal, they chewed him out good in front of everyone. She hounded me afterward, but I told her again and again I was okay, and she finally left me alone.

She visited our class and blabbed about being kind, getting along, and "reaching out for help" if needed. Blah, blah, blah!

I hate attention. It's like getting rotten food in my mouth by accident and having to throw up again and again. You'd think a counselor would understand not to get everyone staring at someone who'd been picked on. Doesn't she know that stuff bothers people?

Wouldn't it make them want to sink through the floor? It makes me feel that way, but she never gets it. She asked me in front of everyone if I wanted to say something about being hit. Stupid cow. Yeah, I have stuff I want to say. "Bleed! Just bleed!"

I didn't hear her talking to me at first. I was thinking about my plans for later, visiting my spot in the woods and working on an animal. Fun stuff. I've gotten a little better at cutting, and I know how far to go in the woods so no one can hear. When I finally heard Wilson say my name super loud, I realized she must've done it more than once already. Staring at her long nose and triple chin, I wondered how she'd look with no skin.

Saturday, May 5

Mom asked me what I want for my birthday. It'll be here soon. I almost told her, "A set of sharp knives," but I knew she'd probably ask me what I needed them for. Besides, last time we were at Grandpa's, I got a really sharp knife—not from him but from an old-woman neighbor of his. Her hearing's bad, and she's half blind, so she didn't notice me in her kitchen.

Sunday, May 13

Today's my birthday. It's been okay. Mom had a surprise party for me at Kids-O-Rama; a pizza and burger place with a bunch of things to climb on and through and a big game arcade. I got a new bike, lots of books and games from Grandpa, a BB-gun from the Bastard (the first thing he's given me that I like), a bunch of new clothes, and some other stuff. Lacie drew pictures for me and sewed me a handkerchief. It looks sort of crappy with uneven stitches running all over, but I know she did the best she could, and that means something. I didn't get the knives I wanted, but I never asked for them. The kids from my class were invited, and some of them showed up. They gave me games, new T-shirts, craft kits, and other things.

I'll have a real party alone later after everyone goes to bed.

I caught a squirrel in the snare yesterday, so I have that to look forward to. I haven't seen as many animals in the woods lately, so I think I'll start putting the snare in another area.

It's weird. I'm a year older now, but I don't feel any different than when I was 10 yesterday. Am I supposed to?

Friday May 25

I haven't gotten to play in the woods much. Mom and the Bastard have been making me babysit Lacie. They told me, "We want you to help out more since you're older, and we're raising your allowance from 10 dollars to 15." Maybe they thought I was going to argue, but I didn't. I just said, "Okay." Lacie was happy, bouncing all over the place, wanting me to pick her up.

Wednesday June 6

They haven't noticed Mr. T's gone. That's the Bastard's cat, a Persian with long black fur and green eyes. He's irritating. Well, he used to be. I didn't plan to kill him, but the stupid thing kept following me into the woods and meowing very loudly. I knew the animals that could be snared would hear him a long way off and be scared away. Besides, I never liked that cat, and he didn't like me either. The Bastard would talk crap to me, stuff like: "You're strange," and "You'll never make anything of yourself!" Then he'd be all coo-ey, petting and babying Mr. T. Stupid cat! I thought about smashing him. I thought about drowning him. I thought about skinning him alive. I stabbed him instead. That shut him up quicker and was something new. I'd never stabbed anything before. As his blood gushed out, Mr. T snarled and tried to scratch me but got weak super fast. My favorite part was watching his eyes as he died. Everything dies differently. Sometimes I take notes.

Sunday July 1

I went to another funeral today: Lacie's. Police said she drowned in the pond close to our house. They explained she must've slipped on some rocks, banged her head, and gone under the water. They said her body must've brushed against something sharp too. They came to our door three days ago to report finding her body. I was watching TV but ran out of my room when I heard Mom start screaming. The Bastard put his head in his hands, yelled, and punched the wall a lot.

Mom cried through the whole memorial service and time we were at the graveyard. She kept hugging me, saying, "It'll be okay. It'll be okay. It'll be okay." I hugged her back and said, "I know." She's my mother, after all.

The Bastard was a little nicer today, which was different for him, and thanked me for all the times I helped Lacie with her homework (she never had much), played with her, dished up food for her, and babysat her. I told him, "It's okay. I didn't mind." What I said was the truth. I didn't.

At home, Mom walked around touching Lacie's toys, touching her dirty laundry, putting Lacie's favorite shirt to her face and crying into it, touching the last cup she drank out of, and looking at pictures she colored. I helped the Bastard do the dishes and laundry and clean up some. It seemed like the thing to do, and Mom couldn't do it.

The Bastard offered to read me a story at bedtime and held me on his lap. He'd never done that before. The story was about a dog that always got in trouble somehow. It was meant for younger kids, I think, but it was fine. Mom tucked me in bed afterward, something she hasn't done in a while. She got in bed next to me and lay there a long time. She said, "I love you so much, Bobby, and I'm proud of you. Promise me you'll stay away from the pond or any other bodies of water. Don't wander off so much, and stay close to home, all right? I don't want to worry, and I don't want anything to happen to you." She was crying. "I couldn't bear it if anything happened to you."

I answered, "All right, Mom."

She whispered, "I wish Lacie was here. She was my baby, and I miss her so much."

"Me too, Mom." I meant it. "If you and Tim had another baby," I said, "I'd have a baby brother or sister." I hugged her before she left my room. Afterward, I looked out the window toward my special place in the woods. I miss it, but I'll go back soon.

Lacie could be annoying, but I do miss her. If she was alive, I could kill her again.

Gabriella Balcom was born in the lone-star state and lives there with her children, whom she adores (but who drive her stark raving batty at times). Her family includes three dogs that think they're human and are convinced they rule the roost (they do, at least part of the time), and two cats that could talk anyone's ears off (they're claiming they're the real rulers and proving it more than the dogs would care to admit).

She describes herself as a lifelong reader, loves writing, and sometimes thinks she was born with a book in her hands. Her background is in psychology and criminal justice, and she works full time in a mental-health field. She writes fantasy, horror/thriller, romance, sci-fi, children's stories, and about a variety of things including abuse, mental illness, and life—the good and the bad. She likes traveling, music, good shows, photography, history, interesting tales of all kinds, plants, and animals (especially dogs, cats, and wolves). She has visited or lived in various states but dreams of traveling to more areas and countries. After all, don't beautiful places exist all around the world? Don't interesting, wonderful people live everywhere? Gabriella believes the answer to both questions is a resounding, "Yes!"

She's a sucker for a good story and loves forests, mountains, and back roads which might lead who knows where. She has a weakness for lasagna, garlic bread, tacos, cheese, and chocolate, but not necessarily in that order.

TECHNICAL JARGON

Signature Sheena Robin Harris

It was just a drip—one tiny little drip from the kitchen faucet. But one droplet of water after another, I was slowly going insane. I Googled it. I even attempted to tackle the problem myself, but as usual, my wife Janie decided my handyman skills were lacking and left me the number to a plumber on the fridge. After two weeks of drip, drip, drip radiating through the house, I'd had enough anyhow. One phone call brought over Ted the Plumber.

When I opened the door to Mr. Ted that Monday morning, my initial impression was pity for the dude. Here he was, the epitome of what people envision when they hear the word *plumber*. Fairly large around the midsection and several inches taller than myself, pretty grimy in appearance and wearing one of those hideous work shirts with *Ted* embroidered on the pocket, this guy was no doubt a plumber. Even his scraggly sideburns proved it.

"Good morning, Mr. Cross. I'm Ted, the plumber." He extended one ape-like hand toward me for a shake and gave me a half grin in an obvious-but-failed attempt to be polite.

I shook his hand quickly and stepped aside. "Come on in. The leaky faucet's right through there in the kitchen."

As he made his way to the kitchen sink a few steps in front of me, I was even more amused. Poor Ted was scruffy-faced, slightly bald on top with too much hair everywhere else, and outfitted in old-man jeans that didn't seem to fit him right, other than around his legs. His spilled-over gut in the front and lacking rear end left him constantly pulling at the denim waistband to cover his crack, but the unsightly crevice still managed to remain visible just below his too-small shirt.

Ted took one look at my kitchen sink and began pulling out tools from his toolbox until he had a small pile on my kitchen counter. He grumbled a little when a screwdriver rolled onto the floor, and I looked away when he bent to get it in fear of being fully mooned.

"Oh, wait. I almost forgot. I need you to sign this before I get to work," Ted said as he pulled a stack of papers and a pen from the bottom of his massive toolbox. "It's my work agreement. Pay no mind to the length of it. Everybody's ready to sue you for somethin' these days, and I have to add a new section every day it seems. I gotta keep my ass covered, if ya know what I mean."

Well, Ted, you need to try harder, I thought but kept my comments and my smirk to myself as I thumbed through what looked to be a twenty-page service agreement. *Damn, all this just for a leaky faucet.* Against my beloved wife Janie's voice nagging in my mind, *"Don't sign what you don't read, John. That's just asking for trouble,"* I flipped to the last page, skipping all the nonsense technical jargon, and added my signature. It was only a leaky faucet, for crying out loud.

"Here ya go, man. I've got some work to do back here on the computer, so if you need anything, just come find me down the hall and to the left."

"Sure thing. This shouldn't take too long."

I watched Ted momentarily as he got to work taking the faucet apart but didn't waste any time returning to the office. Something about Ted the Plumber was a little off, but I couldn't quite read him enough to figure it out.

I took my seat in front of the computer and jumped right back into the content spreadsheet I had to get completed for work by the end of the day. I tried to shrug off the awkward feeling of having some strange, hairy man in my kitchen, which reminded me why

I always just did things for myself when Janie let me get by with it.

No more than a few minutes passed when the music started—loud, obnoxious Christmas music. The volume was so loud that the echoes of the dinging bells and chorused voices rattled my brain in spite of the walls between my office and the kitchen. Apparently, Ted the Plumber was in some kind of festive mood in the middle of July and brought along his own work tunes. It started with "Jingle Bells," next up was "Let It Snow," and then came "Silent Night." By the time "Rudolph the Red-Nosed Reindeer" came on, I was ready to throw Ted out on his holly-jolly ass.

Fearing I would walk in and find Saint Nick in place of Ted at the kitchen sink, I pushed myself up from my desk and followed the ear-raping holiday sounds to the kitchen. This was uncalled for. I needed a leak fixed. I didn't need to be caroled in my own home in the middle of summer by a weird guy with a holiday complex.

There Ted sat at my kitchen table, drinking my last beer from the fridge and eating a turkey sandwich—*my* turkey sandwich. His eyes were closed and his foot tapped as the music spouted off reindeer names. He mouthed every last one right along with the lyrics, spilling bits of *my* turkey sandwich out of the corners of his mouth as he did. He'd even taken the liberty to light the ten-dollar-each cranberry-colored taper candles in the centerpiece that my wife had just bought. *What in the hell?*

"Excuse me, Ted?"

Ted's eyes snapped open to acknowledge I was standing there, but yet he proceeded to grab the beer and take several gulps. He let out a Homer Simpson burp, and I could've sworn I saw his lips actually vibrate with the air off of it.

"Yes?" Ted stared at me but continued to eat my sandwich like he was not making himself at home right in my kitchen, drinking my beer, and eating my lunch to the sounds of the far-off season.

"Is there a reason you're not fixing my sink?" More than a little freaked out by this situation, I chose my words carefully. After all, Ted the Plumber did have a certain *ring* to it, like one of those old slasher movies. Who was to say Ted didn't have a machete in that toolbox of his? I gulped hard thinking of what my guts would look like spilled across our white tile floor while Ted merrily danced around a Christmas tree he'd fashioned out of the soda cans in the recycle bin.

"I'll get to that," Ted said with a laugh and a sweep of his hand. "It takes me a bit to get in the spirit to do it."

Apparently, it takes holiday music, my beer, my turkey sandwich, and candlelight to get you in the spirit, I wanted to say, but instead, I held my tongue and eyeballed him with my best questioning look.

"Um . . . I'm not sure I understand, Ted. Maybe there's a misunderstanding here. I just need you to fix that leaking faucet. That's it. In fact, when I called, you said it would be an easy fix."

"Oh, yeah. It definitely will be. Makes no difference, though. I've been doing this so long, it all looks the same to me. I gotta get motivated to do it. Otherwise, I'll be here all day. I know you don't want that."

The chuckle he interjected after this made my skin crawl with uneasiness.

"I'm actually on a really tight deadline at the moment and need the peace and quiet. Do you mind turning the music down?" I could deal with the loss of my lunch and my last beer, but that Christmas music had to go.

"Sorry, I'm afraid I can't do that, Mr.—Can I just call you Jonathan?" He had his service agreement laid out on the table and flipped to the back page where I'd scribbled my signature.

"Why can't you? This is my home." I felt the anger burning in my gut, but visions of bare-butt-crack Ted with a bloody machete danced in my head.

"It's listed right here under Stipulations in section C. You signed my contract. Didn't you read it?"

Of course, he knew I didn't read it. I barely looked at it. "You said pay no mind to the length like it was just a bunch of technical jargon."

"Well, mostly it is just, as you say, technical jargon. But you should never sign a contract without reading it, Jonathan. If you'd bothered reading it, you would know that the music is part of the service. There's no way around it. It says so right here." He flipped back several pages and pointed a finger at a small section of tiny print.

Thinking maybe comedy would fix this situation, I let out a laugh. "Listen, I've seen *Cable Guy*. If this is a joke, then well played. You really got me, Ted." I forced a second laugh and a genuine smile, trying my best to believe this must be some crazy farce.

Ted did not laugh. Ted the Plumber didn't even crack a smile. Instead, he gulped down the rest of my last beer and gave me an accusing, angry look. "You need to understand something. This is my business, and I take my business very seriously." Ted spun and shifted the empty beer bottle back and forth on the table so that it was making an ugly scratching noise against the wood. "My business is nothing to joke about."

Holy hell. This guy is a lunatic. Scared of what else I'd unwittingly agreed to, I took a step back toward the doorway. "W-well, if you could just keep it down, that would be great."

Not sure of what else to do, I retreated to my office, shut the door, and sat down. *I'm such an idiot.* Surely this man was going to do what I called him to do.

With "Chestnuts Roasting on an Open Fire" ringing through the house, I did what any sane homeowner would do in that situation. I slipped on my earbuds, cranked up some tunes of my own, and tried to get back to work and put Ted out of my mind.

I managed to complete two more lines on the spreadsheet before the real racket started. There were noises coming from my kitchen that were so loud, not even my noise-isolating earbuds could cancel them out. Hesitating and not sure if I even wanted to get a good listen, I pulled out one earbud slowly after hearing one too many crashes and hard hits.

Glass was breaking, there was a drill humming, and it seriously sounded like Ted was doing jumping jacks and banging the ceiling with his fists at the same time. All this to the beat of "The Little Drummer Boy," while Ted belted out the lyrics, which sounded something akin to a dying cow. Whatever was going on in my kitchen, it was way more than repairing a dripping faucet.

The anger that now bubbled up to the surface was strong enough to push those images of my own displayed innards on my kitchen floor out of my head. I swung open the office door, and a sharp *POP* rang out as the knob struck the wall. When all this was over, I'd probably need more than a plumber, but I didn't care. Ted was leaving—come hell or high water, come machete or whatever—I was done.

At the end of the hallway, there was a cloud of white dust so thick it took my breath. The refrigerator was partially blocking the entrance from the hall to the kitchen, but the narrow view I got by peeking through was more than enough. Off in the distance, Ted had used some kind of saw to cut a hole right through the wall by the back door. I could see the trees in the backyard through it. Pieces of my cabinets littered the floor. My kitchen table lay disassembled in a corner, and the chairs were stacked over the disheveled mess. Our kitchen was a total disaster.

All I could think about was which lawyer I could call first and whether or not I should call the cops. Janie would have my balls for supper when she saw the sight before me. She'd always hated the kitchen. She'd even begged me to have it remodeled the year before. But she'd also poured herself into making it look nice, and now it was utterly destroyed. *What have I done by allowing this lunatic in the house?*

Ted continued working with the saw, ass crack shining and now coated with a layer of dust, oblivious to the fact that I stood watching him through the narrow gap from the hall. Ted had even taken the liberty to punch out the one tiny kitchen window we had over the sink, and broken glass littered the white tile floor, which, thankfully, seemed to be still intact.

I squeezed my slim frame through the gap and headed straight for the boombox on the counter. With a single click, I interrupted the chaos of "Feliz Navidad," got Ted's attention, and the saw shut off.

"What do you think you're doing? I done told you the music is part of the service agreement. It says so right there on page—"

"Ted, you need to leave. I don't know what your intentions are here, but I'm calling the cops. It's obvious you either don't know what you're doing or you are completely out of your mind . . . maybe even both."

Ted said nothing. He stared at me with no emotion. The seconds ticked by. I actually heard them ticking from the wall clock that now lay beside me on the floor. It had once hung on the wall where there was now only a huge gaping hole. Every tick dragged by like slow thunder. Ted the Plumber showed no remorse for my destroyed kitchen. Ted the Plumber had nothing to say. Ted the Plumber was potentially planning to chop me into little pieces and stuff me into the garbage disposal before Janie got off work.

How many times had he done just that? There was no way I was his only customer.

Instead of speaking, Ted reached for his toolbox.

Oh God, he's after his machete.

The lid clicked open, and he reached inside, not once taking his eyes off me.

This is how I'm going to die. Chopped up by a psycho plumber in the middle of my own wrecked kitchen. I stepped backward toward the small gap between the fridge and the wall, hoping to escape, but instead tripping over a drawer full of spatulas and falling hard against the wall.

A smile stretched across that grimy face of Ted's so wide that I could see the gold caps on the teeth in his lower jaw.

"Please, Ted. I'm sorry. I have a wife who loves me. I'm a nice guy. I'm so sorry. Don't—"

With one swift movement, Ted pulled his hand out of the metal box. There was a flash of something shiny and silver, and I squeezed my eyes shut.

Please, God. Don't let me die like this. Please, God . . .

"Have a good night, Jonathan. This was fun."

Fully expecting a sharp *thwack* over the head, I didn't budge and didn't dare open my eyes. I heard heavy footfalls out the back door and a jovial chuckle heading away from the house. Then, the crank of an engine and crunching gravel as a vehicle left the drive.

Ted the Plumber was gone. Just like that. I opened my eyes and scrambled to my feet. There on the kitchen counter amid all the broken bits and clutter was a rectangular present, perfectly gift-wrapped in shiny silver paper. Beside it, the same hefty service contract I'd signed earlier was flipped open to the back page.

You've got to be fucking kidding me right now.

I crept toward the present on the kitchen counter like it contained a live bomb. After staring at it there for what seemed like an hour, I pulled the silver ribbon loose slowly and used a wooden spoon to pop off the lid, jumping back and shielding my face with my arms as I did. Much to my relief, the thing didn't explode, so I stepped closer with caution and peered over the edge. Inside, flat on the bottom, lay a single card all decked out in red glitter. I carefully picked it up, flipped it open, and read:

Dear John,

One of these days, you'll learn to listen to me. NEVER sign a contract you haven't read, even the technical jargon. That's just asking for trouble. I hope you enjoyed Ted the Plumber. He's a really good guy once you get to know him. Oh, by the way, that hefty contract you DIDN'T read? You might want to look at it. Do you remember last Christmas when I begged you to get the kitchen redone? Remember? It was all I asked for, but you said no? Well, guess what? As luck would have it, you've just signed the service agreement for Ted's company to complete the renovation, so thanks, honey! It started today, in case you were wondering. Oh, and there may or may not be a clause in there about holiday music. Just saying.

I know you love me,

Janie XOXO

Sheena Robin Harris resides in her hometown of Campbellsville, Kentucky. She is a respected freelance writer by day, with published pieces across the Internet, and a moonlighting fiction writer by night.

"Technical Jargon" is her first formally published piece of fiction, and her debut novel, *Lost in Reverie*, is scheduled for release in Winter 2018.

Sheena's married to her childhood sweetheart, with whom she shares three children, two dogs, a clowder of cats, an army of chickens, and one curious gecko named Floyd. Her mother taught her words are just as powerful as weapons, so Sheena spends her life proving her right. For updates on upcoming works, follow her on Facebook at www.facebook.com/SheenaRobinHarris.Author.

"**Sign here** and here, and right over here," Arthur Young said to the man in the striped jumpsuit. "After doing this, you'll be released and pardoned of your crimes. We will provide the house, tools, and specimens, of course. The only thing we want out of this is what was previously discussed, and whatever is left over is yours to keep as partial payment for your services; that and of course your freedom. After the fair, you can walk away a free man. So, Denton, what do you say?"

His pudgy fingers scratched the underside of his well-groomed hairy chin, then handed the jumpsuit man a pen. He sat back in the creaky plastic chair, his arms resting on his plump stomach.

"Only five days? And Warden Walker's okay with this?" Denton asked in a monster-of-Frankenstein's voice.

"That's right. He agreed to the contract. You will be pardoned and free to go wherever the wind takes you."

The man grunted and scratched his head covered by a snake tattoo which slithered around and disappeared at the base of his neck.

"Seriously, I don't understand why you're taking so much time to decide. I'm offering you freedom from this shithole in exchange for five days of work. You know what, Denton, there are other men I could ask, but I chose you because I know you're the best for the job. But I'll consider the runner-up if you don't sign the paper right now. I've got better things to do than hang out in a padded room with a freak that smells like sweat and cabbage. Now, what do you decide?"

He slid the paper in Denton's direction and began to push off his chair.

"Wait, I'll sign," Denton said and grabbed the piece of paper.

The pen stuck out of his right fist like a twig; his other hand held onto the paper with wide-spread bratwurst-sized fingers. He signed *DENTON* on the line in capital letters, the way a five-year-old would on a Crayola masterpiece.

"Great." The man clapped his hands in victory. "You won't be disappointed, boy. I'll take good care of you."

The following day, Arthur brought Denton, accompanied by a slew of guards, to his new house: a two-story shanty covered in grey mouldy shingles and stained-glass windows. The house was set back in the island's forest, far away from the road and tourist traps. The chubby man with the bulging stomach then unveiled the best part of the deal. Denton's eyes grew bigger than hubcaps as he examined the equipment awaiting his skillful hands in the basement. Butcher hooks dangled from the ceiling on his left, and on his right was a stainless-steel rolling cart loaded with the tools needed for the next five days. Another table sat at the centre of the room; it reflected the glow of a fluorescent strip light hanging above.

Arthur gave him half a day to settle in, then paraded in with three goons carrying the first load of work.

"Tell me, why am I doin' this?" Denton asked as he slid the ten-inch fillet knife underneath the tender skin.

"Yah don't ask questions, buddy. Yah just do your job," one of the goons answered. He had introduced himself as Antonio D. Masconi the previous day. "Antonio D. Masconi, at your service. I'll be yahr shadow for the week, just in case yah felt like skedaddling," he had said as they shook hands.

Denton's right eyebrow had risen high enough to touch his nonexistent hairline. This guy wasn't just Antonio. No. Too important for that shit. He was the whole freakin' shebang: Antonio D. Masconi.

Denton wondered what the *D* stood for. *I bet it's for Douchebag. Definitely, it had to be for Douchebag, no doubt about that.*

Around the five feet eleven inches mark, Antonio did not seem to have an ounce of fat on his body. Perfect specimen for a muscle exhibit in an anatomy class, with a neck the size of a giant sequoia's trunk. Every day, he wore a different cashmere turtleneck underneath his suit jacket and pants, worth more money than Denton had ever dreamed of, pleated in all the right places. Thin whiskers dangled thinly over the top of his raised upper lip like an overtly tanned version of Snidely Whiplash with an added hundred pounds of muscle.

The knife slid some more as Antonio walked closer to admire Denton's self-taught surgical ability. Denton stood straight with knees half bent as he wielded the knife like a samurai would a katana. Lou Reed's "Perfect Day" played on repeat.

For the last two days at dawn, Denton and his Italian shadow would thump down the stairs, then Denton's index finger would press the button marked by a green triangle, and the music would fill the room. Only then would he relax. His tensed shoulders hung loose, his pupils dilated, and his smile, oh, his smile, would grow to an unimaginable size, loosely showing random rotten teeth.

"You're blocking my light," Denton said without looking at Antonio D. Masconi.

The man stepped back and around the stainless-steel table. "Yahr really good at this. Arthur was right 'bout yah. Mad skills."

Denton looked at Antonio, rolled his eyes back until his dirt-brown irises disappeared, then looked back down at his bloody hands.

"Y'know, you could go for a walk. I usually work alone."

"No can do, buddy. Boss said to stay here, I stay here."

"Nice to see you've got a mind of your own."

"Wha'z that supposed to mean?"

"Make yourself useful and nudge them a bit. They can't die on me; the meat won't be as tender."

The goon walked towards the butcher hooks, a bone saw in hand, and, as Lou sang the chorus, he gently nudged the remaining two with great disdain. He slouched forward and stepped back after a violent tremor shook him from toenails to split ends as weak moans erupted from the moribund specimens.

"Can't yah shut the damn music off," he shrieked.

Sweat saturated through his cashmere shirt and suit jacket around the armpit areas. Droplets rolled from his temples; he dabbed them with a silk handkerchief from his back pocket, then shooed flies, swinging it around like a damsel would on the deck of a ship waving goodbyes to loved ones.

"*Shhhh.*"

"*Shhh* what, bud?"

"Listen to them; they're singing along."

"Whatchoo talkin' about? Yahr fuckin' crazy."

Denton looked and grinned as he threw another completed piece aside. He grabbed the skinned remains and brought them to the walk-in cooler. He delicately laid them on top of his last piece (these were his to do whatever with, Arthur had told him, so he took great care), then returned to grab the fourth and next to last specimen of the day, humming to the tune. The load fell and rattled the table. One of these times, the table would break underneath these heavy specimens.

Why did they have to be so big? he wondered. He needed to ask Arthur about this; Antonio D. Masconi wouldn't know—too dumb. He didn't expect him to know anything past wiping his ass clean.

This piece was the biggest yet; every inch of it had been meticulously shaved and washed before arriving at the basement.

A weakening sound, like a faraway drone, came from its ribcage. The scalpel pierced the top layer of skin right under the trachea and slid, like a knife through butter on a warm summer night, down to its navel. The specimen moaned some more as blood flooded the incision line.

"*Shhhh,*" he said repeatedly, tapping its side. "It'll all be over soon."

He grinned and licked the saliva accumulating at the corners of his lips.

"Whatcha gonna do with all tha' meat?" Antonio asked on his last day with Denton.

He didn't really care what Denton did with the lot, but he felt like he should converse more now that the five days were coming to an end. He would soon go back to his wife, kids, and dogs in his 400k bungalow in the suburbs of Morton and pretend that the conference he attended on the mainland was a hit. If Joyce knew what he had spent the last five days doing, she would divorce him—or even worse, turn him in. He'd see the kids (supervision provided by a loveless fifty-something broad in white cotton scrubs and beige tights hugging her cellulite-covered legs) one weekend every month at St. Peter's penitentiary.

"Sausages, if you must know. Sausages, hamburger meat, different cuts of prime ribs, and steaks."

"Nice, very nice," he answered, not really paying attention to the words spoken by Denton. "I got the order from Arthur to take yah to the fair when yahr done today. He wanted yah to see the success we have 'cause of yah. When yahr done, I'll take yah."

"I don't do good in crowds."

"Arthur insisted yah be there." He paused. "Yah have no choice."

The fairground smelled of popcorn, frying oil, cow shit, and diesel. It was the island's last attempt at attracting tourists from the mainland and erasing their past of cholera plague, disappearances, and death. It was known throughout mainland that if you wanted someone gone, you took them on a trip to the island.

Antonio pushed Denton past guards in matching blue uniforms and nodded in an obligatory greeting to the little people. They were always excited to get recognized by a high-ranking guard, at least that's what Antonio thought. They pushed through a small crowd of islanders impatiently waiting their turn for a forty-second Ferris wheel ride, surely a highlight of their summer.

Clouds covered the late afternoon sky to let the wild flickering lights of the rides and game booths glow through. Pop music smothered awkward conversations between family members who hadn't seen each other since the last summer fair; they shouted over the music, laughed, embraced, and teased the kids.

Denton's head throbbed, spun around like the rides; he hated crowds, couldn't stand them. At six feet seven inches, he stood taller than these happy families and disgruntled teenagers looking for a thrill. A toddler ran and bumped into his left leg. The kid fell on his bum and stared at the towering man like he was something out of Frankenstein's lab, then ran off crying to his mother.

Denton wanted to crawl back to the dampness of his basement with the warm glow of the fluorescent lights dangling close to his forehead. At this moment, he even missed the stone walls of St. Peter's, where he'd spent the past fifteen years of his life.

"What now?" he asked Antonio as they walked towards the back of the fairground.

"We're almost there," Antonio answered and pointed to a crowd gathered around long tables.

A banner hung above the hundred-some people. It read: ANNUAL FOOD FAIR.

"You're taking me to a food fair?"

But before Antonio could answer, Arthur welcomed Denton with open arms.

"Denton, m'boy, look at our success," he said excitedly. "This is all thanks to you, kid. I really appreciate everything you've done these past five days."

"What are they looking at?" Denton asked, ignoring the praise.

"They're all waiting to taste our tacos."

"Tacos?"

"Yes, boy. You want one? Antonio, won't you go and fetch our guest a taco?"

"Sure, boss." Antonio pushed through the crowd and came back a minute later with a small plate in hand. "All dressed for our gues', hope that's 'k."

He shoved the plate in Denton's hands.

Denton looked down at it. The V-shaped hardshell was slightly burned at the top and filled with the usual toppings: tomato, meat, shredded cheese, and salsa. He looked closer at the shell; his eyes widened as he stared at the crowd in awe.

"I like you, kid. Been waiting to ask if you'd do me the honour of becoming one of my guards. I don't mean a little shit running around in a blue uniform, I mean at the top with your bud, Antonio. You guys seem to get along quite well."

"Sir," Denton began. "Do they know that—"

"Of course, you would have to come and live at the mansion with me until we can find you a place suited for your position, something much better than that rathole house."

"Do they know?"

"You could have any girls you want. We have a gym and a pool, anything you want. Only the best for my top officers."

"Do they know?"

"Do they know what, son?"

"That they're eating human flesh?"

"Well, of course not! How ridiculous. That would bring them

to your level of insanity, and there's only one like you, am I right?" He chuckled, holding his large stomach hanging over his tight uniform pants. "So, what do you say? Are you in?"

"Sure," he said vacantly shaking Arthur's hand before taking a bite out of the taco.

At the back of his mind, he heard Lou Reed belting out how perfect this day was, because it truly was. The flavours ignited his taste buds: sweet, salty, spicy—every component was there to make the best tasting taco, one worthy of a blue ribbon at a food fair.

And that is just what happened when the four judges sank their teeth in the crunchy yet tender homemade shells.

Gena White was born and spent most of her childhood in Trois-Rivières, Québec. She moved with her parents to Montréal at eleven, where she roamed the city streets and was busy being up to no good. Now, she lives a quieter lifestyle in New Brunswick, Canada with her husband, sons, cats, and dog. When she is not sitting at her computer working on her upcoming novel or short stories, you will find her in the garden or having serious conversations with her many chickens and ducks.

Gena has been leisurely writing on and off since high school but has been serious about the art for the last five years. "The Fair" will be her first published short story. "Collapsed Spyglasses" will follow shortly in the *Flashpoint Anthology* published by Clarendon House Publications. She is presently working on finishing her psychological horror trilogy.

You can find her on Facebook at facebook.com/genawhiteauthor.

AUNTIE LEELA

Signature *Samantha Hamilton*

"I'm so happy," Leela sniffled.

I believed her. Not the tears, which I thought were over the top and, frankly, inartistic, considering she was supposed to be an actress. But I had no doubt that she was happy to be firmly and legally married to my great-uncle Charles. I fished in my clutch to offer her a tissue, but she forestalled me by whipping out a tiny scrap of linen and lace and dabbing it with exquisite care under her heavily made-up eyes.

"It's just so amazing that Charles and I found each other, out of everyone in this big, wide world," she went on, her periwinkle eyes huge with earnestness.

I didn't buy this, either. I should explain that my uncle, Charles White, was the wealthiest man in Wheeler County, Virginia. My cousin Ginny, who moved up north to New York to work on what she always just calls "the Street" (her daddy at first thought she said she was working on "the streets" and was halfway to breaking her jaw when her brother Sam popped up and yelled, "Wall Street, Daddy! *Wall* Street!") – anyway, Ginny once worked out that our great-uncle Charles was worth at least thirty-five million in visible assets.

Leela was a gold-digger; Uncle Charles was therefore her natural prey. It was no more surprising that they had found each other than that a tigress finds a gazelle. But I smiled and nodded and said, "Yes, how lucky for you both," because that is what a well-bred wedding guest says. Gotta say, weddings are not one of my favorite spectator sports.

To go back a couple hours, my mama had made me come early. Now, rich people's weddings are catered—Mama knows that—but she thought it would look well if I went and offered to help, "like family oughtta do." Uncle Charles was our rich uncle, and even if he was getting a brand-new wife, Mama figured there might still be a remembrance in his will. I thought it was highly improbable, but Mama stood firm; so rather than wasting time at home arguing with her, I drove the half hour through rich October foliage and wandered into the big house an hour early. Men and women in tidy beige uniforms were still dragging around folding chairs and squabbling over flower arrangements.

Just as I was wondering whether I could talk one of the barmen setting up into giving me a drink, Uncle Charles came sidling out of the big book-lined room he called his study.

"Ha!" he said on spotting me. "You're too early. No eats yet. And if you're looking for a drink, you're still too early."

I produced my best familial smile. "I just came along to see if I could be any help, Uncle Charles."

"Huh. Your mama send you?"

No point in lying. "Yes, sir."

"Now, which one are you?"

"I'm Courtney Wells."

"Lonnie's girl? Your daddy's a mechanic?"

"An engineer, Uncle Charles."

He was taken aback. "On the Southern?"

All I could do not to bust a rib, but I answered gravely, "No, sir. He builds dams and bridges and such."

"Huh. Dams. Damn. Well, if you really want to be helpful, you can go find Henry and tell him to bring us in some 'dam' drinks. I fancy a 'dam' julep, and the lawyer feller wants coffee. I got to go sign some more papers. There's a mess of papers to be signed at these wedding things."

Well, I reflected as Uncle Charles tottered back to his study, he's a man who ought to know. This would make his fourth wedding in eighty years. First was Daisy, who divorced him for mental cruelty somewhere back in the 1960s; then Claire, who ran off with her hairdresser in 1984, shocking some of the more conservative of the family with their first intimation that all hairdressers were not necessarily gay. The only Mrs. White I remembered was Auntie Gwen, a sweet and very sociable lady who loved gathering the entire extended family around her for holidays and summer vacations.

How she put up with a couple dozen assorted cousins and second cousins tumbling all over the huge house for days or even weeks on end I'll never know, but she seemed to always have time and patience for everyone. I was truly sorry when she died the year I went off to college. Since then, Uncle Charles had been wont to refer to himself, rather disconcertingly, as a "swinging single," usually accompanied by his harsh, barking laugh.

Any rate, I had no problem finding my way back to the kitchens, the lawful domain of Henry Jackson and his wife, Dolly, butler and cook respectively. They had been the mainstays of Uncle Charles' domestic staff since before I was born. More beige minions were in possession, clattering away in efficient and humorless assembly lines, voices occasionally raised as someone came swinging through with a huge aluminum tray. Henry was nowhere in sight, but I finally tracked Dolly to the butler's pantry, where she perched on a high stool, nursing a Diet Coke with a panicky look in her eye.

"Miss Courtney! You came to see ol' Dolly!"

She wore a cheerful flowered apron over an even more cheerfully flowered polyester dress, and in her vast hug, I felt like I was being upholstered. I passed along Uncle Charles' order and, given something to do, she brightened up right away. She bustled importantly to brew the coffee and muddle the mint, and I got a running commentary on "ol' men who don't even know they're ol' men, and what's he want getting married to someone young enough to be his granddaughter, anyway?" I thought she was exaggerating, but when I pulled up Leela's Facebook page, I saw she was admitting to twenty-six and claiming to be an actress. Allowing for the traditional showbiz age cheat, that still made her a year or so younger than I was.

And baby-doll pretty—round forehead and cheeks, pouty lips, huge round eyes, and the kind of figure Aldous Huxley described as pneumatic. There was also a lot more in the way of blonde hair and eyelashes than the average human is born with, the whole effect suggesting a Pamela Anderson knock-off built from a kit.

I was reflecting on how little the family was liable to take to this, when the sound of a pack of rabid Rottweilers echoed from the lofty hall. I raced out, followed by Dolly exclaiming, "Oh, that Mister!"

Mister proved to be an elderly and odiferous Bulldog, braced rigid at the bottom of the big staircase, eyes bulging, baying with everything he had. Halfway up the staircase was the owner of the Facebook page, surrounded by yards and yards of lace and satin so white it hurt the eye. Leela had her copious skirts hoicked up over her knees and was laying on the Tupelo honey with a trowel.

"Shoo! Shoo, now! Nice doggie! You let ol' Leela by!" Then she fixed Dolly with an icy eye and demanded, "You get that damn thing outta here *now*!"

At this moment, Henry came hustling to the rescue from the dining room, where he'd been overseeing preparations. He scooped up the still-baying Bulldog and bore him off toward the back of the house.

"That poor man is wore to a frazzle," muttered his helpmeet, with some justice. Henry's lanky dignity was as frazzled as I'd ever seen it.

"Now, you know better than that, Miss Leela," Dolly called up the stairs. "You know it's bad luck, you coming down like that in your dress and all! Now, you git on back before Mr. Charles sees you!"

"Well, then, send up some more champagne," retorted Leela. "My bridesmaids are getting thirsty."

Now, I don't know if this information will ever come in useful for you, but it is very difficult to make an effective exit when you have to about face and march up a flight of steps while handling three yards of white satin train. Leela accomplished the maneuver in a series of vicious jerks and got up the stairs without either tearing her gown or tripping and breaking her pretty neck, so I guess the performance may be accounted a success.

"Thirstiest bunch of girls I ever came across," grumbled Dolly as we went back toward the kitchen. "This'll make a half-a-dozen bottles even. Don't see how a one of 'em's gonna be standing up with her."

Henry came pelting back across the hall to the dining room without even seeing us.

"Well, now—" said Dolly in frustration.

"I'll take the tray in for the gentlemen," I offered. "Just fix it up for me, Dolly."

Five minutes later, I was wondering how people in the service industry ever manage to open doors while balancing a tray heavy enough to need two hands. It wasn't graceful, but I figured a workaround and wrestled the silver coffee service and the drink fixings into the study. Uncle Charles and a rubicund gent in his late fifties or so were sitting at the big desk, surrounded by a light drift of papers. Uncle Charles looked up in mild astonishment.

"Well, you really did mean to help," he said.

"Dolly and Henry are a little busy."

I found a place to plant the tray and did the honors.

"This here's my lawyer, Andy Coggins. Andy, this here's the niece I was telling you about. Courtney . . . Wells, isn't it? Lonnie's girl. Her daddy's an engineer. You take after him, missy?"

I loathe being called missy, so I replied briefly, "I'm an architect."

"Well, isn't that fine," said the round red lawyer affably. "And are you married yet, Miss Courtney?"

"No, I'm not."

They swapped one of those old-boy looks, and Uncle Charles said, "Well, now, that's unusual. Why is that, honey?"

Any Southern-raised woman knows the answer to that one. "Why, because you were already spoken for, Uncle Charles," I beamed.

It was a good exit line, so I used it that way.

The guests weren't due for another half hour, so I meandered back to the kitchen and found Dolly again in the pantry, with Mister the bulldog whuffling asthmatically on a bed stuffed into the most remote corner. It's not for nothing even homely dogs have those big brown eyes. I snuck Mister a piece of beef tip waiting to be dished up. He looked at me, sniffed the meat, and then pointedly turned his head away.

"He's that fussy," said Dolly proudly. "Won't take a single bite unless me or Henry gives it—or Mr. Charles, of course."

She plucked the scrap from my hand and reached it down. Mister snapped, and it was down his gullet without so much as a chew.

"And oh, Miss Courtney! I got that champagne all ready to go, but Mister's having one of his spells, and I don't like to leave him alone with"—Dolly peered out at the beige-clad horde still assembling dishes and bickering—"*those* folks." She looked at me wistfully. "I don't suppose you could possibly . . .?"

I was about to reply that no, I couldn't possibly. I had been called Missy, I had been snubbed by a dog, but I drew the line at waiting hand and foot on a gaggle of already half-drunk young women in cheap pastel taffeta. Then two things occurred to me: the first was that Dolly and Henry must be stressed enough already. They had been with Uncle Charles for almost four decades and were about to get a new boss. A new woman in charge of the household can make a servant's life hell; it didn't need much imagination to see that. And the Jacksons, while younger than Uncle Charles, were at least well into their sixties; after most of a lifetime as domestics, new work would be hard to come by. It was beholden on me as "family" to help them out. The second thing that occurred to me was that if I showed up with the champagne and an extra glass, there wasn't much the bridesmaids could do to stop me having some, and I was more than ready for it.

So I shoved an extra bottle and glass on the tray and staggered upstairs. (Another couture tip for those interested: if you do show up early to help, wear flats and stick your three-inch heels in the mudroom to slip on once the guests arrive.) Oak Bridge is an antebellum mansion—not the biggest or oldest in the state of Virginia, but architecturally impressive nonetheless. There are three stories, eleven bedrooms, six reception rooms, three porches, and two kitchens, plus cellars and attics.

I had to get up to the third floor, where the female contingent of the bridal party was established in one of two huge rooms that had originally been nurseries. Last decorated sometime in the 1970s, the boys' room had a guns-and-dogs theme, while the girls' was done in tasteful florals. The bride herself was ensconced in a suite on the second floor, the best accommodations the house offered besides the master bedroom.

I stopped on the landing before the third floor to take a breather. I'm in decent shape, but that tray was heavy, and I didn't want to show up amongst the bridesmaids puffing like the Little Engine That Could Use a Drink. And as I stood there, hauling in air like they were about to put a tax on it, the clackety bird noise of half-a-dozen women all talking at once began to come into focus, and I couldn't much help overhearing the following high and nasal voice:

"Yes'm, that's what she told him—not a glimpse of the goods do you get until that paper is signed. Signed and witnessed!"

"But why?" asked a lower, slower voice. "I mean, if she's his wife, she'd get everything anyway, wouldn't she?"

"Leela's taking no chances! There's a raft of poor relations and servants, and I don't know what all else, and she said right out, she said, 'Not a finger do you lay south of the border'—if you know what I mean—'until you have it on paper that I get all the money.' And he just rolled over like a little lamb and said, 'Yes, honey, yes I will.' And he's down there signing those papers right now so he can have his wedding night, the dirty ol' pervert!"

"Well, good for Leela, then," said Ms. Low-and-Slow, and I found I had enough adrenaline running to make it up the rest of the stairs and then some.

I took a moment to tuck my lips back into my cheeks and walked in with a bright, "Well, ladies, I was told we were running low on supplies up here!"

They flocked round like seagulls to pizza crust, with one—by her voice, the legally knowledgeable one of the previous conversation—remarking, "You ain't the same maid as last time."

"I ain't a maid a-tall," I told her cheerfully as I uncorked the first bottle. "I'm just a relation of Uncle Charles, the one who's marrying Leela, don't you know."

At which a knowing smirk circulated amongst the bridesmaids as they contemplated how bitterly disappointed I'd be to know all Charles' money was safely left away from me, and they were really quite gracious as I poured and drained the glass of wine I'd promised myself. Then I got the hell out of there, promptly demoted myself to guest, and went down to where my assorted kin were beginning to arrive.

The wedding itself took place in the ballroom and was as tedious as these things normally are. The bride's colors were lavender, pink, and gold, and with cap sleeves and bouffant skirts, her attendants looked just as hideous as you'd expect—they'd never get another day's wear out of those dresses.

And excuse me rambling, but I have never for the life of me understood why people spend so much money on a function that will leave so little impression on anyone's mind. The bride and groom are normally too exhausted, and the guests too intent on downing free food and booze, to give a rat's left gonad what the color scheme was or how many yards were in the bride's train. I'm convinced this is why people take so many pictures at weddings: so the family can all gather round and look at them later and pretend they remember.

Anyway, Charles and Leela being duly pronounced man and wife, the relations and friends set about the eating and drinking part. There were hors d'oeuvres and beef tips and lobster and strawberries dipped in chocolate (which are somehow never as good as you think they're going to be) and of course a cake, every inch covered in lavender roses. The bourbon came in numbered bottles, and the champagne came from France. There was probably also lemonade and sweet tea, but I wouldn't know.

Once the initial threat of starvation had been at least temporarily staved off, the guests began to mingle. Leela made her little blushing bride speech to me during this time; I gathered that she vaguely remembered seeing me with Dolly and concluded that I was much more important in the family structure than I actually am. She was flanked by two of the less tipsy of her attendants, who simpered smugly the entire time. I was glad when Andy the Lawyer came up to introduce his pleasant-looking wife and I could escape to the bar.

Old Aunt Edie, a near contemporary of Charles, tacked up to me and reached up to bellow in my ear. "What that ol' man is thinking, I do *not* know! If poor Gwennie was alive today to see this, she'd be rolling over in her grave!"

I was still working that one out when my mama sailed up with my cousin Travis in tow and twittered, "Well, how long is it since you've seen each other! I know you'll want to catch up, with so much in common!"

"Well, hey, Travis, what're you up to these days?" I asked heartily.

"I, uh . . . I work at a place installing HVAC systems."

"Well, that sounds interesting."

"Uh . . . No, it's not really."

I couldn't argue. "So . . . um . . . Whatcha been reading?"

"I don't really read. Not books and such."

Pause.

"Soooo . . . what are you listening to? Who's your favorite band right now?"

"Don't care for music much."

Another pause, longer this time. Frankly, I didn't see we had anything at all in common aside from the fact that we were both carbon-based lifeforms. Then I remembered. He was a year or so younger than me, but we'd romped in these hallowed halls in the halcyon days of Great Auntie Gwen.

"Been a long time since we've been here at Oak Bridge, isn't it?"

Here I got a ripple of something resembling enthusiasm. "Hell, yeah, it has. Since Auntie Gwen. The ol' man's too cheap to have us here since then. I remember when we was kids, you was always the best at hide-n-seek. How'd you always manage to win, anyhow?"

"I attribute it principally to my cloak of invisibility," I said solemnly, and earned a look of pure contempt.

"Well, that's just stupid. Them Harry Potter movies wasn't even made back then."

Of course . . . obviously, I couldn't have owned an imaginary object before Ms. Rowling invented it. I'm not sure which of us was more relieved when the music—a portly five-piece band sedately remembering the best of the sixties and seventies—kicked into life.

Well, I danced with most of the cousins of my generation, a geriatric aunt or two, and a succession of rather sticky and manic toddlers, sugar-fuelled on cake and those little flower-shaped buttermints you only seem to get at weddings. I had just sat down to refresh myself with a well-earned glass when a gnarled hand landed on my thigh a good three inches above the familial zone.

Uncle Charles cackled, "Havin' fun, Miss Courtney?"

"I am. Thank you for having me, Uncle Charles."

His rheumy blue eyes swam up to engage my brown ones. "They all think I'm plumb crazy, marryin' that lil' bit of a gal, don't they?"

Someday I will design an algorithm for the number of drinks that have to go down an educated Southerner's throat before he starts talking pure Dogpatch, but that day I just smiled.

"Uncle Charles, if you're happy, I don't see it matters a damn what anybody else thinks."

He smacked my thigh hard enough to hurt, even semi-numbed by alcohol as I was.

"Thass my girl! Thass what I said! You git on up and dance with me, girl!"

And here, gentle reader, I will draw a merciful curtain across the spectacle of an octogenarian trying to meet the needs of "Single Ladies" played at about three-quarter speed. He had put a ring on it.

The next time I was up at the big house was New Year's Eve. I had spent Christmas week at my mama's, and there was no real reason not to stick around till the big party. Back in Auntie Gwen's day, the guest list had numbered well over a hundred, so I wasn't all that surprised to get an invitation now that there was again a chatelaine at Oak Bridge. Mama still thought it meant that I had a look-in on the will; I could have told her different, but what was the point?

I shook out my dress until the sequins lay right and went along to the big house early enough to "help."

The beige brigade were doing their thing, so I went back to the kitchens and got clinched by Dolly, which cracked a couple sequins. Henry was there, dignified as always, and when I asked about Mister the Bulldog, they told me that he was doing well, thank you. Mister wasn't allowed to sleep in Mr. Charles' room on account of his—the dog's—snoring, but he had a little bed right outside the door, and he was quite happy there. Well, except when Mrs. Charles came along. Would I believe it, he'd never got used to his new mistress and barked like a mad thing every time he saw her. Oddly enough, I believed it. It sounded like Mrs. Charles still kept a separate bedroom, which was more information than I needed.

I turned down an offer of tea and cookies and volunteered to help Henry pack up some breakables that had been deemed safer out of the way of the festivities.

As we were out in the hall, making a last sweep for any Lalique or Boehm that had gotten overlooked, Uncle Charles came backing carefully out of his study. I saw right off that he looked frailer and more tottery than I'd seen him just a few months before.

Henry was at his side in a moment, urging respectfully, "Now, Mr. Charles, you shouldn't be down here. You should be upstairs, getting some rest. Your guests gonna arrive soon."

"I'm fine, I'm fine, don't fuss at me, Henry, don't fuss!" Uncle Charles waved a blue-veined hand at him as if the "fuss" was a mosquito. Then he caught sight of me. "Well, it's lil' Miss Courtney, come to help! You can help me to a lil' libation, darlin'. Come along with ol' Uncle Charles."

Henry and I exchanged a quick look. Bloodshot eyes and all, Uncle Charles was still the boss, so I accompanied him back into the study. On the threshold, he almost lost his balance, and I shot out a hand to catch his bony elbow.

"It's nothin', it's nothin'," he groused, confirming my worst fears. He was at the stage of repeating himself, and it wasn't yet seven o'clock. "I jus' got a lil' visit from my ol' friend Arthur, is all."

"Arthur?" I repeated blankly, getting him safely seated.

"Arthur-itis!" he cackled. "Don't you worry none. My Leela done give me a couple aspirins, I'll be fine soon enough. You jus' pour us out a little from that decanter in the middle. Now, that there's good sippin' whiskey. I don't usually offer it to ladies, but you got a career and all that, don't you?"

Which logic evidently made sense to him. I endured about fifteen minutes of absolutely painful small talk—mostly a monologue on his side about how I oughtta be gettin' me married, and there would be plenty of nice boys at the party tonight—before he announced abruptly, "Well, I need a lil' rest. You go 'long, now. Tell 'em I'll be right there."

There was a fleece blanket with a hunting scene printed on it draped over the sofa. I tucked it around the old man and wandered out, promising myself that no matter what Mama said, my days of getting somewhere early to help were over.

By now, folks were beginning to arrive. I remembered that I'd left my coat and clutch in the kitchen and went back to fetch them out. Dolly was a lot more relaxed than she'd been at the wedding; maybe she'd had a glass of New Year's champagne.

"Oh no, honey, I took your things upstairs. Mr. Charles said you'd be staying, so you're up in the girls' room."

Well, that was odd. Staying with my mama, I wasn't more than half an hour away. Still, it was nice to think I wouldn't even have to drive that far.

"I took up a toothbrush and a washcloth and a nightie. You all set whenever you get sleepy, Miss Courtney. Now you just go on out there and shake what your mama gave you, okay, honey?" She smacked my arm genially.

Maybe two glasses.

I greeted my relatives with mixed feelings. Personally, I loathe holidays where drinking is the main event, and most of my kin were serious contenders at that sport. Still, for most of my childhood, I'd spent New Year's here at Oak Bridge; at first watching with amused contempt as the grownups got more and more childish; then, years later, sneaking a bottle or two for ourselves into the basement rumpus room to watch Dick Clark; and finally taking our places in the chain of hands all round the house, singing "Auld Lang Syne." It was sobering, in every sense, to watch the tears creep down the faces of even the meanest, toughest aunts and crustiest old uncles as they remembered those who were no longer there to join the circle. It did things to my tear ducts just remembering it.

About nine o'clock, our hostess made her entrance down the great wide staircase, and I have to admit, it was an entrance in the fullest sense of the word. She must have had to go past Mister, because I recall that hysterical baying from somewhere in the upper regions as she swept down the stairs. But she was a picture—I'm not specifying what kind of picture—in a dress cut so low there was no point in calling it a bodice at all, with a sort of off-the-shoulder negligee of yards and yards of black eyelash lace that draped so softly, you knew it was real silk.

Her husband met her at the bottom of the stairs, looking rather the worse for wear; but if there is an advantage to calling yourself a gentleman, it's that you do the proper thing in the proper season. He escorted his wife around while she greeted her guests, and if he wobbled from time to time, hardly anyone noticed. Folks were mostly focused on how near Mrs. Charles was to popping right out of her gown. But I have to say she did her duty and circulated like a trouper—there were four rooms to go through, and near as I could tell from my own shifting vantage point, Auntie Leela covered her bases.

From there, the party progressed according to program: the volume of sound went up as the alcohol went down, I distinctly caught two elderly aunts crying well before eleven o'clock, and my mama told several embarrassing stories. As the grandfather clock in the hall began to toll midnight, the sonorous sounds of some hundred inebriates singing an old Scottish dirge to the memory of absent friends quelled the shriek and chatter of cocktail talk, and each guest turned to the person next on their right for the midnight kiss.

I'd wound up next to Cousin Travis, and we hastily agreed to make do with a half-hearted, one-armed hug. Andy the Lawyer and his pleasant wife clasped so long and so hard I was somehow certain that a child had been lost. I saw neither Uncle Charles nor Auntie Leela, but that didn't surprise me much. Leela had a lot of ground to cover as hostess; Uncle Charles had been unsteady on his pins a couple hours since and was probably cozily tucked in bed.

Which sounded like a pretty good idea to me not long afterwards. I abandoned the conclave of middle-aged uncles and teenaged cousins commencing a dance party on the glassed-in porch and launched myself up two flights of stairs. On the second floor, I happened to look down the hall and saw Mister ensconced in his state-of-the-art orthopedic doggie bed. He looked up when he heard my step and whuffed softly.

"Good night, Mister," I said equally softly and hit the home-stretch.

I forced myself out of bed about nine the next morning. My two bunkmates—I recognized them as a couple of Leela's bridesmaids—were still asleep and snoring heartily. Having not planned to spend the night, I had no change of clothes and had to shimmy back into my sequins.

At the bottom of the stairs, I saw a dozen or so of my relatives congregated outside the dining room, some already holding a dose of the hair of the dog they had so assiduously wooed the night before. They were grumbling quietly amongst themselves, which was appropriate enough in the house of the hungover, but I couldn't make out why they didn't get them on into the dining room and dig in. Then I saw a uniformed policeman cross the hall from the study to the front door. Something was very wrong.

Avoiding the morning eye-opener crowd, I dodged around the other side of the stairs and trotted back to the kitchens. There I found Dolly sobbing over a vast vat of grits and Henry dithering over a huge Smithfield ham.

Dolly looked up at me and groaned, "Oh, Miss Courtney, Mr. Charles is dead! Mr. Charles is dead, and the police are all over our house!"

Well, if there's one thing a Southern upbringing teaches you to do in an emergency, it's cook. I whomped together something that would pass for gravy and popped the biscuits Dolly had forgotten about into the oven. Then I set to work scrambling eggs and sicced Henry on the toast. Dolly pulled herself together and dished the grits and fruit compote, to the tune of a long, circular eulogy to my late great-uncle. In about twenty minutes, the dining room was open for business, and I could look for some answers.

I didn't get many until a Detective Jeffrey Todd invited me into the study for an "interview." His soft-spoken voice didn't match his a square-jawed bulk, built along the lines of those little plastic robots that used to knock each other silly in that little plastic boxing ring. Even then, he didn't tell me much beyond the facts that Henry had found Uncle Charles dead when he brought in his coffee a couple hours back; that Uncle Charles had departed this life well before midnight last night; and that the cause of death was yet to be determined. What he did do, though, was ask a lot of questions that let me work out what the police were thinking.

I wasn't much help with answers. I couldn't give any coherent timetable for a four-hour party when I'd been moving around and drinking steadily, if not immoderately. I didn't know if Uncle Charles had any enemies, and I had no idea what was in his will, besides what I'd overheard about Leela's stipulation. But by then I knew Detective Todd was thinking homicide.

I told him about Uncle Charles' arthritis and agreed that a man of his generation might well describe any kind of painkiller as "an aspirin," so there was no knowing what he had really taken. Then Detective Todd began asking about, of all things, Mister the Bulldog. Yes, I'd seen the dog bark at Mrs. White on more than one occasion. Yes, the dog was outside his master's door when I went upstairs a little after midnight. We'd exchanged pleasantries. The dog was alert? Oh, yes . . .

And by then, I knew the detective wanted to cast Leela for the role of First Murderer.

The detective stared past me as he turned off the recorder. I guessed he didn't like this one bit. There might be upwards of a hundred possible suspects—some of them influential local officials—and apparently, the main person of interest was off the table.

"Well!" he said so suddenly I jumped. "We're asking everyone to sit tight here while we finish our investigation. Now, Mr. White's lawyer will be here in a little bit. He wants to read the will to the family, so you just get some coffee or something, okay?"

The remains in the dining room included a spoonful of congealed grits, a couple streaks of dried egg, a few scraps of ham fat, and half a piece of soggy toast. I had coffee.

Andy the Lawyer had become Andrew C. Coggins, Attorney-at-Law. Presiding over piles of papers on Uncle Charles' desk, he glanced up over his glasses only briefly as the family filed in. Most of us were pretty subdued—by hangovers if not overmastering grief—but Leela looked absolutely radiant. Henry and Dolly sat hand-in-hand on a sofa toward the back, Dolly still sniffling. I also noticed Detective Todd, discreetly tucked away in a window seat way back behind the desk, a notebook on his thigh.

The whispered conversations died when Mr. Coggins cleared his throat.

"I thought it best to acquaint the family at the earliest possible opportunity with the provisions of Mr. Charles White's will, and indeed, this is what my client personally requested when he signed the will and its associated documents some months ago . . ."

Mr. Coggins went on like that for about fifteen minutes, and there wasn't a sound in the room, mostly because nobody followed a single word he was saying. I'll tune you back in at the point we began to sit up and take notice.

"At the request of his then bride-to-be, Leela Marie Aikens, Mr. White dictated and signed a document which I will now read in full." He adjusted his glasses. "To my bride, Leela, at her specific request, I hereby state and record that on my death, said Leela White is entitled, solely and absolutely, to all the money of which I die possessed."

The smile on Leela's face was positively indecent. I mean, really, like that post-coital moment when everything is all blissful and dreamy. I had to look away. Unfortunately, what my eyes lighted on was my cousin, Travis, industriously picking his nose. I focused back on Lawyer Andy.

"Also dated, signed, and witnessed on the same day is an addendum: 'I mean this bequest to be taken literally and at face value. My wife, Leela White, is entitled only to the cash money in my possession at the time of my death.'"

No one can tell me lawyers aren't frustrated actors. Mr. Coggins's timing was perfect. He took off his glasses, arranged them on the desk, and began, "Now, my client was a very unusual man. Some might even say a little eccentric . . ."

Leela began to look like that post-coital moment when you can't remember whether or not you used a condom.

Coggins continued: "Mr. White did not approve of keeping large sums of cash around. Except for gifts and gratuities, he had rarely used cash at all since credit cards came into general use. In fact, it was his practice, for many years now, to review his bills at the end of each month and then have me sell enough of his many corporate holdings to meet those debts, with very little over. This being the first of the year, that process had taken place just before the holidays. With the permission of the police, Mr. White's personal effects have been examined by myself and another trustee, and we have verified that the amount of cash money in the possession of Mr. White at the time of his death, and therefore the amount bequeathed to his wife, came to a matter of . . ." He replaced his glasses and consulted a paper on the desk. "Twenty-six dollars and forty-seven cents."

"*What?*" Leela rose like a rocket with an ear-splitting shriek. She seemed to find speech difficult. "Do—do you mean to tell me that I—I—I *shtupped* that crazy ol' bastard for a matter of twenty-six dollars and forty-seven cents?"

"Not only that, you murdered that poor ol' bastard for a matter of twenty-six dollars and forty-seven cents."

Swear to God, I had no idea those words were coming out of my mouth until there they were, floating in the stuffy air of the study like the smoke from one of Uncle Charles' cigars. I found I had also stood up, and a dozen or so of my blood kin were gaping at me like fish in an overcrowded aquarium. But two heretofore unrelated facts had just met up in my brain. One was inspired by Cousin Travis, the other by Mister.

A third person got to his feet: Detective Todd. "Now, that's a very interesting thing to say, Miss Wells," he said. "Would you care to explain?"

"Mr. Todd, would you care to step outside?" I answered sweetly.

He came along to escort me, and his grip on my elbow was so firm I wasn't sure if it was courtesy or custody.

When we were out in the hall, I said, "Look here. Your idea, and mine, is that Leela gave my Uncle Charles a lot of heavy-duty painkillers and then got him good and liquored up and then just waited for him to . . . well, forget to breathe. That right?"

"Well, we won't know what drugs he took until the autopsy—forgive me, ma'am—but even if that's true, I don't think we could bring a case that she deliberately killed Mr. White."

"But what if she went up and helped him along a little bit? What if you could prove that?"

"Miss Wells, we have testimony from several people, including yourself and Mrs. White herself, to the effect that Mr. White's dog had taken what you might call a violent antipathy to Mrs. White, and she couldn't have got past the dog into the old gentleman's bedroom without everyone in the house knowing about it. Or are you saying the dog was drugged, too?"

"Well, no. Mister wouldn't take anything from anyone except Henry or Dolly or Uncle Charles. I saw that myself. But I know how Leela could have gotten to Uncle Charles' room without waking the dog. Come on." I explained as I walked him through the hall back to the kitchens: "When my Auntie Gwen was alive, us kids used to play all over the house; when it was rainy out, we'd play hide-and-seek, and I always won. In fact, it was my favorite game, and I'll show you why."

I took him clear to the back pantry—not the butler's nook but a seldom-visited storage area beyond the old original kitchen area. I hunkered down to the third shelf from the bottom—well under the sightline of the average adult—and pulled out a couple jars of preserves.

Dolly's cherry preserves, I thought wistfully, would have gone great with those biscuits at breakfast.

I handed them off to Detective Todd, who looked at them, confused, before reaching around to set them on another shelf. Meantime, I felt along the right side of the shelf, just at the back, and then dug two fingers into the little recess I found there. And when I heard the little spring release, I stood up and pushed a section of the shelving right back. There, neat as you please, was a doorway just wide and tall enough for one person to go through.

"I found this one day by accident. Hiding back there the first time was way dusty and not much fun, but I never got found until I got bored and came out. After that, I smuggled down a flashlight and a blanket and borrowed a couple racy books from Uncle Charles' library and went on a real vacation whenever I wanted. I'll show you—"

Detective Todd stopped me. "Miss Wells, I'd rather you just tell me for now."

I looked down where he was staring and saw a black thread caught in the rough wood of the doorframe. Evidence? My heart beat faster.

I gabbled, "So anyway, one day I got curious, and I went exploring with all the dust and the spiders and the ghosts or whatever all's back there, and I went up a flight of stairs, and then there's another catch just like this one, and then I was in Uncle Charles and Auntie Gwen's room, and I wasn't supposed to be there, and so—"

For the first time, after twenty years, it suddenly struck me why it might be convenient for the master of the house to have a quick and private way down to the kitchens, but I filed this revelation for future reference.

"And so," I finished lamely, "I came back down. But that's how Leela could get past Mister, and no one the wiser."

Detective Todd stuck out a palm to put me on Pause, pulled out his phone, and gave orders. Daniel was to keep everyone in the library, and Tammy and Willy were to come along to the back of the house with their kit.

Then he turned to me and said kindly, "Well, now, if I send you back to the library, your kinfolk will be asking you all kinds of questions. So if you'd rather stay out here—"

"Oh, yes, Mr. Todd, I most certainly would."

So, while the crime scene team made their way up that cobwebby old staircase, I wandered only far enough to find a leftover bottle of champagne and a glass. I figured I'd earned it.

Of course, I can't take credit for the subsequent arrest and prosecution. Leela's footprints and fingerprints and scraps of French lace were all over that secret staircase, but that in itself wouldn't have meant much. Nor would the fact that the decades-old dust from the little corridor was all over her negligee and shoes. After first denying she'd been anywhere near her husband's room, Leela lawyered up and said she didn't remember, and then she said that yes, she guessed she might have taken that route from the party to check up on her dear husband without waking up that goddam stupid lil' monster of a dog.

But then, when the pathologist found the identical dust from the old staircase *in* Uncle Charles' nostrils, along with 160mg of OxyContin in his system, they had a case. Leela began cussing in earnest and incriminated herself up one side and down the other. She'd given her dear hubby a couple of "aspirin" for his arthritis, and then a few more a couple hours later, making sure his glass was never empty. About ten thirty, she had Henry take him up to bed and tuck him in. She'd just nipped up between circulating from one room to the next and held her hand over an unresisting face until the elderly and drug-depressed body gave up the ghost.

Well, Leela White is young and pretty. I expect her lawyers will keep appealing the case until she's not, or until her GoFundMe page fails to.

Andy Coggins told me later that if Leela had stuck it out for a year, Uncle Charles had a second will ready to sign that left her the whole shooting match. But the will he signed on his wedding day . . . okay, it seems showing up early to help kinfolk actually *is* the right thing to do.

And I do hope that next time Virginia is in your vacation plans, you'll stop by the Oak Bridge Inn, Proprietor Courtney M. Wells, and try some of Dolly Jackson's famous cherry preserves.

Samantha Hamilton started her career as staff writer and editor at Fleet Street Publishing and has since worked as a disc jockey, teacher, bartender, ad copywriter, producer, and psychic. This story represents her return to fiction writing. More of her work is available through Clarendon House Publications, and readers can visit her novel in progress on Facebook at Pink Lady–novel.

ENDLESS SKIES

Signature J. M. Ames

The trees swayed below as the *USSS Ward* soared over them. Nightfall had drained them of color; their emerald leaves shone silver in the predawn starlight.

Teri slipped her trembling hand into Michelle's. "I can't believe it's come to this."

They peered out the portal at the passing scenery, Teri's mouth agape.

Michelle squeezed her hand. "We'll find a way to carry on."

"How? I don't know how to fly this damned thing, and neither do you. I'm just a medic, and you're just a mechanic."

"Hey, I'm an amateur botanist too. Look, the *Ward*'s AI knows what to do. It's set to search out habitable planets. It'll find *something*. It has to. Besides, I *do* know the basics, like how to accelerate and steer, so we can evade anything that the sensors can't detect." Michelle grabbed the steering stick protruding from the control board and wiggled it. "Every one of these ships is designed to hold two thousand passengers for sixty-eight years. It's just the two of us. We'll never run out of food, water, air, or power—not even when we're a pair of old geezers. We'll be fine, I promise. We still have each other."

"But the others, they—"

Michelle shook her head. "They didn't make it in time. You saw the reports, all the bodies piled up in the streets. If you hadn't found those gas masks, we never would've made it to the *Ward* in time."

"None of the other ships made it out, did they?"

"No. At least not any American ones. We were the first out, and Control went silent right after."

"Just us, then. The human race dies with us." Teri's face crumpled, and her body shook with sobs. "We failed. Thousands of us signed away our lives to colonize other planets should the worst befall Earth, and now that it has, only the two of us make it out. How are two women alone going to bring back humanity? We're the last humans, ever."

"If we're the last humans, we better make damned sure we get the most out of our lives together, don't ya think?" Michelle winked and slipped her arm around Teri's shoulders. "Look, I followed you into the ARC program to keep you safe, and that's exactly what I am going to do. I promise you."

Teri frowned and looked away.

The hum of the gravity drive intensified. The shifting G-force made Teri nauseated, as it always had in training. Air vents hissed, and the ship vibrated as it departed Earth's atmosphere. They gazed out the portal at what had been their home—umber, verdant landmasses and cerulean seas, spotted with swirling ivory clouds. A bright purple blaze raged on what remained of the United States' eastern seaboard, where the first bombs had detonated. A sapphire haze spread across a third of the globe, a luminous hand of doom snuffing life's flame from everything it touched. Earth would be barren within hours.

"I still can't fathom that it's all gone. The training camp, our college, that rundown bowling alley where we all used to drink cheap beer and burnt coffee while that sleazy pig of a clerk leered at us." Teri's voice cracked, and she covered her eyes with her hands.

"All men are sleazy pigs." Michelle's smile faltered when she realized her half joke failed to lighten Teri's mood. "You know what I'm going to miss most? You and me, sunning nude on Liberation

Beach, bathed in nothing but the cool breeze. Always makes me happy when I think of it."

Teri rolled her eyes and waved her away. "You're a goofball."

Michelle's heart sank. She broke out into a cold sweat and reached into her pocket for her Vraylar, the pills she used for her schizophrenia. Her stomach dropped, and her face blanched. All she found was a small bag of marijuana and rolling papers. In her rush to escape, she had left her medication at the dormitory.

Fuck! I have got to try to keep myself together somehow.

She plopped into one of the beanbags in the corner and pulled her guitar onto her lap. Her shaky hands struggled to roll a tight joint. An argent beam of moonlight illuminated the scene as if it were a performance onstage.

"I think we need some sweet leaf to free our minds of this bullshit, don't you?"

Teri sighed, nodded, grabbed her bongos, and joined her.

Teri's heavy-lidded, bloodshot eyes were locked onto Michelle's. "What did you mean earlier, when you said you followed me into the ARC program?"

"Huh? I don't think I said that. It doesn't matter." Michelle waved her away. "What matters is this haunted journey we'll be spending the rest of our lives on together."

"Did you join because of me? I thought you were a fellow Repopulist, dedicated to the survival of the species when the Final War broke out. We all signed the same contra—"

"I am. I just . . ." Michelle couldn't hold Teri's gaze and looked away. "I dunno. I never thought anyone would be stupid enough to start a war that would kill the whole planet. I guess this is what happens when war pigs are running the government."

Teri's eyes searched Michelle's. "Honestly, neither did I. Not after that near miss in the early twenty-first century, but it happened. And that doesn't explain why you're here with me now."

Michelle finally met her gaze. "Do you really not know? Teri, I've been in love with you since college. I would fuckin' die for you. I know you don't feel the same way; I know it will never happen. You like men and all. But I'm happy just to be your frien—"

Teri's lips stopped Michelle's mid word, her tongue hungrily probing. Light kisses traveled up Michelle's jawline to nibble her earlobes before brushing against her neck. Teri unzipped Michelle's uniform and peeled it away in seconds, before Michelle flipped Teri on her back and removed hers.

Michelle took the role of the kisser as her hand found Teri's naked breast and squeezed gently. Her hand slid between Teri's legs, and her eager mouth took its previous place on her erect nipple.

Teri bit her lip, arched her back, and moaned.

Michelle's tongue danced down Teri's stomach and then farther down, tasting all there was to taste of her new lover. She looked up at the flushed, panting face of the woman she had loved for over a decade and felt the happiest she had in her whole life.

Finally, I get to be with her. She's mine, and mine alone. Forever.

"I love you so much, Teri," she whispered before returning to the task at hand.

Two eyes shining in the blackness greeted Teri when she awoke. Gooseflesh bloomed across her skin, and her breath caught in her throat.

"M-Michelle?"

"*Hmm*?" Michelle rolled over and cupped Teri's breast, lightly squeezing. "Right here, honey."

Michelle's soft snores resumed almost immediately.

Another eye appeared, and it took Teri a few moments to realize they were merely stars outside the portal.

I'm getting paranoid. I guess that's just a symptom of the universe I live in now.

She pushed off Michelle's arm with a frown and went to make

them coffee. Lost in thoughts of their new and permanent isolation, she shuffled into the galley. She froze when her gaze drifted to the bay window on the far side of the ship, and her belly felt as if filled with iced gelatin. They had sailed through these endless skies much farther than she had thought. The great crimson eye of Mars consumed most of the window.

It's like the fiery oculus of some great, celestial God.

Between it and the *Ward* was another ship, drifting toward them.

Soft lips brushed the goosebumps on the back of her neck as Michelle's arms wrapped around her waist, making her jump.

Teri pointed out the window. "Look, another ship! Do you think there could be—"

The commlink crackled to life, startling both women. Teri couldn't quite stifle the scream that shot from her.

"*USSS Ward*, this is Captain John Anthony of the *HMSS Zeitgeist*. How many of you are there? I-I'm the only one here. Thought I was the only human left anywhere. None of the queen's fleet made it out . . ."

Teri smiled widely at Michelle. "Maybe this isn't our extinction. Maybe we *can* start over again as we travel the universe together. With a man to reproduce with both of us, I think we're saved!"

"Yes, saved . . ."

Michelle's smile faltered then broke when Teri turned to chatter excitedly on the commlink.

"Captain John Anthony, this is Doctor Teresa Iommi. I have with me Technician Michelle Osbourne. We were the only ones to escape the States. Have you heard from any others?" Teri felt so excited, she had to consciously slow down her talking.

"No, I'm afraid I . . ."

Michelle's head swam, and all sound faded. She could hear the joy in Teri's voice. Joy that she could once again be with a man, which would in turn push Michelle to the sidelines of the dreaded friend zone yet again. Her knees buckled as she crumpled to the cool floor. Sobs wracked her body in small, silent quakes.

No, not again. I can't lose her again. I've waited too long for her, been dying for her love. I finally got to have her. How dare she do this to me again? Do I mean so little to her? That fucking bitch is mine!

A sudden, cold clarity calmed her. There was no question of what had to be done. Michelle picked herself up from the floor and staggered to the controls. She wiped her eyes with the back of her hands before entering the manual override codes and grasping the steering stick.

Teri chattered away, so focused on advising John with how the U.S. had fallen that she hadn't noticed the ship's change of direction.

Once the *Ward*'s trajectory was aimed at the *Zeitgeist*, Michelle locked the steering and set the acceleration to maximum. She crept behind Teri and prepared to tackle her if she realized what was happening and tried to stop their electric funeral.

A flash of white shone bright and brief to the right of the *R.F.S Dvoretskiy*, just above the Martian horizon.

"Serzhant! We've detected an explosion off of the starboard side. It looks as if a pair of ships has collided."

Serzhant Uil'yam looked up from his astral charts. "Were they ours?"

"*Nyet*, all of our ships are accounted for."

Uil'yam raised an eyebrow. "*Hmm*, I thought only our fleet escaped in time. While that may be interesting, comrade, it is no concern of yours. Now carry on, and get the *Dvoretskiy* settled into temporary Martian orbit, then send the coordinates to the rest of the ships for Volk 1061c. The *Dvoretskiy* has deemed that is the closest planet likely to sustain human life."

J.M. Ames is an author native to Southern California, where he lives with his family. He published his first short story, "The Last Ride," in 2016 and has been writing nonstop since. When not working his day job, listening to Black Sabbath, or enjoying his fatherly adventures, he writes short stories and novels, including an upcoming series.

You can get up-to-date details on his website: jm-ames.com.

AMERICAN DREAM

Signature *Melinda Logan*

"No, my son not for sale."

Miguel jerked his head up when Mama mentioned his name and noticed the man staring in his direction. He was happy when his younger sisters tugged on his arm.

"Miguel, come play with us!" the twins sang in unison.

Miguel turned his attention back to his sisters, thankful for the distraction. They were kneeling on the bedding where they slept every night in a corner of the cramped apartment. One of the twins cradled their only toy in her arms, a tattered ragdoll that Abuéla made for Mama when she was a young girl. The other twin had a frown on her face as she waited impatiently to hold their treasured doll, even though time had faded the rainbow-bright colors to muted pastels.

Miguel began to tickle his sister in hopes to cheer her up. Before long, both sisters were squealing with delight, the heirloom forgotten as they smiled and shouted in high-pitched voices.

"Tickle me!"

"No, me!"

They were jumping up and down in a frenzy; their hot breath, sour from hunger, blasted Miguel in the face as the twins surrendered to the floor in a mass of sweat and giggles.

"Miguel, bring home sweets tonight, pretty please," one of the twins begged.

"Chocolate, chocolate cake, pretty please," the other one added.

Miguel silently prayed that Mr. Johnson, who owned a bakery around the corner and who let him work odd jobs in exchange for baked goods, had some old cakes tonight that he could bring home for his sisters.

The sound of his baby sister's familiar cry of hunger muffled against his mama's chest caused Miguel to turn his head towards the kitchen table. The familiar groaning and grumbling of his stomach wasn't enough to distract Miguel from the uneasy feeling he got from the glassy eyed stranger seated across from Mama at the makeshift kitchen table made from an oversized cardboard box.

Miguel recalled how happy his mama was when he brought home the box.

"Oh, Miguel! I couldn't ask for a better son! Your papa would be so proud of you."

When he was further rewarded with a wet kiss on the forehead and a ruffle of his ebony hair, he knew that it was worth the painful strain that his rail-thin arms took when he dragged the box from the alleyway and up five flights of stairs to their apartment.

She retrieved the rolled-up serape that served as a pillow, unrolled it, and spread it out to cover the top of the box, letting the fringe ends fall over the sides. The brilliant shades of yellow, orange, and red humming with energy contrasted sharply to the bleakness of the lackluster surroundings.

"This was a wedding gift given to me when I wed your papa." A weak smile crossed her lips as she touched the woven fabric with loving hands.

She wasn't smiling now as she fanned herself with a piece of paper and clutched the fussy baby to her breast. Her face strained with emotion as she watched the man place a stack of money on the serape and push it towards her. The green bills seemed to materialize out of thin air as he placed another one on the table and slid it in her direction.

"No, not for sale!" She jerked the paper fan hard back and forth.

A bead of sweat began to pool on the man's forehead, and the calmness of his demeanor began to crumble. When the pointy features of the stranger's face began to twitch and contort, he reminded Miguel of the rats that scurried over their legs at night while they slept.

The man took a deep breath and seemed to gain his composure once again. "I'm not buying your son. I want to employ him. He'll be working in a place with other boys just like him. He'll be off the street." The man sounded slicker than a used-car salesman.

"*Waa!*" the baby began to wail as Mama shook her head once again.

"What are your children going to eat tonight, tomorrow, the next day?" the man continued, his voice laced with confidence.

"Cakes, cakes, we want cakes!" his sisters began to chant in high-pitched voices barely audible over the baby's piercing cries.

"Your son is begging in the street, working until his hands and feet are blistered, only to be paid in stale, moldy bread and cakes that aren't fit to feed a cockroach." His voice raised in an attempt to be heard over the wailing of the baby and persistent chanting of the twins. His eyes followed a cockroach, right on cue, as it darted across the table.

As Miguel silently observed the scene, he remembered the last words his father spoke to him before he left. Miguel recalled how his papa had bent down before Mama and planted a tender kiss on her belly that was starting to swell with new life.

"You're the man of the house now. I want you to promise me that you'll take care of your mother and sisters."

Miguel's chest swelled with pride that his father would entrust him with such a responsibility. He never thought he could fill his father's shoes, but he would try very hard to keep this promise to his father.

"We will be together very soon and live the American dream together." His father had spoken his last words and embraced Miguel in a tight bear hug.

Miguel never saw his father again. He wanted to be the man his father envisioned, and there was only one way he knew how. He silently walked over to his mama.

His mother looked up at him with a tear-stained face and said, "No, Miguel. I will not allow you to go."

He placed a reassuring hand on her shoulder and said, "Mama, I am the man of the house now, and it is my decision to make."

"You made the right decision, son," the stranger said as he grinned like a Cheshire cat.

"No, Miguel, you can't do this," Mama said in a strained voice.

The man pulled out a solitary piece of white paper and placed it on the table.

"What is this?" Miguel asked.

"A contract that your mama has to sign."

Miguel knew he would only recognize some of the words on the paper, and his mama would know none. He silently wished he had stayed in school, where they taught him English, instead of dropping out to make money and find food.

"There's one condition of the contract that will ease your mind. After you sign the contract, your son and I will walk to my van and wait for about five minutes. If you change your mind within those five minutes, all you have to do is come outside. Once I see you, I'll know you changed your mind and will immediately rip up the contract."

He walked around the table and slipped a pen in Mama's hand and placed the paper in front of her.

His finger landed pointedly on a space on the paper, and he said, "Please sign here."

Mama squeezed the pen so tight, her knuckles were turning white.

"Mama, it will be okay. Please sign it," Miguel whispered in her ear.

She rubbed her head with the back of her hand, took a deep breath, and signed the paper.

Without warning, the man snatched the contract from Mama and wrapped his hand tightly around one of Miguel's wrists. The twins began to cry, not understanding what was happening. The baby started to howl louder than ever. Mama was still staring down at the table in a trance as Miguel was pulled out of the apartment by the death grip on his wrist. He could barely feel his feet touch the stairs as the man hurried down them. When they reached a white van—that was more rust than metal—Miguel found himself tossed into the back, landing on a pile of dirty blankets and shoeboxes neatly stacked.

"Make yourself at home." His words dripped with sarcasm as he watched Miguel through bars of metal that divided the front of the van from the back.

Miguel felt panic rising up in his chest. All he wanted was to get out of this van and back to his mama. He scrambled around the back, looking for a way out. All the windows were blacked out except for one small corner of the glass.

"Here she comes, right on time."

Miguel had a rush of hope as he remembered what the man had told them. He could barely see with one eye through the glass, but it was enough to afford him a view of his beloved mama running toward the van.

As his mama approached the van, Miguel heard him say, "You see, I'm a man of my word."

The next sound Miguel heard was paper ripping and his mama letting out a guttural cry. The last thing Miguel saw was his mama standing in the road with outstretched arms, sobbing, while bits of white paper showered around her.

When the van sped off, Miguel lost his balance and fell to the floor, knocking off some of the shoebox lids. He felt bile coming up in his throat as the contents of the toppled shoeboxes came spilling out.

He was surrounded by pictures of naked boys.

Melinda Logan is an author and illustrator originally from the Windy City, who now calls Alabama her home sweet home. Melinda wanted to create a children's book series with a unique twist, so she came up with *Music Town Tales*. It is a series of children's books that feature musical instruments as characters. *Victor Viola Moves to Music Town* (Volume 1) and *Victor Viola Moves to Music Town* coloring and activity book are available now. She is in the process of completing the next volume for the *Music Town Tales* series and a novel set in Alabama.

To find out more about her writing endeavors, check out her website: www.melindaloganauthor.com and Facebook page: www.facebook.com/AuthorMelindaLogan.

When she's not writing and drawing for her own projects, Melinda assists her husband as a writer, actor, and producer in his short films and commercials, of which there are numerous to date. Their documentary, *West Blocton: Small Town, Big Heart*, won many accolades. They won first place for their entry in the Home Run Inn Pizza Halloween Short Contest.

To find out more, check out their YouTube Channel: www.youtube.com/user/mjlogan2001.

Dusk descended behind East Haven as Tommy Wallace watched the iron gates close in the rearview mirror. The colonial house gleamed from small spotlights planted in the mulch, showcasing the ultra-white paneled siding and black shutters of the two-story structure; every exterior floodlight sparkled with elegance. The McAllisters were a reputable family but being on their property—with its luscious greenery and immaculate water fountain—instantly shamed him for his quaint, one-bedroom apartment and twisted his nerves.

I shouldn't be here, he thought as he parked the police cruiser next to the three-car garage and quietly exited the vehicle.

Tommy wiped his sweaty palms against his slacks and swallowed a nervous lump down his tightening throat; his heart pounded heavily with each step as he traversed the slate driveway.

He had first met Mindy McAllister last winter right after he joined the force, when the university hosted a candlelight vigil for four students who disappeared in the Catskill Mountains. She was huddled with a small group of girls close to the mound of cards and flowers, but his eyes grasped her attention across the path, and she threw him a gentle smile. He offered her a cup of hot chocolate to combat the cold, which she graciously accepted, and made small talk before returning to his post.

Their paths crossed again in the spring at Blue State Coffee in New Haven while on his lunch break. He bought her a cappuccino and spent an hour with her, telling bad police jokes and accidentally-on-purpose touching her fingers. At the end of their impromptu date, she gave Tommy her cell number and kissed his cheek before disappearing into the cool afternoon sun.

He wrestled with his desires for a week before sending her a simple text: *I can't stop thinking about you.*

He knew her father well—Clive was his boss and not a man he wanted to upset—so going to her place was out of the question, and he was too embarrassed to ever take her to his quarters, so their lust exploded wherever possible: motel rooms, university bathrooms, his police cruiser. The locale didn't matter but watching her walk away after every excursion stabbed his gut.

When Mindy invited him to her estate for the evening, Tommy had more than a few reservations, but he jumped at any and every chance to see her, if only for a few moments. He brushed his hands across his uniform once more, smoothed his hair, and pushed the doorbell.

Mindy opened the door, her short blonde hair bouncing around her perfect jawline. She wore a red-and-white striped tank top and frayed blue jean shorts, revealing a vast majority of her smooth, summer-kissed skin.

"Hi," she said, standing tiptoed to kiss him on the cheek.

"You look amazing, and this place . . . Wow."

Her cheeks reddened, and her lips parted to reveal her bleached teeth. "Come in. My parents just left. We have the whole place to ourselves."

"Are you sure this is okay?" he asked, surveying the house's interior: the elongated staircase, the grand living room with oversized furniture to the right, the formal dining room on the left. A monstrous crystal chandelier hung high overhead, enchanting visitors upon entry. "Your dad's not going to come home early and shoot me, is he?"

Mindy placed his hands around her waist and gazed into his dark eyes. "You're safe. I promise."

Her soft, cherry lips impacted Tommy's, giving him an instant erection.

"I have a bottle of champagne on ice," she said, pulling him past the staircase. "I thought we could watch the fireworks from the terrace."

"Sounds perfect."

They walked hand in hand onto the wooden space overlooking a beach filled with spectators awaiting the fireworks show. Tommy grabbed the champagne bottle and poured the bubbly into two crystal glasses.

Mindy smiled and sipped the liquid, staring at him with desire as the beverage tickled her throat. She found him irresistible in his police uniform. She was initially drawn to the badge—his tight, muscled body too, if she was being honest—and the clandestine rendezvous had been a huge turn on, but ecstatic butterflies fluttered in her stomach whenever his name appeared across her phone, and she found herself wanting more, which was the reason she extended the invitation for the evening.

Tonight, she was ready to say those *three little words* and hoped he would feel the same way.

"You are so beautiful," he said, caressing her cheek with his thumb. "Thank you for having me over."

"Thank you for coming. I know you're still worried about my dad finding out about us, but I think I'm ready to tell him . . . if you are."

A swig of champagne entered the wrong pipe and sent him into a short coughing fit. "Are you sure?"

"I don't wanna hide anymore," she said, setting aside the champagne glasses and falling into his kiss. His facial stubble tickled her mouth, lubricating her insides.

The first firework exploded over the bay, but Mindy was too intoxicated by Tommy to notice the display. She grabbed his hand and led him through the French doors and upstairs to her bedroom.

Mindy and Tommy collapsed on the bed and untangled their lips only long enough for him to remove his undershirt, revealing his hairy pecs. He rubbed his hand up her soft skin and slightly squeezed her petite breast; his other hand caressed her thigh as he tasted her sweat.

Fireworks continued booming outside, sporadically lighting the darkened room with multicolored flashes.

He unzipped his pants and stopped moving when glass broke from the sidelines. Tommy jerked his head toward the bedroom door as Mindy clung to his shoulders, but nothing stirred; he thought the sound had originated from the closet.

She turned on the lamp, allowing Tommy to grab his gun and silently maneuver to the door.

"Tommy—"

He placed his index finger across his lips and reverted his attention to the still closet. He grabbed the handle, steadied his weapon, and jerked open the door, revealing an oversized walk-in space. He turned on the light, checked behind the hanging garments for any suspicious items, and found the culprit.

Mindy held her knees against her chest until he reemerged, holding a picture frame—glass shards huddled in various sizes across a familiar face. A young man was posed against a burgundy 1967 Chevelle Super Sport, his arms folded, a sly smile forever frozen behind the glass fragments.

She met Dean Carrington last fall after he scored the winning soccer goal against Stonehill College and quickly found herself in the back seat of his hotrod, twice a week, until his girlfriend witnessed a *Chevelle-session* in the school parking lot before winter break. Lenoir Sheldon locked eyes with Mindy that night before evading the scene, but never confronted them, and Mindy had kept silent about the bust. She had started to care for Dean, but when she gave him an ultimatum, he refused to terminate his relationship with the redheaded bitch.

"What happened?" she asked.

"It must've fallen from the top shelf. It was behind your shoes."

"It couldn't have fallen. It was in a box on the floor."

"I checked, and there's no one in there. Maybe you just misplaced it."

She continued staring at the picture, lost in memories. "Maybe."

"Isn't that one of the missing students from the university?"

The story exploded on social media when Dean's wrecked and abandoned vehicle was found in the Catskill Mountains. Leaked pictures of the Chevelle revealed massive amounts of blood covering the roof and back seat. Later reports confirmed the blood belonged to Dean and his friend, Luke. The search lasted for weeks, and Mindy found herself glued to the television every night at six o'clock to hear the latest developments, but no bodies or evidence ever surfaced, and the story dwindled after the vigil.

"Yes, that's Dean. We dated for, like, five seconds and broke up before he disappeared."

A wave of jealousy swept across Tommy's chest. "I didn't realize you knew him that well. Did you know the others?"

"I knew *of* them. The two other guys were Dean's best friends, James Conrad and Luke Sheldon. I never got a chance to meet them . . . because Dean was also involved with Luke's sister."

Tommy raised his eyebrows in surprise. "Did you know he had a girlfriend when you started seeing him?"

Mindy's face reddened, and she reverted her eyes to the picture, resenting the question. "I'm not perfect, Tommy. I knew about Lenoir, but I really did have feelings for Dean." She wiped a tear from her eye and set the broken frame on the nightstand. "Maybe I went about it the wrong way. I feel incredibly guilty now that they're all missing, and probably . . ."

Tommy touched her face and pulled Mindy into his chest. "I'm sorry. I didn't mean to upset you."

"It's okay. Let's just forget about it. Besides, weren't we in the middle of something?" she asked, groping his crotch to resurrect his thick rod.

Her kiss fell upon him again in a heated frenzy. Tommy removed the rest of his clothes and pulled her under the sheets. The fireworks climaxed as the couple's bodies synchronized.

Mindy bolted upright and expelled a high-pitched scream, startling Tommy from a deep sleep. They had inadvertently fallen asleep after lying in each other's arms, and she was now sitting in the middle of the mattress, sweat dripping from her shoulders and forehead, her body shivering. Her breaths came in rapid spurts.

Tommy turned on the lamp and touched her shoulder.

"What's wrong?" he asked, rubbing her arm and checking the clock on the nightstand.

"Red eyes!"

"Baby, you had a nightmare. That's all."

He lay her on the pillow and noticed fresh blood on Mindy's oversized sleep shirt from the lower abdomen. Tears dripped down her cheeks as Tommy raised her top to reveal a five-inch long cut.

"How did this happen?" he asked, grabbing his undershirt to apply pressure against the wound.

"I-I don't—know."

"Hold this tight. I'm going to get a washcloth and the first-aid kit. I'll be right back."

As Tommy walked across the room, he observed a small glass shard tinting the cream carpet with its red, wet edges. He glanced back—the broken picture frame still rested on the nightstand. He had seen no signs of forced entry, and an intruder would have tripped the McAllisters' high-grade security system. No one else was in the house. Every conjured explanation was quickly dismissed. The only scenario which halfway seemed plausible was Mindy had accidentally cut herself while trying to deflect the nightmare, but even that possibility left him perplexed.

He shuffled aerosol cans and lotion containers under the

bathroom sink, found the coveted items, and rushed back to the bedroom.

Mindy lay motionless on the bed, her sobs muffled by the pillow. Tommy passed the stray shard, knelt beside her, and examined the wound. The cut was shallow but still bled profusely. He poured peroxide on the rag and placed it on the gash, kissing her warm forehead to dispel her fear.

"Are you okay?" Tommy asked, breaking the silence.

"I guess so," she whispered. "What happened?"

He placed the gauze over her wound. "I was hoping you could tell me. You had a nightmare and somehow cut yourself with a piece of glass from the frame. Do you remember anything?"

She shook her head and closed her eyes but vividly remembered starting the bathwater. Steam had fogged the mirror as she stepped out of her panties and onto the pink rug next to the tub. She stooped to shut off the pipe and saw eyes staring at her through the ripples. A shadow erupted from the water, grabbed her arm, and pulled her under the water, sending her shrieking into consciousness.

"I'm going to run downstairs and get you a glass of water. Just relax and take deep breaths."

He kissed her lips, pulled on his pants, and exited the room.

Mindy lay silently and touched the bandage. With each passing second, the house seemed quieter—darker than before. The lamp flickered and threw bizarre shadows across the ceiling and walls, adding to the unease. A cold air moved over the bed, sending goosebumps up her arms. Then the light dissipated completely, blanketing the room in obscurity.

"Tommy?" she yelled. She knew he couldn't hear her calls from the kitchen, but her chest heaved with nervous tension.

The closet door slowly creaked open. Mindy's eyes widened, and her heart pounded faster against her ribcage. Her neck hairs stood on end as an electric breeze poured into the room. Then the door slammed against the adjacent wall with a loud *thump*, and a dark shadow emerged, floating closer to the bed. Mindy held her breath as tears clung to her frightened eyes.

The presence converged at the footboard and seemed to smile.

Tommy was already climbing the stairs when he heard Mindy's terrified scream. He rushed up the steps—spilling water onto the hardwood with each stride—slammed the glass on a half-table in the hall and stumbled backward upon reaching the doorway.

Mindy levitated above the bed, her limbs flat as a board. He turned on the overhead light and forced his shuddering body into action. He ran to the bed, grabbed her right ankle, and pulled, but she remained in place.

"Tommy, help me!" Mindy shrieked. "Help me, please!"

An invisible force crashed into his chest before he could respond and shoved him into the wall, breaking her family's portrait. He caressed his aching skull but focused his attention back to Mindy. Her body swiftly inverted and sailed into the opposite wall next to the window. The overhead fixture rapidly glinted.

Her shirt crumpled above her breasts and collected on her chin. The bandage ripped itself from her flesh and dropped to the floor, revealing the still-fresh cut. Tommy slowly leaned against the wall to balance his equilibrium and froze in horror as the lone shard from the carpet drifted toward Mindy's abdomen and dug into her skin.

"No!" Tommy yelled, darting toward the animated piece.

He was expelled to the floor again as the object bore an *A* into her skin. Mindy's cries increased as the sliver began a new pattern: a circle encompassing the letter. Tommy watched helplessly as the rogue fragment finished the design.

The bloodied glass and Mindy simultaneously fell to the floor. Tommy's body released from his imprisonment, allowing him to scramble to her side. She scantily caught her breath between giant moans. The cuts bled in tiny rivers as Tommy cradled her in his arms.

"I'm so sorry," he said. "I tried to get to you. Are you okay?"

She remained silent, her eyelids refusing to blink.

Tommy found his bloodstained undershirt and pressed the material against the symbol. "We have to get you out of here. Can you walk?"

"I . . . think so."

Tommy helped her stand and rushed her to the stairs, throwing his arm around her shoulders to deflect more potential harm. As they descended, the front doorknob clicked, stopping the couple midway.

Clive McAllister entered the house, his face wrought with anger. After seeing Tommy's police cruiser parked outside, Clive's blood pressure skyrocketed, but a new rage filled his body upon seeing Mindy running toward him and away from Tommy with blood soaking her shirt and tears flooding her face.

"You sonofabitch," Clive yelled, rushing past Mindy to connect a fist across Tommy's jaw. Clive jumped on him, landing multiple blows.

"Daddy, no!"

Loraine McAllister placed her cellphone in her purse as she entered the house, her blue sequined dress hugging her plump hips. Mindy raced up the stairs and blocked Clive from inflicting more damage to the battered man. Blood dribbled from Tommy's nose and mouth, and his eyes circled in confusion.

"What's going on here?" Loraine asked, appalled at the scene. "Mindy? Clive?"

Clive vehemently descended the stairs and stood next to his wife, his chest furiously pumping air.

"That sonofabitch attacked our daughter," Clive said, his face a bright red.

"No, that's not what happened. Tommy didn't do this to me," Mindy said, holding her abdomen.

"I'm really sorry, Chief," Tommy said, slowly walking toward the front door while holding Mindy's hand, "but we have to get out of here."

"You're not going anywhere, asshole, except to jail."

Loraine placed a hand on Clive's shoulder to hold him at bay. Her brow creased with disapproval and worry settled in her eyes. "Mindy, tell me what's going on. What happened to you? Who is this man?"

"Tommy's my boyfriend, Mom."

Clive cawed at the announcement and shook his head in protest. "Are you kidding me with this right now?"

Tommy hugged Mindy closer to him. "I'm sorry, Chief, but is there a rule that says no one on the force can date your daughter?"

Clive continuously shook his head, a stupefied grin planted on his face. "You just wait, boy. I'm gonna—"

"Stop it!" Mindy interrupted. "Listen to me. There's something in my room. It attacked me."

"Something?" her mother asked.

A short, elderly woman—no more than five feet tall—entered the McAllisters' home, a purse tucked under her arm. She was in her late sixties, with thin, graying hair and watery brown eyes, and she examined each person intently, as if scanning their souls.

"Oh my," the stranger said with a southern drawl.

"Who is this woman?" Mindy asked.

Tommy kept glancing up the stairs, alert despite the soreness.

Loraine McAllister approached the lady and placed her arm around the woman's shoulders. "This is Juanita Sinclair. We met her tonight at the charity ball. She had some very interesting stories to tell, one of which involved you being in some kind of danger."

"Maybe I should speak my piece before things progress," Juanita said, looking at Mindy's bloody shirt and adjusting her hearing aid. "Like your mama said, my name's Juanita. I'm from a small town down south called Shady Valley, and I've recently had experiences with strange occurrences. About a year ago, I began having visions—nightmares—involving people I knew, and then strangers. Going ignored, the subjects of those dreams wound up missing, or worse, so I've learned not to disregard my calling. Strange as this sounds, I dreamt about you recently, Mindy, and you're in terrible danger."

"I'm sorry, I hate to interrupt, but we have to get out of here," Tommy said, tugging Mindy to the exit. "Ma'am, thank you for the warning, but you're a little too late."

The front door slammed, and the house's electrical system wavered; faint crackling sounds buzzed through the currents. Tommy tried the door, but it resisted. The security alarm came alive and blaringly pierced their ears. The house trembled with the power of an earthquake; pictures fell from walls, vases shattered on the hardwood floor, a bookcase in the living room fell with a heavy thud. The foyer's crystal chandelier violently rattled from the second story, snapped, and plummeted onto Clive's head, crushing his skull.

Loraine's screams were imperceptibly heard over the thunderous shaking and high-pitched alarm. Mindy clung to her mother, like she was a child again. Tommy ran into the kitchen, but the patio doors were suctioned as well. He grabbed a chair from the table and rammed the legs into the door's glass, but the chair deflected. Tommy repeated the process with the windows, but the glass had acquired shatterproof strength.

The noise ceased forthwith, leaving the group in darkness with ringing ears. Juanita retrieved a flashlight from her purse and shined the beam around the room, skipping over the blood pooling under the chandelier.

Tommy grabbed his gun from the holster. "Everyone get in the living room, and stay on the floor. I'm going to try to shoot out the kitchen window."

"Tommy, no," Mindy protested through hysterical sobs. "What if it backfires?"

He gave her a what-else-am-I-supposed-to-do look and kissed her forehead.

Juanita nodded and brushed the McAllister women into the living room, her beam guiding the path around the chaos. The ladies huddled together by the couch, with Loraine and Mindy sobbing in each other's arms. Their tears meshed as they knelt to the floor.

Tommy posed several feet from the window and aimed his service weapon. He steadied his arms, exhaled to calm his nerves, whispered a silent prayer, and pulled the trigger. The bullet hit the window, then ricocheted past Tommy, zipped down the hallway, made a sharp left turn, and barreled into Loraine's forehead. Mindy's eyes grew wild and frightful as her mother's blood splattered her face; her head flopped on the couch cushion. Tommy scooped his girlfriend from the tragedy and carried her into the dining room.

"What do we do?" Tommy asked, looking at Juanita. "I thought you were supposed to help us."

"I don't know it all, sweetie," Ms. Sinclair said. "I don't have an answer for this."

"Then what are you doing here?"

Mindy escaped from her boyfriend's hold and slowly retreated toward the foyer, gazing sporadically into the air. Her surroundings became foreign as walls instantaneously transformed into giant trees, and hardwood floors turned to vegetation, but then everything returned to normal. The room transitioned back and forth—lasting only a few seconds with each rotation—shocking her into horrific fear.

"Tommy?" she asked, her voice quivering.

He touched her shoulder, and the alternating images ceased. She stared into his brown eyes, and then recoiled as his irises shot bright red. His face took the form of a deer with sharp, towering antlers; razor teeth peeked from the growling sneer.

Her boyfriend's normal features reappeared, and she raced into his arms, expelling an almost inaudible screech which chilled his flesh. They sank to the floor. Tommy supported his frazzled girlfriend and rested her head on his shoulder.

Juanita dabbed her eyes with a handkerchief, then stuck the cloth in her purse. She steadied the light on the shaking couple as she sat in a chair.

"You saw it, didn't you?" Juanita asked.

"Saw what?" Tommy retorted.

"The creature," Juanita said, her breath catching in her lungs.

"That's what I came here to warn you about. You see, she's been afflicted with a curse, one that will stop at nothing to get to her. It's an unholy beast that will come for us all."

"How do you know this?" Tommy asked. "I thought we were dealing with some kind of pissed-off ghost?"

"Oh, there is a presence here, and it's out for blood, but it has summoned an abomination. I don't know why, but we have to keep her out of the woods."

Mindy raised her head to look at the prolific psychic, fear chiseled across her face.

"What did you say?"

"In my vision, you were alone in the woods, running from a creature that had a man's body . . . and a deer's head. After days and days of research, I finally came across the little-known legend of the Deer Man."

"Deer Man?" Tommy asked. "You're kidding me, right?"

Juanita ignored his remark and cleared her throat. "The legend dates back to the eighteen-seventies when a young boy named Oliver Quincy wandered off into the heart of the Catskill Mountains."

"That's where they found Dean's car last winter," Mindy interjected.

"Little Oliver crossed paths with Ethel Townsend, an accused witch who'd been banished to live in the woods. Deprived of human contact for decades, Ethel lured Ollie to her underground cave and, repulsed by his rambling cries of wanting to return home, entered into a blood pact with something demonic and unholy—an unbreakable and infinite contract, if you will—to afflict the boy with a curse that transformed him into the first Deer Man. Oliver Quincy became her pet, her slave, and, when he matured, her lover. Ten years after his disappearance, Ethel took a bucket of goat's blood and marked the Quincy cabin with the letter *A*, encompassed by a circle. That mark bound Oliver to kill his entire family."

Mindy lifted her shirt to reveal her bloody mark. "Did the symbol look like this?"

Juanita focused her flashlight on the cuts and nodded.

"Mindy, we need to dress your wounds before we try to escape again," Tommy said. "We're wasting time listening to this ridiculous story, and you've lost a lot of blood."

Mindy shook her head. "I'm not going back into my room."

"I'll grab what we need." Tommy kissed her lips and disappeared around the corner.

Mindy turned to Juanita and quietly asked, "How do we stop this?"

"Well, darlin', the Deer Man can be killed, but you have to be very careful. The curse passes to whomever kills the creature, if it's the last of its kind. The only way to stop the beast from coming after you is to remove the mark, which is quite impossible in this situation, I'm afraid. But maybe if we cut a line through a side of the circle, it might do some good?"

Tommy returned with the first-aid kit and an arm full of Mindy's clothing. When he entered the dining room, Mindy was holding up her shirt and standing in front of Juanita, who held a knife to Mindy's abdomen. Tommy dropped the items and drew his gun.

"Tommy, it's okay," Mindy said through clenched teeth. "This may be the only way to stop it."

Juanita sliced a line across the symbol's curve and asked Tommy for the disinfectant and a fresh bandage. Tommy held onto Mindy's shoulders as Juanita carefully readdressed the lesions.

"I can't get a signal on my cell, and the landline is dead," Tommy said. "You think this will stop whatever's going on?"

"We sure hope so," Juanita said, taping the last edge of the bandage to Mindy's skin. "But stopping the spirit will be more difficult."

Mindy dressed herself and put on her tennis shoes. Her cuts stung with each movement, but she forced herself to work through the pain. She grabbed her blue-jean jacket from the foyer closet—trying to ignore her father's dead body under the shattered chandelier—and pulled her arms through the openings. Despite the summer's heat, the events inside her home left her with a chill she couldn't escape.

Tommy used his baton and pounded the front door handle. The knob bent with every blow but resiliently adhered to its post. Mindy stood close to Juanita, closed her eyes, and mumbled a prayer under her breath.

The dining room's recessed lighting sparked a dim glow. After one final strike, the lights intensified and remained consistent, and the door handle clanked to the floor. He beamed triumphantly, exhilarated with glee as he yanked open the door and reached for Mindy's hand. She intended to join him but couldn't move her foot.

Mindy fell backwards and slid across the foyer, her leg angled upward as her other limbs wildly floundered; her left hand plowed through her father's blood. She reached for Tommy's hand but missed, then slipped up the wall and into the upstairs hallway.

Tommy trampled the stairs toward Mindy's bedroom, which now contained a heavy whirlwind; clothes, books, shards of glass, and papers churned in the air. Mindy clung to the closet doorjamb and screamed. Tommy ducked to avoid the swirling objects and grabbed Mindy's hand. He placed his left foot against the wall and heaved, but the whirlpool edged her farther into the closet, now a black void. Her squeals climbed above the rushing winds as Tommy continued to tug her arm. He seized the handcuffs from his belt and secured the restraints around their wrists.

Just as he gained an inch from the hole, the lamp smacked his skull, and his hold slipped. Mindy disappeared into the vortex with a loud shriek and dragged Tommy along for the ride.

A raindrop met her cheek, and then another. Mindy fluttered her eyes and stared at the dark clouds. Her head spun as she desperately tried to force her body to commit to her will. She steadied her muscles and stood, her thoughts rummaging for answers.

Tall trees masked the air, climbing to the sky for escape. Thunder rumbled in the distance, and a strong wind brushed her face. Lightning briefly illuminated the woods, allowing her to gawk at the swaying shrubbery dancing along the storm's prelude.

Mindy shivered and rubbed her arms. Her fingers brushed the silver handcuff clinging to her wrist; the set was severed at the chain. She inhaled uneasily to shout Tommy's name, but her voice caught in her throat, fearing the unknown in the shadows. She took three quick breaths, fighting her fear and preparing her lungs.

"Tommy!" she screamed, hoping to hitch a ride on the wind's current. "Hello?"

The reply was another roar across the heavens, followed by a faint, hellish howl.

The skies broke, and rain heavily descended to the earth, sending Mindy under a giant tree for shelter. She stood motionless, rapidly scanning her surroundings with each illumination, hoping to gain insight or see Tommy running in the distance. Her peripheral glimpsed a woman's silhouette nestled against a neighboring tree. Mindy held her breath and closed her eyes when the light dissipated. She could feel the shadow's stare blazing into her face from behind the scenes; goosebumps erupted over her entire body.

The light flashed, prompting Mindy to involuntarily open her eyes for exploration. A pale-faced, decrepit woman shrieked inches from Mindy's face; her white eyes glaring with pus and maggots, her skin cracked and ostensibly transparent. Mindy scuffled from the apparition, certain she would only take two steps and collapse, but her shoes found traction and propelled her into a sprint.

Tree branches reached for her through the wind and clamped onto her jacket, temporarily hindering her escape. She imagined herself in the *Snow White* cartoon, running through the woods with no sense of direction after her encounter with the Huntsman. But there were no friendly animals or awkward dwarfs to assist in Mindy's quest, and her handsome prince was MIA. She twisted free and caught her heel in a muddy patch, catapulting her body several feet before landing face down on stable ground.

Mindy reared and stared at a deserted road. Her eyes widened and searched for headlights from either direction, praying this would be the road back to civilization, but the night remained void. She picked a direction and splashed down the double-yellow line.

Exhaustion soon forced her to pause. She stooped to slow her breathing and settle her racing heart. The bandaged graffiti stung, but adrenaline kept the burn from completely registering with her tensed nerves. She continued inhaling deeply until she gained control of her senses.

A low growl arose from behind, and an odd-shaped figure emerged onto the road, watching Mindy as she scanned the highway. When the electric pulse lit the sky, she clearly saw the creature with sharp teeth and pointed horns.

The Deer Man.

Mindy retreated a couple steps, and the beast trotted in her direction. She turned and bolted down the lost highway.

"Somebody help me!" Mindy screamed, traversing the desolate road. "Tommy!"

The Deer Man howled and dashed toward its prey.

Mindy pushed her body, her mind desperately searching for a resolution. She saw a heap lying in the road ahead and abruptly stopped at Luke Sheldon's mutilated body, his stomach gashed and hollowed.

Mindy's throat felt hoarse and her lungs burned, but she managed another blood-curdling shriek as she approached a body hanging upside down from a rope. Dean Carrington's corpse swung in the storm's current, his blue skin stained with his own entrails.

She turned away from his marred body and vomited, her heart dropping to her stomach. She looked behind her—momentarily forgetting her own peril—and saw the charging monster. The road seemed to expand indefinitely through the mountains, and no cars were coming to her rescue, so she made a split-second decision to lose the beast in the woods. She cut through the bushes and debris at top speed, avoiding the thick tree trunks as tears swept her cheeks.

She hid behind a cedar tree after a few moments, unable to locate the creature. Her cuts bled profusely, her bandage now stained crimson.

From somewhere below, she heard a faint voice beckoning, "Help me."

Startled, Mindy held her breath and focused her hearing for a direction as a female repeated her plea.

"Hello?" Mindy yelled.

"Please, hurry!"

Mindy darted through the setting, anxious to find the orator. The repeating cries glided through the woods until she found a partially concealed cave; a faint light burned at the end of its long corridor. Mindy timidly traversed the musky passageway, afraid a false move would alarm the mountain's demons. The light deepened as she trekked toward the strip's end, which concluded in a grimy room with burning torches. Bones littered the ground, human skulls draped the walls, and the grotesque smell of death filled her nostrils and turned her stomach. Markings similar to the one on her abdomen defaced the ceiling, sketched in blood. Five torches outlined a dirt mound. Tommy rested on the altar, his hands and feet tied to stakes.

"Tommy," Mindy whispered.

Bones crunched and rattled under her wet shoes as she slid to his side. He was unconscious, dried blood crusted on his face. She wrestled with the knots as he slowly opened his eyes at the sound of her voice.

"Mindy?" he asked, disoriented. "What's going on?"

She untied his right hand. "Tommy, thank God. We've got to get out of here."

"Where are we?"

"I don't know, but we have to go before—"

A woman's laugh vibrated the skull wall, and Mindy's back

tingled with chills, as if someone were walking over her future grave. She eyeballed the corridor and squinted to focus her stare as a familiar face rounded the corner.

"Lenoir?"

Lenoir Sheldon leisurely walked into the room, a smile drawn on her blue lips, her dirty disheveled hair glued to her skull. Old blood stained her tattered sweater, and her skin was pale and slightly transparent, but she moved with precision.

A look of satisfaction displayed across Lenoir's brow. "Mindy McAllister. I've waited a long time for this moment."

"You're . . . alive?" Mindy became shock-stilled, momentarily forgetting her struggling boyfriend.

"Do I look alive to you?"

Mindy didn't reply but remained focused on the undead while slowly receding to Tommy's right foot. She placed her fingers on the knot and pulled.

"I wouldn't do that if I were you," Lenoir warned. "I've got big plans for your new boyfriend."

"Lenoir, we have to get out of here. There's a literal monster outside."

"Oh, you mean James? Don't worry about him. He'll be along shortly."

Mindy's eyes trembled. The mystery of the four missing students had been solved, but the truth was more terrifying than she could have possibly imagined, and she immediately wished she could forget.

Lenoir laughed. "I've had so much fun torturing you tonight. I waited for the perfect moment to make my move, but I didn't think you were ever going to invite your handsome friend to stay with you. Daddy didn't approve?"

"Tommy has nothing to do with this."

Lenoir's appearance morphed into the decrepit woman from the forest and screeched like a banshee preparing for battle; her eyes were white and veiny. Mindy ran behind the altar and quickly loosened Tommy's left hand. Lenoir's apparition charged into Mindy, slamming her against the wall.

"This is all your fault!" Lenoir shrieked, returning to her normal form. "You ruined my relationship with Dean. He broke my heart, but he got his comeuppance, just as you soon will. You're a selfish, manipulative bitch, and now it's time to pay."

"I'm manipulative? I think you take the cake on that one," Mindy said, her body quivering, trying to distract Lenoir long enough for Tommy to finish untying the knot. "I loved Dean, I did, but he loved you more, so how is any of this my fault?"

Lenoir stood in front of a half-decayed body; the corpse's clothing matched her attire.

"You never loved him," Lenoir said. "You were only interested in one thing. If you hadn't seduced him, he never would've lied to me, we never would've gone on that road trip, and we'd still be alive."

"Lenoir, I'm sorry for the way things happened, but don't punish Tommy for my mistakes. Please, let him go."

Lenoir laughed. "I'm afraid I can't do that, Min. That's not how this works. You see, you're going to die, and he is going to be my bitch."

Mindy dashed toward Lenoir and, to her surprise, hooked a fist to the redhead's semi-solid face. Lenoir cackled, relishing the clash, and plunged her translucent hand into Mindy's chest. Lenoir's icy fingers grasped her beating heart.

Lenoir's eyes widened with delight as she squeezed harder. "I was just going to let James kill you, but this is much more rewarding."

Mindy gasped as her chest burst in inexplicable pain and tried to push away Lenoir, but the grip was ironclad.

Tommy freed his last restraint and stood beside the altar with his revolver extended. A gunshot loudly reverberated throughout the crypt. Without removing her stance, Lenoir raised her free palm, and the bullet reversed course, cutting through Tommy's shoulder. He fell to the ground, holding the wound.

Mindy's chest ached, and her head felt distant. She was about to lose consciousness, but the grip suddenly released and was followed by a shocked yelp. Mindy inhaled deeply as her heart regained a painful rhythm. She coughed against the dingy air, tears burning her eyes.

Lenoir struggled against Dean Carrington's hold. She pulled at his arm laced around her neck and thrashed like a wildcat caught in a hunter's net. Mindy copiously blinked her eyes, but the image remained unchanged.

"D-Dean?"

"You have to burn her bones," he said, struggling to keep Lenoir restrained. "Burn down this whole place."

"Dean, I—"

"I'm sorry—to both of you—for everything," Dean said, struggling to keep Lenoir controlled. "Do it!"

Tommy grabbed two torches and touched the flames to Lenoir's rotting carcass, her ragged clothes and hair catching the initial sparks. Lenoir twisted in Dean's grasp and bellowed as her spirit erupted in blue flames. Dean smiled at Mindy and mouthed, *Thank you*, as he and Lenoir dissolved into the air.

Tommy gathered the remaining torches and stacked them together on Lenoir's body. Once the flames spread, he and Mindy limped along the corridor and into the humid night.

Tommy stroked her hair and kissed her trembling lips. They rested against an overturned oak, and Mindy glanced at the cave's entrance every couple of seconds to ensure nothing emerged. She was scared to relax, afraid her body would decommission for days if given the chance, leaving Tommy to haul both of them to safety on his own. She focused on her injured boyfriend, whose own tears escaped his unsteady eyes.

"Are you all right?"

She smiled through her own pain. "I'm okay. Are you?"

"Yeah, it's just a shoulder wound."

The wailing of a siren came into range, echoing louder as a car approached above the destitute couple. Blue lights flickered across the trees, and a spotlight scanned the ravine. Their faces glowed with relief, and they quickly climbed the Catskill toward the vehicle. The light found the bloody duo and followed them to the road. An overweight officer exited the car, keeping one hand on his hip while blinding their vision with his flashlight.

"Tommy Wallace? Mindy McAllister?"

"Yes?" Tommy answered.

"My name is Sheriff Murphy. You're safe now."

"How did you know about us? No one knows where we are. *I* don't even know where we are."

"Son, you're in the Catskill Mountains. New York State. We received a call from a woman by the name of Juanita Sinclair in Connecticut. She told us you were in trouble and where to possibly find you. I wasn't sure I believed her story, but, by the looks of it, she was right."

Sheriff Murphy ushered them into the back seat, turned off the flashing lights, and made a U-turn. Mindy collapsed into Tommy's chest and closed her eyes, taking deep breaths to steady her nerves. Tommy's heartbeat soothed her worries and brought her to a restful state.

"So what happened out there?" the sheriff asked, breaking the silence. "Did you see it?"

Tommy looked at the sheriff through the divider and caught his eye in the rearview mirror.

"We saw plenty tonight." Tommy retorted. "Could you narrow that down a bit?"

"Deer Man. Is it real?"

"No," Tommy replied. "There was no Deer Man."

The sheriff huffed his disappointment and turned on the radio. Deep Purple rocked the stereo with "Smoke on the Water" as he sped his passengers down the mountain, lightly tapping the steering wheel in rhythm to the beat.

Tommy rubbed his sleeping girlfriend's arm and kissed her

scalp. His muscles were exhausted from the night's events. His eyelids closed, lulled by the tires' roar and Mindy's warming body.

"What the—" Sheriff Murphy yelled.

The car grew weightless, and the pair crashed against the partition. The car careened into an embankment, mangling against a giant Eastern Red Cedar. Tommy and Mindy slowly repositioned themselves through the pain, blood escaping their orifices. A small engine fire outlined Sheriff Murphy's crushed body; a tree branch impaled his head through the broken windshield.

Tommy banged against the door and busted his right shoulder after the fourth ram. He then noticed the divider was bent and rigorously wiggled the structure as smoke seeped through the windshield, blurring their vision and filling their lungs.

A pair of antlers shattered Mindy's window, propelling her into Tommy's body. The Deer Man snarled and snapped its teeth as Mindy's screams pierced the car's interior. The creature clutched her foot and yanked her across the broken glass.

Tommy grabbed her arm, extended his gun at the beast, and squeezed the trigger.

"No!" she screamed.

Blood gushed from the hole in the Deer Man's forehead, and James Conrad collapsed out of view.

Mindy's body shook uncontrollably, showered with the monster's blood. She turned to Tommy and screamed louder as his eyes glowed red.

"What's . . . happening . . . to me?"

His head throbbed with each heartbeat, wincing his brow and gritting his teeth. His lungs rapidly gasped for air.

"You're becoming one of them," she cried. "Juanita said the curse passes to whomever kills the last Deer Man. James must've been the last one."

Tommy groaned, sweat gushing from every pore of his body. "You have to . . . end it. P-please."

He placed the gun in Mindy's juddering hands. She looked at

the weapon and then back at Tommy; tears exploded from her puffy eyes. She violently shook her head in protest.

"Tommy, I-I-I can't do that. No!"

"If you . . . kill me . . . it'll be over. The curse won't pass to you . . . if the transformation doesn't happen, right? Please . . . don't let me become one of them."

She examined the gun and held her breath to stall the inevitable breakdown.

"I love you, Mindy. I only regret . . . not telling you s-sooner."

Her heart plunged to the depths of her stomach and shattered into jagged fragments, like the glass covering the seats. She forced a half-hearted smile, wanting his last image of her to be one of strength.

"I love you too, Tommy, with all of my heart."

She leaned against the man she loved and kissed his hot, quivering lips. He smiled as she retracted, nodded his head, and closed his eyes. Mindy raised the gun and steadied her aim at Tommy's forehead, her heart leaping from her chest. She took a long, deep breath, fluttered her eyes to clear her watery vision, and squeezed the trigger.

The *pop* deafened her ears but couldn't drown her screams. Tommy's body lay crumpled on the seat; his blood saturated the windows.

Mindy dropped the gun on the floorboard and howled into the dawn.

M.R. Ward was born and raised in Knoxville, Tennessee. "The Road Back" is the sequel to his first short story, "The Open Road," which is included in the anthology, *A Journey of Words*. His third story, "Tootsie," will be published in Smoking Pen Press's 2018 anthology, *A Wink & A Smile*.

He is currently working on his first novel and has more bizarre tales planned for the future.

He is an avid fan of horror movies, loves dogs, and can't start his day without coffee.

Follow him at www.facebook.com/mrwardauthor.

THE WOMAN NO ONE SEES

Signature *Leah McNaughton Lederman*

Esther was fourteen when she joined the ranks of the family cleaning business alongside her mother and older sister, Johanna. Year after year, they'd pile into the minivan with the vacuum cleaner, dust mops and brooms, and various spray bottles organized haphazardly into buckets.

Squeegees and feather dusters poked akimbo from the mop pail like some sort of grotesque housecleaning mascot. Her mom and Johanna called it the Mop Lady and liked to laugh about it—"Did the Mop Lady take that gum?"—but when Esther caught a glimpse of the Mop Lady in the corner of her eye, it startled her. Every time.

She had a cleaning caddy for herself that she kept neatly organized, armed with the supplies she'd need to dust and polish any surface. In her head, Esther called it the cleaning holster and sometimes entertained herself having Windex quickdraw contests with her reflection.

Tonight, they were cleaning some building that had been repurposed at least three times, judging from the faded shapes on its front where different businesses had hung their logos.

No matter what the structure, it was their job to clean it, to make it look like no one had ever been in there.

Vivian wanted to shift her chair farther from the woman next to her, but they were those interlocked hotel conference chairs, so she was stuck. Normally, the personal space thing didn't bother her so much, but she was here trying to take notes, trying to further her future, and this lady kept muttering nasty comments under her breath about the speaker, Allen Engle, and "this bullshit pyramid scheme."

It's not like that, Vivian wanted to hiss back at the woman. Allen was a great spokesperson with a powerful presence. She could admit that the products sometimes left a little to be desired, but mediocrity didn't bother her. It wasn't any better or worse than what she'd found at big-box stores.

"We're selling things people want, and we're bringing it directly to them," Allen had told her. "The truth is, it's not all magnificent. But we are consumers of crap, let's just face it. We need these products to fill the part of our soul we're trying to stuff Cheetos into, you know?"

Oh, she knew. He didn't have to tell her twice. No one needed these cosmetics, these facial masks, these hair crimper-slash-curling-irons or three-brushes-in-one. But they were marketed with "a nurturing care and a personal touch that no store could ever hope to duplicate." Even if it was a line from the sales guide, it was one she believed in.

Like Allen always said, "Vehemence was a family, and it was a family dedicated to making women feel good about themselves. Everything else in the world made them feel like they fell short. Here was something that could really empower them."

Vivian wasn't entirely convinced she needed a straightening iron to empower herself, but she didn't know what else would, aside from maybe being the one who was selling them.

And so she sold. She sold enough in the first year to attract the attention of some of the higher ups, and she'd been invited to two regional conferences now. This time, they'd even paid for her room, and she was going to share a meal with a few of the speakers, including Allen. She'd bought a mock-turtleneck sweater from the consignment shop just for the occasion.

Vivian knew better than to lie to herself about why she was so excited. Allen was a charismatic speaker, and his looks added to his allure. The first thing she'd noticed about him was his dark, flirtatious eyebrows set in contrast to his short sandy hair. He must have known they were his best feature because he used them to emphasize and exaggerate his expressions.

God, I'm such a cliché, she thought, shaking her head. Single mom at a product sales conference, getting her vitals twisted up over some collared shirt and tie.

And khakis.

They were a machine, the three of them. When Mrs. Eisenmann had called them about the new property, to warn them it was high maintenance and that they should set aside at least two hours to clean it, their smug smiles were warranted.

"Don't you worry, Mrs. E." Esther's mom flicked her cigarette ashes into the bowl by the phone. "You know me and my girls will have the whole place sparkling in under an hour."

Some places were amazed the three women could complete the job so quickly. The manager at the law office went so far as calling the security company to verify their log in and log out times.

They had a rhythm, that was all—even in the way they entered the building. Each plotted the quickest course to their destination, and they mobilized, turning on lights and turning off alarm systems in a methodical cadence, then getting to work.

Mom handled the bathrooms, Johanna went straight for the dust mop, and Esther took care of the trash. When the last of the garbage had been emptied, she'd whip out some polish and a microfiber rag from her bucket and march into the offices. No photo frame untouched; keyboards and mousepads wiped—then lifted, to reach the surface beneath them.

They weaved around one another, offering encouragements when there was something particularly gross or unheard of and making comments like, "Uh oh, the popcorn bandit is back!"

They knew the secretary was off her diet again when the floor under her desk was littered with the pethy microwaved snack.

Allen stood up halfway and waved to her from his table in the corner of the hotel restaurant. His teeth practically sparkled in the dim lighting.

"Vivian, hello!" He touched her elbow and placed a friendly kiss on her cheek.

The gesture seemed exotic to Vivian; it was something people did in Europe or in the movies. She'd been expecting a handshake and now was more flustered than she wanted to admit.

"You'll have to forgive Shawn. She got called back to Cleveland this morning. She really wanted to sit down and talk with you, too—" He frowned and pointed at the look of doubt on Vivian's face.

She didn't believe him, but she certainly liked the way it sounded.

"No, no, it's true. And they're talking about you back at HQ. The rising star!" He raised his eyebrows and gave the waiter a nod from across the room. "I hope you don't mind white."

"White?" Since the peck on the cheek, Vivian had only managed to communicate through an awkward series of grimaces and bashful smiles. *Use your words, Viv.* "Oh, wine? Yes—yes, that sounds lovely. Thank you."

Allen sipped from his water glass, never taking his eyes from her.

Certain he was waiting for her to say something else, Vivian offered a few head nods and inhalations that never quite formed into words. The whole thing—the kiss, the lighting, the wine—it didn't feel like the "business success dinner" the Vehemence secretary had described on the phone.

"Vivian?"

"Yes?"

Allen gave her an appraising look. The homely brunette was very nearly receding into her turtleneck sweater, head down and shoulders hunched. He completely understood why Leonard thought she'd be the perfect person for the job. The perfect mixture of self-doubt and self-loathing, plus a dash of hot mess.

"Please don't be nervous." He smiled softly to himself, remembering that he was the perfect person for his job, too. The finesse.

Thinking his expression was meant as a comfort, she took it. It worked, too. She felt heartened. "I swear, Allen, I'm not usually this awkward. I just, well . . ."

The waiter filled their wine glasses, and Vivian stared at the microscopic beads of water forming a cool cloud on the outside of the glass. She watched Allen's eyebrows waggle with their own vocabulary as he first took a curious sip, then an appreciative one.

Once he had set his glass down, she counted slowly in her head all the way to ten before taking her own first sip. The crisp liquid's bite on her tongue was worth the wait. She set the glass down and began counting again in her head, being sure to nod at intervals and "*mmhmm*" as Allen began his monologue. Three sips in, she felt the warmth of the alcohol spreading its hot fingers around her blood vessels. It climbed them like ropes, hand over hand, into each of her extremities.

"Vivian? Is everything okay?"

She took another swallow of wine before realizing he was waiting for a response to something he'd said. "Yes, I'm sorry. There's—you're saying there's a new product line?"

"Well, a new demographic. And you're the perfect candidate for launching its inaugural run right here in town. What do you think? Want to hear more?"

Vivian nodded one more time, this time with a wide, warm smile covering her face.

"That's what I hoped for, Viv." Allen motioned to the waiter again. "Let's order some dinner. You like crab cakes?"

It had been about four weeks—four separate cleanings—of the new place when Mrs. Eisenmann stopped by their house to tell them the facility manager was nervous about the size of their cleaning entourage.

"I told him you all were our best team,"—Mrs. Eisenmann took the cup of tea Esther's mother offered—"but I guess he's the nervous type. Start-up company and all."

Johanna rolled her eyes. "Old Mr. Uglykids just has pent up energy."

The older woman nearly slid off the couch, eyeballing Esther's giggling sister. "*What* did you call him?"

"Ha! You didn't know? We got pet names for all of them." Johanna counted off on her fingers. "There's Popcorn Lady, Casanova, Hoarder . . . now we have Mr. Uglykids."

Esther smiled and said quietly, "He's a great addition to the collection."

Johanna's giggle morphed into an ugly squawk. "Have you met the dude who's in charge? Oh my God, the pictures on his desk." She snorted again. "They are *startlingly* ugly children. No wonder he's got a beef. I'd be mad too, if my kids looked like that."

Esther snorted in spite of herself, and the sisters laughed even harder when they made eye contact with one another.

"*Girls!*" Their mother's smoky baritone startled them, and they both sat up straight. Once their mother was satisfied they'd calmed down, she turned her attention back to her employer. "I don't understand. He doesn't want all three of us there?"

It was Mrs. Eisenmann's turn to roll her eyes. "It's a strange facility, and he seems a strange man, but he pays the top rate. Can just one of you clean it?" She set her tea down on the table, throwing a sidelong glance at the teenagers. "And ladies, no more nicknames, okay?"

The second their mother stepped towards the front door with Mrs. Eisenmann, Johanna and Esther melted off the couch and ran from the room in hysterics.

The waiter filled their wine glasses again when he brought out their dinners. Allen went with the crab cakes and onion rings; Vivian supposed she might look sensible if she ordered a salad, so she went with the Cobb. She tried to eat it one tiny piece at a time like the actresses in romantic comedies. But wouldn't they do the thing where they order a giant greasy burger and not gain a pound and go into hysterics after belching at the table? What kind of woman did Allen prefer?

"I'm telling you, you have got to try one of these." Allen bit down on one of the onion rings, and the onion slid right out of the crusty casing, giving him a greasy slap on the chin. He wiped it with a grunt.

Vivian scraped at some lettuce. "Oh, I've got plenty here, thanks. But tell me more about these new products—"

"*Mmm,*" Allen interrupted her, though his mouth was full of food. He put his finger up to indicate she should wait while he swallowed, which he did with a painful grimace. "Sorry, hot bite. There is no new product. We're just switching up our audience."

"Oh?" She popped a cherry tomato in her mouth and hoped it looked cute.

"That's right. We here at Vehemence, we're a family, you know? We want—" He stopped mid-sentence and hung his head. "Gosh, just listen to me. I don't need to go into sales mode with you. You're already a part of the family, you know that."

He flashed a smile and reached across the table to pat her hand.

Vivian was halfway through glass number two. His touch was

warm, and she leaned forward as an invitation for more of that sort of thing.

"You don't need to sell me anything, Allen. Just tell me what to do."

"What we want to do is cater specifically to lower income brackets. The market's locked on your standard suburban housewife. But what about the women who get overlooked, the ones no one seems to see?" This time he grabbed her hand with both of his and looked into her face. "I see you, Vivian. I know it's a struggle, raising a child by yourself—"

Vivian pulled away reflexively at this, using the hand he'd touched to take another gulp of wine. Marky was upstairs in the room right now, watching *Seinfeld* reruns. She couldn't afford a sitter, and besides, neither one of them wanted to pass up the indoor pool and free HBO.

"So, you're marketing to single moms?"

"It's more than that, Vivian. Bigger. *The women no one seems to see."* He paused for effect and Vivian nodded, trying to understand. "Sure, it's the single moms. But it's the ones in the programs, too, your alkies, junkies. Battered women in shelters."

Vivian was mid-sip when he mentioned "alkies" and looked up at him from her glass, but Allen was lost in his pitch.

"These women deserve access to our products—we want to take our business to them. It's sort of a 'fake it till you make it.' If they can feel better about themselves on the outside, maybe things will improve for them on the inside."

The waiter approached to clear their plates, and Allen motioned for two more glasses of wine, though he didn't take his eyes off of Vivian while she processed the information. She had a face like she smelled something funny but couldn't quite place it. He wondered how many aces he'd have to pull out before she agreed. She would agree soon enough. And not even with an ace—maybe not even a face card.

"It's not like they don't have access to our products, I don't think. It's just . . . it's not a priority. These women got a different view on what comes first."

"Of course, of course." Allen nodded gravely. "But don't you think they deserve to have the choice? It's not on their radar, because it's too far away. We want to put the product in their proximity."

Vivian gestured with her wine glass as she spoke. "Okay. But how exactly do you plan to target them? You're saying they're not already in the sales funnel?" She hoped that was the right terminology.

"That's where you come in. We want you to do a little . . . outreach."

Vivian took a few swallows of wine, then set the glass down and traced her fingers on the stem.

"I don't know, Allen. Am I even qualified? And I'm not sure I have the flexibility . . ." She trailed off and took another drink.

His partner, Leonard, had been right about the wine, Allen thought, watching her wave down the waiter. The woman really could put it away.

"It's delicate, but from what you've told me about your background, you might have some . . . perspective."

Vivian looked down at her hands. It was time to take a step closer.

"Are you worried about time away from . . . it's Mark, isn't it?"

He watched as her eyes snapped up. *Bingo.*

"How did you—? I never told you his name."

"Shawn told me." He gave a little wave of his hand. "Like I said, we've been talking about you. He's upstairs now, right—in the room?"

Vivian froze. "Wait, what? I mean, I checked into it, and by law—"

Allen leaned forward and took her hands, both of them this time. "Hey, hey. Vivian, it's okay. Look at me." He waited until her eyes landed on his face, then continued. "We want you to have this opportunity because you and Mark deserve it. It's going to change things for both of you. Say, change of title, give you a spot on the payroll?"

She sat back in her chair, her thoughts a bit soupy after the third glass of wine. Maybe it was the fourth.

"So, I get a permanent position. You—the company—gets to move in a new direction with a new demographic."

Allen gave a curt nod but said nothing. He stared at her intently, his eyebrows raised in question.

"What if it doesn't work? What if I fail?"

"Honestly, Viv? I don't see how you could. Let's shake on it."

Vivian took a sip from her freshly filled wine glass and pointed at him, glass still in hand. "And here I thought you was going to kiss me again."

When the dusting was finished, Esther would typically join her sister with a mop, the two of them swaying in a silent, focused rhythm as the soggy tendrils of Mop Lady's hair rolled languidly across the surface of the floor. It made Esther think of the woman with the alabaster jar, using her hair to wash Jesus' feet. The white noise of the vacuum would hold them all in their own thoughts, the two daughters mop-dancing, their mother pushing the sweeper back and forth with a pendulous flourish.

There was none of that, now that Esther was cleaning the facility by herself. She didn't mind in the least; in fact, she welcomed the solitude. It let her snoop a little. Usually, if she even looked at a picture too long, her mom would bark from across the room or land a heavy palm across the back of Esther's head.

But now, she did more than look at pictures. She took them from their frames to see what had been scrawled on the back; she rooted gently through unlocked drawers and peeked in the fridge. All of these people, leading their lives completely unaware of her.

At the same time, though, they traveled in separate dimensions than she did. They were just as invisible to her. The thing she daydreamed about more than anything else was what she would do if she ever ran into one of the faces from the photos in person.

Out front, the minivan honked. She'd taken too long. Snapping to attention, she conducted a guilty walkthrough, inspecting her work and eyeing carpeted corners for any fuzzy speck that would malign their cleaning reputation.

And there was one, right there along the back wall leading to their janitor's closet. Esther bent to pick it up but saw it was just a miniscule blotch of sinkwater-gray paint. She scratched at it, but it was good and stuck. It must have splashed there when they painted the wall. From the looks of it, it had been a while.

Her mom would be impatient, so she'd have to leave it for the next time. She ran out to the car, and as they drove away, she still wondered about the people who worked there during the day. She wondered if they thought about her.

That's when she noticed the section at the back of the building without any windows. Esther mentally traced her route through the building. Each of the three offices on that side had a window, and then, if she were walking down the hall, it would turn and lead to their janitor closet. When she'd been standing in that hallway by the newly painted wall, she thought that was the end of the building. Here, from the outside, she saw that it extended beyond that. There was easily enough space for another room, maybe two.

It was harder than Vivian thought it would be. Over the next several weeks, she scoured the area for women's shelters, psychiatric wards, places where she might find the women Allen wanted her to find.

At the local behavioral health center, she didn't even make it past registration; if she had moved a little more slowly, she was fairly certain the nurse would have kicked her on the way out. The ladies at the women's shelter office listened to Vivian's spiel and handled a few of the products.

One of the outreach coordinators, Linnea, was a stick-thin little thing with a pierced nose and jet-black hair so straight it looked like daggers exiting the Celtic hair barrette. She picked up the three-in-one hair styler.

"This looks like a fancy hair doohickey. It doesn't just fall apart after a few tries though, does it?"

"Oh, absolutely not. I've had mine for two years now, and it's what I used to flip my hair out before coming here." Vivian patted her hair. "You really need to see how quickly it heats up, too. Do you mind if I plug it in?"

"Sandy?" The young woman threw a questioning look at the mousy, brittle-haired woman leaning against the doorframe, and Vivian guessed that Sandy was in charge.

"We're slow enough. You want to play dress-up, you go ahead."

Sandy's pleated jeans didn't fit her quite right, making it the faded-green T-shirt's job to cover the flesh waves spilling out over the waistband.

Linnea and Vivian crowded the electrical outlet like co-conspirators, making their plans for Linnea's hair.

"So, plait the hair this way if you want to straighten it, turn it on the side for a flip-out . . ." Vivian reached back into the box. "And look, it's really almost four-in-one, since you can attach this crimper."

"I hear crimping is coming back in," Linnea said, laughing. She let out a giggle when she released the handle and found three inches of her hair perfectly ridged like a potato chip.

Sandy rolled her eyes as she watched them, but there was a smile on her face. "Yeah, our ladies might get a kick out of this. A self-esteem boost, confidence at job interviews. Your company—what's it called again, Adamant?—is doing a great thing, making these donations."

"It's Vehement." Vivian frowned. "I'm sorry, maybe there's been a misunderstanding. We're rolling out a reduced-price feature for women in difficult situations, but we're not exactly *donating* . . ."

The tenor of the room changed then. Linnea set the crimper down and stole a look at Sandy, who had unfolded her arms and was now leaning forward on the desk where Vivian sat.

"Look, I appreciate what you think you're trying to do, but you're missing the mark."

Linnea nodded in agreement. "We run on *donations*, and hell, we're barely running. Companies giving us their discontinued or expired makeup. Rich ladies give us their old suits. Half our ladies are lucky if they have a winter coat. You want them to pay ten dollars for a—" She scoffed, midsentence. "A *hair crimper*?"

Vivian started to gather her things, the shame radiating from her like heat waves. They were right. They were absolutely right, and that's what she had tried to tell Allen, but he wouldn't listen.

She managed a stifled, "Thank you for your time, ladies," before leaving the room, her head buried in her bag like she was searching for her keys. She was trying to hide the tears she knew were coming.

Not so many years before, she'd been in a facility just like this one. St. Margaret's. That was when the state had taken Marky from her, after Brian had died. The ladies at Maggie's had given her a place to sleep, and volunteers ran workshops on job application skills, parenting. They'd given her a way to stand on her own two feet again.

Here she was, thinking she'd come back to a women's shelter as some sort of success story, or like, her way of giving back. And the whole thing had fallen flat. She'd screwed the whole thing up. Of course they were right. This was a horrible place to give a pitch. It was completely inappropriate.

But what was she going to do? Vivian had visited local AA anon and NA chapters, the hospitals, hell, even a few bookstores. None of them wanted anything to do with her "skeezy pyramid scheme," as the bookstore owner had called it.

It was going to be a tough phone call to Allen and Leonard the next morning, that much she was sure of.

Dusting was Esther's favorite. No giant pail of soapy water to slosh down the hall, no extension cord to unravel. Not even an On button. Just a light rag, dampened with Windex—sometimes orange cleaner.

It smelled slightly sweet and slightly sharp, and she secretly loved when she smelled it on her clothes at the end of the night, mixed in with the little bit of sweat she'd worked up. Sometimes she'd set it to Spray and give one pump into the air before walking through it, like it was Bulgari perfume. She was pretty sure Bulgari was expensive because it came in a very fancy bottle and lay inside an even fancier box. Esther knew this because the receptionist kept some in her top drawer.

After cleaning the place by herself the first time, Esther took a piece of candy from the bowl on the desk and sat in the spinny chair. The box's lid shimmered from inside the partially open drawer. It wouldn't close completely on account of all of the other junk the lady kept in there.

In subsequent weeks, Esther would carefully lift the lid and remove the bottle from its perfectly molded indentation. It was heavy and crescendoed into a swirled mob of clear crystal at the top.

She'd close her eyes and breathe deeply at the opening, inhaling her way to some gondola in a foreign country where people rode bikes everywhere, and the car horns sounded different, and the pigeons were white instead of gray. Then she'd wrap her finger in an unsoiled portion of her rag and Windex her fingerprints from the bottle before placing it sweetly back into its case, making sure the nozzle pointed the same direction as she'd found it.

Her heart always ached when she walked away. She was a ghost, as a cleaner, an unthanked face who dealt with people's personal belongings on a daily basis. But this particular item she coveted from a place deep within her she had not known existed; a place that was as foreign to her as the white pigeons in her perfume-induced daydream.

"We're not philanthropists, sweetheart."

Leonard's voice had a way of making Vivian understand how a dog felt when someone petted it backwards against the grain. It sent a shudder to her kneecaps and back. She'd never met him in person, but Allen brought him in on some of their calls. Something in his voice seethed contempt. She could never say the right thing, as far as he was concerned.

"No, I don't think we should be giving product away, neither. But this model isn't really working, or our approach—"

"This is *your* approach, isn't it? We've given you a lot of freedom and leeway—and a hell of a paycheck—but we're not seeing any results."

There was an audible sigh and then some muffled sounds on the other end, like someone had covered the phone's speaker. Allen's voice came over next. Gentler. More patient. Vivian hugged her phone closer to her ear to drink it in. She hadn't been given a lot of kindness over the past few weeks.

"I told you I wanted to reach a new group, the women no one sees. You can reach them. We need you to reach them. So, what can you do differently, Viv?"

This stopped her. She'd tried to straighten it all out in her head, but the truth was, she wasn't so business smart. And she'd needed a few drinks to steel herself for this conversation, so she wasn't at her sharpest.

"Well, I-I . . . I was thinking . . ." She was thinking that, for the life of her, she still didn't understand why they'd tasked her with something so monumental.

Leonard snorted. "You're done thinking. It's not your forte. Here's the plan: You need to get us a test group. Asses in seats. Ten of them."

Allen cut in again to explain. "We want to have a product demo, and we want your ladies to be our guinea pigs—don't use that phrase with *them*, of course. But listen, when I said I didn't think you'd fail, I meant it." He paused, then his voice gained a sharper edge. "There's no room for it."

Vivian was sitting on the edge of the tub, hunched over. Her insides squirmed. A test group? What product demo? This wasn't what she'd been asked to do.

She passed Marky on her way to the kitchen. He was sprawled on the couch in his dad's old Browns jersey, laughing and talking into his headset to a few of his friends as she grabbed the bottle from the top of the fridge. He was too busy scrolling through his phone to even notice the aliens from his video game splattered on the screen.

She took a hot swig without bothering to find a glass.

"I don't want to let you down, Allen. Leonard. You want new clients, and I'll—"

Leonard interrupted her. "Forget clients. I'll speak slowly so you understand. We need disadvantaged females. Your job is to get us a demo group."

Vivian felt the anger rising in her. Her mentors at St. Margaret's had told her not to let people treat her like she was stupid. She deserved better.

"I can do my job better if you wouldn't change the objective midstream!"

This time Allen's voice was as sharp as Leonard's. "The objective has changed, Viv, since we're done with your screwing around. Just get asses in seats, ten of them, in two weeks. This has to happen because my ass is riding on it, which means your ass is riding on it."

Vivian sank against the wall, staring at the ceiling with big bubble tears in her eyes. She couldn't deliver. It was that simple.

She sniffled and gave a breathy, "Okay, Allen. I'll try."

"Try?" Leonard's sneer was palpable in his tone. "It's been

pretty nice with this hefty new paycheck, hasn't it? Fattened up that chunky boy of yours some more. What is he, twelve?"

Her stomach went cold, and Vivian felt the chilly tingle rise up her spine to her neck where the hairs rose up like antenna, sniffing the air. That was the thing that had been digging in her mind like a splinter ever since having dinner with Allen at the hotel. She'd thought about it a few times since then, thought about how she drank too much and flirted like a buffoon. Thought about whether or not she'd ever talked to Shawn, or anyone, about Marky. She was pretty sure she hadn't. And she sure as hell hadn't told anyone that he was a chunky twelve-year-old.

Something was wrong. Who were these men?

"This conversation is making me uncomfortable. What are you trying to say?"

"What we're trying to say is that we don't like to be disappointed," Leonard said.

"What the hell, guys? I thought this was a family. Isn't that what you're always spouting?"

Allen let out a slow laugh. "And tell *Marky* that the Browns suck."

The line was dead.

This wasn't good.

Vivian took off her hoodie and threw it to the floor, then jammed the faucet on cold, full blast. Bending over the countertop, she dipped her head into the sink and felt the water gush onto her scalp. It ran down her face, making icy rivulets of foundation and mascara on her cheeks.

There isn't time to waste, she told herself.

"Marky?" she called, walking into the living room. "I'm going to need your help."

The two of them crouched in front of the laptop for the next few hours. Vivian had a hard-enough time making friends in real life, she'd never fussed with social media. She needed help to set up a group and send invitations, but only after Marky had created a profile for her.

She tilted her head at the screen. "So, I just put my stupid mug up there and ask people to like it?"

"Well, you don't want to *ask* for likes. That's what creepy people do, and it always sounds desperate." Mark looked at his mother. "Here, take your hair down. Let me take your picture."

Vivian rubbed her face with her sleeve to wipe away any melted makeup.

"Oh God. In this? And I just soaked my head in the sink."

"Jesus, Mom. Why'd you do that?" He smirked, then saw her face.

She was tired and stressed out. This new job seemed to be wearing on her, even if it had gotten them some pretty sweet electronics.

"Mom, you're really pretty. You have a trustworthy face. People will see it and see what you're doing . . . They'll be happy to join up." He reached over and scrunched her hair a little. "There. Now, just smile a little bit, not some big stupid grin. No—that's a grimace. You look like you're about to take a dump!"

Vivian laughed in spite of herself; the easy, open-mouth laugh she could only share with her son. He snapped the photo right away, capturing the moment perfectly on the screen. She looked like she was having fun, enjoying where she was in life. And, in the split second that laugh had taken place, she probably was.

That whole weekend, she gathered and posted promotional material—inspirational quotes, product information. It was flimsy but enough to limp on. When it came to sending invitations, she scoured local pages that offered the same type of support and wellness information as the brick-and-mortar facilities she'd visited in the last few weeks—women's shelters, pages devoted to drug abuse recovery, victim support, that sort of thing. The results were immediate. Vivian crunched caramel popcorn and watched the screen as notifications lit up every few minutes or so.

Monday afternoon, she reached next to her on the couch for the phone and dialed Allen.

"Tell me you've got something, Viv."

"I think I did it, Allen. There's three dozen people signed onto my Facebook group, and I'm waiting to hear back from double that."

"Wow, darlin', sounds like you really turned that around. Soak it up while you can, this sweet scent of success." He no longer had any emotion in his voice, and it chilled Vivian. "Oh, I'll let you go. Looks like Marky is home."

Vivian whipped her head around and saw the clock. It was just after three o'clock and there—she drew the shades back on the second-story apartment window—the school bus had stopped on the street out front.

"Listen, sorry we had to put the pressure on you the other night. I guess even families fight sometimes, right?" Allen gave a dry chuckle. "Maybe I can work in some sort of bonus for you. You've earned it."

"What the hell is this, Allen? What do you want with Marky?" She had sunk to her knees on the floor, covering her face with her free hand. "Please, just leave us alone."

"I don't want anything with Marky. But it's just a damn good way to make sure this gets done, don't you think? Do the job, Viv. See you next week."

Vivian threw the phone before she heard anything else, then ran to her bedroom to hide her frantic tears. Marky couldn't know anything was wrong.

Standing in the bathroom-turned-custodial-closet, Esther waited for the stained yellow bucket to fill with sudsy mop water. It was easy enough to stay busy, pressing her finger through the cloth into the corrugation of each cleaning product bottle. They'd been there for years, she guessed; some of them had crusted themselves to the rickety shelves.

Curious, Esther opened a tricenarian Pine-Sol to see if it would smell the same as a fresh bottle, but she fumbled the cap. It clacked along the chrome bars of the shelving unit before careening into the hollow death rattle only a plastic cap can make as it comes to a standstill.

She bent to retrieve it behind the forgotten, grody toilet and stopped. Some type of warranty was stuck to the tank, but the tape had yellowed, and where the paper leaned away from its adhesive prison, someone had written on it in tiny, faint print.

It was a dismal, nondescript building, with faded spots on its exterior. Vivian double checked the address on the index card before walking in. It was almost over.

Twelve women had confirmed their arrival at the facility for a demo of Vehemence's new product line. She'd gotten "asses in seats." That conversation still rang in her head daily. Something was wrong, she knew it. They'd changed the plan on her, for one thing. And the other thing—well, she'd sent Marky to stay with her brother in Michigan.

This wasn't what she'd signed up to do. But she'd done it, and in the end, that was what mattered. It was a good day.

"Vivian, right?" The woman at the front desk eyed a clipboard. "They want to see you before you go in. Right this way please, ma'am."

Vivian wasn't used to a well-dressed woman calling her *ma'am.* It felt pretty good. The receptionist took her to an office where Allen and another man—Leonard, Vivian guessed—were seated behind a table.

"Morning, Viv," Allen said, offering a smile.

Leonard looked bored.

"I guess this is it, right? The ladies should be here soon." Vivian began to stammer when neither man acknowledged her. "Will you need me in the demo room or should I just be greeting . . ."

She trailed off when Allen got up to close the door. "Is something wrong?"

"I guess it gets tricky now," Leonard said. It was definitely Leonard. That thin, nasally voice made her hairs stand on end. He walked to her side of the table. "We want you to be a part of the demo, sure."

Allen's eyes danced between Leonard and Vivian. "Your face is pretty recognizable. The other women know your face from the group profile."

Vivian frowned. "Well, sure. But I've got a trustworthy face, right?"

The two men were quiet for a moment before Allen said, "We're afraid it could skew results."

None of it made any sense to Vivian, what they said next. She hardly understood social media, let alone what the hell would go on during the demo, but they were telling her the women might be angry with her when they saw her, if they recognized her.

"Maybe I just don't participate?"

"Oh no." Leonard chuckled dangerously. "That simply isn't an option."

The details, the explanations, all of them fuzzed out after the first punch to the face. It knocked her from her chair and left droplets of blood on the floor.

"What the *hell*?" Vivian blubbered and threw out some other choice words. The best ones she knew.

Allen bent over and guided her back to her seat, speaking softly. "It will hurt, Viv. But this will work out better for you. Trust me."

He took one of her hands in his and kissed it softly, shushing her tears, then slapped her sharply with his other hand. Her cry came out like a bark, and she sobbed incoherently after that.

"Both eyes and a cheek, that oughta do it." Leonard's snakeskin voice interrupted Vivian's tears. "Now, how about that hair?"

She thought of Marky while they lopped her hair off in great chunks using some scissors the receptionist delivered. He used to play with her chocolate tresses back when she could still call them that, before age and stress and drink turned them into the brittle wands she had now. He would lay on her lap in just his diaper, and she'd tickle his belly with the full, weighty strands of her hair.

The receptionist—a surly woman now, no more of this *ma'am* stuff—led her down a hallway into a nondescript office. A man in a medical coat ran a quick examination, shrugging as he jotted down some numbers, then jabbed a syringe of something into her shoulder.

Rough hands shoved her into a metallic, sterile-looking room. Vivian couldn't make much out through her swollen eyes but heard the furtive whispers of a few female voices before the door shut and everything went dark.

March 16, 2014

Maybe no one will ever read this, but I have to say I'm sorry.

These women are here because of me, and I don't know what's going to happen to us.

It was just a job. But now they have us in these cells. I can't talk to any of them, can't even look at them. What if they know I'm the one who brought them here?

God forgive me, I know the one girl needs some medicine. She wasn't stable and made for an easy sell. The others I just lied to. I told them if they bought this stuff from me, I could get them selling it too. Money for rent and food. Birthday parties. I used his lines on them, and it worked.

It's like prison but worse. Orange suits. Broth. One by one they take a girl, and when she comes back, she's . . . different. They're testing something on us and keep saying they're getting us ready for the demo.

I reached out to poor people and addicts and victims. He said the women no one sees, but he meant the ones no one would miss. If you read this, remember us. We were here. God forgive me.

It was several months later, and Esther stole into the building from the rooftop. After she'd read the mysterious letter and learned of the false wall, she'd taken time each week to find a way in. She had to get to it, that's all she knew.

There was no way she'd just bust in through the wall—too much to clean up. And she didn't want to tell anyone. What if it was nothing? Besides, Esther loved a secret. She wondered if she'd found someone else invisible, like her.

Once she knew to look, it wasn't hard to get to. There was an extra room in back. She couldn't get in from the inside wall or the outside wall, so she tried it from above, dropping in from a vent. Like MacGyver, Johanna would have said.

She hadn't been surprised to find the bodies. A few sprawled across metal cots, a few on the floor; the women's faces were dusty, skeletal sloths stretched into various grimaces. There were eleven of them.

It took her a few weeks to come up with a plan. First, she made sure she didn't clean there anymore. And not Mom or Johanna. Then, she knew she needed to send them off properly, the women.

Esther kneeled beside one of them and studied the ancient-looking grimace as she felt the bottle of Bulgari perfume in her pocket. She'd avoided tripping the alarm when she stole it outright but knew the finger would point to the cleaning crew. They'd lost the job.

For someone without access to money or fine things, it was worth it. The bottle's lure was too strong, and it seemed to Esther the only way to honor the contents—the women—of this tragic chamber.

She opened the perfume, the strong scent of a foreign world bathing the silent place. Like the woman with the alabaster jar, she poured its contents, a trickle at a time, at the feet of each body. It was all that she had to offer.

And yet, it was clear to her, it wasn't enough. Their faces cried out to her, R*emember us. Take us with you.* Esther took her fingernail and scraped at the dusty skull in front of her, holding the empty perfume bottle beneath it. She did this to each body, each face, until the bottle was brimming with it, though she couldn't tell if it was ashes or dust.

Same thing, she thought.

Then she pocketed the vial and made her way out of the silent, reluctant tomb.

Leah McNaughton Lederman lives in the Indianapolis area with her husband, their two sons, three cats, and dumb dog. She started her own parenting mal-advice column in her hometown's *The Toledo Free Press* and has had short stories published by *Bloodlotus Online Literary Journal,* the Indianapolis indie magazine *Snacks*, and Indie Author's Press *Issues of Tomorrow.* Her story, "Lithium Sandwich," in Scout Media's anthology *A Matter of Words* is the prequel to the story you've just read.

You can find out more about her work at www.leahlederman.wordpress.com or on Facebook at www.facebook.com/ledermanediting.

SUPPORT

Signature *Jake Ratcliff*

The woman takes one big drag on her cigarette before she stubs it out in the ashtray. The ember tip flares in her eyes, and as she presses it down, she makes sure it's flat—flatter than it has to be, like the butt has wronged her somehow and she's stomp-stomp-stomping it out.

She shouldn't be smoking in here. It's illegal to smoke in this room, but I take one look at her, and I can't say no, not after what she's been through, what she's gotta go through. A few cigarettes feel like a small mercy.

Her name's Dorna, which I think is a really stupid name. Her son's name is Albert, which is better, but not really.

She's crying in front of me, her hands trembling as they reach into her bag for one more cigarette.

"Please, miss, please, just one more," she begs, and far from saying no, I take the lighter from her and help when her hands are too shaky to do the job themselves.

Her son is lying two rooms over, more tube than man. Coma. Somewhere in the paperwork it says how he ended up there, two rooms over, how he came into the hospital with his veins half empty and his bones more shard than solid. I haven't looked, so I don't know. Car crash? Jumped off a bridge? Maybe he was gay, and when people found out, they beat the shit out of him. I don't know, and I don't care.

Dorna says something about her oldest son, Albert's elder brother. Or at least she tries. She chokes on the words, and a fresh wave of tears shoot out her eyes like a .44, and she takes a drag on her smoke, like filling her lungs will help her get the words out. She inhales, and she holds and she holds, and her eyes close, and I get a good look at her. She was attractive before, handsome. You know the way some women get to a certain age and they can be handsome. Right now, I think she looks more like she's in anaphylactic shock, with her eyes giant and red. Her lips are so vibrantly red from where she's put on so much lipstick, I figure if I leant forward, I'd be able to see my reflection in them. Her cheeks are so red, the blue veins crossing them are almost glowing. Too much smoking, that's what happens. The smoke just destroys the veins and capillaries, and those things don't heal either. They'll be that way forever. It'll get worse as she ages, and smoking will only make it worse.

But, in this case, the smoke seems to do her good, and she exhales slowly, her shoulders slumping.

"What's your name?" she asks me.

I've told her a dozen times.

"Dr. Somers—I mean, please, call me Ellie."

"You got pretty hair, Ellie."

My hair's scrunched up in a loose bun I shoved together with half a sandwich falling out my mouth. She's stalling.

"Mrs. Donoghue, we—"

"Please, darlin', call me Dorna."

I grimace, but she doesn't notice. Dorna Donoghue. Alliterative. Like a fucking superhero. If superheroes cried in hospital rooms and smoked cigarettes like they'd get your son off life support.

"Dorna," I say, trying real hard now to keep my shit together. I'm such an asshole.

I place my hand on the papers, but she looks up at my hair like it's the halo of Jesus Christ himself, and she brings her cigarette up to her lips and sucks on it and sucks on it for so long I worry she's going to choke herself to death. The thought doesn't terrify me. If she collapses and needs medical treatment, it would save me from this awful conversation. I'm a bad person, not a bad doctor.

She stares at the corners of the room, and when I tap my fingers on the documents, she looks away from the table and fixates on my hair even harder.

"Mrs. Donoghue, I'm sorry, but we really need to—"

"*Dorna,*" she says, and her voice cracks like a needle skipping over a vinyl.

I don't mean to use her last name, just professional habit. She gets my name, and we're friends; I use her last name and that means, well, it's supposed to make her think she's in charge. That she deserves respect. All the respect she deserves exists in the dying son she has two rooms over, not because she just so happens to have a small fraction of my attention.

"Dorna." I smile. "I'm sorry."

I have to hand it to her, she wants us on the same page, both on a first-name basis. Now we're besties. Sorry, I'm tired. I hate these conversations. I'm an asshole.

"I know this isn't an easy decision," I offer, like she hasn't heard it before, like I haven't stolen that line from every film ever conceived since the dawn of celluloid.

I sigh.

She closes her eyes, shakes, her fingers tremble towards her mouth, and she places the orange butt into her mouth, only to discover she's smoked the cigarette to the filter. Now all she's inhaling is burnt plastic. Red acrylic clings to the other end of the butt between her lips, and it stains her fingers from where her lipstick is too thick. She places the butt—smouldering one end and dyed red the other—onto the table slowly with surgical precision.

I watch like she's performing some death rite.

Her eyes fall on the paper.

Albert Donoghue. Coma. Life support. Can't breathe on his own, so a robot's doing it for him. Hidden in the dossier it says somewhere that he stopped breathing for a few moments too many, and his brain took the brunt of it. If he wakes up . . . well, as a professional, I'm not allowed to say vegetable.

Her eyes flash up to mine, her lips slightly open. Her eyes, glazed over from crying, are bloodshot and desperate, the way you'd imagine a deer to look in the moments before the car crushes it.

"Mrs. Donoghue . . ." I pause, because that's what you're meant to do. "It's looking less and less likely that your son is ever going to wake up from his coma. In the unlikely event he ever does, there would be some serious questions that would have to be asked about his standard of living." I inhale.

Her face looks like one of those theatrical masks, the one where the mouth is like an upside-down *U*.

I continue. "Right now, I've got a little girl up in ICU who needs plasma. His heart could save someone's life." I slide the paper over towards her. "I just need you to sign."

We're supposed to say, *Please, ma'am, take your time. Take all the goddamn time you need.* But I don't. And sure, a part of that is because patients are dying—patients who actually need me. But honestly, right now, I need coffee.

She sobs and blubbers. A part of me fights off another part of me that really wants to ask what eyeliner she's got on because that shit would withstand a *Titanic*-level catastrophe.

In another dossier, there is a photo of the patient—I mean Albert—when he came in. One eye is sealed shut from all the raised bruising, and the other is bulging out of its socket like Rodney Dangerfield. His cheek is slit open, and you can just see a small patch where the skin split over his brow so severely you can see the white of his skull.

I took this picture out of his file before I brought it into this room.

Right then, Albert looked the worst I've ever seen anyone look. And right now, his mother looks worse.

She stares down at the slip of paper, the dotted line. My signature is above it, hastily scrawled out with one hand while I downed my eighteenth cup of coffee that day, told three interns to fuck off, and concentrated as hard as I could on Not. Needing. To pee.

"Ya know, Ellie," she says, and she fumbles around in her crocodile-skin purse for what I can only assume is yet another cigarette. When she finds it she holds the pack, stares down at the slogan imprinted on the side: SMOKERS DIE YOUNG.

She does nothing. Stares.

I hope she can appreciate the irony of outliving her son; the tobacco prophets, proved wrong again!

She continues: "When Albert was seven, he said he wanted to be a . . ."

She's talking, I can see her lips move, the smudged red opening and closing like a maw where interesting things go to die. I pretend to listen. I pretend *real* hard. A part of me knows I can't tell her to stop, because she's talking, and talking is good; she's opening up, and she's starting to trust me, and she's not all holed up in her little self-pity shell—though Christ knows I won't say she doesn't deserve a bit of self-pity right about now.

As a doctor, I'm trained to treat patients physically. Give me a punctured lung, please God, and I can fix it; give me a talker, and I'm lost. Give me a Barbie doll up some forty-seven-year-old guy's ass rather than make me sit and have to listen to this woman wax lyrical about what a good person her son was. Is.

In his state, the difference between Is and Was is a signature on a piece of paper.

Life and death controlled by a switch, the same you'd find on any old coffeemaker. On and off. Robots wouldn't have to rise up to destroy us, just turn off all the life support and watch the families slowly talk themselves to death.

"Have you got kids, Ellie?"

The question draws me out of my digression.

"No," I answer.

I reach across the table grab the pack—SMOKERS DIE YOUNG—and help myself to a cigarette. She reaches across the table, and I cup my hand around the flame—not because there's a breeze, but because I've seen it done in movies. That's what you do, right?

I exhale gently, the blue smoke rising to the corners of the room to join hers, wafting there, like a spectre watching over us.

She doesn't stop me or say anything. She retracts the lighter and takes another drag on her cigarette.

"Can I tell you a secret, Ellie?"

I inhale. Nod. Exhale. "Please."

"I wish I'd never had kids."

I'm supposed to say: *Why ever not, Mrs. Donoghue, please tell me everything, Mrs. Donoghue, open your soul to me, Mrs. D., so that I can hide it in and get to know the real fucking you.*

Instead, she takes a drag on her cigarette, and then stamps it out with her finger. I pass my half-smoked cigarette to her, and for a second, our fingers touch. Her hands are stumpy, her fingernails polished and gleaming and perfect and probably fake, but I stare at them anyway. My nails are bitten to the quick—I realise what different lives we lead.

Her hands are shaking; she struggles to take the cigarette, and I worry she might burn herself. The last thing I need is a further delay for her to look after her stupid, fat, fake, burnt fingers, or for me to have to go get some painkillers for her to put in her stupid, fat mouth.

I forgot for a moment why we are here, and I look down at the manila dossier again, and a bulb in my head goes: *Oh yes, you bitch, her son is dying. You have to convince her to let him go, so he can save a lot of other patients.*

"Dorna, I know this is hard, but—"

"Because," she raises her voice, cutting me off, staring at the glowing tip of the cigarette, and I feel that's because she doesn't want to look at me. "Because," she repeats.

She sticks the already reddened butt of the cigarette between her teeth, now stained in the same powdery crimson. The tip ignites. She exhales.

I exhale too, trying to stop myself shaking too much. The expired residue of the cigarette smoke tastes like shit in my mouth, and I wonder how the hell does anyone ever like these? If I'm honest, all I'm getting from it is a stupid head rush, and I feel fifteen years old again, like I just stole the cigarillos my granddad used to smoke and hid out at the back of our garden for what turned out to be an experiment in who could vomit more, me or my friend.

"Because,"—she's still talking—"then . . . then . . ." Her hands are shaking something awful. She's almost at risk of knocking over the ashtray. ". . . I'd be used to going home to an empty house."

I place the pen in her hand, and she takes it. This simple act feels like stepping on the moon for the first time, and I think, *Fuck you, Neil Armstrong. Next time, why don't you try something actually difficult, like getting a mom to turn off her son's life support? How's that for a giant leap?*

She stares at the pen in her hand, and I can see the countdown in her eyes, wondering, now that she's pulled the pin, how long she has till it explodes. She puts the pen down and crosses her arms over it so she can't see it, but she has the form in front of her, and the pen is nearby.

I nod. I want to tell her she can stay in with him as long as she wants before she signs, after she signs, till it's time—but people who are on the heart transplant list aren't renowned for having all that spare time. We need those organs. I need her to sign so I can leave and she can start her life of mourning and I can carry on my job of not letting people die.

Yes, the irony of seeking permission to kill someone has already hit me. I'm a doctor; my job is to decide the lesser of evils. One person dies so that another four can live. That's just math. *Sir, you have to choose your wife or the baby. Yes, we're going to lose one, and you have less than three minutes to decide whose death you want to be responsible for, for the rest of your life, before we lose them both.*

Thankfully, that wasn't a conversation I ever had to have, but I watched it happen. I was an intern. I think I can understand what Dorna means when she says she wishes she'd never have had kids.

"Dorna . . ." Fuck knows what I was gonna say. "Thank you. For the cigarette."

"Anytime, darlin'."

Now I'm stymied. I have to take control, but this isn't a crash victim, this isn't respiratory failure, this isn't something I've practiced!

"Dr. Somerset," she says. "Can I see him? Can I see my son?"

The first thing you notice in the room is the expansive rasping, like a giant gasping over and over again. It's so loud. The room has a stale smell, a non-smell that is typical of hospitals but made even worse here because all the air in this room is fake. Immediately, your throat goes dry, like your body knows this air is wrong; there's too much of it, it's too cold.

His body is pale and naked, though of course he's under blankets. His hair has grown longer, and over the weeks, his face has healed slightly. His lips are still chafed red where they split, and there's still a bruise on his brow, but the worst of it's gone. I haven't checked, but I've been a doctor long enough to know he hasn't had time for all his bones to heal. Especially not once the surgeons had to snap out his ribs to re-inflate his lungs. They did what they could and then passed him on to the great and powerful Machine.

More stoically than I would ever have expected, Dorna pulls the chair over the top of the bed, and she sits beside him, her face turned down. I hear, over the robot breathing, a gasp escape her red lips, loosening the red plastic on her teeth, and a lump of it falls out her mouth, but she doesn't notice or doesn't see.

I stand just inside the door, leaning on the frame with my arms crossed, the form and the pen clutched against my chest. More than the robot, I can hear the clock ticking just to my side. There's a TV in here—one of those cathode monitors where the backs are longer than the screens are wide. It's on, the screen flickering, but someone's turned down the sound. If I thought it would matter, I'd hunt down whoever left the TV on and the sound off, like that's any good to someone who can't open his eyes.

I exhale. Dorna.

Dorna's crying, but it's soft this time and kind of pathetic. The tears congeal in her eyes and fall like fat raindrops onto his pillow. There's a noise coming from her throat like a mouse caught by its tail screaming and screaming. She's shaking again, her bottom lip quivering. She can't see me.

I roll my eyes. I slap my imaginary wrists again and tell myself to do my job and stop being such a *fucking bitch*.

Now she's uttering, "My boy, my precious boy," like a mantra and pushing his hair back, not that it's very long. I think she just wants to touch him.

Artificially, I can see his chest rising and falling.

"Ellie," she calls my name. Back to a first-name basis.

I step off the doorframe and wander over with the form held in front of me so she knows I brought it with me. When we left the other room, she didn't even look at it.

"What will happen if I sign?"

This question seems like a step in the right direction, though I noticed she used the non-solid *if*, rather than the unquestionable *when*.

"He won't feel anything," I say. "Because he's in a coma and on life support, he'll pass pretty instantaneously. It'll be like stepping into another dream."

Another dream? Who the fuck am I, Lewis Carroll? Another dream doesn't even mean anything. Christ.

I continue: "We'll take a bit of his plasma. We're pretty sure he's a match, but we'll have to run a test to be sure. His heart will be taken straight away. There's a girl who's a perfect match. She's been on the list for a couple months, and she won't last much longer."

"What's her name?" Dorna asks.

"Chloe," I say. "Chloe Forrester."

"How old is she?"

"Seventeen."

"What's wrong with her?"

"Congenital heart failure."

"If not Albert's . . ."

I shake my head, though she can't see. "She'll die."

"That doesn't make it any easier."

"I know," I say, managing to say it softly. "I'm just letting you know what'll happen. Dorna, Chloe has a chance. Or, I mean, she might."

Dorna looks up at me and then back down at Albert, his soft features, the minor bruises, the tubes clamped between his teeth. He would have been handsome, or at least easy on the eyes.

"That doesn't make it any easier."

"I understand."

Her body tenses, and I wonder if she's going to snap at me or disagree, but she doesn't. She's right though, I don't understand.

"If I *don't* sign. What then?"

"He'll stay on life support, likely for the rest of his life. You'll be able to see him four times a week, for a maximum of two hours. We'll feed him through that tube,"—I point it out—"and this machine will fill his lungs twenty-four hours a day, seven days a week."

"And Chloe?"

"Will pray that tomorrow someone has a car crash and their heart isn't affected, and they are, by some other miracle, a perfect match. It could be months before we get another match—"

"And Chloe won't last that long, I get it." She took the words right out my mouth.

"No."

Her voice breaks, and she asks in a haunted, quiet sob, "Is Chloe Forrester more important than my son?"

Yes.

"Mrs. Donoghue, the odds of Chloe finding another heart are zero. Your son is one hundred-percent of her chance. He has less than one-percent chance of waking up."

That's just math. The lesser of two evils. Her for him.

"And the rest of him?"

In cases like this, we tend not to store organs. I don't want to tell her that his kidneys might not be a match for anyone on the list, and if they aren't, they just go in the medical waste bin with all the other waste. Same goes for his liver. For everything else, when they cremate him or bury him or ritualistically sacrifice his dead body, he'll be an empty shell.

"It's judged on a case-by-case basis."

And then she asks me the question that they always ask, the question they should never ask, the question we doctors hate, because we understand logic, we understand chance, and we understand not to get involved.

"What would you do, Ellie? If he were your son, what would you do?"

Pull the plug.

"It's not up to me, Mrs. Donoghue."

She looks back at her son and touches his cheek, and she grazes her fingers on the tube going into his mouth (and down his throat).

I think she's made her mind up.

"Such a handsome boy," she says, and she's crying again now, properly.

I lean down and place the form on the bed in front of her, the pen on top of that.

"Want me to leave?"

She doesn't wipe her eyes, and I noticed her mascara's still in place. Somehow.

I need to sleep, I realise. I need to leave, I need to get out, I need to see someone, I need to get drunk, I need to go to the most expensive restaurant in town and order the biggest steak they sell with as much blood as they're allowed to serve it with and the kind of wine they don't put on the menu. Something red. Something that'll go underneath cocktails, and lots of them. I haven't had sex in months. I haven't seen my friends in weeks. I think my cat's probably upset at this point that he never got to eat me, because as far as he's concerned, I'm probably dead.

She nods.

I leave. I return to the interview room, and it stinks of smoke and sweat, and I stumble, catching myself on the table. I hate this. I hate all of this.

I clear away the ashtray, hoping no one notices. A part of me doesn't care if they do.

When I return, Dorna is resting her head on his chest, probably pressing down so hard the machine is struggling to do its job, but it doesn't matter anymore. The form is stained with droplets of salty tears, and underneath mine, she's scratched a few curves that might be a name.

"Dr. Somerset," she says, without looking at me.

"Yes?" I ask, grabbing the form.

"Has anyone told you you're a bitch?"

"Yes, Mrs. Donoghue. I'm sorry. You did—"

"If you tell me I did the right thing," she says, without looking up or moving off her son, "I'm going to jump out that window."

I leave the room, the form clutched in my hand like I've found the Arc of the Covenant.

As I walk through the doorway, Dorna looks up and asks me, "Chloe Forrester. She'll make it now?"

"Yes. Of course."

"It doesn't feel that way."

She looks around the room, up and down and left and right,

and she gazes out the window. I feel like she's got more to say, and even though I want to dash off now I've got the form, I don't.

She says, "Now I have to go home. I have to tell Albert's father I killed our baby son. Tell his brother he's an only child again."

Shivers run down my spine. I leave.

I take the form where it needs to go, and the process of officially killing Albert Donoghue begins.

THE TWELFTH MAID

Signature *K. M. Reynolds*

The heavy brass knocker thumped against the solid oak doors, and Mary swallowed nervously, a ball of electricity resting in the pit of her stomach. A minute passed as she fidgeted on the stone steps, warring with herself about knocking again. The wind picked up, tossing the bright fall foliage that surrounded the mansion. Mary shivered, wrapping the front of her cardigan tightly around her slim frame. After another few moments, she reached for the cool metal handle, preparing to knock again. As her hand touched the knocker, the door began to open, seeming to groan with the effort. She jumped, the sound causing her skin to ripple like gooseflesh.

A handsome man in his early thirties smiled out at her from the now-open doorway. Mary returned the smile, eager to make a good first impression. A cursory glance revealed an expensive, tailor-made suit, hair impeccably groomed, and dark eyes that burned as though with a hidden desire.

Mary's skin prickled again, and the ball of electricity in her gut seemed to quiver.

"Come in, come in!" His voice was like a perfectly aged wine—smooth in all the right places. "I'm delighted to have you. Mary, is it?" He stepped gracefully to the side, allowing Mary to enter the foyer. "I am Mr. Archer Hammond, the proud owner of this estate. But you may call me Archie." He winked at her, his deep eyes still glowing with an almost devilish light, his lips pulling to the side in a smirk.

Mary smiled again, hoping her face did not betray her racing heart. "It's wonderful to meet you, Archie." Spinning slowly on her heel, she took in the impressive foyer. "You have a lovely home. I think it's the nicest home I've ever seen!"

"Thank you, my dear." That mischievous smirk appeared again, and Mary's knees grew weak. Archer gestured to the hallway on the right side of the foyer. "This way, then. Let's get you all settled!"

Mary nodded in agreement and followed behind, marveling at how Archer seemed to glide across the floor.

My, what a stunning, graceful man, she thought, feeling her cheeks flush a bit as she remembered the way he had winked at her. *I could fall into his eyes and just stay there forever.*

As they walked, she began making mental notes of the various doorways they passed. Some were open, and she saw a laundry room, a large sitting room, and what looked like a billiard room as they strode past.

Archer paused in front of a large set of double doors, turning to face Mary. "Won't you step into my office?" He reached behind his back, grasping the door handles, and pushed them open with a flourish. "This is where I spend most of my time during the day, taking calls and clients," he informed Mary as he receded into the room. "If you need me, there's a very good chance I will be holed up in here."

Mary took in the rich décor of the spacious room, from the oil paintings on the walls, to the leather couches. On one of the walls, from floor to ceiling, a massive bookshelf resided, filled to capacity with various tomes. Mary noticed several large volumes about human and animal anatomy, a complete encyclopedia, and what appeared to be the entire works of William Shakespeare. A smaller bookshelf rested behind the impressive mahogany desk, overflowing with smaller books.

Archer took his natural seat behind the desk, settling into his chair with a contented sigh. Mary chose one of the high back chairs that sat facing the desk and perched on the edge, leaning forward slightly and clasping her hands tightly on her lap. Archer rifled through his desk, brow furrowed, quietly muttering to himself. His face lit up as he retrieved a thick file from deep within the desk.

Mary blinked as the stack of papers hit the desk in front of her with a plop.

"Alright, Mary. This is a standard employment contract. I have them set to expire and be re-signed every three months, because I understand how unpredictable this market can be." He gave a wide grin, and for a moment, Mary was reminded of a shark. "I hope we are a good match—I've had to get rid of almost a dozen maids in the past few months, most for breach of contract." He paused, his own dark eyes locking with Mary's grey ones, causing a shiver to run down her spine. "I'll let you peruse this, and when you get to the last page, we can discuss it. It's a bit . . . unusual. Most people have questions."

Mary nodded meekly, her mouth running dry. Her mind buzzed as though it contained a beehive, her thoughts tumbling one over the other like a waterfall. She picked up the thick contract, her eyes running over each section thoroughly, searching for red flags. Page after page she turned, finding nothing out of the ordinary. The sections covered her household duties, protocol for sick days and emergencies, her rate of pay, causes for termination; all of the basics.

She flipped to the last page, and her eyes widened a bit.

"Non-Disclosure Agreement and Gag Order?" she queried, looking up at her future employer. "I'm a maid; why would I need this?"

Archer smiled again, his thin lips stretching over his teeth, somehow showing even more of his pearly whites than the last smile had.

Mary shifted uncomfortably in her chair, suddenly feeling very small and alone.

"Well, Mary," Archer began, his voice cool and calm, "as you know, this is a large estate, and I am a very wealthy man in a great position of power." He paused, looking pointedly around the study. "As a maid, you will be here daily and may see and hear things that could undo me as a professional if word was to get out. You will see my clients as they enter, and you will have the inside scoop on so many inner workings here at the house. Of course, you understand why I can't risk you talking about any of it outside of the confines of this estate. Client confidentiality, my own personal security, all of that."

The explanation was logical, and a wave of relief and confidence washed over Mary. She still felt slightly uneasy, but she chalked it up to normal *new job nerves.*

She gazed once more at the Non-Disclosure part of the contract, skimming to the bottom. "This contract can only be broken on pain of death! Oh, my."

A nervous laugh escaped her lips, and she looked at Archer with questions dancing behind her grey eyes.

Archer offered no verbal response; he merely met her gaze and shrugged.

"I guess you do take this seriously." She laughed again, this time out of amusement. "I guess I get it. You've got to drive your point home." She flipped back to the first page of the contract, glancing over the page once more. "May I have a pen?"

Archer produced a fountain pen with a flourish, and Mary began to initial each page of the contract. She reached the last page and paused, the pen hovering over the paper. That last line seemed to leap off of the paper, screaming a warning. She blinked, pressing back any feelings of uncertainty.

This is an advantageous position, and the money is unbelievable. It's just a phrase, she reminded herself. *You can do this.*

Now determined, she signed her name at the bottom of the document and passed the pen back across the desk.

Archer quickly turned the contract towards himself, penning his signature just below her own.

"There. Now it's official!" He rose from his chair, extending his hand, which Mary accepted. "It's a pleasure to have you on board, Mary."

"The pleasure is all mine, Mr. Hammond," Mary replied, once again mesmerized by his burning gaze.

"Oh, please. Call me Archie," he reminded her, giving her hand a playful squeeze. "Now, shall I show you around the estate?"

Still grasping her hand, he moved from behind his desk to stand beside Mary. He tucked her hand into the crook of his arm, cocking his head slightly as he awaited her answer.

"Of course, Mr. Ha—Archie," she corrected herself, a rosy blush coursing across her cheeks.

Being this close to him was almost intoxicating. Those dangerous eyes, his smooth, lilting voice; for a moment, Mary felt like she was under a spell.

The pair left the study behind and began the tour of the sprawling manor. The kitchen, the gardens, the various bedrooms—it was enough to make anyone's head spin, and Mary was doing her best to create a mental map of the place. They ambled through a hallway that ran behind the kitchen, and Mary noted a large metal door.

"Where does that go?" she queried.

Archer patted the hand that still rested in the fold of his arm. "Ah, that's a basement storage door. Nothing of import. You won't be needing to go in there for a while, and I'll take you in when it's time. It gets pretty messy in there. I wouldn't want you getting hurt!"

Mary cast a furtive glance back over her shoulder at the strange door, her curiosity piqued.

"*Ah!* Here we are, one of my favorite rooms in the house, besides my den, of course."

Mary gasped audibly as they entered the library. Books of all sizes and colors lined the walls, the smell of parchment and ink hanging in the air. There were large French windows overlooking the gardens, bathing the room in glorious natural light that twinkled off the decorative crystal chandeliers. Around the room there were several large taxidermized animals, each seeming ready to spring to life at any moment.

"You have so many books! I don't think I've ever seen this many books in a home before."

Her eyes were wide, and she released Archer's arm, turning around and around, a smile dancing across her face. She brushed a pale-blonde strand of hair from her face, tucking it neatly behind her ear.

"I can see why you love this room so much! And these animals; goodness, they are quite impressive."

Archer nodded, a smile brightening his own features. "Words are the very fabric of society. Words make us who we are. They teach and mold us. We can use them to heal, or as weapons, at will. There's nothing quite so powerful as well-crafted words. So, I collect them." He gestured grandly. "These are all words of significance, and I am more than happy to share them with you. Feel free to borrow any book you wish to read. Just please return them in good condition. Many of them are first editions."

Mary was giddy with excitement, all trepidation washed away. She fought the urge to jump up and down with glee. Instead, she grasped one of Archer's hands in both her own.

"Oh, thank you. Thank you so much! I promise that if I ever read any of them, I will take great care to be gentle!"

Archer nodded to a large black bear that stood frozen on its hind legs in the corner. "As for the animals, I stuffed them all myself! I have a bit of a fascination with taxidermy and anatomy, as I'm sure you gathered by my personal books in my office, and now these animals."

Mary took a closer look at the bear, noticing its gleaming eyes and razor-sharp claws.

"How fascinating! I've never given the study of anatomy or

taxidermy much thought, but perhaps I can learn more while I'm here."

"Of course, dear Mary. I would be delighted to teach you some time. I can see that we share a love of words, and I think we will get along famously. I do hope this works out as a long-term arrangement!"

Somewhere in the house, a grandfather clock began to chime.

"Oh, look at the time! I have a client coming shortly. Let me show you to the door." He began leading her out of the library and back the way they had come. "Now, I know this place can be a bit of a maze, so don't panic at first. I'm sure you will get the hang of it all in no time." He led her through an archway, and she could see the foyer up ahead at the end of the hall. "So, you will start tomorrow. Eight a.m." They reached the foyer, and he grasped her hand, raising it to his lips. "It has been a pleasure."

Mary flushed again, and managed to squeak out, "Yes! Eight a.m. I will be here. Thank you so much."

She turned and practically ran for the door, keenly aware of the place on her hand that had brushed his lips. Reaching the door, she turned and gave a quick wave before exiting the house. As she scrambled down the steps, a portly gentleman was ascending. He gave her a curt nod as she passed, and she realized that he must be the client that Mr. Hammond had mentioned.

At the bottom of the steps, she paused, desperately attempting to organize the various emotions roiling within her chest. Having no luck, she continued to her car, sliding into the driver's seat. Her heart was pounding as she put the keys in the ignition and turned them, the engine purring to life. As she pulled out of the main property gate, she let out an excited squeal. She had never had a job this prestigious before; to go from a hotel maid to something of this caliber was almost unheard of.

She wore a smile the whole drive home.

The first three weeks of work went extremely well for Mary. She was punctual and productive, able to move through her daily tasks with ease. By her third day, she had learned the layout of the estate and could find her way around easily. Every night, she dined with Archer at the table, at his request. This was a bit strange, but she always accepted, finding no real reason to decline. It was the bright spot in her day, when she got to spend one-on-one time with the master of the house. They would laugh and talk of literature and world news, and every meal was sumptuously prepared.

She often felt she was alone in the house, although she knew there were other staff members. The silver-haired butler, Frederic, moved like a ghost. He would complete his duties in silence, vanishing without a single word. Based on the old family portraits scattered throughout the building, Mary knew the butler had been serving the Hammond family for decades. She knew there was a small kitchen staff and groundskeepers, although she had never spoken to any of them. The cook, Irma, was a true artist in the kitchen. Archer sang her praises at every meal, and she would stand silently in the corner, observing. The garden staff was quite large, though Mary had never seen any of them up close. They were elusive and never came indoors. They always seemed to be covered in dirt, which Mary supposed was just the nature of garden work.

At the end of the third week, Archer approached her as she was dusting the light fixtures in the library. He was disheveled, smeared with fresh blood, and there were beads of sweat on his brow. He placed a hand on her shoulder, and she started in alarm as she turned and took in his unusual appearance.

"Mary," he began, breathlessly, "I need your help in the basement room. I've made quite a mess."

Mary felt the cold knot of dread tightening in her abdomen as she took in his wild visage, her heart beginning to pound.

"Please, come now. I don't want any stains to set."

Mary acquiesced, following him to the heavy metal door in the hallway just outside the library. He swung the door wide, cool air seeping out of the gaping doorframe. On the heels of the cold came the smell. The odor was pungent—like a mixture between compost and a butcher's workshop.

Mary grimaced instinctively, fighting the urge to cover her nose and mouth with her hands. *This is what death smells like,* a little voice whispered in the back of her mind.

She faced Archer, alarm etched on her delicate features, her eyes wide. She timidly brushed a blonde wisp of hair out of her face and finally spoke, her voice tremulous. "Archie, what's down there?"

"Come, come. You'll see, soon enough. I apologize in advance for the mess; I was trying a new technique, and it got a bit out of hand. I wasn't quite anticipating this."

He descended the stairs, the darkness enveloping him. Halfway down the stairs, the light clicked on. He turned and looked back up at Mary, reluctantly lingering in the doorway. "Well?"

Mary inhaled deeply, simultaneously curious and terrified, and began the descent. The chill of the basement enfolded her, and she shivered. The smell grew more pungent with every step she took. Archer was waiting at the bottom of the stairs, scowling at whatever lay waiting in the cold. She closed her eyes as she took the remaining stairs, her hand gripping the banister. With her feet firmly planted on the floor, she opened her eyes, stifling a scream as she registered the sight in front of her.

A large sow hung on meat hooks over a metal table, her throat slit and her eyes glassy. The wall closest to her was sprayed with fresh blood, with more blood filling buckets that sat haphazardly around the table. The gaping wound in the sow's neck still dripped crimson, silently splashing on the table below. Mary tore her gaze from the ghastly scene in front of her and turned back to Archer. She tried to form words, but her voice failed her, leaving her to soundlessly gape while gesticulating wildly.

Archer held out his bloodstained hands, apologetically explaining, "I enjoy preparing our own meat for the kitchen. Typically, I receive the animals fresh from the slaughterhouse, and I portion the meat myself. But I wanted to try the butchering process, too . . . I seem to have underestimated just how messy it actually is." He hung his head sheepishly. "I know how this must look. I would be scared, too. But please, I need to find a way to clean that wall, if it can be done. I was ill-prepared."

Mary stared a few seconds longer before gathering herself enough to respond. "Do you have cleaning supplies down here?"

"Yes, there's a bunch of supplies in there." He gestured to one of the large steel cabinets that lined the walls. "I'm not sure exactly what we have in there, but I know there's quite a variety. I use this room mostly for my taxidermy and for meat carving. The garden staff also use it to store their supplies." He gestured at the wall, where several rakes, hoes, and shovels were hanging, all caked with dirt. "There's a little door around that corner there, that leads out to the back gardens."

Mary made her way slowly over to the cabinet, keeping her eye on the exsanguinated pig. The whole affair was deeply unsettling, and she could feel the remnants of her lunch churning, threatening to make a reappearance. That tiny voice in the back of her mind was back, urging her to run and never look back. The hair on the back of her neck prickled as she turned away from the gore, opening the heavy cabinet doors.

She began muttering a list to herself as she scanned the plethora of items. "Gloves, rags, water, dish soap, ammonia . . ."

She grabbed a large metal basin and used it like a basket, collecting the supplies she needed. There was a large utility sink on one side of the room, and she carried her items over to it. She donned the gloves and headed to the wall, rags in hand. She began to blot at the stains, absorbing as much of the still-wet blood as she could. She saturated two rags before enough was removed to begin the next step in the process. She quickly mixed the warm water, dish soap, and a bit of ammonia together in the large bowl. Using a clean rag, she gently wiped at the remaining stains, repeatedly rinsing the rag in the tepid mixture. She was pleased to see much of the blood coming off the wall, leaving behind only the faintest of traces.

She cleaned in silence, her mind beginning to wander. *How did I wind up in this position? This is crazy. This scenario didn't even cross my mind when worrying about the things I would have to deal with in this house.*

She remembered her first encounter with Archer; his dark eyes and deep air of mystery and the strange electric tingling throughout her body. He was exciting, but he was dangerous.

"Deadly," she whispered under her breath.

"What—" Archer began, causing Mary to shriek and drop the rag.

"Oh my *God*, Archie!" she squealed out. "I forgot you were here!" One hand over her heart, the other over her trembling mouth, she hissed, "Don't do that again!"

"I'm sorry, Mary. I'm *so* sorry, my dear, I didn't mean to frighten you like that," Archer apologized.

Mary looked down at her uniform, now streaked with blood where she had clutched her apron. "Oh no."

As if in response, Archer stripped off his own blood-drenched shirt and apron and tossed them aside, unabashed that he now stood half naked in front of Mary.

"It's okay, we'll have to wash these, too. We will just wash your apron along with my clothes."

Mary blanched, startled by Archie's sudden brazenness. She averted her gaze but not before she had taken a good look. His arms and chest were toned and firm, and his abdominal muscles were lightly defined, rippling under his skin as he moved. He sported a light tan, and Mary caught a fleeting glimpse of a tattoo on his shoulder before she looked away. The electric buzzing deep in her gut returned, and she trembled, not with fear, but with excitement. She could feel her face flushing, and she grabbed the bloody clothes off the floor.

"I'll go wash these," she blustered, marching off to the laundry room while Archie simply stood there, an amused smirk on his face.

That night, lying in her bed, Mary thought about the events of the day. Finding that sow was completely unexpected, if not absolutely terrifying.

"This must be exactly the sort of thing that non-disclosure agreement is there for," she whispered into the dark. Part of her longed to terminate the contract and never return, while a darker, more conflicted part of her, wanted answers. *Plus, I can only break the contract 'on pain of death', according to what I signed,* Mary reminded herself. *I have no clue what that means, exactly, but after what I saw today, I am not putting anything past him.* She immediately silenced her racing thoughts, correcting herself. *No. While he may slaughter a pig, I know he wouldn't actually hurt a person. He's far too educated for that. He may be eccentric, but I don't believe, in my heart, that he is dangerous.*

Despite her reassurances to herself, the urge to run fast and far was overwhelming. However, in the end, the urge to find answers won out, and she determined to stick out the contract for the remaining two months, no matter what else happened.

The next several days at the estate passed without incident. Neither Mary nor Archer brought up the incident with the sow in the basement, and after a while, Mary began to wonder if perhaps she had dreamt it all. That little voice in the back of her mind was her constant companion now, urging her to go back into the basement and seek answers.

Finally, on a blustery Friday, an opportunity presented itself.

"Ah, Mary!" Archer greeted her cheerfully as she entered the estate, hanging her coat and scarf on a hook. "The basement room desperately needs a bit of a touch up today, if you don't mind?" Her expression must have given her away, because Archer quickly added, "It's just a basic sweep and mop and a bit of a tidy. No big messes today."

Mary smiled, quelling the nausea that rumbled faintly deep within her. "Of course, Archie. I can absolutely do that today." Her mind was racing with the possibility of discovering what else was in the basement.

The pair walked to the basement door, Archer unlocking it and holding it open as she descended. Once the lights flicked on, he closed the door, joining her in the cold room.

Much to her surprise, the basement seemed quite clean, though there was a bit of dirt where the garden staff had been moving things in and out of the garden. She quickly located a broom and began to sweep, humming to herself. She kept an eye on Archer, who sat on the last step. He watched her as she moved about the basement, cleaning the stray dirt and organizing any misplaced tools. Time and time again, her gaze wandered to the far wall, where the metal cabinets and deep-freezer chests were lined up.

Her curiosity got the best of her, and she asked, "What's in the freezers? I didn't notice them the first time I was down here."

Archer stood to his feet, striding over to the three large freezers. He opened one, motioning for Mary to approach while explaining, "I keep my animals in here, the ones I intend to preserve. Here, take a look!"

Mary stopped in her tracks, turning back to her task at hand. "Oh, no thank you, Archie. I'd rather not see them, if it's all the same to you."

Archer smiled knowingly, closing the freezer lid. "I get it. They are far prettier once they've been stuffed and cleaned."

Mary finished tidying the basement in silence, feeling slightly better about the mysteries the room held. She wished that Archer would leave, but he sat there, ever watching, like a hawk watches a rabbit. After the two had ascended the stairs, he finally took his leave, retreating back into his office. She did not see him again until dinner was served.

Over the next two weeks, the basement cleaning became a regular task for Mary. Every few days, Archer would ask her to clean, and then would sit and watch her as she tidied. The room seemed innocuous enough, now that she knew the multiple uses it held. Despite the various assurances that everything was aboveboard, she couldn't help but wonder why Archer always stayed to watch her work. He did not do this in any other area of the house, and that small voice in the back of her mind continued to warn her that something was not quite right about the basement. She knew that she would need to investigate the room alone if she wanted any real answers.

One evening, Mary was walking down the hall when she heard the thick sound of the bolt on the basement door being unlatched. She ducked into the library, peering cautiously out of the doorframe.

Archer emerged from the basement, once more streaked with blood. This time, the blood was much darker, as though it had been settling for a while. He seemed preoccupied, muttering under his breath. He let the door swing shut behind him as he walked away, totally engrossed in his own thoughts.

Mary slipped into the hall and furtively approached the door, her eyes constantly roving to prevent being caught unawares. She tried the handle. It was unlocked! Her eyes widened, and she couldn't believe her luck. She pulled on the door, for the first time realizing just how heavy it was.

Once more, the cool air and smell of death washed over her, but she did not hesitate. She descended quickly into the darkness, knowing that her time was limited. The lights clicked on as she neared the floor, and she braced herself for what she may find today, since she had not been invited down. To her shock, there was . . . nothing.

She scrutinized the room, slightly confused. *Where did the blood come from then?*

Not wanting to waste any time, she strode confidently to the first steel cabinet and swung the doors wide. Inside, carefully placed, were specimen jars. The jars varied in size, but they all had something in common. They all contained organs.

Human organs, she realized, observing the eyes, hearts, brains, and various other vital body parts that floated in the jars, each meticulously labelled.

"This is a strange collection," she mused, running her hands lightly across the jars.

She moved to the next cabinet, opening it. More of the same. Next in line was a large deep-freezer chest, and she grunted with effort as she lifted the lid. Upon looking into the freezer, she was immediately filled with regret. She stifled a scream as her knees buckled, sending her to the floor. What she had seen there, staring up at her, was a face.

She stayed perfectly still on the floor, desperately trying to calm her erratic breathing. She gathered her strength and stood, leaning on the freezer for support. Bracing herself, she looked into the freezer once more. Laying there, with a gaping hole that stretched from her sternum to her pelvis, was a woman. Her face was contorted in horror, her eyes and mouth open in a soundless scream. Her organs had been removed, leaving a bloated carcass of skin and bone behind.

Bile rose in Mary's throat, and she ran to the utility sink, barely making it before the contents of her stomach boiled over. She stood at the sink, quivering and gasping for air, praying that she would wake up from this nightmare. She ran the water, splashing her face and rinsing her mouth to rid herself of the evidence. She slowly returned to the chest, closing the lid.

There was another ice chest immediately to the left of the first, and she reluctantly lifted the lid. She stifled another scream as she stared into the severed heads of ten other women. Their bodies were nowhere to be seen, their faces all displaying various levels of decay and freezer burn.

"Eleven. There are eleven dead women in this basement," Mary whispered into the empty basement, tears now streaming down her face. "The organs in the cabinets—they must belong to these women. He is murdering women." The little voice was screaming now, drowning out all other thoughts.

Run, run, run!

Mary closed her eyes and shut the second cooler, fighting the urge to collapse again. Archie's words the day they met rang in her head: *"I've had to get rid of almost a dozen maids in the past few months, most for breach of contract."*

Her world began spinning, and the last line of the contract seemed to float in the air before her—*on pain of death.*

"Maids. He's been killing his maids." Her knees buckled again, and she fought to stay upright. "I have to call the police."

"I can't let you do that." His voice rang out in the silent basement, and Mary whirled to face him, desperately searching for the closest object that could be used as a weapon, finding nothing.

The pair locked eyes and moved as one, circling each other in a deadly dance.

"Mary, oh, Mary. What a shame. I really liked you!" He clucked his tongue, narrowing his dark eyes in disapproval. "Now you'll wind up alone in the cold, just like all the others. If only you hadn't gone poking about where you didn't belong. We could have been so happy together."

Tears were still pouring from Mary's eyes, and she fought to control the quiver in her voice. "Archie, I'm sorry. I signed the contract, I won't tell. I just want to go, please let me go. I promise, I won't tell a soul." A sob escaped her lips, and she fell to her knees, pleading for her life. "Please, Archie, I'm begging you. You know me! I'm smart; I know what will happen if I tell."

Archie slithered toward her, his athletic body weaving like a cobra about to strike.

"Sweet Mary. Kind Mary. I wish I could do that for you."

He reached her, pressing her head against his thigh as she wept, relishing in the fear pouring from her trembling frame.

"*Shhhhh, shhhhh, shhhh . . .*"

He ran his fingers through her pale-blonde hair, sending shivers of revulsion down Mary's spine. He knelt down, his fingers still tangled in her shoulder-length locks, and looked into her tear-filled eyes, tightening a hand around her neck. He smiled as she struggled to breathe, futilely beating her hands against his broad chest.

"I wish I could do that, my dear. But it's just not possible. It wasn't possible for the other eleven, and I can't make an exception for you. I'm sorry."

Those were the last words Mary heard before the world went dark.

Archer released her hair now, her body slumping to the floor. The dull sound of her head connecting with the concrete floor echoed across the room.

He smiled ruefully, placing his hands on his hips. "Twelve."

K.M. Reynolds is a multi-genre author with a particular penchant for thriller, romance, and fantasy. She has been writing poetry and short stories since 1998 and had her first piece published in 2005. In 2017, she decided to shift her focus to longer pieces of fiction and is currently working on a fantasy-romance series, *The Echarian Chronicles*, with the first book scheduled for release in May 2018.

K. M. lives in South Florida with her husband, her children, and an assortment of animals. She has a deep passion for literature, theatre, and visual art. She spends her free time reading and writing and is an avid audiophile. She enjoys thunderstorms and firmly believes that it's never too late in the day for a good cup of coffee. She has been fortunate enough to travel all over the world and draws inspiration for her work from her real-life experiences.

For updates on upcoming works, visit her website: www.RaisingReynolds.com/Author-KMReynolds or follow her on Facebook: www.facebook.com/AuthorKMReynolds.

Your first demon is always the hardest. Once you've gotten that out of the way, the rest all falls into place. That's what her father said. Her famous father, the renowned exorcist, Ozymandis Archibald Scott Featherstone the Third, heir to the Eye of Michael, slayer of ghouls, and bane of the undead.

Unfortunately, she was only Olivia Alice Sylvia Featherstone the First, heir to a modestly-sized teapot collection from India, slayer of not much, and bane to all decent suitors in the British Empire. And she had never banished so much as a stove gremlin, let alone a fully-embedded demon.

"You'll do just fine, Olive," her father reassured her. Then, because he was famous after all, he reminded her to please behave herself, and try extra hard not to embarrass the family name.

It was something she repeated to herself over and over during the short hansom carriage ride across London. She wore her best working gown that day, a dark green dress embroidered with the family crest on the bodice and pearls sewn into the generous neckline. The crest itself was of a blessed dagger of St. George piercing a viper and surrounded by alchemical symbols for the elements and for strength of soul. The whole thing looked ridiculous, but at least no one could accuse her of trying to imitate the bejeweled and beflowered costumes of that tart, Charlotte Van Hellsing. Roses indeed . . .

The hansom rocked to a stop in front of the duke's London residence, reminding her of the task at hand. Olivia imagined Charlotte's face the next time Lady Whitelock had them for tea, when she could finally tell a story of her own. Perhaps today's demon could even put up a fight, so she could give an exciting account.

The door of the carriage opened before she could touch it, and Olivia found herself greeted by a stout footman with a toadish, unpleasant face. He offered her a stern smile that did not reach his eyes and offered his hand.

"Miss Featherstone," he said. "We were expecting your father."

She accepted his help and stepped down from the carriage, fan clutched to her chest with her free hand.

"Father sent me in his place. Has there been any change in the boy's condition?"

The left side of the footman's mustache twitched, but there was otherwise no indication that she'd been heard. "This way, ma'am."

Olivia followed him inside, trying not to gawk. Even by affluent standards, the widowed Duchess of Oaksbury managed an impressive London household, funded by an estate earning over twenty thousand pounds a year. The Featherstones might not be too far from her in rank, but their stations were far from equal.

The footman led her through a grand entrance and to a parlor featuring white French furnishings with gold leaf trim. The duchess herself sat on a reclining chair, a cold cup of tea in her hand. She was young, not ten years Olivia's senior, but she carried herself like a woman many times that. She stared at the teacup with unfocused eyes but came back to the world with the footman's awkward cough.

"Miss Featherstone, Your Grace," he announced, his rounded spine straightening for one brief moment. As soon as his employer acknowledged the words, his back folded upon itself once more. He settled against the door, a deflated balloon awaiting its next assignment.

"Miss Featherstone," the duchess repeated, and her eyes sharpened as they fixed on the nervous young woman at the door.

Olivia dipped in a quick curtsey. "At your service, Your Grace."

"I asked for your father's service, not yours. Is he unwell?"

Her cheeks burned, and Olivia reminded herself of her manners. "I have trained since I was a child, Your Grace," she explained in a wavering voice. "My father should have sent word yesterday that I would be taking his place in this matter."

"This is not a situation for one with a . . . delicate disposition." The duchess did not bother to hide the curl of her lip as she looked Olivia over like a horse that just threw a shoe.

Olivia was prepared for such a reaction but felt her blood pressure rise nonetheless. She clasped her hands behind her back and offered her sweetest smile to the duchess, that miserable bejeweled cow. Her voice found strength. "Then it is indeed fortunate you sent for a Featherstone and not a Van Hellsing, Your Grace."

The Duchess of Oaksbury pursed her lips but did not press the issue. Good.

"May I see to the young duke?" Olivia continued. "I would not wish for his discomfort a moment longer."

Her new employer nodded, seeming to accept the arrangement for now, though her face was still dour and disapproving. "Thomas!"

The toad-like footman reappeared beside the novice exorcist with a speed and silence that defied both his girth and basic laws of science. He needed no further instruction beyond the sound of his name. He motioned for Olivia to follow him out of the parlor and toward a grand staircase that lay in the center of the home.

As if insisting he was a simple ordinary footman, Thomas lacked the miraculous speed conjured not a minute prior. His body huffed and swayed up the stairs, allowing Olivia ample time to follow in his shadow. He remained silent except for a few labored grunts, and she did not encourage conversation either.

The banisters left a streak of gray on her gloves, and the candles alongside were burned down to their bases. Had the whole house, décor and servants all, gone to disarray due to the child's affliction? Now that she thought of it, Olivia had yet to see another soul in the residence. Not even a lady's maid or scullery girl flitting through rooms.

Once on the third landing, they walked through a set of doors that separated the family's rooms from the rest of the house and down to the last set of double doors of the wing. The duke's private rooms.

"The duke's condition has not changed since you called for me?" Olivia asked. She felt the comforting presence of her blessed rosary within her dress pocket and tried to slow the ever-increasing pounding of her heart.

"It changed somewhat since we called for your father," Thomas corrected.

"In what way?" She was too preoccupied with what lay beyond those doors to be bothered by the affront.

"His Grace has had a sudden craving for the blood of rabbits. Lambs as well, once we ran out of rabbits."

Oh. Well then.

"You should not have given it to him," she groused, reaching for the brass doorknob.

"I will be sure to reprimand Her Grace for it," Thomas volleyed before snapping a mediocre attention stance and walking back the way they came. Miserable fat toad.

"Let's hope, for the boy's sake, they are better at shopping than following directions," Olivia muttered to herself.

She drew one last deep breath and pushed open the great mahogany doors. It was time to prove her worth.

The stench was what hit her first. Her father often described it, but no words could have prepared her for the true horror. It was as though one wrapped a corpse in swamp-drenched rags, urinated on it, and left it in the summer sun to fester for a week. Like the bloated carcass of a plagued sow had finally popped open and spilled itself all over a meat factory's floors.

Like a child possessed by the evilest of Hell's demons.

The Duke of Oaksbury, the duchess' seven-year-old son, lay in his luxurious bed, nested in a cocoon of goose feather pillows and heavy down blankets. Yet for all the wealth surrounding him, the boy took no comfort. His cherubic cheeks were bright with fever, and the spirit sweat soaked through to the top blankets. His dark curls were plastered to his forehead, and he swayed his head from side to side, muttering in equal parts Latin and Demonic. He would not have lasted another week like this. Leave it to the rich to sequester the afflicted from the world until absolutely necessary.

Fortunately for all parties, the items Olivia and her father told the duchess to purchase were all laid neatly on the chest at the foot of the boy's bed: a bundle of white sage and lavender, a crucifix—hopefully blessed by a bishop, three white candles, and a bowl each of salt and pepper.

"What is your name?" Olivia asked as she inspected the quality of each item. The routine of checking helped settle her frayed nerves and grounded her soul for the coming ordeal.

The boy's eyes opened, and she looked into the most beautiful pair of blue eyes she'd ever seen, pale ice rimmed with red and puffed up from his tears.

"Edward," he said in a thick rasp.

"Not you," she scoffed, plucking up the candles.

She felt his continued gaze as she walked around the bed to place a candle on the nightstands on either side.

"Come on now. What's your name?"

Then the boy laughed, and she nearly turned to look before remembering herself. The last candle remained on the chest by the boy's feet, each of them imitating the suffering of Christ on the cross.

"Dantalion."

Olivia's brows furrowed and now she did turn to look at the little duke.

"Dandelion?"

If it were possible for a dying boy to look appalled with insult, he did so then.

"Dantalion, you deaf girl. Great Duke of Hell, prince of thirty-six legions of the swarm, the seventy-first of the great seventy-two demons of the Morningstar's Court of Daemons."

She wasn't trying to be rude, but Olivia still heard *Dandelion*, and so *Dandelion* it would have to stay.

"Well, whatever it is, I have no interest in your legions or how you rank among your brothers. You are to leave this boy in peace and return to your pit."

The boy laughed again, his breath reeking of brimstone and death. "And here I thought they'd hired a professional. Am I not worth that much effort?"

"I doubt it." Olivia lit the sage bundle next, laying it in a ceramic bowl beside the last candle. "But I am a professional nonetheless. I just thought I would ask first."

"A polite exorcist?"

"A merciful one."

The laughter boomed out of him then, far too loud and deep to come from such a small body. It echoed throughout the large room and reverberated off the walls. He laughed far too long for anything considered civil, and it had her fuming where she stood. There wasn't anything malicious in his merriment, and that was the worst part about it.

"Oh, really now, this isn't funny. Please be an adult about this, won't you?"

The woman put her hands on her hips and narrowed her gray eyes at the boy-beast. The sage tickled her nose and threatened to make her sneeze, but she refused to do so. He would not have the satisfaction of seeing any of her discomfort.

"My apologies," Dantalion said, his raucous laughter finally dying down to a more reasonable level. He propped himself up against the headboard, fluffing the pillows at his side. With folded hands in his lap, the child was the perfect image of a dutiful student. "Please proceed."

It would do.

Olivia smoothed down the front of her dress, making sure the sigil on her bodice was visible. He must not have seen it yet to be so fearless of what was about to happen. Demons much more powerful than he could be frightened out of a possession with the mere mention of the Featherstone name alone.

He didn't look impressed. His loss.

Olivia picked up the bowl of salt and began the cleansing circle. The prayer flowed from her lips as naturally as if this were her hundredth ceremony instead of her first. The disruption caused by this Dandelion demon melted into the background. This ceremony was one she'd practiced since childhood, and the familiarity was comforting, even in this unholy setting.

The circle began on one side of the bed, leaving just enough room for the exorcist to move. It circled the bed and created a seamless white horseshoe in the room. The last step was to close the circle over the headboard, and the demon would be bound. Well, nearly so. He had only two choices left to him at that point: return to Hell to rejoin his brethren, or remain where he was, buried within the skin of a dying boy. No escape to another host. No way out.

So why didn't he try to escape the circle before it was closed? Why was he just sitting there as if she were about to put on a puppet show rather than banish his soul? It was almost disappointing.

"You cannot win," she explained, leaning over the bed to dust the headboard with the purifying salt. "You may as well give up now before I'm forced to destroy you."

"Destroy me?" the demon snorted, though he did eye her with new wariness. "You cannot destroy me, girl. You couldn't destroy a dinner party, let alone a Duke of Hell."

Olivia brushed back some of the loose brown waves that had fallen free from its pins.

"You're wrong on both counts, I'm afraid."

She slipped the bishop-blessed rosary around the boy's little head, and still Dantalion did nothing to stop it. That did not mean he was remaining indifferent.

The angelic faced darkened, and his ice-blue eyes narrowed dangerously. "The boy will die too."

A soft hum of acknowledgement was the only indication that Olivia had heard him. She stepped back when she was satisfied with the binding circle and returned to the foot of the bed. Her hands patted the many inner pockets of her dress until she came to the right one. She really should find one pocket for her rosary and just stick with it.

"Featherstones may be powerful, but they cannot keep me from exacting my revenge."

It took a moment, but Olivia was able to untangle the mess of chain and stone in her hands. Her father was right; a rosary blessed by the pope himself should be treated with more care.

"I will drag his soul to Hell as payment for your impertinence!"

"Yes, yes." *Now where did that bowl of pepper get to?*

"And when I return, I will slice open your pretty neck and drain you of your lifeblood!"

She wrapped the rosary around her right wrist and picked up the located bowl. Facing the possessed little duke, she lifted her chin in defiance. It was time to show the world what a Featherstone could do.

"Hush now, Dandelion, it is time to begin."

"Dantalion, stupid girl!"

"I said hush."

The possessed boy's lips curled up in a sneer so much like the duchess' own that Olivia briefly wondered if the child weren't simply a brat playing at possession for attention. Was he even worth curing if it wasn't a ploy? No doubt he would grow up to be as unpleasant as the woman downstairs sipping her cold tea. Not that it mattered really; it wasn't about the boy in the end. This demon needed to be purged from the world and that was that.

The Latin came to her when she called, smooth and lyrical. Her chest rose and fell with each measured breath, each word a song and a prayer and a command all in one. Ozymandis was right; once she settled into the ritual, it all came together. The demon's body stiffened with every word that passed between her lips, and his eyes narrowed into dangerous slits. He was angry. Afraid. It was working!

Olivia held the cross high enough for the demon to see and continued her prayers. At the end of each command, she pinched some pepper and tossed it onto him. The sage, meanwhile, smoked with a thick pale cloud gathering along the ceiling. It would likely take weeks for the room to properly air out.

The longer Olivia chanted, however, the more her nerves began to reemerge. Everything was performed according to her father's strict standards. Her accent was flawless, and she'd tossed the exact amount of pepper called for.

Yet when the last *amen* faded into silence, the demon still sat before her, his arms crossed, pepper in his hair, and a sour expression on his face.

"Was that it?" he asked.

For the first time, she had no quip to toss back. Was that it? Well of course that was it! Why wasn't he writhing in agony and accepting banishment to the burning pits of Hell's fire?

Her gaze immediately went to the salt circle, but it was unbroken. The candles were still lit. The purchased rosary smoldered a little on the boy's white smock but not even that appeared to distress the demon.

"Because if that was it, it was awful."

Olivia turned the cross in her hand, looking at the brass Christ, as if He had something to do with it. Then she looked back up at the boy in bed.

"What did you say your name was?"

A slow smile began to form on his cherubic face. "Dantalion, and it wasn't that."

Cheeks and eyes burning, Olivia dropped her gaze to the floor, to the bed, anywhere but at the demon now tickled with amusement. Her first assignment and she was being humiliated by a Duke of Hell in the body of a seven-year-old.

"What was it then?" she asked in an embarrassed mumble.

"Go home, little girl. You're wasting my time."

Olivia couldn't give up, she couldn't just abandon an innocent boy and dishonor her family on her first exorcism. The first one is always the hardest, that's what her father said. She just had to get through this first one and it would all come together.

He muttered something under his breath and her head snapped back up.

"What was that, hellspawn?"

"I said," and then he laughed, "they should have sent for a Van Hellsing. I'm worthy of a professional exorcist."

Her eyes met Dantalion's, and while she nearly caved to his patronizing joy, his words convinced her otherwise.

"I will go home," she said, slow and clear. "But I will be back. You haven't seen the last of me, Dandelion."

"For the sake of your dignity, I better have."

For her dignity indeed . . . Olivia turned and stalked towards the bedroom door.

"Hey, girl! Break the salt circle at least!" he cried in her wake. "It is unbecoming to leave a mess."

She ignored him. Van Hellsing, he said! Van Hellsing! Well of course he would say that; he was a demon. Of course he would prefer a second-rate exorcism from some second-rate tart. Though if Charlotte was second-rate and had already defeated her first demon, then what was Olivia?

"Is he well again?" the Duchess of Oaksbury cried when she reached the bottom of the stairs. The anxious mother's eyes were puffy and red, and her lined mouth held none of its earlier scorn.

She clutched a lace handkerchief to her breast, completing the perfect picture of an agonized mother.

Thomas hunched by the door, Olivia's hat in hand. He didn't make the perfect picture of anything.

"Do not open the door no matter what you hear," Olivia said as she brushed by.

The duchess tottered after. "But my son. Is he well?"

"I will be back in the morning. Do not open that door, Your Grace. The duke's life and eternal soul hinges on it." She accepted the hat and tied it on, hoping they couldn't see the trembling of her fingers. "And no more lamb's blood!"

"Yes, of course." The duchess looked as though she would like to say more, but Olivia was already out the door and walking to the curb to flag down a hansom.

All she wanted was to disappear back into the city and get as far away from Oaksbury as possible.

Olivia hardly remembered the ride home and found herself selfishly grateful that her father was not home when she arrived. How could she face him in the wake of her humiliation? Worse, she knew he wouldn't yell or chastise her. His disappointment alone was enough to break her. So rather than wait downstairs for his eventual return, Olivia sequestered herself in their library and buried her defeat in an endless amount of books and tea.

For hours, she poured over the ancient tomes, searching for a solution to her predicament. Her demon was easy enough to find, though his name still looked like a plant's. The more she read, the worse her situation became. He was right, her problem wasn't in the name at all. What it actually was, however, remained a mystery.

At some point in the late afternoon, she heard the door downstairs open and their butler greet the master of his house on his return. Olivia froze where she sat, afraid that her father would come in any moment and inquire about her day. Her heart stopped altogether when his light steps tapped on the stairs. Yet, he paused outside the door to the library; he moved on and left her in peace. Bless that man.

Book after book, Olivia continued to read and take notes and mark pages to be re-read later. She worked until the light outside faded and her candles burned down to misshapen stumps. Nothing in any of the books so much as hinted at a remedy that she had not already thought of.

The problem, then, had to be Olivia.

When she could avoid her father no longer and her last candle had snuffed itself out, Olivia slipped the last tome into place and left the sanctuary of the library. She was grateful for the privacy Ozymandis allowed her, but it could not be granted forever.

She dressed for dinner with extra care that evening, not wanting a single hair out of place. Nothing could give away her distress; she could not bear it. When at last she was satisfied, she finally descended the stairs.

Ozymandis was already seated at the table when she appeared, a cheerful expression on his youthful face. He stood as she approached and offered her a chair with a flourish. He might be many things, but no one could deny the man his charm.

"There you are!" he said with an excited grin. "I was hoping you would come down tonight."

Olivia offered a weak smile in response and sank into her seat. "I'm sorry, Papa," she said. "I lost track of time in the books."

"As one will, as one will."

Her father returned to his own seat and rang the bell for dinner service to begin. He was still handsome for his age, even after raising a daughter alone and working for so long as an exorcist. What wear his body took showed nothing more than stray white strands in a head otherwise full with deep brown hair and regal lines in his face. His green eyes were still bright and his steps lively.

Olivia hoped she aged half as well throughout her career. If she even had one, that was.

Ozymandis served them both once the food was on the table,

granting her a generous portion of everything. She knew what would come following this and prepared herself as best as she could.

"So then," he began, as predicted. "Tell me everything, Olive. Did you do our name proud?"

"Of course," she said with as bright a smile as she could manage. "I had the best trainer, did I not?"

"That you did," he agreed. "I'll tell that idiot Abraham he'll have to do a better job with Charlotte. We'll put them out of business, you and I!" Her father leaned forward and laced his fingers before him on the table, his dinner forgotten in his eagerness. "What was it?" he went on. "A ghost? A creature of the swarm?"

"A duke," Olivia admitted. She took a bite of fish to allow her more time to think.

"A duke, eh?" His eyebrows rose, clearly impressed. "My daughter defeated a duke."

"Not . . . quite." Olivia shrugged and smiled again to assuage any lingering doubt. "He's nearly gone, but I need to finish the job in the morning. He's . . . quite difficult."

Her father finally began to eat, though he didn't seem to taste any of it. He was far too intent on her words to so much as look at his food. "Do you need my assistance?"

"No!" Olivia cleared her throat and giggled awkwardly, waving a flippant hand. "No, of course not. Do not worry yourself, Papa."

Ozymandis nodded and beamed again, shoving an enormous chunk of bread into his mouth. "My daughter, defeating a duke."

She watched her father eat with affection. The poor man had been a bachelor too long to be fit for society. Too busy providing for Olivia and selling his services to half of the isle to worry about silly things like table manners. He insisted on a governess for her own education on femininity, which was probably the only reason she could pass so well in society. He always insisted on the best for her, for his little Olive.

And she'd disgraced him.

Dinner passed as it usually did, with Olivia listening enraptured to her father's stories. That evening, he told her favorite one of all: the werewolf hunt where he was a young man and met a fierce Valkyrie of a woman who stole his heart instantly. A woman who could never quite be tamed, not even by the high society she married into. A woman who fought to her very last, saving her husband and infant daughter from Beelzebub, the Lieutenant of Lucifer himself.

And when the last slice of lemon cake was devoured, Ozymandis finished his story the way he always did. It was her favorite part.

"And you will be the fiercest Valkyrie of all," he concluded, no doubt in his animated face.

This time, the words failed to fill her with the usual excitement and pride. This time, it all fell flat, and the burning shame returned with a vengeance, a wound with no salve. Duke or ghost or sprite, it didn't matter. Olivia didn't have the gift, and perhaps never would. Tomorrow, everyone would know it. Her father would know it.

"May I please be excused?" she asked.

Ozymandis' face fell in disappointment, but he nodded. "Of course, Olive. You must be exhausted."

"I am." That wasn't a lie at least.

Wishing her father a good night, Olivia retreated to her room and tried to calm her mind long enough to rest.

Sleep did not come for her that night no matter how she tried. Possibilities and theories raced through the girl's mind, each more ridiculous than the last. She had to exorcise the demon by the end of the next day or not only would her reputation be forever tarnished, but her father's as well. Failure was not an option, but it was the only one available to her.

That was, until her epiphany at midnight.

As the last chime of the grandfather clock rang, the beginnings of a plan started to come together. It was mad, no doubt a result of stress, exhaustion, and lemon cake. Yet it could work. It would work. It had to or all truly would be lost. With stakes as they were, it was her best chance to get the demon duke out of the human one. There was really no choice to be made at all.

Olivia rose from her bed and tiptoed back to the library.

Two hours later, she returned to her bedroom, a pile of supplies in her arms. She lay it all on top of her bed and pushed the rug away from the center of the room. With enough room to work, Olivia picked up the book she found and opened it to the right page. Of course the exorcism section was vague and completely useless, but summoning? Oh, the summoning ceremony was detailed, neat, and easy to follow.

She started with the chalk, drawing the summoning circle on the floorboards. It was an elaborate design that carried with it containment and protection runes meant to keep Olivia safe from whatever, or whoever, she drew into it.

Once it was sealed, she lit five candles and placed them equidistant from each other. To the North was a green candle for Earth, East had yellow for Air, South was red for Fire, West was blue for Water, and in the center sat white for Spirit.

The last thing she did was draw a larger circle with salt that surrounded both herself and the chalk. If anything went wrong, she could at least keep the disaster contained.

"Alright, you horrible thing," she muttered. "Let's see Charlotte do this."

Olivia knelt before the summoning circle and began her chant. This was not holy Latin she was singing but something much older and darker. King Solomon himself would have approved. Talentless she might be, but Olivia Featherstone well made up for it in temperament and studiousness. Were she a man, she might have been a doctor or professor. As it was, she was forced to settle for possessed children and summoning demons in her bedroom.

As she chanted, Olivia saw the chalk brighten as if lit from beneath. The candles flickered and waved in a nonexistent breeze. The center candle burned brightest of all, and as it grew taller and taller, to the height of her chin, a black flame took the place of yellow.

"Who dares summon the great Duke of Hell, Commander of

the Swarm and Satan's High Legions, Seventy-First of the Fallen and Lord of the First Hierarchy, Dantalion the Terrible?"

Dantalion emerged from the flame in his true form: a tall, thin man with golden flames in his eyes and long, spindly fingers. He looked as if a spider had been given human form, but not a very convincing one. The clothing he wore was that of a gentleman, fancy and preposterous.

"You aren't of the First Hierarchy," Olivia snorted. "That's Astaroth."

The demon looked at her for a moment, his mighty visage wilting. "It's you," he said with a disappointed sigh.

"It is. I've called you here to strike a bargain, Dandelion."

The sad demon straightened back up. "How is it you can say Astaroth's name but not mine?" He pointed to the open book before her. "It's written right there!"

"I'm in no mood for your tricks, demon." She sniffed.

"It's not a trick, you illiterate dalcop! Look!"

She held up a hand to silence him. There was very little time and much to do. "There's no need to be rude. I've summoned you here for a purpose."

"Purpose? What purpose? Haven't I been punished enough with your presence?" Dantalion's fire-filled eyes widened suddenly in alarm. "You tricked me into leaving my vessel!"

Olivia paused and blinked in realization. It would have been the perfect solution had she thought of it. Her father could have been at the Oaksbury residence right at that moment, sealing the boy from Dantalion's evil hold. Stupid girl . . .

Rather than give the duke the satisfaction of her most recent failure of the day, she simply waved a flippant hand. "Indeed," she said. "And if you want to return to your vessel, you will hear what I have to say."

The demon crossed his long arms and raised an eyebrow. He did not look fooled.

Olivia cleared her throat and continued. "As I said, I have a bargain to offer you."

"Go on," he said.

"Possess any vessel you want in the city."

He was quiet for a moment, clearly amazed at her cleverness. "What?"

"You heard me. Possess whoever you wish. I will not stop you. I can even help you pick them out."

Again, Dantalion appeared stunned. Well, a more stunned version than before. More stunnier.

"And when they call for an exorcist?" he asked, as though to a child.

Now, Olivia thought, *time for the finishing touch. For the stunniest he'd ever been.*

"You let me exorcise you."

"I'm amazed," he said.

She beamed.

"You are truly stupider than I ever gave you proper credit for."

Olivia glowered down at the insolent creature. "Explain," she said.

"Explain? What is there to explain? You'll 'allow' me to possess someone if I 'allow' you to exorcise me? Were you dropped on your head as a baby or is this a more recent affliction?"

It appeared the silly beast needed things watered down for him to understand. "I will, and you will," she said. "That is how this will be from now on."

"And if I tell you where you can put this scheme of yours?"

Olivia lifted her chin and pointed to her bedroom door. "Then I tell my father, and by the time he's done with you, you'll be lucky if there's enough left of you to return to Hell in failure. If you knew the Van Hellsing name, then you know the name Featherstone."

Now the demon was paying attention. The look he gave her was much more respectful than before, and she liked it that way.

"How do I know you won't just send him at me anyway?"

"You'll ensure it," she said in triumph. "I can't get rid of you on my own, and we both know it. No one else does. So you make sure to give a good show whenever I exorcise you, and no one will ever have to ask for anyone else."

Dantalion thought for a moment, eyeing her with wary gold eyes. Yes, this respect was much better.

"You're devious enough to be a demon yourself. All that for some fame?"

"For more than that, but I'll accept fame."

"I get a month in my vessels."

"A week."

"Three."

"Now you're being greedy."

"I'm a demon!"

Olivia scowled but nodded her head. "Two and not a day more."

"Done. Now seal it, girl. I have a human to haunt before your little scheme begins."

She reached for a small silver knife that lay in the crease of the book to mark her place. The sting lasted only a moment, well worth the reward. She squeezed the tip of her finger until a drop of blood appeared. This she fed directly to the open flame where the candle spat red sparks, flickered, and finally burned black once more.

Dantalion smiled. "You would be dangerous if you had any power."

"You don't know what power I have."

The demon spread his arms in an exaggerated bow. "Indeed not. Until tomorrow then, poppet."

The candle's black flame filled with gold and finally returned to its normal size as he disappeared. Olivia could feel the room lighten and sighed with relief as the demonic presence left. Had she the ability, she would have vanquished him the moment he appeared in the summoning circle. Unfortunately for her, the protection the circle offered her against Dantalion also protected him from her.

There was no choice but to allow him to return to the child. For now.

The next morning, she prepared herself with all the solemnity of a soldier packing for war. Today would be a historic one for her and her kind, no matter how it ended or who knew what. Demons were hardly known for their trustworthiness, but his word was all she had. It had better be worth something.

She left before the sun or her father rose, sure she could not keep her secret if faced with him before the deed was done. Success was at last within reach; she could not afford to lose her nerve now.

With no other carriages on the street competing for space, the hansom arrived in only minutes. When Olivia was received at the duchess' door, Thomas looked rumpled and disoriented as if he'd just woken. Perhaps her early start was a touch too early.

"What are you doing here at this hour, Miss Featherstone?" he mumbled.

She could have believed the rudeness was the result of the hour, but Olivia knew better. Still, she was here now, and there was no point in arguing about time or manners.

"I am here to finish the job you are paying me for." She sniffed, handing over her hat and cloak.

He took them dumbly and allowed her to show herself in.

The duchess was halfway down the stairs in her nightgown and shawl by the time Olivia saw her.

"This is too irregular," she grumbled but did not hinder the younger woman's progress.

"How is His Grace?" Olivia asked.

"The same," the older woman grumbled, following her up the stairs. "Are you sure you know what you are doing?"

Olivia hoped so.

"Of course."

They stopped outside the door to little Edward's room, and Olivia looked at her companion with pointed impatience. The duchess lightly coughed into her handkerchief and waited.

"Your Grace, I don't think it is wise for you to see—"

"Open the door, Miss Featherstone."

Did karma truly awaken this early in the morning to punish her for her demonic bargain? It seemed so.

With no logical reason to refuse a mother her diligence, Olivia opened the door to the duke's room. She held her breath without meaning to, unsure of what would face her on the other side. If possible, she felt even more nervous than the day before. Blood pounded in her ears, and sweat trickled down the center of her back. An audience was not something she'd planned on while making this deal. She didn't even know if the deal would be honored.

She led the way into the room on stiff legs, the duchess following close after. The boy was already awake, sitting upright in bed and watching with calculating blue eyes that glittered in the golden light of dawn.

Dantalion was still at home.

"This could get dangerous, Your Grace," Olivia said in one last ditch effort to get rid of the duchess.

"I am not afraid," the elder woman said, dashing that effort against the cruel stones of reality.

"Of course you're not," Olivia muttered beneath her breath.

"What was that?"

"Nothing, Your Grace."

She broke the salt circle and stepped inside, motioning for the duchess to come with her. The possessed boy watched with amusement, curling the edges of his lips. He thankfully kept his mouth shut while the exorcist recreated the salt circle in full and made a smaller one around the doting, invasive mother.

"Come to finish the job then, little girl?" he asked when she was done. "Perhaps you will be more successful than yesterday."

The duchess shot her a withering glare that Olivia stubbornly ignored. He could say whatever he liked so long as he kept his end of the bargain and the existence of it a secret.

"Laugh now, Dandelion," she said, raising her crucifix, "but I will banish you."

"Dantalion."

She scowled and resisted the urge to stomp a foot. *Just make it look good,* she mouthed silently.

His grin widened.

The song didn't come as easily to her this time, not like it did before. She stumbled at first, fumbling over the words she learned as a child. She could feel the duchess' eyes on her and pushed it to the back of her mind. No matter how it was done, she still had a job to complete.

To the demon's credit, he gave a great show. Once the exorcist found her rhythm and the chant came out stronger, Dantalion began to writhe and groan. As they continued to play their respective parts, the ceremony grew in intensity and volume. Her voice rose higher and higher until she was shouting the words instead of singing them. The demon, too, wailed and twisted the little body he inhabited, selling this exorcism with all his shriveled brimstone heart.

"Oh, you're too powerful for me, Featherstone! My soul is burning!"

Perhaps he was a tad heavy handed about it.

The child's body arched back and lifted from the bed, hanging in mid-air like a broken doll on a string. Then a white beam shot through the boy as though pierced by the light of Heaven itself. With a final inhuman shriek, the demon fell limp and sank back to the pile of blankets and pillows.

Olivia was impressed.

The duchess screamed.

"Edward! Oh, my Edward!" the duchess simpered, leaving the safety of her salt circle to embrace the boy.

The very-human Edward opened his clear-blue eyes and clung to his mother, sobbing tears of relief and terror.

"Oh, Mother, it was horrible!" he cried. "I thought I was going to die!"

The exorcist smiled at the pair and tucked her instruments away before quietly excusing herself. Payment would be taken care of through lawyers, so there was no reason to linger. She doubted the duchess or her son even noticed her presence or departure, and Thomas seemed only too glad to hand back her things so she could be on her lower-class way.

"Shall I call a hansom for you, Miss Featherstone?" he asked.

"No need," she chirped, securing her hat. "It's a beautiful morning. I believe I shall walk home."

"Of course you will."

Then he shut the door behind her, and they were rid of one another at last.

The city was just beginning to stir as she made her way down the sidewalk. Horses sleepily walked by with their carriages, and businessmen shuffled past, just barely tapping their hats to her in silent greeting.

She didn't care; there was nothing that could bother her now. She'd done it. Perhaps with a less orthodox method, morally ambiguous one might say, but she had done it. The Featherstone name would continue on as a paradigm of demon banishing and monster slaying. Her father would not be ashamed, and she would not have to suffer that smug look from Charlotte ever again.

"Glorious morning to you, Miss!"

Olivia chuckled softly and made room for the young man who approached from behind to walk at her side. He was a handsome man with a sharp tailored suit, cane, and hat.

"Good morning," she greeted.

"So how was it?" he asked, all teeth and dimples.

"A bit theatrical but perfectly adequate. Who is this gentleman then?"

Dantalion twirled his cane and shrugged, offering an arm to help her cross the street. She accepted.

"I have no idea," he said. "He was reading a paper when I happened upon him. Didn't like the way he tied his cravat."

Well, a Duke of Hell the beast might be, but it appeared he'd fixed the offending cravat.

They continued in companionable silence until she neared her home, at which time she tilted her head to consider the demon. "Will you ever tell me what it was?" she asked.

He released her arm at her doorstep and stepped back. "I'll tell you now if you like," he said, grinning again.

Olivia nodded and folded her hands in front, waiting. "Go on."

"You are tone deaf, poppet. You couldn't compel a priest from the nunnery with that voice."

To her credit, she held back her response to his vulgarity. "Tone deaf, you say?"

"Hopelessly so." Dantalion offered her a flourished bow, doffed his hat to her, and straightened once more. "Until we meet again, Miss Featherstone."

"Two weeks," she reminded. "Not a day more."

"Two weeks." He nodded. "Till then, poppet."

"Until then, Dandelion."

He shook his head with a sigh and continued down the street, whistling a merry tune to himself.

Olivia watched him disappear into the morning crowd and waited until she could no longer hear him before heading inside. She'd expected to feel guiltier, bargaining with demons as she'd done, but she didn't. If anything, joy bubbled within her and left her as giddy as a little girl. When dealing and haggling with such precious things as souls, it was best to remain flexible and open to possibilities. To use every resource available, even if they were a touch unconventional. A Featherstone never made a name for themselves by being anything less than extraordinary, and Olivia was determined to be the best of them all.

To hell with songs and salt, this exorcist had much more valuable resources at her fingertips.

M.L. Garza comes from a proud line of authors and artists and has been making up worlds and adventures since she was old enough to talk. She plays with computers for a living and loses herself in her stories during her time off. When not huddled in her writing cave, she can be found on the beautiful shores of Hawaii, a cup of tea always in hand. She has a love for speculative fiction, especially that which explores other cultures and underappreciated mythologies.

Her work has appeared in anthologies, stand-alone projects, and the big screen itself!

"Okay, on the count of three, we both do it," said Bard.

"You mean one, two, three, go? Or go on three?" said Belligan, who was clearly starting to have second thoughts about the arrangement they had made.

"One, two, three, go," said Bard.

"Okay . . . So, one, two, three, blam?" asked Belligan.

"Yeah, that's how it's gonna work," said Bard, his annoyance starting to seep through the cracks of his cool demeanor.

The dusty attic was illuminated by a camping lantern that hung from a single crooked nail in the crossbeam in the ceiling, and the dull cone of light that it emitted cast dark shadows from the deep-set features of Bard's face, making him look older than his twenty-five years.

"Just like that?" asked Belligan, the gun beginning to shake just a little bit in his hand.

"Yeah, just like that. Is there any other way to do it?" answered Bard, staring straight ahead.

"No, I guess not. It just seems so sudden. Shouldn't we at least say a few words or something?" asked Belligan.

"Like what? Who's gonna remember those words when our brains are painted all over the wall?" snapped Bard.

The thought of his head turning into a steaming pile of red mush made Belligan's stomach turn violently, and his enormous round face scrunched up viscerally into an ugly wince at the horrifying image Bard's words had planted in his mind.

"Fuck man, don't say things like that. I don't want to think about it!" cried Belligan.

"So, don't think about it then. That's why it's just one, two, three, blam. If you start thinking about it, you're going to fuck something up. Now, are we gonna do this or what?" asked Bard, who was rapidly running out of patience for Belligan's sudden, cowardly foot dragging.

"Yeah, yeah, yeah, I'm still in to do this shit. I just gotta make sure that I'm in the right frame of mind before we make it official, ya know?" replied Belligan, his tone unconvincing.

"The trigger ain't gonna pull itself. You sure you got the balls to see this through? If you can't do it, just say the word, and I'll shoot you before I shoot myself," said Bard.

"Are you actually offering to shoot me? I don't even know what to say to that," scoffed Belligan, dumbfounded.

"Just say the word, and I'll put this bullet in your brain, no questions asked," Bard offered for a second time, his tone softened to convey the humble sincerity of his offer to kill Belligan.

"I don't want you to fucking shoot me! What are you, insane?" shrieked Belligan, who was becoming more and more incredulous as the reality of Bard's suggestion began to set in.

"It would be a kindness," said Bard.

"A kindness? Shooting me in the head would be a kindness?" said Belligan, who let his jaw drop in an ostentatious display of shocked disbelief. "You and I clearly must have very different ideas about the definition of kindness."

"Why not? Don't you want to die? Isn't that the whole point of a suicide pact? What is a suicide pact, if not a kind of verbal contract to guarantee that each person's life ends by any means necessary? I was very clear in the wording of the ad: *One way or another, neither of us is leaving this attic alive.* If you can't pull the trigger yourself and put an end to your life, then the terms of our pact dictate that I must do it for you. I don't want to have to do that, but what would my word be worth if I didn't hold up my end of the deal?" asked Bard.

"I didn't sign up to get murdered by you; that is not what I agreed to at all. You never said that I couldn't change my mind," said Belligan defensively.

"Wait a minute. So, you came here with the intention of shooting yourself, but now you're losing your nerve, and I offer to do it for you, but you don't want me to? Are you fucking serious? Make up your fucking mind. Do you want to die or not?" screamed Bard furiously, the thick vein bisecting his forehead, throbbing in an angry asynchronous rhythm.

"Yes, I still want to die, goddamnit! I just want to do it on my own terms," wailed Belligan.

"Well, we haven't got all night, so just be a man about this, and pull that fucking trigger!" Bard shouted.

"What about going on the count of three?" asked Belligan.

"Yes, of course we're still going on the count of three," said Bard.

"So, it's one, two, three, blam! Right?"

"Yes, yes, for the hundredth time, yes! One! Two! Three! Blam! Goodbye forever," said Bard.

He couldn't take it anymore. If Belligan decided to pull out now, it would fuck everything up. No one beside Belligan knew that he was suicidal. Bard couldn't just let him walk out of the attic knowing the most intimate secret of Bard's life, able to blab it carelessly to the entire world when he had been so careful to keep it hidden, had planned every detail perfectly so that no one would be able to get wise and try to stop him before he had a chance to do it. He also knew that he didn't have it in him to shoot himself right in front of Belligan and leave him to deal with the mess in his own house. The only solution was to stick to the original plan, which Belligan was doing his best to get out of now.

"Look, I'm sorry, alright? I've just never done anything like this before," said Belligan, the irony of his statement lost on both men.

"Then just don't think about it. That's the thing about suicide; if you do it right the first time, you'll never have to do it again. We'll both start counting, and then after three, it will all be over. You'll never have to worry about anything ever again," said Bard.

"Okay. Fuck! Let's fucking do this shit!" screamed Belligan, spit spraying wildly from his red lips.

"You sure you're ready?" asked Bard.

"Fuck yeah. I'm ready, let's do it," answered Belligan.

"Okay then, on three," said Bard.

"I thought it was right after three," said Belligan.

"*Right after three*, pull the trigger," said Bard, as if he were explaining it to a slow-witted child.

"Right, got it," said Belligan with a forced edge of confidence to his voice now, which Bard guessed was his way of overcompensating for the terror that was clearly screaming through his body like wildfire.

"One . . ."

The gun began to shake even harder in Belligan's hand now, sweat beading at his bulging temples and running down the fat rolls on the back of his neck.

"Two . . ."

Bard and Belligan locked eyes, and the tears that could no longer be contained began trickling out fitfully from the corners of Belligan's eyelids.

"Thr—what the fuck, dude? You're not counting!" barked Bard suddenly, his tone of voice bordering on adolescent sulking.

"Wh-what? Since when am I supposed to count?" sniffled Belligan.

"We're doing this thing together, I need you to count with me. That's the whole damn point, so we don't have to do this alone," said Bard.

"No, you're the counter. You're the mastermind behind this whole arrangement. You do it," said Belligan, folding his meaty arms defiantly over the rotund mass of his stomach.

"Who made me the counter? Just say the words with me, and it will be easier," said Bard.

"Come on, man. I can barely keep my head straight right now. It's just, this is all happening so fast, and I don't know how to handle it," said Belligan, his voice choked with emotion.

"Jesus Christ, why did you even agree to the pact? Do I need to pull up the series of emails between us on my phone to remind you of how certain you were of this decision just a few hours ago? You responded to my ad, you assured me that you were beyond certain that you were ready to end your life, you drove three hours to meet me here for the explicit purpose of committing suicide together. It's too late to back down now, Belligan. It's time to either shit or get off the fucking pot."

Neither man had anything to say for a good while after this, so they both waited in uncomfortable silence that felt like it might never end for something to happen from the other man. Bard had been kneeling for nearly ten minutes now, and his bad knee couldn't stand the pressure anymore, so he rose to his feet and shuffled the gun tensely in the palm of his hand, listlessly watching the reflection of the dull lantern light dance upon the barrel of the gun. Belligan set his gun aside, reached for the bottle of Johnny Walker that sat near his feet, and wept softly.

It was probably 4:30 by now. Bard's mom would be coming home from work soon, and he saw his window of opportunity steadily slipping away, making him feel the familiar sting of regret in his gut once again. He'd managed to make a mess of most areas of his life, and now it was looking like he wouldn't even be able to kill himself properly.

Belligan drank off the bottle long and hard, like there was a fire inside of him that only whiskey could extinguish. When it was empty, he dropped the bottle and began to weep some more, the ample, doughy frame of his body shuddering hypnotically to the rhythm of his gasping sobs.

"I'm sorry, man . . . Really, I am. I want to do this. I don't want to hurt anymore. I'm just scared of whatever comes next," said Belligan between pathetic gasping sobs.

"Once you pull the trigger, you won't hurt anymore. You'll never feel anything again. Let the bullet do what the booze never could," said Bard.

"I'm just scared, Bard. I can't remember being as scared about anything in my entire life," said Belligan.

"I promise you, Belligan, whatever awaits you in the next life can't be any worse than what you'll have to deal with if you keep on living. I've never asked to know your reasons for entering into this pact, but the fact that you are here now is proof that the pain in your life has reached a level that is no longer tolerable. How the hell could whatever awaits you on the other side be any worse than what you've already been through?" said Bard, who could feel the hint of possible tears welling up in his eyes as his own haunting reasons for wishing for his life to end came flooding back into his mind one by one.

"Okay. You're right, goddamnit. It's now or never, so let's do this before I change my mind again," said Belligan, the confidence in his voice now genuine and unmistakable, as if he had suddenly become aware of having crossed over the threshold from fear to acceptance and knew that he was finally going to go through with it.

"Brilliant. Let's get to it then. One, two, three, blam, just like we planned," said Bard, a little too zealously for what seemed appropriate given the circumstance.

Both men again assumed the awkward position of death, knelt low on both knees, with their guns pointed at their right temples.

Belligan's hand was still shaking hard, but now it seemed like the hand was being swayed more by the forces of rage and desperation than by fear.

"One . . ."

Both men in unison this time: "Two . . ."

Eyes locked. Straight steady focus. One final breath.

BLAM!

The world instantly fuzzed away in a blinding white blur, and as Bard's eyes began to slowly adjust and the white noise all around him faded away, they revealed a horror scene laid out before him in harrowing clarity. Suddenly, Bard found himself with a gun in his hand, a dead man bleeding out on the floor of his attic, and absolutely no recollection of the savage atrocity that had just unfolded before him. Bard couldn't think. Couldn't speak. Couldn't move. His feet seemed to be locked firmly in place by the force of sheer panic and fear that suddenly swept through him in a huge roiling tidal wave of doom. It wasn't humanly possible to process all of the questions that began invading his mind. He'd never seen so much blood before. So much black-red blood on the floors, on the walls, on him . . . everywhere. Clearly, something very wrong had gone down here, but he couldn't remember a thing, and there was no time to think about that now.

The towering wave of doom was cresting now and poised to crash down upon Bard at any second, when he suddenly heard the sound of the garage door opening and his mom coming home from work. Just then, the temporary traumatic amnesia was swept away, and the full memory of what had happened only moments before crept back into the swarming hornet's nest that was Bard's mind.

It was supposed to be one, two, three, blam. Not one, two, blam, thought Bard.

Before they'd even gotten to three, Belligan had been lying motionless in a pool of blackest blood and what used to be his brain. Bard began frantically wrestling with Belligan's heavy corpse in an exhausting attempt to drag it into an empty corner of the attic and cover it with an old blue tarp, instinctively trying to hide the evidence of the horror that he had just witnessed.

In the house below, he could hear his mother tromping from room to room, yelling his name as if he might eventually answer her if she shouted it out enough times. His heart thundered like a jackhammer in his chest, and his mouth was an arid desert. It didn't seem possible that this could be happening. He thought that he'd had every detail of the suicide pact sewn up perfectly, but Belligan had somehow managed to find the one stray thread and ended up unraveling the whole thing in an instant.

Bard looked down at his blood-splattered clothes and the gun he still clutched in his right hand and decided that there were just two choices for him now, as far as he could see. The plan had always been to do the deed when his mom wasn't home, to minimize the trauma that stumbling upon his fresh corpse would surely cause her. He had parked his car a few blocks away from the house and walked back, so when she came home, she wouldn't have any reason to think that he was there. She had never once been up to the attic in his entire life that he could remember, and he couldn't imagine any reason for her to think to look for him in the attic now. He could try to wait it out until she fell asleep and sneak out of the attic to clean himself up, and then the next day when the house was empty again, he would figure out what to do with Belligan's body. This option meant that Bard would have to reformulate his plan entirely on the fly and did nothing to resolve the fact that he still wanted to put an end to his own mortal suffering but would first have to deal with the problem that Belligan's fresh corpse now created for him.

The more he thought about the logistics of altering his plan at this stage and what it would entail, the more he began to doubt the chances of it working out without his mother discovering him covered in a stranger's blood. There was no practical way that he would be able open up the hatch door of the attic without her hearing him. Even if he waited it out all night in the attic and was able to sneak Belligan's body out in the morning once his mom had left for work, what the hell was he going to do with that thing once he got it out of the attic? And supposing he was able to dispose of this bloody albatross of a corpse without leaving any clues, surely whenever the police began investigating Belligan's disappearance, they would eventually discover Belligan and Bard's correspondence via the website where they had first connected with one another. There were just too many things that needed to go exactly right for this new plan to work out, and with the way his frenzied mind was racing a mile a minute now, he doubted that he would be able to do what would be required of him without making some kind of fatal blunder that would bring it all crashing down.

Then, he began to weigh the second, far more terrible option left to him. It was the option that superseded all of his best laid plans, his unspeakable ace in the hole, the option that could eliminate the unbearable, soul-crushing pain of his current reality in an instant and replace it with the great unknown that awaits a man on the other side. One quick squeeze of the trigger and he could be free of it all; but was he really the kind of man who could blow his brains out, knowing that his own mother was watching TV in the room below him? If there was just an infinite void of nothingness after death as Bard had always firmly believed, why should he worry at all about the horrible trauma that witnessing his final act of self-indulgence would inflict on his mother? How could he be haunted by a guilty conscience if he no longer had any consciousness? The more he thought about it, the more he questioned what he had to feel guilty about anyway.

He'd lived in this house alone with his mother for the past fifteen years ever since his dad had skipped town for good, and in that time, it seemed as if they'd become relative strangers with only a passing interest in each other's lives. She was the kind of person who couldn't possibly see beyond the minutiae of her own life, and maternal love had always been more of an abstract concept than a human emotion for her. His life had been spinning out of control right under her nose for years, but she had been either too clueless or uncaring to even notice. Once the initial shock and inconvenience of his death had subsided, she would get back to her same daily routine and only pretend to miss him whenever someone asked about him.

Bard reached up to switch off the lantern hanging overhead and sat down beside Belligan's corpse in the darkness in the hopes of quieting his reeling mind. Without any light in the attic, the blackness of the space began to take on a new depthless dimension, like the gaping maw of some titanic beast that was waiting to swallow him whole. There was no stillness to the darkness that enveloped him. It swirled and throbbed and pressed down on him from every angle until he felt like he couldn't breathe, as if all the air in the cramped room had been replaced with this malevolent, sentient darkness that was trying to invade his body and crush him from the inside out.

Bard could suddenly feel the tide rushing swiftly around his ankles again as the next towering wave of panic began to swell deep inside his brain, poised to crash down upon him again at any moment. He sprang up awkwardly to his feet and groped blindly for the lantern, but he had become completely disoriented by the overwhelming darkness of the attic, and as he shambled about trying to find it, he managed to trip over the legs of Belligan's corpse and came crashing down in a loud thump on the wooden floor, his face splashing in the shallow pool of blood that had gushed out of Belligan's head.

In the left pocket of his jeans, he felt the two sudden jolts of vibration coming from his phone that alerted him whenever he received a text message. Bard reached into his pocket and pulled out his phone, the abrupt glaring brightness of its screen piercing into his eyes, making it impossible to see who the text was from until his vision had adjusted; but even before he could make out who the message was from, he knew it was his mother.

The house below him had grown eerily quiet; the final wave of panic was about to crest.

Where are U? I think I just heard a really loud noise up in the attic . . . Kinda freaking out. Should I call the cops?? WHERE R U???

And then, as if it had been the most obvious decision of his life that had been staring him in the face the whole time, Bard finally knew what he had to do.

Ian Thomas Bishop is an author who hails from Orange County, California. He has spent most of his life as a musician who always enjoyed writing for fun in his free time and is honored to have his first professionally published story, "Bard's Folly," included in Scout Media's *A Contract of Words*.

When he is not working on one of his stories, he enjoys spending every possible moment with his wife and son and two cats, playing guitar in his rock band, New Evil, and relaxing on the beach with a good book and a couple of beers. He is a passionate supporter of Liverpool FC and often wakes up in the wee hours of the morning to watch them play on the other side of the planet.

His writing spans across many genres, but he primarily enjoys writing literary fiction, speculative fiction, and fantasy. Aside from the many short stories he is always working on, he is currently working on an epic-fantasy novel that he hopes to publish sometime in the future.

Melissa Jacobs stood on the pavement, staring up at the imposing building looming over her: The Gallows, a rather ominously named wine bar where she was now the new full-time bartender. Well, for the next three months at least; longer, she hoped, if all went well. The job came with a room, so this was perfect.

Taking a deep breath in, she pushed open the heavy, old wooden door and entered the bar. It took several moments for her eyes to adjust to the dimly lit room, and she squinted, searching for Karl, the barman she had met when she was here two weeks ago for her final interview. She spotted him at the end of the bar, drying glasses and talking to an elderly gentleman who sat on a tall bar stool, throwing peanuts towards his mouth and missing nearly every one.

Relieved to have spotted someone she knew straight away, she walked over to Karl and the old gentleman, heaving her duffle bag over her shoulder.

"Melissa," Karl called as he noticed her approaching. "Hey, how was your journey?"

"Hi, Karl. It was good, thank you. As good as any five-hour coach journey can be, anyway, with a hyperactive three-year-old sitting in the seat behind you," she said, laughing. "I swear, if I had heard one more line about those damn wheels on that damn bus, these fine Doc Martens of mine would have been walking the rest of the way here."

"Oh, not good," he replied, shaking his head, not very successfully trying to suppress a laugh. "I'll just finish here, and I'll give you the grand tour. Won't be a minute," he said, and continued drying the glasses and then poured the gentleman a pint of ale in a ceramic tankard.

Melissa placed her bag underneath one of the wooden tables at the side of the room and began walking slowly around. The walls were clad in wood panelling, which added to the darkness of the room. Wonderful, quirky mirrors of all shapes and sizes were hung around the walls, perhaps in the hope of bringing light into the place, but it didn't seem to be working all that well. Here and there hung old black-and-white photographs of people and places from a bygone era, dressed in old-fashioned clothing, standing by old farm machinery and horses.

Melissa stopped by one photo. It looked to be a photo of this building, with a tall, grey-haired man wearing a long dark cloak standing on the front porch. His arm rested proudly on the wooden railing to his side. The man's dark beady eyes seemed to stare straight at her, and she shuddered, taking a small step back.

"Nathaniel Locklie," said a voice from behind her, making her jump. "Sorry. He's a strange one, isn't he? I swear he looks directly at you wherever you stand in this room. This was originally his house, you know," Karl said as they both made their way back to the bar so that Karl could show Melissa around. "Seriously, this will take all of five minutes, there isn't much to see. You already know where the kitchens are, and they are closed now for the evening. Follow me this way," Karl said, walking around to the back of the bar. "This is our storage room/cellar/office," he said, unlocking a heavy wooden door with a key hanging from a chain on his belt.

Karl slapped at the switch on the wall, and the room flooded with bright fluorescent light. The large square room was filled with various barrels of beer and cider. Along the wall on the right stood seven barrels of real ale, resting in their racks. At the back of the room stood a small desk with a tall metal filing cabinet next to it.

"Over there," Karl said, pointing to the left of the desk, "is the safe. All the takings go in there at the end of the night till they can be banked the next day. You get it?"

"I do," Melissa replied, following Karl back out of the room and waited as he locked the door again.

They walked back around the front so Karl could continue to work. Melissa found a stool at the end of the bar and sat down, glancing back at the old photo of Nathaniel Locklie. Karl was right; it was as though he was staring straight at her, even though she was now in a totally different position than before.

"He sees you," Karl hissed from right behind her ear, and she jumped, almost falling from her stool.

She slapped him hard on the arm as he bent over, laughing loudly.

"So, this was his house?" Melissa asked, her heartbeat returning to a safer rate.

"Yes. Nathaniel Locklie was the City of London's official hangman back in the eighteen hundreds. He executed over three hundred people, including women. It is said that he enjoyed his work a little too much and would rig the gallows so that it took several minutes for the condemned to die. One took over half an hour. He liked to put on a show for the many spectators, who came to watch in the hundreds. He would swing on the body, back and forth, until their neck would break, then cheer triumphantly."

"Well, he sounds delightful," Melissa said, frowning.

"Around eighteen sixty-eight, it was decided that hangings would no longer take place in public, that they would be conducted within the prison grounds. It was also decided that Locklie's services were no longer required. Locklie was furious, claiming they were breaching his contract. He hadn't executed the full three-hundred-and-fifty stated, and he was so good at his job, in his sick and twisted opinion. Nevertheless, Locklie's contract was terminated, and he swore that there would be repercussions. The gallows were dismantled and were ready to be burned, but they were given to

Locklie instead. He had asked for them, like they were dear to him or something. I think they were sick to death of him by that point and just wanted him to be gone. So, they let him keep the gallows. He used them to build what is now part of the front porch of this building."

"Well, okay then," Melissa said, shifting a little uncomfortably on her stool.

The elderly gentleman signalled that he was ready for another drink, so Karl hurried along the bar and refilled his tankard.

Melissa sat, thinking over what Karl had just told her. What a truly horrible man Nathaniel Locklie must have been. She stared back around at the photo again. He seemed to sneer back at her, pleased to have aroused such feelings within her. She quickly turned back around to find Karl standing directly in front of her, making her jump yet again.

"Let me give you your keys. I'm sure you want to get settled in to your room," Karl said, laughing.

Melissa collected her duffle bag from under the table and followed Karl around to the back of the bar again and past the store room to a flight of stairs.

"Right to the top, second door on the right. The first on the left is my room, just in case you need me," he said with a wink.

"Good to know," she said with a small smile. "I think I'll stay up there for the night if you don't mind. I'm totally beat," Melissa explained as she began her ascent up the narrow staircase.

"No problem. I'll see you first thing in the morning," Karl said, giving her a mock salute, and with a big smile, he returned to the bar to finish off for the evening.

Melissa unlocked the door to her room and pushed the door open. It creaked loudly on its hinges, and she winced at the sound.

Going to need some oil for that, she thought as she switched on the light and walked inside, letting the door swing closed behind her.

She dropped her bag down onto the bed and checked her

watch. It was only 9:30 p.m., but, after all the travelling, she felt as though it were much later than that. It only took a few moments to unpack the few belongings she had brought with her, always one to travel light.

She sat on the edge of the bed and untied her well-worn and beloved pair of Doc Marten boots. They had literally gone everywhere with her, these past few years. It was silly to be attached to something as mundane as a pair of boots, but that didn't change the fact that she wouldn't be without them. She felt that they brought her luck. Something had always turned up just when she needed it, as long as she wore the boots. A place to stay, food, money, and even this job.

Placing them carefully beneath the edge on the bed, she quickly brushed her teeth in the small bathroom and climbed into the bed. The sheets were freezing cold, and it took a while for Melissa to warm up.

As tired as she was, she decided to read for a while. She always found it hard to sleep the first night anywhere, and tonight would unlikely be an exception. So she grabbed her book from the bedside table and began to read. Half an hour spent in the realm where hobbits and wizards dwell was enough to put Melissa firmly inside her comfort zone, and she felt her eyes growing heavy. Reaching over, she placed the book on the table and switched off the lamp. Rolling over onto her side, she pulled the covers up underneath her chin and snuggled farther down the bed.

Just as she felt herself drifting off to sleep, she heard a noise. The sound of scratching on the walls. No, it sounded as though it was coming from inside the walls.

Great, she thought, *now we have mice.*

Though she found the scratching oddly comforting for a while. It made her feel a little bit less alone.

Melissa had fallen into a deep sleep for several hours, when she was awoken by the sound of the mice. Only this time, there seemed to be hundreds—maybe thousands—of them scampering about and scratching. The sound came not only from the walls all around her, but also from beneath the floorboards and in the ceiling. She felt completely surrounded.

As Melissa listened, she heard what sounded like the swish of material as though someone were walking in her room. She held her breath, not daring to move. The sound moved closer and closer, coming towards her, as she lay frozen in her bed.

Just as the sound seemed to approach her pillow, all of the noises stopped at once. No swishing of material, no sound of the scratching or scampering of a thousand tiny feet. Silence.

Suddenly, she felt a cold, bony finger trace a line across her neck. Screaming, she jumped from her bed and rushed towards the door. Slapping at the wall, she found the light switch, flicked it on, and spun around. The room was empty.

No bony-fingered person or a single mouse to be seen. She stood there, doubled over, trying to catch her breath. She had never been one to suffer from nightmares in the past, but surely that had been one hell of one right there?

Composing herself, she walked back across the room to her bed. She kneeled down onto the floor and slowly lifted the covers to check underneath. She was a firm believer that you could never really be sure there were no monsters until the underneath had been checked. There was nothing scarier than a couple of dust bunnies and a few dead flies.

Making a note to clear them away in the morning, Melissa climbed back onto her bed and lay back down. It was her first day on the job tomorrow; she would not let some stupid nightmare spoil this for her. So she pulled the covers around her tightly and closed her eyes, deciding not to turn the light out so that only the good dreams would come.

Melissa woke the following morning to the sound of birds chirping outside of her bedroom window. She lay there for a few minutes, remembering the events of the night before. With the thin streak of sunlight shining across the opposite wall and the beautiful sound of the birds just a metre or two away, it was hard to take any of it seriously. Just nightmares caused by being overtired and the strangeness of staying in a new place and add to that the terrifying tales of Nathaniel Locklie, it was no surprise that she hadn't really slept that well. And then there was the matter of the new job that she was about to start in . . . she checked her watch—less than fifteen minutes.

She jumped from her bed and raced into the small bathroom, having the fastest of showers and a quick brush of her teeth. She threw on a clean set of clothes and made her way down the stairs to start work. She could hear people talking, and someone laughed from inside of the bar, whom she was pleased to recognise as Karl.

"Well, good morning," he called from behind the bar.

She was beginning to wonder if he had even left the night before.

"Coffee?" he asked, looking at her with furrowed brows.

"My God, yes please," she mumbled. "Is it that obvious?"

"You look more tired now than when you went to bed last night; you looked pretty shattered then as it was."

He smiled an apology and switched on the coffee machine.

"Yeah, I didn't sleep well at all. Nightmares or something," she muttered, hoisting herself up onto a bar stool and resting her chin on her hands.

Karl brought over a large mug of steaming coffee and slid it across the bar to Melissa.

"I'm guessing strong black this morning," Karl said, then gestured to his left. "This is Maria. She works the bar with me on the weekends and cleans the place every morning."

"And a thankless task it is too," she said, smiling at Melissa from the other end of the bar.

"Nice to meet you. I won't shake hands, 'cause . . ." she replied, holding her hands in the air, covered in bright yellow rubber gloves.

"Nice to meet you too," Melissa answered with a grin.

Whether it was the much-needed coffee or the company, Melissa wasn't sure, but she was feeling much better. In fact, she was starting to feel a wonderful little buzz of excitement in the pit of her stomach.

Melissa enjoyed her first day working at The Gallows. There had been no major hiccups, other than a smashed wine glass and the elderly gentleman from the day before refusing to drink from the glass she poured his pint into.

"I should have warned you about that. That ones on me. William will only drink from his own ceramic tankard. He's pretty cool though, once you get that bit right."

"Good to know. Anything else that I should know about?" Melissa asked.

"I don't think so. So, how did you find your first day?" Karl asked, looking honestly intrigued.

"You know, I have had the best day. I think I am going to really enjoy it here," Melissa answered, trying not to sound too excited.

"Good. I think you will fit right in. Fancy a celebratory drink before we finish for the night?" he asked, grinning at her and doing a little jig to music apparently only he could hear.

"That sounds like a plan," she said, laughing as she finished wiping down the last of the tables towards the back of the room.

She rinsed out her cloth and slumped down on a stool at the bar, exhausted but happy.

Karl slid a bottle of Budweiser along the top of the bar as if he were the bartender from some old western movie. He whooped loudly as she caught it. He joined Melissa and slumped down onto the stool next to her.

"Not bad for your first day, Mel. Not bad at all." And they chinked their bottles together in the air and both took a good, long swig of beer.

They stayed chatting at the bar till the early hours; Melissa found herself able to talk to Karl about almost anything, and she found that the buzz she felt in the pit of her stomach wasn't only due to the excitement of a new job.

Karl paused as he turned to leave and kissed Melissa on the cheek, and she felt her face flush slightly.

"See you in a few hours," he said and headed off out the back to his room.

Melissa sat at the bar for a few moments longer, a smile across her face. This really did feel right. This place was everything she hoped it would be. Maybe she would finally be able to settle down.

She turned to get off the stool when the old, black-and-white photo of Nathaniel Locklie caught her eye. She walked slowly over to it. Narrowing her eyes, she stared at the picture. Her breath caught in her throat as she looked at the wicked man glaring back at her. She was certain that something had changed. He appeared to be grinning at her, his uneven, broken teeth exposed between his thin lips.

She looked closer and saw one of his hands was now raised up slightly, and it appeared to be pointing one long and bony finger towards her. She stepped back, knocking into a chair behind her. Breathing hard she stared at the photo. Nothing happened.

Come on, Mel. Clearly that was too many beers for you tonight, she thought.

"Time for bed," she muttered and collected the cash from the till to store in the safe for the night.

She locked up the front door and walked back through the bar, switching the lights off as she went. With each step, she felt more and more as if someone were behind her, and she picked up the pace a little.

Stopping outside of the store room, she grabbed the bunch of keys from the string on her belt and searched through them until she found the right one. It took a couple of attempts for her to successfully insert the key into the lock, but she finally did and pushed the heavy door open, slapping hard at the wall in search of the light switch.

The room was once again flooded with fluorescent light, and she squinted her eyes against the glare. One of the barrels hissed, making her jump. It was as though it were annoyed at being disturbed at such a late hour. She chuckled quietly at just how jumpy she was and, shaking her head gently, walked over to the safe on the far side of the room. Placing the cotton bag containing the day's cash takings on top of the cluttered desk, she bent down to unlock the safe.

The second that she touched the cold metal dial, the room was plunged into darkness. Crouched down in front of the safe, she strained her ears for any sign there was someone there. The room was silent. The darkness within the room felt heavy, as though it were pushing in on her from all sides.

She began to stand upright when she did hear a sound. A sound that she remembered from the night before. The scratching and scampering of hundreds, maybe thousands, of tiny feet. They seemed to be all around her, coming from all four walls and from all over the floor and above from the ceiling. Her heart pounded noisily in her ears, and she swayed a little on her feet.

Reaching over blindly in the dark, she found the edge of the desk to steady herself. Her hand sweaty, it slid across the top, and she stumbled forward a step. The scratching and scampering noises grew louder, and it sounded as though they were almost upon her when she heard the swishing of material. It sounded as though someone were inside the room with her, their clothes moving as they walked, dragging along the ground.

The room suddenly flooded with bright light again, and Melissa shielded her eyes with her hand. Just as she glanced up, the room was plunged back into complete darkness again. Her heart felt as though it were about to pound straight through her chest, and she struggled to gain control of her breathing.

Once again, the room became ablaze with light, and through the glare it looked to Melissa as though something hung down from the ceiling. Then the room was thrown back into pitch darkness again.

Melissa whimpered quietly, her legs threatening to give way beneath her. She covered her eyes with her hands, not wanting to see this time if the lights came on again. The scratching and scampering continued all around her, and she waited, hunched over, shaking. Raising her head and lowering her hands slightly, the lights sprang on again as though they were waiting for her to see.

Melissa lifted her head and screamed as she looked above her. There, hanging from the ceiling on large metal hooks, were dozens of bodies. Spread out, filling the whole of the room as though this were a butcher shop instead of a store room.

The light switched off once more, tremors swept through Melissa's body, and she crumpled to the floor. She felt something scurry across her hand, and she bolted upright and stumbled forward, bumping into something heavy. Melissa shrieked as the room lit again, and she found her face an inch away from the face of a young woman, hanging upside down by her feet. The lights began blinking, two seconds on then two seconds off, then on, then off, again and again.

Melissa floundered through the store room, stumbling into the bodies—each one, then bumping into the body hanging next to it. With corpses swinging wildly all around her, Melissa lurched through the room, desperately trying to find the door.

A body struck her hard on the back, and she lunged forward. Reaching out to stop herself from falling, her hand grasped hold of something. She quickly realised it was someone's leg; oddly, she noticed that they were missing a shoe.

Looking up, she felt every drop of blood drain from her face as Karl hung there, staring down at her, blood dripping from his open mouth.

It sounded to Melissa as though it were someone else who screamed. Some primal scream born out of sheer terror, but as the pain rushed through her throat, she realised that it was her. The pain brought with it a rush of adrenaline, and she fled towards the door, pushing Karl's body aside.

Fumbling with the door handle, crying out in frustration, she finally managed to open the door, and she threw herself out of the room. Landing heavily on the floor, Melissa crouched over on her hands and knees, her breath rattling in her chest. Slowly, she raised her head upwards, and looming over her was the tall and ominous figure of Nathaniel Locklie.

Looking down at her, he cocked his head to the side with a jerk and grinned.

Melissa spun around, her feet scrambling, trying to find purchase against the slippery floor. She sprinted forward a few steps but felt something cold slither around her neck. It pulled tight and she felt herself being lifted off of the ground. Her legs kicked wildly, and her fingers scratched at the rope as it tightened further still. Higher into the air she rose, gasping for air.

Melissa threw herself back and forth but to no avail. Sparks invaded her sight like a macabre fireworks display. Her eyes bulged from their sockets, and her face turned a deep shade of scarlet. Suddenly, a heavy weight landed upon her back, and she began to swing forwards and backwards.

"Number three hundred and fifty," he hissed, his breath tickling her ear as she looked towards Karl hanging a short distance in front of her. "I said there would be consequences," the hangman screeched, and his audience swung softly back and forth in approval.

Maria finished cleaning the main bar area and tidied everything away in the storage room. She shivered a little as she locked the door again. She had never liked that room—something always felt a little off, like she was being watched. And she was sure that they had mice. She had heard them scurrying about on several occasions.

Walking back towards the bar, she glanced up the stairs on her left with a smile. She had seen the way those two had looked at each other.

Fair play to them, she thought, and entering the main bar area, she grabbed her bag and car keys from one of the tables and walked towards the front door. She paused by the old, black-and-white photo of Nathaniel Locklie.

His wicked grin seemed more sinister than ever this morning as he leaned back against the wooden railing. Upon his feet, poking out from beneath his cloak, were the toes of a well-worn pair of Doc Marten boots.

C.E. Rickard grew up in a small, rural village in Oxfordshire, United Kingdom. She began writing short stories as a child, incorporating her love of all things supernatural into her writing even then.

At the age of thirty-nine, Catherine was diagnosed with the hereditary eye-condition, Retinitis Pigmentosa. The realisation that her sight was fading and that she would eventually become blind turned out to be exactly the boost she needed to actively pursue her dream of a career as a writer, and she is loving every minute.

She published her first short story, "Little Girl Gone," in 2017 in *Ghost Stories*, a Zimbell House anthology.

Facebook.com/C.E.Rickard.author

August 14th

I stare at her, not sure what this is or how to respond to it. All I did was ask if we were dating. She said she'd think about it over the next few days, which I thought meant *no*, as I've never dated anybody. I can't say I was expecting her to bring me this . . . whatever this is.

"You want me to promise not to talk to or look at any other woman?" I stare at her across the table, confused.

"Yes." She's matter of fact.

"You can check my phone whenever you want? Why?"

"This might sound dumb, but to make sure you aren't seeing somebody else on the side. Believe it or not, it's happened to me before," she says, leaning forward.

I catch the flicker in her eyes, and I instantly know I don't want to do anything that would remind her of a past relationship.

"Oh, okay. *Answer your text within a reasonable time?* What does that mean?" I ask, feeling my phone in my pocket. "What if I'm at work or something?"

"It doesn't matter. I want to make sure you are where you say you are. All I'm saying is, message me within seven minutes so I know you're at least thinking about me."

Samantha smirks as she reaches across the table and touches my hand. I like the contact, her warm skin against mine as she laces our fingers together.

"Okay, I get that. This says—it says I can't ditch you for my band. We practice like four times a week."

"That's probably not going to work for me. I want to be able to see you and spend time with you. How are we going to do that if you're always with your *band?*"

Our Final Tomorrow is a huge part of my life. I've told her that.

"I can talk to them . . ."

She bats her eyelashes, a smile spreading across her face.

". . . See what I can do," I mutter, looking down at the paper.

"Good. Go on," she orders.

"I have to take you on a real date three times a week. That doesn't sound bad." I glance at her, but she's no longer paying attention. "I have to agree to love you no matter what happens between us? What do you mean?"

I look at her and I'm reminded of my mom and her making me promise to love her no matter what.

She crosses her arms, and her head tilts to the right, something she seems to do a lot. "It means exactly what it says. No matter what happens between us, you're agreeing to love me. Can you do that?"

"I mean—I think so."

"It's yes or no, Dean."

"Y-yes."

I don't mean to stutter, but her big brown eyes bore into me, and my heart slams into my chest. I say what I have to so I can be with her.

"Good. You have to agree to let me move in with you. I think it'll be best if we're living together, that way you won't have time to think about cheating or doing something stupid."

"I would never do that to you," I assure her.

"Well, I don't know that. It's happened before. You have to earn my trust. I'm not going to give it to you freely."

I nod and look at the last thing she wants me to agree to. "You're my top priority?"

"Yes, if you want to be with me, I need to be your top priority. I refuse to be second to anybody or anything. If I'm your girlfriend, then I need to be the most important person in your life. Can you agree to that?"

I trace my fingers over the paper and stare at the words that are typed up.

"I know this is probably silly, but it'll make me feel better. We've been on several dates, and we've hung out countless times, so if you sign this, it means we're officially official."

She shakes the pen in front of my face, waiting.

"What if—"

"What if you don't want to sign it?" She cuts me off, like my mom used to do. "If you don't want to sign then I guess we're not a couple. You go back to your meaningless life, and I'll find me a man that will actually want to be with me and will adhere to my terms."

She leans forward, and I catch a whiff of her strawberry scented hair. What does she mean by *my meaningless life?*

"I mean, look at me; who wouldn't want me?"

She flashes her perfect white teeth, and I take another look at the contract she gave me.

"Okay."

I don't know if she hears me because I hardly hear my own voice as I look over the list. I know nothing about relationships, but I know I want to be with her. I know since I've been hanging out with her, the storm in my head has seemed to calm down.

"Come on, make up your mind. I don't have all day to sit here." She snaps her fingers, waiting for me to make my decision.

My mom was great at making up rules for me, which is what this reminds me of. Maybe these rules won't be as serious as Mom's were.

"I'll sign it."

I don't think anybody else would date somebody like me, so I'm doing it. If it wasn't for my friend, Matthew, I would have never met Samantha on my own. I can't say no to this.

"Okay, here."

She holds up the pen, and I take it, ready to take the next step in what I'm hoping is the only relationship I'll ever have. After our last date, I felt a strong attraction to her, like she was the one. She's smart, confident, and seems to know exactly what she wants.

"I can honestly say you made a smart decision." She takes the paper after I sign it, folds it up, and puts it in her purse. "Now you're my boyfriend. Wasn't so hard, was it?"

"Matthew said he figured things would work out between us," I tell her, stuffing my hands in my sweater pocket, not exactly sure what to do now.

"You're so cute. Listening to your friends."

September 17th

Her ice-cold hands are heavy as they press down against my throat, and her long fingers grip tightly. I immediately push her arms, but she's stronger than me. Her nails dig into my skin, and my breath is trapped.

As my lungs begin to burn from lack of air, I push her harder, remembering the words my dad ingrained in me growing up: *Never put your hands on a woman.* There's no escape as black spots dance in my vision. I try to speak but no words come from my mouth. I'm going to die. The woman I love is going to kill me. Why?

I close my eyes, fear taking over. I'm going to die. I'm going to die.

All at once, I can breathe, and I fight for air as I'm released. My heart slams against my chest, and I can't help but place my hands where hers were.

She's saying something, something I don't understand. I want to get up and leave, but I'm weak. My legs don't work; my head is fuzzy. Why can't I get up? Why did she do this?

"Are you okay?"

Samantha stands above me, and I can't do anything but look at her.

"Dean? Dean?"

She's inches from my face. Her perfect red lipstick is all I can focus on as her hair grazes my cheeks.

"Can you get up?"

She grabs my wrist, yanking me into a sitting position. The room spins, and all I want to do is lay back on the floor. Samantha pushes my hair back from over my face and smiles that perfect smile. I don't want her to touch me but I can't stop her.

"I didn't mean to do that." She places both hands on my face, her body inches from mine. "You forgive me? Dean, you forgive me, right?

She taps my face forcing me to look at her.

Speaking is impossible; my lungs burn. Do I forgive her? Should I forgive her? Did I upset her? Was this my fault?

"Hello?" She waves her hand in front of my face, stopping the thoughts in my head. "I swear, if you would have let me see your phone, like I asked, this wouldn't have happened. You know my rule."

Her rule? The contract? This is about the contract she had me sign?

"I told you there would be consequences. You didn't believe me, did you?"

I don't know how I ended up in the bathroom, but I don't like what I'm looking at in the mirror. Red eyes stare back at me, and I can't help but notice the bruising on my neck. How am I supposed to hide this from everyone? How am I supposed to face Samantha after what she did? I shouldn't have broken her rule. If I gave her my phone, this wouldn't have happened. This is my fault for not remembering.

"You okay in here?"

She walks in without knocking, and I don't dare look at her. I wasn't expecting this behavior from her.

"I can't believe you wouldn't let me see your phone. Are you hiding something from me?" She snakes her arms around my waist and looks down at me. "Yes or no?"

I shake my head because it hurts trying to speak.

"Then it shouldn't have been a problem that I wanted to see it."

She kisses my neck where her hands once were, and I force myself out of her arms. This isn't okay. I'm not going through this again.

"What, Dean? You're not afraid of me, are you?" She corners me against the wall and tries to kiss me again. "Come on, it wasn't that serious." She lets out a laugh and grabs my face between her hands. "You agreed to love me no matter what. Don't let *this* interfere with that."

"You . . . You—"

"I didn't do anything that you didn't deserve."

She pushes her lips against mine and slips her tongue into my mouth.

Did I deserve this? Is it my fault? Should I break up with her?

"Kiss me back, Dean."

She snaps me out of my thoughts, and I do as I'm told. This won't happen again. I won't let it. I'll remember her rules.

"I-I'm so sorry, Sammy," I manage to say through the pain in my throat.

"Of course you are. I didn't do anything wrong, you did. As long as you remember the *contract* you signed, we'll be fine."

She hugs me tight, and I can't help but do the same, needing her to love me.

"Leaving isn't an option. You'll regret it if you do."

Is this what I signed up for to date her?

Rayona Lovely Wilson is a dedicated and hard-working writer who lives with her husband and three young children in the Central Valley area of California. When she's not busy cranking out words to create a new story, she enjoys being a jungle gym to her children and rocking out to bands like Korn and My Chemical Romance. She also loves spending time with the rest of her family, telling stories and driving everyone crazy.

Rayona has been writing since she was twelve years old; it was one of the things that got her through a lot of the hardships she and her family were going through. It became her outlet, something she found herself doing at any hour in the day.

Her main focus in writing is contemporary new-adult drama fiction, where she wants to reach the younger crowds.

Rayona's first published short story, "Of All People, It Was Me," appears in the anthology *Askew Volume 004* (2017), and her novel, *She Loves Me Not*, was published in December of 2017.

You can learn more at her website: www.facebook.com/shewhoscribbles.

THE MAIN EVENT

Signature *David Williams*

"Keep the change, good brother."

Andre Steele stepped from the taxi, dragging his bag behind him. He turned and faced the huge building to his left—Springfield's multi-purpose arena. All his dreams were about to come true. Andre was approaching thirty years old and had worked in the wrestling business since he was eighteen. He had worked his way through many different positions in different promotions within the business, from selling tickets, refereeing matches, and even being part of the ring crew. Throughout his years in the business, he had continued training and learning from the boys. He felt his time had finally come. He had paid his dues, and now he was about to sign a bona fide wrestling contract.

Andre walked through the doors of the arena and approached the first person he saw with a lanyard around his neck. This turned out to be a beast of a man with giant arms the size of Andre's head. He had an earpiece looped around his right ear, which ran to a radio pack on his hip. Andre was six feet four, but this guy towered over and intimidated him.

Andre sucked up his nerves and spoke. "Hi there, I'm Andre Steele. I'm here to see Carlos Goldstein. Do you know where I can find him?"

The man-beast studied Andre up and down, then up again.

"The jobber locker rooms are that way, kid." He pointed over his shoulder with his thumb. "You don't need to see Carlos."

"Yes, I do. I'm here to sign a contract with the company."

The man-beast laughed so loud Andre heard the sound reverberate throughout the foyer. Once the man-beast had calmed, he radioed a colleague to inform Carlos he had a visitor.

"Someone will come and take you to Carlos, kid."

Andre moved away from the man-beast and waited in the foyer where some fans recognised him and asked for pictures and autographs. Andre loved interacting with his fans and spent some time talking to the small crowd that had gathered.

"Hey! Hey, hot shit," the man-beast shouted. "Your chariot awaits."

Andre thanked his fans and told them to enjoy the show.

A security guard named Steve accompanied him to Carlos Goldstein's office. As they approached the office door, they heard raised voices and arguing. Steve threw out his arm to stop Andre in his tracks.

"Wait here until Carlos is finished in there, Mr. Steele."

Andre nodded and thanked Steve for bringing him up. He couldn't hear what the argument was about, but he recognised the shadowy figure through the blinded window. The hat on top of the person's head was a giveaway. It was "Cowboy" Dean Anderson, the company's top babyface and most popular wrestler.

Andre studied the office door. The company's logo was next to Carlos Goldstein's nameplate. Springfield Championship Pro Wrestling was one of the biggest companies in Illinois, second only to Windy City Pro Wrestling in Chicago. Andre daydreamed about becoming the champion of the company and the payday that would bring him.

He was staring at the door when it burst open, and Cowboy Anderson stormed out. As he passed Andre, he muttered something.

Andre retrieved his bag and took a deep breath as he walked toward the open door. He knocked on the door's windowpane as he peered through and saw two men: one sat behind a desk and the other stood at his left side.

"Mr. Goldstein, sir?" Andre tried to sound confident but thought his nerves had gotten the better of him.

"The jobber locker room is downstairs, kid," the standing man bellowed.

"No. I'm here to see Mr. Goldstein. My name's Andre Steele. I'm meant to sign a contract with you today."

"Ah, Andre. Yes, please come in," Goldstein interjected. "This is Freddie Holt, he's my business adviser."

Andre closed the door behind him and approached the desk with his hand extended. "I just want to say, Mr. Goldstein, sir, I'm extremely grateful for the opportunity to join your company. I look forward to working with you to bring many years of success to all involved."

Goldstein ignored the hand hanging in the air in front of him. To his left, Freddie Holt held a disgusted smirk. Andre heard him mutter something that sounded like, *Fucking mark.*

"How about we talk business first, Mr. Steele? We'll shake hands once we've concluded our deal," Carlos Goldstein said, removing a thick document and placing it on the desk in front of Andre. "This is your contract, Mr. Steele. As we're so close to bell time, I'd ask you to read it thoroughly in your own time. I need you to sign the contract before I can sanction you to wrestle tonight, however. Now some of the boys do wrestle a little stiff and might catch you out from time to time, but as long as you're under contract with us, you're one of the boys, and they'll keep you safe in the ring."

"Do you have a pen, sir?"

Freddie Holt threw a pen onto the table, and Andre flipped through the pages briefly before readying to sign his signature on the back page.

"Now, you must understand that you'll have to pay your dues here. I expect you to help the ring crew before and after a show. You'll probably be in a couple of squash matches before I decide what I'm going to do with you long term. You can't expect to be thrust into the title picture."

"With respect, Mr. Goldstein, I've worked in the wrestling business for almost twelve years. I think I've paid my dues at least five times over. Is there a way for me to prove to you I'm worthy of a bit of a push?"

"Listen, kid. You've just fucking got here. Some of these guys have been here for more than fifteen years. The only way you're going to get a push is if one of my top dogs drops dead. Unless something happens to Cowboy or Butch, you'll do exactly what I ask you to do."

Andre thought about this prospect for a moment before signing his name on the dotted line and printing the date next to it. He pushed the papers toward Goldstein and threw the pen at Freddie, who launched forward and squared up to Andre's face.

"Watch yourself, mark," Holt barked.

Goldstein shot up from his chair and separated the two men. He straightened his suit and extended his hand to Andre.

"Now we shake hands, Mr. Steele. Our business has concluded. Welcome to the company. Freddie, take our fucking picture, will ya?"

Andre traversed to the front of the arena where the man-beast orchestrated the incoming crowd.

"Hey, hot shit," Andre shouted to the man-beast. "I'm a signed wrestler now, motherfucker."

Before the man-beast could react, Andre skipped his way toward the locker room area. Goldstein hadn't told him whether he was to be a babyface or a heel, so he slipped into the babyface locker room and found a space to prepare for his match. When Goldstein had invited him to sign for SCPW, he'd said Andre would wrestle Hillbilly Bob. Bob's gimmick was exactly as it sounded—a stereotypical hillbilly, redneck, trailer-trash character.

Andre surveyed the locker room and saw the other guys going through their pre-match rituals and routines.

He spotted a few wrestlers he had worked with in other promotions and some he had never met before. In the far corner near the shower area, he spotted the top babyface, Cowboy Dean Anderson. He was undressing from his normal clothes and preparing to shower before his match.

Andre recalled what Goldstein had told him: *The only way you are going to get a push is if one of my top dogs drops dead . . .*

Remembering hearing Cowboy argue with Goldstein about something earlier and deciding to kill two birds with one stone, Andre slipped from the locker room and followed the signs to the almost-empty catering area. Andre grabbed a bottle of water and a doughnut and continued to walk toward the kitchen hatch. No one was inside. He saw a large knife block on the counter opposite the hatch. Andre entered the kitchen and picked the biggest knife in the block and slipped it into his jeans, against his hip.

As Andre travelled toward the locker room, he smiled and shook the hands of people who recognised him and posed for pictures, using being seen as a potential alibi. He slipped through the door of the backstage area and returned to the locker room where he wrapped the knife in a towel from his bag. Andre glanced to where Cowboy sat, completely naked now, and took a deep breath.

Andre undressed, grabbed his towel, and entered the shower area. Two cubicles were available, and Andre hoped the next person to shower would be Cowboy Dean. He entered his cubicle, started the water, and soaked his entire body and hair. Just as he was about to turn off the water, he heard Cowboy enter the cubicle next to him. Andre crouched to his knees and slipped underneath the partition near the door of Cowboy's cubicle. His backside faced Andre. Perfect. A knife in the back would be better all around. Andre wouldn't be seen, and maybe he wouldn't kill Cowboy after all, just injure him.

The knife felt heavy in Andre's hand, as if the water from

the shower had absorbed into the handle and weighed down the weapon. He moved closer to Cowboy and raised the knife, level with his chest. As Andre moved to drive the knife through his victim's back, Cowboy turned around and now faced Andre.

"What the fuck?" Cowboy shouted.

Andre pushed Cowboy's naked body against the cubicle's wall and powered the knife through his chest, then pulled it out and slashed his face for good measure. He watched as Cowboy's body slumped to the wet floor, which turned a watery red colour. Andre used the water flowing from the shower to wash the knife and slipped under the partition. He counted to ten before wrapping the knife in the towel again and opening his cubicle's door.

The rest of the locker room hadn't heard the commotion, but Andre noticed the bloodied water spreading toward the cubicle on the opposite side. He calmly walked to his bag and removed another towel to dry himself, while stashing the weapon deep inside the bag. He wrapped the clean towel around his waist and began his pre-match dressing ritual, starting with his jockstrap and socks.

Andre realized if he was the person who noticed the pool of blood in the shower area, he was less likely to be a suspect. He stood and approached the wall next to the shower area's perimeter and set up to stretch. He counted to twenty.

"Hey! Hey, something happened over here," he bellowed around the locker room.

Some of the guys rolled their eyes, while others didn't even look up from what they were doing. Stavros Anistonakis, better known as Ares in the ring, noticed the red-tinted water flowing from the cubicles.

"What the hell? Guys, someone is bleeding in the showers." The increasing urgency in Stavros' voice caught the attention of the rest of the room.

The whole room converged on the shower area to see what had happened.

Andre stood at the front of the crowd and banged on the

cubicle's door. "Hey, who's in there?" His voice wavered as he called out.

"Fucking move, kid. Let me."

The left arm of a man Andre didn't know threw him out of the way, while the right arm and shoulder smashed through the door.

"Holy shit, it's Cowboy. Someone call 9-1-1."

The man who had smashed through the door, Freddie Holt, turned to Andre. "Did you see what happened here, kid?"

Andre shook his head. His eyes didn't leave the pale, bloodied body laying against the cubicle's tiled wall. Andre felt a sharp blow to his face. Freddie had slapped him.

"Look at me when I'm talking to you, mark," he barked.

Andre looked at Freddie and tried not to show his face's excruciating pain.

"No, I didn't see anything."

"Okay, kid. Go and find Carlos. Tell him the Cowboy has been attacked and to get down here right away."

Andre pushed through the crowd to his bag and changed into his normal clothes as quickly as he could. He raced through the locker room door and straight into the torso of a giant. His momentum sent him tumbling to the floor, which made the giant tower over him even more. Andre held the side of his head and looked at the giant's face—Tony "The Butcher" Ortiz, or just Butch. Butch stood seven feet seven and barely could stand straight in the locker rooms. Andre couldn't believe Butch, the company's top heel, was in the babyface locker room.

Butch grabbed Andre's arm in one of his massive hands and dragged him to his feet.

"Watch where you're going, little buddy." His voice sounded softer than Andre had expected. "I heard something happened to Cowboy. Where is he?"

Andre pointed toward the showers.

Butch shook Andre's hand and walked with purpose to where Andre had directed him.

Andre power walked through the door for a second time and went to find Goldstein.

Andre knocked on Goldstein's office door but didn't wait for a response. He opened the door, and an image he expected would live long in his memory greeted him. Carlos Goldstein stood with his trousers around his ankles and one of the ring crew on his knees in front of him.

Andre entered the office and closed the door behind him.

"Hello, person I've never met. My name is Andre Steele. I'd ask for your name, but I don't like when people talk with their mouth full."

Goldstein fumbled his trousers back around his waist and ordered his friend to leave the office at once. Andre heard him mumble something about needing a lock on his door.

"What do you want now?"

"Freddie sent me. Something happened in the locker room. Cowboy was attacked."

"What do you mean *attacked*? Is he okay?"

"Last I heard, someone was calling 9-1-1, and Butch was going into the babyface locker room. Freddie said you need to come down right away."

"I'll be down in a few minutes." Goldstein looked sternly at Andre. "You saw nothing in here, you understand me?"

A smile rose to Andre's face. "I don't think you're in the position to be making threats like that, do you?"

"If you breathe a word to anyone, I will end your career, Steele."

"I'll keep quiet, but only if you do something for me."

"Oh yeah? What's that?"

"Cowboy isn't going to be able to compete tonight. You're going to need someone to take his place in the main event. Let that someone be me."

"You think you can blackmail me and force your way to the top of the card?"

"I've just walked in and found you playing hide the sausage with one of the ring crew. If you want me to keep that quiet, then yes, put me in the main event. Otherwise, this closet you call an office will be busted wide open."

Goldstein pondered this proposal. "Okay, fine. You've got your main event match. If you can put on a good match with Butch, then maybe I'll have something to think about for the future. Go and speak with Butch, and tell him the changes."

Andre returned to the locker room and saw Butch carrying the limp, bleeding body of Cowboy Dean Anderson out the back door, where the paramedics were opening the back of the ambulance. Andre heard later the paramedics couldn't lift Cowboy onto the stretcher, and Butch, being the only guy bigger than Cowboy, had to help.

Goldstein appeared shortly after and spoke to the paramedics before they drove Cowboy to the hospital.

"They're saying there's a fifty percent he'll survive," he told the entire locker room. "One thing I do know is Cowboy wouldn't want us to not put on a show here tonight."

A mixed reaction swept through the locker room; some mumbled agreement, and others muttered that the show should be cancelled.

"As they say in showbiz, the show must go on. And so will ours. The card will remain the same. The only changes will be as follows: Freddie, you'll face Hillbilly Bob instead of Andre, who'll replace Cowboy in the main event against Butch."

The mumbling and muttering in the crowd of wrestlers behind Andre grew louder and more discontented.

"What? The fucking mark gets pushed to the main event ahead of everyone else?" Freddie screamed at Carlos. "That's bullshit, Goldy, and you know it."

"That's my final decision, Freddie. If you don't like it, you can get the fuck down to the hospital and stay with Dean. Now, seeing as we have about fifteen minutes until the first match, I suggest you all get on with getting ready."

The crowd of disgruntled wrestlers dispersed. Andre stayed and stared into Carlos' eyes.

How much further can I push him?

"There's one more thing I want, *Goldy.* Make my match a title match, and book me to win the title. Do that and your secret is safe."

"Not a chance, Steele. I've already done what you asked me to do. There's no way you're winning the title as well."

Andre moved closer to Carlos, enough to whisper into his ear. "When I signed the contract today, your words were if one of the top dogs drops dead, I could take his position. Just before our meeting, Cowboy was seen arguing with you in your office. It doesn't take a genius to figure out where I'm going with this. If Cowboy dies, I'd say you're a shoo-in for prime suspect."

"You twisted motherfucker. You attacked Cowboy so you could take his spot!"

"Now, now, boss. You can't go throwing accusations around like that. But if you want your secret to stay locked in the *closet* and for me not to tell the officer standing outside the door that I heard you arguing with Cowboy earlier today, you'll do what I've asked you to do."

"Ladies and Gentlemen, boys and girls, children of all ages," Carlos said into a microphone as he stood in the middle of the ring, "due to an incident backstage, we have a few changes to our main event match tonight. I regret to inform you all that Cowboy Dean Anderson will be not be able to compete tonight."

The entire arena turned on Carlos. The crowd joined in a chorus of jeers and boos, with numerous spectators throwing their plastic cups and bottles at the ring.

"Rest assured, folks . . . rest assured we have a main event for you which promises to be just as incredible. The Butcher will be putting his SCPW Heavyweight Title on the line against the company's newest recruit, Andre Steele. The ink has barely dried on this guy's contract, folks. That's how new he is to our family."

This was met with a better reaction than Carlos expected.

"So, without further ado, please welcome Andre Steele!"

Andre's music started, and he strutted to the ring. As he walked down the ramp, he passed Carlos walking up.

Carlos stormed through the curtain as Freddie burst into the backstage area.

"I've just had a call from the hospital. Cowboy didn't make it. He's dead."

Carlos bowed his head and muttered a quiet prayer. He turned to the curtain and saw Butch waiting for his music to cue his entrance.

"Hey, Butch, come here."

"What do you need, boss?"

"We've just had word that Cowboy didn't survive the attack. Pass the word on to Steele when you get into the ring. Then beat the living shit out of him. Beat him to within an inch of his life."

"Whatever you say, Goldy."

Carlos fished through his inside pocket and removed Andre's contract. Once he heard the bell ring for the start of the match, he walked through the curtain and down to ringside. Most of the crowd didn't notice his presence.

Butch and Andre grappled each other in a collar-and-elbow lockup, their faces close together.

"Carlos said to tell you Cowboy didn't make it," Butch said in a low voice, then maneuvered Andre into a headlock and faced him toward the corner where he saw Carlos.

"Hey, hot shit! Watch this," Carlos shouted to Andre as Butch whipped him into the corner.

Andre turned his head toward the voice and watched Carlos rip his contract into shreds.

"Oh fuck . . ."

David Williams was born in 1988 and bred in Liverpool, England but currently lives and works in North London as a support worker for adults with learning disabilities. "The Main Event" is his second published short story; his first published story, "Get Your Kicks on Route 66," appeared in Scout Media's *A Journey of Words* in 2016. He hopes to one day finish the novel he has been writing since 2013.

You can find him on Facebook at facebook.com/davidwbooks, his website davidwbooks.com, and twitter.com/davidw_books.

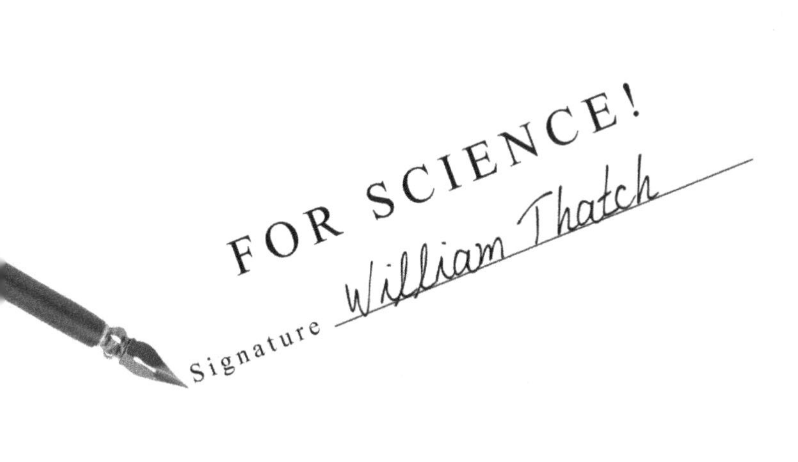

I'd like to think of myself as both a humble man and the world's greatest at everything. Especially at being humble. No one is more humble than I am. They've made statues in honor of how humble I am. Huge in the humility department, I can't stress that enough.

It was these qualifications that led me to answer an advertisement online. *Scientists looking for test subject to advance human understanding,* the ad read. I threw the paper in the trash and was about to walk away when I noticed they were offering twenty dollars and a hot sandwich.

The men in lab coats had the same reaction to me that every other doctor I'd ever met had.

"Sir, put your pants back on," the first scientist said.

"Make me," I fired back.

Three minutes later, after a short struggle with muscle-bound orderlies and a needle filled with some sort of numbing agent, they had made me put my pants back on.

These guys were good.

"Patient is feisty," said the second scientist with deliberation as she wrote those words down on a clipboard.

Or, I mean, I guess that's what she was writing. You never really know what doctors are writing down, do you? Secretive people.

Too secretive, if you ask me. They could be drawing pictures of dinosaurs getting it on, for all we know.

I tried leaning over to see if it was words or erotic dinosaurs, but whatever was in the needle was still working its magic, and I fell to the floor.

"Also, well hung," I added, a mouthful of drool escaping onto the floor.

"Delusions of grandeur," she said, writing that down next.

On the scientist's orders, an orderly picked me up and sat me down on a chair.

"Now, you are aware of the risks in this experiment, yes?" the first scientist asked.

"Ye—no," I replied. "Haven't the foggiest. Itchy, watery eyes?"

"No," the second scientist said.

"Uncontrollable bowel movements?" I asked.

"No, nothing like that."

"Low resale value on my home?"

"Sir, this is not a guessing game."

"You didn't say *no*."

The scientists sighed, rubbed their temples in frustration, and conferred with each other about whether I was the right subject. It was finally agreed upon that not only was I the best subject, and the greatest subject ever, I was also the only applicant to be a subject at all.

"All right, you're aware we may not be able to reverse the condition, yes?" the first scientist asked.

I stared blankly at them.

"That the condition would be permanent," the second scientist clarified.

I blinked hard. So hard my eyelids hurt. My head hurt a little too. I didn't understand their big words. Also, it hurt from where I'd face-planted onto the floor earlier.

"Sir, you are aware of what we're testing here today?" the first scientist asked.

"Not a clue. I'm here for twenty dollars and the sandwich I was promised," I said.

They both sighed again. Must be a scientist thing. Like all the smarts build up pressure in their heads, and the sighing is like a release valve. Or something. I don't know; I'm not a doctor.

The two of them proceeded to explain to me that they were trying to solve the question of what happens to us after death.

"Explosions?" I guessed.

"Still not a guessing game."

"That's what you think."

They continued explaining their experiment over the top of my continued guesses.

"Global warming! Global cooling? Global gonorrhea!"

They had the orderly inject me with something else. This time I felt as if I was melting in my seat as my muscles relaxed to the point I couldn't move my jaw. That did not stop me from trying to guess, however.

"So, our goal," continued the second scientist.

"*Raaaaaaaaaaaar.*"

"Is to induce a condition known as death."

"*Raaaar?*"

"Once in this state, we'll give you a few minutes to experience this state before bringing you back. Hopefully."

"*Ra-Ra-Rar?*"

"Yes, hopefully."

"We're not sure where you'll end up," the first scientist chimed in. "We'll need you to pay close attention, not just for the experiment, but also there's a lot of money riding on this."

The first scientist pulled out a white board with a bunch of names, their guesses for what they thought would happen, and the odds for each. The usual suspects were there—Heaven, Hell, Purgatory, coming back as a ghost, coming back as a ghost and traveling around the world with Adolf Hitler. That last one had better odds than I would have expected.

"You're not going to win," the second scientist said to the orderly.

"I know what I saw!" the orderly shot back.

"Hitler was not tea bagging baguettes in France!"

"You take that back!"

"Make me."

The orderly injected the second scientist with whatever was in his needle, and she collapsed to the floor, drooling. The orderly then stood there, scratching his head for a minute, unsure of how he was going to make her take it back. Words were not as easy to put back as pants were. The orderly soon slumped his shoulders in defeat. I guess that's why he wasn't a scientist. Didn't know when or how to make someone do something.

"Anyhow," the first scientist said, "we kill you, bring you back, you tell us what you experienced. Do we have an agreement?"

I roared as loud as I could and pissed myself. The pissing myself wasn't part of the response, I had simply lost control of my bladder.

The scientist conferred with the orderly and then the orderly stuck me with another needle. I felt muscles tightening in my jaw as a result.

"Dreadfully sorry about that. Anyhow, deal?"

"I want the twenty bucks and sandwich up front," I said, bartering.

The scientist considered it for a moment. "Twenty up front, sandwich upon return," he said, also bartering.

I didn't like his counteroffer. I much preferred my original offer. That's why I offered it first. I always wanted my payments up front because people could screw you good by getting what they want from you and then not holding up their end of the agreement. I knew this very well because that's what I was planning to do to the scientists. Get my sandwich, twenty dollars, and then excuse myself to the bathroom, shove them to the ground, and walk away at a brisk pace.

I've been told my plans have unnecessary extra steps, and

I always stop talking to those people. I don't need that kind of negativity in my life.

The deal sounded bad. So, I decided I wasn't going to accept it.

"I accept these terms and conditions," I said.

Dammit.

My tongue felt quite heavy after the effects of the needles they had been sticking me with. I had perhaps the worst slip of the tongue I had ever had just then, and I needed to correct it immediately.

"I am of sound mind and tongue and have not misspoken in the slightest," I said.

Sonofabitch!

The first scientist, as in the one not on the floor still drooling, pulled out a piece of paper with a lot of legalese on it. I still didn't want the deal, but I had given my word, and I was feeling a little too embarrassed by my mistake to go back on it. So, I signed the contract saying they could kill me and revive my corpse.

My mother had always told me, "John—" which was really strange because my name isn't John, "—never challenge scientists to make you do something because they will end up killing you." I always thought she was just being overly dramatic. Fool me once, as they say.

The first scientist gave the contract the once over and set it aside.

"Shall we begin?" he asked.

"I guess," I said.

My heart really wasn't in it. I had expected to be running away with a twenty-dollar bill in one hand and my mouth full of sandwich by now, gleefully cackling at my fooling these eggheads until I choked on the sandwich. Instead of choking to death on a sandwich, I was now going to die some other way. And that really bummed me out.

I wondered how they were going to kill me. Did the orderly have some other needle, one filled with death juice? Or did they have some fancy science machine that was going to carefully zap me with death sparks? Maybe they would have me wrestle a ferret or something to the death. The suspense was killing me, so I asked.

"So, I hope it's not rude of me to ask, but how are you going to kill me?"

"Oh, don't worry about that," the first scientist said. "Before we get there, I want to show you something." He led me over to the window and pointed. "You see that building over there?" he asked.

"Yes," I lied.

Then he shoved me out the window.

Fool me twice, I guess.

On the way down, I decided it was important to spend the last few seconds of my life thinking of the things and moments and people that meant the most to me. Unfortunately, as one hurtles to the ground at terminal velocity, one only has the time to shout curses and soil oneself. My curse of choice was *Egads!* It wasn't the worst thing I'd ever said—that was actually informing a small group of children what kind but inappropriate things I would be doing for and to their mothers, and in one case, a father, that night—but it was all I could think of.

When I landed on the sidewalk with a sickening splat and jarring bone-and-spine-and-everything-else crunching sound, I was relieved that I didn't feel anything, and that my death would at least be painless. Then the shock wore off, and I cried, "Egads!" in agony for hours while a small group of people gathered around me to watch.

What do you call a group of people anyway? A group of fish is a school. A gathering of crows is a murder. A bunch of cows is called your mother. I guess if it were up to me, I'd call a mob of people a bunch of dumbasses.

As I was saying, the dumbasses had gathered around to watch me die.

"Maybe we should help him," one of the dumbasses said.

"No, I think I read online that you're not supposed to get involved in things like this," another of the dumbasses replied.

"Is there a doctor here?" asked the first dumbass.

"I'm a doctor!" shouted someone.

"Can you help him?"

"Oh, good God, no," Dr. Dumbass said. "The lawyers would be up my behind so fast—"

"It's true," said a legal dumbass, peeking out from behind Dr. Dumbass. "I'm just waiting for him to make a mistake."

After several hours of my shouting, "Egads!" the orderly came out and put his hand over my nose and mouth. He closed my air passages for a few minutes until my cries of "Egads!" grew quieter and quieter, and then louder at one point when one of the dumbasses stepped on my femur, which was sticking out of my spleen, and then quieter again until I stopped saying "Egads!" altogether.

Everything was dark and still for a while. At first, I thought something had gone terribly wrong—aside from the being shoved out the window and breaking my everything.

My senses started to return one by one. First, I got my sense of taste back, but since that's heavily tied to the sense of smell, I didn't notice it right away. Then I got my hearing back, noting the loud screams of unyielding agony and a few people shouting, "Egads!" and "Why, I never!" and "Goodness, this sucks!"

Next sense I got back was the sense of touch and feeling. And what I felt was my body still mangled. Or at least that's what I felt I felt. I could have been wrong. I couldn't see that my body was mangled, and I wasn't about to trust just one sense. Perhaps, if I could taste my body being mangled or hear the ends of all of my broken bones rubbing together, I'd buy it, but just an intense pain brought on by everything being displaced? That's not scientific. That's not scientific at all!

Then I got my sight back and, whoo boy, was that body mangled. I got a good look at it, too, as one of my eyeballs had been popped from its socket and got a good look at the front of my body and the back of my body simultaneously. Maybe the scientific community would have preferred double-blind studies and control groups, peer reviews and the whole nine, but I live a little more freely than rigorous testing methods. Deciding that both feeling and seeing my body mangled was enough scientific consensus to come to the conclusion my body was, in fact, still mangled, I began crying, "Egads!" again.

A few seconds later, I got my sense of smell back and realized I could also taste things. I mean, I really didn't care at the time. The whole being twisted like a literal human pretzel thing was more pressing. But, for the sake of telling the whole story, I did get that last sense back.

I also found a quarter in my pocket, but that's neither here nor there.

I spent a couple of minutes trying to shout "Egads!" with different tones and inflections in hopes someone would come and help me, but no one did. When I finally got the point that everyone here, wherever here was, was a selfish, ungrateful dumbass, I decided I'd have to pull myself up by my own bootstraps.

I reached out with my arm that wasn't shoved down my own throat and grabbed the straps of my boots. They immediately broke. Whoever thought that was a good piece of advice was a bunch of dumbasses.

Ever so slowly, I began putting my body back together. I removed my arm from my throat, the femur from my spleen, put the eyeball back in, then took it back out, flipped it right side up, and put it back in. I untwisted my stomach, my testicles, and my ribcage. I took the butterflies out of my stomach and placed them back into my liver, caught my funny bone while it was dancing an amusing jig a few feet away and put it back in my arm, and then relocated my jaw from my shoe to my mouth. There were a whole lot of things where they shouldn't be, some where they should be but in ways they oughtn't be, and some things I don't think I was supposed to have, like plutonium. I finished off with one good stretch that popped every joint back into place with one satisfying and unnerving *pop*.

I then sat and cried for a few hours in pain.

Finally, I got a hold of myself and tried to figure out where I was. Those egghead dumbasses would be expecting a full report, and I intended to give them both a piece of my mind, which I found lodged in my underwear, and my account. They were paying me well for these services. I intended to deliver the goods.

The first thing I noticed was the smell and taste of sulfur in the air. It was so pungent, I wondered how I hadn't noticed it before. Then I remembered the agonizing pain I had been in. The sulfur was simply terrible but was inconclusive. Several places smelled and tasted like sulfur. Dallas, for instance.

Deciding I couldn't rely on smell and taste alone—a piece of advice I was once given by a one-eyed judge in a cactus judging contest—I decided to employ my sense of balance. I promptly fell over. That was the wrong sense to use, I suppose. It was probably a bad idea to use just one sense at a time anyway. Science demanded all senses.

Wherever I was, it felt hot. Like, really hot. As if everything was on fire around me. Ignoring the cries of pain and pleas for mercy, I could hear crackling like one would expect in a fireplace. I was beginning to get an idea of where I was, but there was one more sense to employ. So far it sounded, smelled, tasted, and felt as if I were in an uncomfortably hot location. But, as I said, science demanded all senses.

So, I opened my eyes to find that everything around me was on fire. So, I guess I didn't need all senses to come to that conclusion. Stupid science, requiring unnecessary steps.

Fire consumed everything. Faces were melting off the people I could see. Then, it was so hot, the faces melted back onto the people. Cloven-hoofed beasts with trident-shaped ends to their tails were moving coffee tables into people's paths so that they were constantly stubbing their toes. Worst of all, everyone's favorite sports team always lost whatever game they were playing.

I put on my thinking cap, which looked a lot like my regular cap but I wrote THINKING on it, and thought about it. At first, I was convinced I was in Jersey. It made the most sense. Jersey sucked just a little more than Dallas. It ranked a fraction of a suck more. Barely beat it out, really. You could call it a tie, but that'd be unscientific.

I thought about it, long and hard. Then I giggled to myself and said, "That's what she said." When I stopped giggling, I came to the obvious conclusion about where I had ended up in the afterlife.

I was in Heaven.

Why it hadn't hit me sooner, I wasn't sure. Maybe there were more missing pieces of my brain in my underwear somewhere. But I am such a fantastic person, I couldn't have ended up anywhere else. I had died and gone to Heaven. A lot of dumbasses said I'd end up somewhere else. I sure showed them.

The scientists back on Earth were looking for details, I figured. So, the more in-depth details I could provide, the better. They might even give me a bonus. I had my fingers crossed for a toothpick to hold the sandwich together. Doubtful, but a guy can dream. I mean, for now. It's probably only a matter of time before the government bans it.

I spent a while walking around and taking it all in. I didn't do much traveling, but, for the first time, I sure got to experience being a tourist. I bitched about the weather not being like it was at home. Then I bitched the pizza didn't taste as pizza-y as it did back home. Even the demons flaying people were doing it all wrong. They weren't putting their backs into it at all. It was as if they didn't care about good quality flaying here in Heaven. I guess when you get eternal life, you feel you can be lax on the brutal, medieval, and inhumane treatment of people. Back home, where people still cared about quality, flaying was done right or not at all.

I went and saw all the tourist attractions. I visited the Seven Deadly Sins theme park, gorged on as many sandwiches as I could, flew into an uncontrollable rage and punched a few people, then took a week-long nap. Best theme park I'd ever been to. Better than Six Flags. My behavior was encouraged here at Seven Deadly Sins.

Six Flags had gotten all pissy and on their high horse. *"They were children!"* they chided me. Some people hate seeing others have a good time, I tell you.

Next I went to see St. Peter and those famous pearly gates you always hear about. Closest thing I could find was about six hundred and sixty people (I lost count at some point, sorry) all linked face to ass in a giant circle. Everyone was crying and trying to express that they didn't want to be there. Again, a lot like Dallas. I guess it was meant to be a more abstract gate and fence motif. I got the fence part, but I think they skimped on the actual gates part.

I ran into Genghis Khan briefly. That's when I felt the most like a tourist. I spoke really loudly in short, jagged bursts to make sure he could understand me while I asked for more places to visit. He pointed me in the direction of a famous suburb where all the celebrities went. The sign read, SPECIAL PLACES.

It's really a fascinating place, but I think whoever is vetting who gets in has gotten lazy. There was a Special Place for people I would not have expected to be here in Heaven with good, pure, honest folk like me. Some were just reserved for people who hadn't gotten here yet. Bill Cosby was the big one. Some were empty but lived in—Adolf Hitler's comes to mind. The note on his door said he was visiting France. Which was strange to me; I thought he'd already been there. Maybe that was more of a work thing than pleasure. The vetting was so bad that the Zodiac Killer had a place there. I mean, I think it was him. I couldn't read the weird lettering on the mailbox. It was nice to see Richard Nixon being honored, though.

You know what the best thing about visiting the Special Place neighborhood was, though? I found a house with my name on it. I was touched. My very own special place in Heaven. People frequently told me I had a special place somewhere, but they never said here. Bunch of dumbasses.

I left when I had my fill of seeing who all had earned a special place here. A few blocks away, I came across the oddest landmark I'd ever see here.

It was a mountain of blindingly white clouds ascending upwards against a bright blue sky, outlined by the relaxing warmth of a brilliant sun. Terrible, I tell you. It really ruined the aesthetics, didn't match the whole hellfire and brimstone décor that the rest of Heaven had worked so hard to create. Some people just don't know when to quit fixing up a place.

At the base of this atrocious art installation, two people were arguing. One was a pale grey man with his head on fire. That hairstyle choice was a bit overdone here. No originality in this place. The other, to my surprise, was that sweet old lady, Betty White. You know, that actress from *The Golden Girls*? I always knew she'd end up here.

"But I'm not dead yet!" insisted Betty.

"That's what they all say!" said the man, using a stick to roast a marshmallow above his head, with a thick Jersey accent.

"I'm really not! I'm still petting my dog in Beverly Hills!"

"That's the exact excuse Liberace used. 'I'm not supposed to be here, I'm petting Betty White's dog.' Youse guys need to come up with a better excuse."

I decided to interrupt the conversation because I was more important than both of these people. I hadn't gone and done something stupid to die. I was here on a mission. A science mission.

So I confidently stepped up to the two of them and shoved the old woman to the floor like the Champion of Science that I am. She shrieked something about her hip. The guy's eyes lit up as he recognized me. He asked me if I was that guy that valiantly pushed over children on my way out of a burning building that one time. I said I was.

"I knew I recognized youse!" the man with the flaming head said. "We have a special place for you here."

"I know, I saw!" I replied. I was so excited to be recognized.

"Did you see the mural in the bathroom? I did that."

I was a little less excited to be recognized now. The mural featured several demons taking turns giving me swirlies in an overflowing toilet bowl. Art is subjective, I suppose. Still, it left me feeling like Heaven wasn't a very nice place.

"Never mind that," I said, pushing him to the ground to make my point. "What is this?"

"That? It's the stairway to Heaven," the guy said as he pulled himself up and dusted himself off.

I said, "*Hmm!*" loudly and shoved the man over again.

That made no sense. We were in Heaven already, weren't we? I mean the Most Amazing Champion of Science wouldn't have ended up anywhere else. That was absurd. I was amazing and fantastic, a true friend to science and dumbasses alike. No, this had to be some stupid art thing, like in that one painting where the stairs kept turning and leading back onto themselves.

The man pulled himself up again, grumbling something about not being paid enough.

"So, if I went up there, I'd end up back here," I said.

"No," he said.

"No?" I asked.

"No," he re-said.

". . . Yes?"

"No."

". . . Maybe if I really believed in myself?"

"Still no."

"If I wished upon a star?"

"Probably not."

I went *Hmm!* loudly again and shoved him over once more.

"So, then, if I went up there, where would I go?" I asked.

"Heaven," he said.

"Right, here."

"No."

"You keep using that word, but I do not think you know what it means."

The man with his head perpetually on fire explained he was an English professor. He lived every day with people misusing punctuation, even in verbal conversation. So, I guess maybe he does know what it means. I think more rigorous testing is needed to be sure, but I didn't have the time, and my arm was getting tired of pushing the man over.

"Let's say what you're saying is true," I said to soothe the man's ego, "which it isn't. Where, then, are we?"

"Hell," he said, getting up once more.

Something rang true in the man's words. A truth I hadn't considered and perhaps didn't want to hear. So I punched the man squarely in his stupid melting nose. Teach him to tell me things I don't want to hear.

I started looking around for signs he might be right. For starters, everything was on fire. That contradicted most depictions of Heaven. There were an awful lot of demons flying around, vomiting on everyone's heads. People kept walking into rooms and forgetting why they went in there in the first place. Dogs didn't want to cuddle; cats would lure you in with the promise of rubbing their fluffy, fluffy bellies and then scratch you when you tried. Goldfish slapped passersby in the face, and parrots parroted back some awful, racist things.

There was one thing that settled it for me that I had not ended up in Heaven. As I looked around the landscape of putrid, flowing rivers of liquefied crap and mountains of gnarly, curly pubic hairs, I had noticed there was a complete lack of sandwiches. There wasn't even a taco stand—the half-assed attempt at a sandwich by people who don't know what good food is. This was truly Hell.

Also, there were a lot of people being tortured. But I feel like there could be some of that going on in Heaven. Some people are into kinky things.

This revelation upset me. I didn't like revelations. I didn't like it in book form, and I didn't like it in world-changing epiphany form. What was the big idea, sending Everyone's Favorite and Most-Well-Known Scientific Champion of Science to Hell? I had a half a mind, not just because of earlier, to give God a piece of my mind (of which I felt a few stray pieces rattling around in my pants).

"You, there!" I pointed at the man I kept shoving down.

He hadn't bothered to get back up. Smart guy. I'd buy him as a professor.

"I want to go up there and give someone in charge a what for."

"Wouldn't we all?" he said. "But you can't. There's something up there that stops us from going in."

"Like, magic?"

He looked at me like I was stupid.

"Don't be stupid," he said. "No, it's just a really thick door."

"But, if I could find my way past . . .?"

"I mean, I guess. It's been a millennium, give or take, no one's figured it out yet."

I didn't let things like well-established understandings of the universe stand in my way. Only chumps did that. I might be dead, on a mission for science, losing small pieces of my body as I walked, and that one femur was back in my spleen. But I wasn't a chump.

"Thank you," I told the man. "If I need you, where can I find you?"

"I live in that big building over there, where they put all of us Grammar Nazis," he said. "It's easy to find; we're right next door to the building of Actual Nazis."

I took a look and was impressed to find the Actual Nazi apartment building was in the shape of a swastika. It seemed like an architectural impossibility, but what do I know about architecture? Nothing, which is why I keep my mouth shut about it. I do know the Trump Towers standing beside it were gaudy, though.

To properly thank the man, I pulled him up from the ground, dusted him off, and shoved him back down again. Something to remember our time together. One for the road, as it were.

And so I marched up the stupid, relaxed incline of the dumb cloud stairs, ignoring how every step shifted just slightly to make sure every step was the right height for my stride. I held out both of my middle fingers to the warm, but not too warm, rays of sun and happiness that peeked out from behind the cloud stairs. I shouted numerous obscenities—including a few I learned from the racist parrot back there—at the incredible blue sky. I hated it all and was completely justified in doing so, I felt.

At the top, I found the door the man was talking about. It was a door all right. He wasn't lying about that. I've seen me some doors in my time, and this was the most door-looking door I had ever had the chance to adore. On this door was a big sign that said, DO NOT ENTER. He didn't tell me about that. I'm gonna count that as a lie through omission. How could he, after all I'd done for him? I swore I'd never trust that man again.

I looked hard at the words DO NOT ENTER. Everything about this hellish place called Heaven annoyed me. First, it gave me a beautiful sight and feeling while I got in some exercise, and now it was going to tell me what to do? I'd never let rules stand in my way before, and I wasn't about to now.

I know the man with his head on fire said no one had figured it out in a millennium, but as I've established whimsically already, he lied to me. So I couldn't trust that anyone had ever tried this before. As such, I employed the most scientific method I could think of. After all, I had been deputized by two scientists to act on behalf of science.

I grabbed the door handle and twisted it. The door came right open.

Below I heard a crowd start mumbling. I made out one dumbass saying, "How come we never thought of that?"

On the other side of that door was Heaven. Not that fake Heaven that was on fire all the time and kept trying to get me to wear itchy pants. Instead, children frolicked in fields of flowers with their dogs, dogs always caught the cars they chased down, cars were always running over your enemies, and your enemies lost their children and pets in fields of flowers. It was a real bad place for your enemies, I guess. And I hated it all.

I hated it all because they had decided I wasn't good enough for their stupid club where no one ever had their eyes gouged out. Call me petty, but if you don't want me in your club, I want you to suffer pointlessly for an eternity. So, I decided to do what I did that time I was refused entry into Oprah's Book Club.

I couldn't find a horse, so I snapped the horn off of the nearest unicorn and beat it to death. The children were mortified by my actions as the pointy end was repeatedly shoved through Ulysses the Unicorn's ribcage, and he screamed in whatever language dumb unicorns screamed in. The looks on the children's faces was so reminiscent of Oprah when I beat her horse to death.

After that wanton murder, I still couldn't understand why I was sent to Hell upon death instead of Heaven.

So I kicked one of the kids in their shin and went running down the street stabbing people with the unicorn horn. Unfortunately, as this is the afterlife, the people would die an agonizing, painful death and then just get up like nothing happened.

"I say, what gives?" said one of my victims, trying to rub the bloodstains out of his trousers.

"Why won't you stay dead?" I shouted and resumed stabbing him.

"How would—*oof!*—that work? I'm—*aaagh*, my liver!—already dead!"

I stopped stabbing him and thought about that.

"I guess I'm not sure what I was expecting," I said.

"It isn't as if there is a Super Heaven you could have sent me to!" he said with a chuckle laced with blood.

"Or is there?" I asked myself aloud. "And maybe you just suck so bad, they don't want you there."

The man thought about that point thoughtfully. He thought and he thought and then he thought some more. Then I realized I had killed him again, and he hadn't revived yet. So I moved onto stabbing the next person.

"What's the meaning of all this, then?"

I looked up from my latest pincushion in time to see a stern-looking angel tapping his foot.

"It's not what it looks like!" I insisted.

"It looks like you're taking out a lot of anger by trying to kill people," the angel said.

"Okay, then that's exactly what it looks like."

Not knowing what else to do and still pretty upset at the whole clerical error that sent innocent old me to the wrong afterlife, I began stabbing the angel.

"Stop that," the angel said. "This is exactly—I said stop it—why we didn't want you here—my cornea!—in the first place."

"Why wouldn't you want me here?" I demanded, surrounded by the groaning and dying corpses surrounding me.

The angel went on to list the myriad of supposed wrongs I'd done just since I had died. I'd beaten a unicorn to death, kicked a small child, shoved over a couple of people, including an old lady, flipped off the aura of God, said terribly racist things to the aura of God, punched several people in the face, and had left the door between Heaven and Hell open.

"I did what now?" I asked.

Turning around, I saw that I had indeed left the door open. The door that had for a millennium kept the hellions at bay with the words DO NOT ENTER had been left wide open. Boy, was my face red. Probably because of all the fire bursting forth from the underworld and incinerating nearby buildings. Demons and Nazis and everyone's least-favorite celebrities were spewing forth and kicking all the children in their shins.

I turned back to the angel and tried to smile, hoping it would be enough to charm the angel into forgetting I had done that. He—or she? I don't know, it was kind of androgynous. I could have figured it out if it walked around without pants, but people frown at me when I suggest that—frowned.

"The big man is very displeased!" the angel chided.

"Oh, yeah? Well, maybe I'm very displeased with the big man!" I replied.

The angel looked taken aback. "What could He have possibly done to raise your ire?"

"Well, for starters, He sent me to Hell."

"For good reasons!"

"I doubt that!"

"How can you doubt it? I haven't even told you the reasons!"

"I don't need facts to know what I disagree with!"

This confused the angel. He tried reasoning with me that I wasn't making sense. He asked if my brain was intact, and I said it was. That's called lying. I do that a lot. I've already lied several times in telling this story. There were really three scientists back at the beginning, but two served the same function, so I just merged them into one composite character. The third scientist's name was Bob.

Anyway, the angel rubbed his temples. People do that a lot after talking to me, I find.

"Look, He is very displeased—"

"Oh, yeah? So am I!"

"You've made that clear. He wants to see you."

"Oh yeah? Well so am I!"

We both stared at each other for a minute, trying to decide if either of us wanted to comment on my inappropriate response. The staring only ended when Betty White cartwheeled up to us and crane kicked the angel in the groin.

I pushed her over and then went running. I wasn't sure how I was going to find God in a place as big as Heaven. The buildings were all so big and magnificent, you couldn't get a good look. So, I did what anyone would do when they were in a new town and didn't know their way to a specific location. I began burning down the buildings. In addition to being big and magnificent, the buildings were also highly flammable. That seemed like a structural problem to me, but again, I'm not an architect. Also, it seemed like an ironic problem for them to have, considering the enemy being Hell and their penchant for fire.

It didn't take nearly as long to burn all of Heaven down to ashes and embers. Once I got going, the legion of Hell thought it was the cool thing to do and began setting things on fire as well. I had to put myself out a couple of times. The rapscallions get carried away sometimes. But eventually, the entire landscape was smoldering, except for one place.

The God Cave.

In hindsight, I really should have been able to spot it sooner. There was a huge neon sign above the door that read, THE GOD CAVE. The door itself read, KEEP OUT. DOING GOD STUFF. People in the afterlife are a very trusting bunch of dumbasses. And way above it in the sky were a series of neon signs that pointed directly to the God Cave and said things like: THIS WAY TO THE GOD CAVE and SEVEN BLOCKS TO THE GOD CAVE and YOU CAN'T MISS THE GOD CAVE, THERE ARE HUNDREDS OF SIGNS POINTING AT IT.

It's a wonder how anyone finds their way around in this poorly planned place. It's a good thing I came along to burn it all to the ground. Now they can rebuild and maybe make things make sense.

I opened the door into the rock formation, and I will say, I had never been more surprised in my entire life. Or afterlife, I suppose. Being dead creates a lot of grammatical questions. I figured I should track down that English professor and get his take at some point.

When I imagined God, I imagined looking into a mirror. I could not have pictured what I found . . .

. . . It's almost too horrible to say . . .

God was . . . a nerd.

The God Cave was a giant room dedicated to Batman paraphernalia. The Bat symbol covered every surface. Every action figure was set up and staged in epic battle poses. Glass cases were dedicated to every issue of every comic book ever created, and some terribly drawn fan fiction featuring God saving Batman from certain doom were pinned up on the walls. All the films were playing on repeat. Frank Gorshin stood in the corner, tired and unenthusiastically saying, "*Na-na-na-na-na*!" to the tune of the "Batman Theme Song."

God himself was wearing the old grey-and-blue Batsuit. You'd think that would be embarrassing enough on its own, but a big gut bulged out the uniform. He whipped around, his cape flapping at the motion.

"*Mom!*" he whined. "I told you not to come in—wait. Who are you?"

"I'm pissed!" I said.

". . . Like drunk, or . . .?"

"No, I am upset! How dare you send me to Hell?"

"Didn't you use my name in vain?"

"That's a goddamned stupid rule!"

"Pretty sure we caught you stealing at one point."

"That is an outrageous claim!" I said, stuffing my pockets with Batcookies. "I have half a mind and should sue you!"

"You've, like, never gone to church. Not even once a year on Christmas to pretend, like most Christians."

"You guys make it so boring sounding," I whined.

"I dunno, sounds like you were sent to the right place."

That upset me even more. I mean, saying I belonged in Hell behind my back was mean enough as it was, but to say it to my face? This guy had a real attitude problem. At least I have the good sense to do that sort of thing behind people's back.

"Well, you're wrong," I said. "This is like the hugest mistake you could make! Hell knows how valuable I am. They made a Special Place for me and everything."

"I feel like that's kind of the point."

"You know what? I could do a better job at being God than you!"

"*Pft*, everyone thinks that," He said. "But you have no idea how whiny people can be. 'Oh, if you're God, why is there cancer in children?' 'Why couldn't you prevent that earthquake in Haiti?' 'If God's so great, why did they make *Batman & Robin*.' I came to the director in his dreams the entire time they shot the movie, and he ignored me!"

"I feel like that's kind of the point—"

"Don't use my logic against me!" He shouted, tossing a Batarang at my head.

I deftly avoided it by accidentally leaning forward and taking it in the face.

"Egads!" I cried. "You let me be God this instant!"

"Make me," He said, readying a Batarang.

So, it's been three months since I overthrew Heaven and became God of . . . I'm not sure, I guess. The job didn't come with a manual. I tried asking Human Resources, but they said they really just assemble the dumbasses. I kept telling them I'm God, and they muttered something about something. I'm God; I don't have to listen to people. Eventually HR stopped taking my calls. So I guess they don't have to listen to me either.

I've tried to rule as fairly as possible. I answer only the prayers of the rich and famous so that when they die, they'll come hang out with me and buy me expensive things. You'd think God would just have everything already but nope. I have to pay for things myself, and it doesn't pay well at all. I tried giving myself a raise, but Congress wanted to tack on a raise for themselves, and I said no dice. They've been awful lax in doing their jobs lately. I didn't feel they deserved a raise.

When the poor ask for help, I tell them God helps the ones who help themselves (who aren't rich and famous). Then I occasionally give one of them tuberculosis or rickets. Put the fear of Me into them.

I'm not sure what's taking those scientists so long to bring me back. I've got a fully written report waiting for their approval. Until they do, I'm enjoying being the ruler of everything. I'm thinking of bringing back the dodo for one last limited run. Like how pumpkin spice lattes are only a thing in the fall season. I'm thinking, make the dodos only on July Fourth. Celebrate with a bang and a terrifying resurrection of the world's most adorable and extinct bird.

Maybe that'll get those egghead dumbasses to bring me back to life.

We hope you enjoyed A Contract of Words, an anthology of authors selected from all over the world. Scout Media looks forward to bringing you the next installment in our 'Of Words' series, A Flash of Words (where each story follows the flash fiction word count limitation). To quench your reading thirst until its release, we offer you this flash-fiction-length story of a contract/promise, written by five-year-old aspiring author, Natalie Kocheran:

A PROMISE

Natalie Kocheran

The little girl with pigtails sat in the waiting room with her daddy. She had a bouquet of flowers for her mommy, who was having a baby. Her little feet swung back and forth. Her daddy told her to stop kicking the chair.

The nurse came out to get Daddy. Daddy smiled and told Daisy to stay with her Aunt Newla while he went to see Mommy first.

Aunt Newla smiled and patted Daisy's shoulder. "Would you like to walk to the fountains until it's time for you to go?" she asked.

Daisy nodded. Her pigtails bounced around. Grabbing Aunt Newla's hand and holding tight to the flowers, she led the way down the hall toward the large window that overlooked the fountain.

She pressed her face against the window. She loved how the water fountain's water flew through the air and landed in the base.

Aunt Newla began to talk to another nurse.

Daisy thought she heard crying. She began to investigate, keeping Aunt Newla within eyesight. She peered in the doors as she went, until she found a little girl sitting in a hospital bed crying.

"Hello," she said.

The girl sniffled and wiped her nose on her sleeve. "Hello."

"I'm Daisy." She smiled, thinking now they weren't strangers, and she could talk to her.

She bit her lip. "I'm Cutie Pie."

"Why are you crying?" Daisy took another step closer.

"I don't know anyone here. My mom and dad died, and I don't remember anything." Cutie Pie rubbed her eyes, fighting back tears.

"Well, you know me." She reached into the bouquet and pulled out a pink rose. "I'll be your friend. If you promise to keep this flower, I'll always be your friend." She handed it to her.

Her fingers wrapped around hers and the flower. Tears ran down her face. "Thank you, Daisy."

Daisy yelled and pulled her fingers back. A drop of blood dropped from her fingertip. Sheepishly, she smiled. "I got a boo-boo like you now." She motioned to her hand wrapped in a bandage. "I guess I didn't remove all the thorns like Aunt Newla asked."

"Daisy. Daisy." Aunt Newla's voice sounded from the hall. "There you are." Her heels tapped across the floor. "I was worried you had wandered off."

"It's okay, Aunt Newla. I made a friend." She turned to her aunt but threw her arms around Cutie Pie. "She's my new best friend. We made a promise." The three-year-old giggled, proud of herself. "And I gave her a flower to make her feel better."

Lightning Source UK Ltd.
Milton Keynes UK
UKHW01f0629230618
324656UK00001B/19/P